R0084820190

02/2017

a season of
daring
greatly

ELLEN EMERSON WHITE

a
season of
daring
greatly

GREENWILLOW BOOKS
An Imprint of HarperCollinsPublishers

A Season of Daring Greatly
Copyright © 2017 by Ellen Emerson White

All rights reserved. No part of this book may be used or reproduced in any manner whatsoever without written permission except in the case of brief quotations embodied in critical articles and reviews. Printed in the United States of America. For information address HarperCollins Children's Books, a division of HarperCollins Publishers, 195 Broadway, New York, NY 10007.
www.epicreads.com

The text of this book is set in Garamond.
Book design by Sylvie Le Floc'h

Library of Congress Cataloging-in-Publication Data is available
ISBN 978-0-06-246321-0 (trade ed.)

17 18 19 20 21 PC/LSCH 10 9 8 7 6 5 4 3 2 1
First Edition

 Greenwillow Books

For my father,
for so many reasons

a season of
daring
greatly

CHAPTER 1

She was going to annihilate him.

Paralyze him.

Petrify him.

Or maybe, okay, just make him—nervous. All she really wanted was for him to swing and miss; she didn't necessarily have to turn him into a permanent emotional cripple.

Probably.

And she bloody well didn't want to throw the curve. Why waste the good hook, if she didn't need it? A little heat in the guy's eyes, and he'd be so sure he could rip it, that she would be able to enjoy a pleasant breeze.

Which would be refreshing, on a warm spring afternoon.

Now, Leonard wanted her to waste one low and outside—

but he was only a sophomore and he lacked the Instinct of Death. So, she shook him off—and knew he was going to ask for the curve *again*, which he did.

When she didn't respond at all, he finally—took him long enough—put down the sign for the fastball.

Okay, then.

She touched the bill of her cap, then took a deep breath.

Her enemy was so eager that she could almost feel how hard he was gripping the bat, ready to take her out of the yard—but, frankly, the batter didn't interest her much. He was an impediment. A minor distraction. A vague annoyance.

Right at eye level. Deceptively tasty. He wouldn't be able to resist hacking at it.

She came to her set position, rotated the baseball a few times inside her glove—it felt lovely—and then let her fingers automatically find the four-seam grip she could form in her sleep—and sometimes did.

Leg drive. Release point. Downhill.

She wound up, and felt her arm slot in just the right sweet spot as she let the ball fly—a good, hard, rising fastball, her right leg coming down with a nice, smooth follow-through on the dirt, her left leg landing a second later, so that she was already poised to field a comebacker, when he swung—and missed. Violently.

She saw the umpire's arm come up to signal the third strike, and although Leonard had to elevate anxiously out of his crouch to snag the ball, it landed in his glove with quite a satisfying smack.

Oh, yeah. She was bad. Game over.

Her teammates were all congratulating her, although she couldn't really hear anything, because her head was still buzzing, but they were happy, and there were a lot of high fives and claps on the back.

Leonard came out to the mound and stuck the ball in her glove, and she nodded.

"You called a good game," she said. "Thanks."

He grinned sheepishly, because they both knew she had called her own game, every step of the way—but, no one would ever say that she wasn't magnanimous in victory.

"That last one had some serious heat," he said. "The herd was pretty loud about it."

The herd. The flock. The clan—all otherwise known as the group of major league scouts, a number of whom showed up more often than not when she was scheduled to pitch, along with college coaches, and a few agents, usually. There were almost certainly a bunch of reporters, too, since there always were, and she'd heard cameras clicking constantly during the game. A much bigger crowd than usual today, since it was her last high school start, and the draft was coming up, and—well, anyway, she had made a point of *not* looking in the stands, because it was better not to know—although she had caught her mother reading a book at one point, sitting at the top of the metal bleachers directly behind home plate.

They lined up to shake hands with the other team, and again, she couldn't really hear what anyone was saying, although she smiled and nodded and pretended to make sincere eye contact. Adrenaline was freakin' *noisy*. But, she couldn't help stiffening when she passed the guy who had bunted—some punk infielder—for the one damn hit of the game.

"Sorry about that," he muttered.

"It was well-placed," Jill said, evenly.

Although it had been a totally bush-league move on his part.

If, in fact, well-placed.

The beefy first baseman she had just struck out—he'd fanned three times, actually—gave her a perfunctory hand slap and scowled at her. "You get asked on many dates?"

"Of course not," Jill said. "I'm *tall*."

That made him smile a little—although one of the guys behind him mumbled, "*Dyke*," and a couple of the others laughed. She didn't even bother responding, since she heard some version of that every time she played, and it was both tedious and predictable. She shook hands and exchanged hellos with the other team's coaches—who were both polite, at least, if not effusive—and was very relieved when the fake bonhomie was over, and she could go into the dugout and take a couple of minutes to try and come down from the intensity of the last seven innings.

Her cooler was at the far end of the bench in the old wooden dugout, and she started unbuttoning her uniform shirt—which felt quite heavy and damp—as she worked her way down the splintery steps.

The ice packs she had brought were nice and cold, and she assembled her shoulder and elbow wrap, and then strapped it over her compression shirt.

"Anything hurt?" her head coach, Mr. Portman, asked, from behind her.

She shook her head, adjusting the straps again, since—of course—the damn thing had been designed to fit a guy.

"You had a live one today," he said.

She nodded. Good, loud pops in Leonard's glove, and there had been more than a dozen pitches he couldn't handle at all, including several curves. A shutout—which should have been a no-hitter, eighteen Ks, two errors, three passed balls on strikeouts, and a walk—except that the ump had blown the ball three call, which had definitely been a strike.

Well, all right, whatever. It didn't matter.

Much.

She always kept a couple of frozen washcloths in the cooler, too, and she pressed one to her face, taking a few deep breaths.

Okay. Okay. Decent game. Not her best, but solid.

"You back yet?" Mr. Portman asked.

She shook her head, focusing on the cold cloth.

"Well, let me know when you are, so I can tell you what a

great game you just pitched," he said. Mr. Portman was a nice guy, who was a history teacher who coached baseball, rather than, say, the other way around. A very *good* history teacher, as it happened.

She nodded, then sponged off her face with the cold cloth, and draped her Mariners jersey over her shoulders, buttoning the top button, so that it hung sort of like a dashing red-and-white baseball cape. Which was maybe a little theatrical, but a lot better than wandering around in front of cameras in a very tight, sweaty compression shirt.

Then, she took another deep breath, let it out, and shook her head to try and release the last residue of the "Kill them all!" game fever.

"How many photographers?" she asked.

"At least a dozen, maybe more," Mr. Portman said.

All right, then. Jill checked her hair, able to feel that the chignon was still reasonably well in place. She'd never been a big fan of the perky ponytail-stuck-through-the-back-of-the-cap look, and her friend Lauren had come up with what she described as an "if Audrey Hepburn were a *serious* jock" look, which she had been using during games since tenth grade. They had had to experiment—Jill didn't have any innate gifts whatsoever when it came to things like hair and makeup—but, it had turned out that a low chignon served the purpose of resting neatly below her hat and, more to the point, kept her hair the hell out of her eyes when she was trying to play.

And an added benefit was that her grandmother no longer sighed as deeply when she appeared in her baseball uniform, but would take a small, brave breath and say, "Well, you've brought a touch of elegance to it, at least."

Most of the team was packing up their gear bags and looking very cheerful, since they had just won their fourth game in a row.

Bobby, their undertalented, but always hustling, sophomore second baseman put a bottle of Gatorade in her hand and she drank half of it in about four seconds.

"Thanks," she said, and finished off the rest in a few long gulps. "That was a great double play in the third."

Bobby grinned and exchanged high fives with Antonio, their more talented, but quite tiny, shortstop.

Her infielders had turned two double plays, and seconds after the putz who bunted had taken his lead, she'd picked him off. She'd also lost three outs on the dropped third strikes, too.

But, still. That damn bunt. She should have anticipated it— and she should have gotten off the mound about twice as fast. Or maybe just figured out that the kid was going to do it in the first place, before it happened.

She could probably talk a couple of her teammates, or maybe their assistant coach, Ray, into sticking around, and hitting her bunts for a while—but, it would either look like false hustle, or as though she was a gung-ho jackass. The latter was, possibly, not too far from the truth.

Ray, who had graduated from their high school about six years earlier and now worked as a line cook in his parents' seafood restaurant, when he wasn't coaching or umpiring in various baseball and softball leagues, was loading a huge duffel bag of equipment just a few feet away.

"Could we possibly do bunt drills tomorrow?" she asked.

He laughed. "Gary"—who was the head coach—"and I were taking bets on how long it would be before you brought that up."

Well, okay. Now she maybe felt a little embarrassed. "Who won?" she asked.

He looked at his watch. "Me, by about a minute and a half."

With luck, money was involved, because she'd heard that the coaches didn't get paid very well, especially considering how much work was involved.

"And yeah," he said, "we can do drills."

Good.

She'd avoided the crowd outside the field long enough— she needed to go out there and smile and chat, making sure to stay on the right side of the line between confidence and arrogance. It was tempting to ask one of the freshmen to carry her gear for her. Obnoxious, maybe, but tempting. Hell, when *she* had been a freshman, the seniors had her lugging around everything in sight, even after she made All-State.

And, after all, it was a well-established tradition for the best player on the team to have minions. It was just the natural order of things.

She took some lip gloss out of the side pocket of her gear bag, and put it on as quickly and discreetly as possible. Her mother and grandmother had turned out to be right—she looked better in photos, when she put in at least a *tiny* bit of effort. Smiling was an effective tool, also.

"What a girly girl," Malik, one of their other pitchers, said, sounding very cheerful.

Not discreet *enough*, apparently.

"Getting ready for your fans?" he asked.

Well—yeah, pretty much. "Yes, Mr. DeMille, I certainly am," she said.

Malik laughed, uncertainly.

Same response she got for most of her jokes. Which either meant that she was hilarious and just woefully unappreciated—or that the jokes in question weren't very damn funny.

Such was life.

She tucked the lip gloss into the back pocket of her uniform, and then picked up her gear bag—she always brought two of her own wooden bats to every game, among other things—and the cooler.

"You want me to haul that for you?" Sprout—his real name was James, but he was short as hell, and rarely got off the bench, except to pinch-run—asked. The other two freshmen were already carrying their slugging senior outfielder's duffel and backpack, and an unwieldy bag of catcher's equipment.

Okay, he had suggested it of his own volition, so now, she could generously say no.

"Thanks, but I'm all set," she said.

Mr. Portman looked up from the scorebook, where he seemed to be updating various team statistics. "Give her a hand, Sprout," he said. "There are a lot of people out there waiting for her."

True enough. She smiled at Sprout. "Thanks. I really appreciate it, James."

He gave her a huge grin back—probably because she was pretty sure she was one of the only people he knew who *always* called him James.

Okay, then. She'd had a very intense coach in Little League who was always screaming things like "Leave it all out on the field!" while a bunch of nine-year-olds, including her, looked back at him in confusion and would drop their gloves and caps on the ground, for lack of a better idea. But, she still liked that particular expression—not because she needed to be reminded to hustle, but so she could remember to keep whatever happened in a given game inside the white lines, and not spend the next hour—day—*week*—brooding about it. She either played well, or she didn't. No big deal. She just had to make sure that once she stepped through the gate, and was officially off the diamond, the game was over.

Forgotten.

Yesterday's news.

Onward, and upward.

She followed Sprout through the opening in the chain-link fence, where there were a startling number of people hanging around. A large crowd, even.

Bunt?

What freakin' bunt?

CHAPTER 2

All things being equal, baseball was the easy part. Throw the ball, catch the ball, throw it again. Hit the ball sometimes. Run occasionally. Try to create—well, maybe not order, so much as a reasonable *flow*—out of the chaos and unpredictability of any given game.

And, sometimes, she liked to try and remember to have *fun* while she was doing it.

When she had first started playing, especially back in Little League, the only people who showed up at games were a few parents and siblings. Maybe, once in a while, someone walking a dog would pause behind the backstop, watch half an inning, and then amble away. She would hear a lot of "Oh, isn't that *cute*, a little girl pitching" remarks, which were harmless enough, and even faintly amusing. The most intense insult she ever got in those days would be along the lines of "Why is that lefty with the ponytail playing shortstop?" And then, she would gun a runner out at first, and the person would usually say to his or her companion, "Oh. *That's* why."

When she was twelve, she was already five-eight—and throwing the ball almost seventy miles an hour. So, she was invited to play on a 14U team, which did some traveling around southern New England, but was fairly low-key, as travel teams went. Either way, coaches were, uneasily, starting to notice her.

Her parents had never been crazy about the idea of her playing fall ball, or going to showcases, or working out constantly at the local baseball training facility, because they thought that it crossed the line into obsession, cost far too much money—and, also, that she would run the risk of maybe having her arm fall off.

Well, okay, mostly her mother. Her father had been a chipper guy, whose first response to almost *everything* was usually along the lines of "Sure, why not?"

Had been. Which *sucked*, on so many levels.

She missed him profoundly, and even four years later, most of the time, it still felt like it had happened an hour ago.

Anyway, it was funny, because her teammates' parents were usually strongly encouraging, or even *pushing*, them to play nonstop, while her parents—okay, yes, primarily her *mother*—had always been more likely to suggest that she stay inside and read a book, or go to the movies, and just generally *not* become a one-dimensional person.

Which sort of backfired, because by the time she got to high school, in addition to baseball, she was playing basketball and tennis, and going skiing, and working out on her own, and running several miles a day and so forth. She always got books about baseball for her birthday and on Christmas, she read every online article she could find, and she studied dozens of the wildly different training theories about increasing strength and agility and stamina. Her mother would say things like, "My God, she is an *unrepentant* jock," with an anxious where-did-we-go-wrong look. "Yeah," Jill would say, "but, a multifaceted one."

Although, in her own defense, she *did* like to go to the movies. A lot.

She was a junior when, during a spring practice on a very cold day, her fastball hit ninety for the first time. After that, an unending stream of college coaches, professional scouts, reporters, self-described "advisors" who were usually sports agents, and ordinary baseball fans started cluttering the stands, and lining up along the fences at every single one of her games. She got so many college recruiting, travel team, and other baseball-related calls that her mother had had to change their unlisted phone number more than once, her email inbox was constantly overflowing, and texts and uninvited voice mails always littered what her brother Theo called "The Celebrity Cell

Phone," as opposed to her private one. Sometimes, particularly aggressive agents, scouts, or coaches would appear at their front door, leave notes in their mailbox, or park near the house, waiting for a chance to waylay and wheedle her. Total strangers would come up to her—even on the beach, or at Starbucks or wherever—to share pitching advice, and tips, and explain why almost everything she was doing was wrong, and how she could be even *better*, if she would just do whatever it was that they thought would be more effective.

And she would smile, and nod, and be impeccably polite— and pretty much ignore every word of it.

Today, waiting outside the diamond, along with the usual group of parents, as well as a bunch of people from the high school, there were—as was almost always the case—a few little girls, who would stare at her with complete, utter, and somewhat unsettling awe. And yeah, the usual collection of baseball people was even bigger than usual. She recognized quite a few of them, and suspected that the skinny guy with glasses and a notebook might be from *Sports Illustrated*, because apparently, they were planning to do a big pre-draft story on her. There were several other reporters, but they were mostly local. She also noticed an unfamiliar tall man in a dark green polo shirt, who carried himself like an aging athlete. He was standing with the scouts, and she'd seen him with a radar gun between innings at one point, so he was probably from one of the teams, and she had just never met him before. But, she definitely saw people from the Orioles, the White Sox, the Mariners, the Rockies, the Mets, the Astros, and the Brewers—and even though she was used to having them show up, it was still pretty cool.

Could he be from the Red Sox? No, she'd met the Red Sox area scout plenty of times, and they had even worked her out with a bunch of other Rhode Island high school and college players up at McCoy Stadium in Pawtucket, although she was almost positive that they didn't have much interest in drafting her.

"Hey, Number Twenty-eight!" a male voice yelled from somewhere up near the top of the bleachers. "You suck!"

Yeah, yeah, yeah. Everyone was a critic.

"You *wicked* suck!" he said, and the guys sitting near him—most of whom were on the football team—laughed.

She made a quick gesture towards her mother, who was making her way through the crowd.

"Right," the guy said. "You *stink*, Number Twenty-eight!"

Better.

"With friends like that," her mother said wryly.

Best friends, even. One of her best friends, anyway. She'd known Greg since kindergarten, and luckily, he had never gone through that "girls are icky and have cooties and I can't be seen with one" phase, so they had been able to sail right through junior high and high school with no strife whatsoever. It also helped that he was the school's top quarterback, and that they had always spent hours doing things like long toss and running together.

"How was your book?" Jill asked.

Her mother flushed a little. "You were on deck. I don't have to pay attention when you're on deck."

As a rule, her mother would read or grade papers during games, except when Jill was actually pitching or hitting. "What if I have complicated *rituals*? And tics?" Jill asked. "You might miss seeing them."

Her mother nodded. "Yes, that would be awful."

Such enthusiasm. "You really *should* be capturing every minute on video, so we can watch the games over and over at night, and on weekends, and just, you know, revel in it all," Jill said.

Her mother looked considerably less than captivated by that idea.

"Hey, Number Twenty-eight, you gorgeous creature!" Greg shouted, and threw a Twinkie at her.

Oh, excellent, she was starving. She caught it, and started to open the wrapper—but she would look like an idiot if she were gulping down junk food in front of the scouts. So, she stuck it into the elbow part of her ice wrap, instead.

"Where's Theo?" she asked. Her big brother, who she had seen leaning against the right field fence, staring at his phone for the first couple of innings, before he wandered off.

"Off writing a poem, or some such, I expect," her mother said.

Jill grinned. Theo was a sophomore at MIT—and suddenly

madly in love with a fellow aeronautics and astronautics major, who was his first serious girlfriend. She was from Seattle, but had gone away to spend the summer with her grandparents in South Korea. So, Theo had been moping—and texting and emailing and Facebook messaging—constantly, ever since he'd come home at the end of the semester.

"'Filthy' is good, right?" her mother said in a low voice.

With the presumption that she meant that in a baseball context. Jill nodded. "Yeah. Who said it?"

"The one in the green shirt," her mother said. "He described your curve as 'positively filthy.'"

Well, *that* sounded pretty damn encouraging.

People were starting to swarm around now, but she saw that a little girl, maybe eight years old, had ventured to within about fifteen feet, but didn't seem to have the nerve to come any closer.

Maybe it wasn't a good sign when one's very presence frightened small children.

Jill walked over. "Hi," she said.

All she got back was a shy half-smile, and the girl glanced at a man—presumably her father—who gave her an encouraging nod.

"Did you enjoy the game?" Jill asked.

A much more vigorous nod this time.

"Well, I'm glad you could come," Jill said. "Do you play baseball?"

The little girl shook her head.

Sprout had left her gear on the bottom row of the bleachers, and she opened up the bag, looking for a ball that was in decent shape. "Here," she said, and handed it to the girl. "I'll bet you can get someone in your family, or a friend, to play catch with you."

"I don't know how," the girl said, her voice so quiet that Jill had to lean down to hear her.

"No problem," Jill said. "You'll learn." She took the ball back to demonstrate. "Hold it this way when you throw, and you'll be in good shape."

The girl beamed, and tried it for herself.

"That's right," Jill said, and adjusted her thumb slightly. "It's perfect, just like that. Have fun, okay?"

"Thank you," the girl said, and then hurried off, holding up the baseball to show her father, already practicing her new grip.

Mr. Friedman, the generally harried school athletic director, was waving her over, and Jill shrugged apologetically at her mother and headed in that direction. She would rather go sit with her friends for a while, but it was nice of him to run interference for her—which was taking a lot more of his time this year than it had in the past, since post-game informal press conferences had become the norm. There were always at least two local police officers at all of her games now, too, and usually several more. People from her father's National Guard unit would also show up, and while some of them probably only came to see her play, she was pretty sure that others wanted to act as an extra level of security, against the occasional loons who would arrive at games with protest signs or scream "You're ruining baseball, you bitch!" and other sorts of invective at her.

She nodded at the people in the crowd she already knew, and let Mr. Friedman introduce her to everyone else. Some of the other players—from both teams—were lurking around wistfully, and she felt a little guilty that it was so very clear that the scouts and coaches and agents and media people were only there to see *her*.

"Anything going on with your arm?" the guy from the Astros asked—and everyone's attention noticeably sharpened.

Yeah, the ice packs probably looked ominous. Jill shook her head. "No, I'm fine, thanks. But, I got it for Christmas"—from her baseball-loving Uncle Bob—"and it's *nifty*, so I like to wear it after games."

Funny, how their postures all instantly seemed to relax.

"How do you feel about losing the no-hitter?" a woman from the *Narragansett Times* asked.

Cheated. Bitter. Enraged.

Or maybe just—irked.

Besides, *what* bunt? She'd already forgotten about the damn thing.

Completely.

"All that matters is that we won," Jill said. "The guys played great defense behind me, Leonard called a really good game, and Francisco got the big hit today. So, you should really be talking to those guys, not to me."

Which did not result in a stampede to go interview any of them, unfortunately.

So, she spent the next twenty minutes or so exchanging pleasantries, introducing her mother to various people, cordially rebuffing the agents and managers who offered, as always, "to serve in a purely advisory capacity during this complicated time in your life," telling the college coaches that yes, as things currently stood, she still planned to honor her verbal commitment to Stanford, and so on. The scout from the Orioles asked if she were open to the idea of going down to Baltimore for a last-minute pitching session, and the one from the Brewers wanted to know if it would be possible to set up a workout at the URI baseball complex. She said yes to the latter, as long as it was on her regular bullpen day, and suggested that the guy from the Orioles come, too, if he wanted.

NCAA amateur status rules, and pre-draft protocol, were so damn complicated, that if she accepted every offer she had gotten to go to Camden Yards or wherever—and perform like a little show pony in front of a group of frowning front office people and high-level scouts—it would have cost her mother *a lot* of money. Travel teams, and showcases, and private lessons were also incredibly expensive, which was another reason she had mostly avoided doing any of that. And it had always made her feel sad to watch guys with minimal talent who wanted to play *so much*, and worked incredibly hard, day after day, all year long, and spent thousands of dollars—and would be lucky if they even ended up walking on at an obscure DII college someday.

For some reason, the African-American guy in the dark green polo shirt seemed to be hanging back, quietly observing. As far as she could tell, the other scouts were treating him with a certain amount of deference—which was intriguing.

Once everyone else had pretty much drifted off—although a few of the agents and reporters were still lingering nearby— the man approached her, holding out his hand.

"Hi, I'm Bill Norcross," he said, with a slight Texas accent. "Cincinnati Reds."

She had met the Reds' regional scout before—a guy named Jerry—and filled out the usual team questionnaire, and took a fairly long written psychological test, in addition to the universal one the Major League Baseball Scouting Bureau had already had her do at one point. Most of the other area scouts had asked her to complete similar paperwork, including medical information and the results of her most recent eye exam.

"Hello, sir." She shook his hand. "I'm Jill Cafferty."

He didn't do a double take—but he definitely blinked, and glanced down at her hand. Which people always did, and she had to force herself not to hide her hands self-consciously. Because, okay, they were *large*.

"It's hereditary," she said, making a concerted effort not to blush. "In fact, um, historically, many of the Bryant"—her mother's maiden name—"women play the harp."

"We've had some wonderful pianists, too," her mother said, from somewhere behind her.

Her mother's hands were pretty big, but not as big as hers were. It was embarrassing, when people noticed and stared—but *awesome*, when it came to things like being able to throw a serious curveball, and just generally getting a lot of extra movement on her pitches.

Mr. Norcross stepped forward. "Dr. Cafferty, I'm Bill Norcross, with the Cincinnati Reds."

"It's very nice to meet you, Mr. Norcross," her mother said. "And I certainly appreciate your coming to watch my daughter pitch."

"I'm glad I got a chance to see her. You can read reports and look at film all day long, but seeing a player in person is a whole different thing." Mr. Norcross grinned. "They weren't exaggerating, either. Perfect mechanics, repeatable delivery, command of all three pitches—" He shook his head. "Hell—I mean, uh, *shoot*, you've even got some pop in your bat."

She had been hit by a pitch, but she'd also had a double to the gap in left-center, and a line drive right down the first baseline—a clean single, which she had stretched into another double. After which, she stole third, and scored on a sacrifice fly. "Are you an area scout, sir?" she asked.

He smiled slightly, and shook his head.

That meant that he must be a cross checker. No MLB team went to the trouble of sending a national cross checker, unless they were *genuinely* serious about drafting someone. She felt her heart speeding up—and hoped that he couldn't tell.

"I'm actually the director of amateur scouting," he said.

Here? In Rhode Island? At this crummy little late season makeup game that didn't even matter, because her school hadn't made the playoffs this year—much to her frustration?

Wow.

Or, more accurately, *double* wow.

The best bet was to refocus, and she gestured towards the radar gun one of the other scouts was packing into a laptop bag. "Where was I today, sir?" she asked.

"Pretty consistently sitting between eighty-nine and ninety-one, but I had you at ninety-three at least twice," Mr. Norcross said.

She must have had some extra adrenaline going, because ninety-two was generally where she topped out. "How about the change?" she asked.

"Mostly about eighty-five," he said, "but I saw you as low as seventy-six."

That was really good, but not as much consistent separation as she wanted.

"How often were you holding back, because the kid catcher couldn't handle the pitches?" he asked.

Too often. Teams had gotten more baserunners on third-strike passed balls than actual hits against her this season, which had privately been very frustrating, because every time she had to adjust for him, she was hurting her own prospects. "He tries really hard," she said.

"But, you have to throw at maybe seventy-five percent more often than you want," Mr. Norcross said.

She nodded.

"Out of curiosity, what did you do wrong today?" he asked.

With scouts, it was safe to assume that every question was a test of some kind. When they had first started showing up, early in her junior year, she had always been really nervous and not sure what to say. Now, though, she just told the truth. "I think I balked on the second pick-off throw, and I tipped a couple of the curveballs, but I don't know if they figured it out," she said. In fact, she was pretty sure that no one other than the scouts had noticed. "And I probably should have buzzed someone, after they plunked me in the third."

That got her mother's attention. "Would you have, if I hadn't been at the game?" she asked.

Yes. "Probably, yeah," Jill said. "But, only from the midsection down."

Her mother frowned at her.

For Christ's sakes, the other pitcher had blatantly thrown

at her, probably because she had driven in two runs during the previous at bat. "They really shouldn't throw at me," she said, mildly. "I don't care for it at all."

Her mother was still frowning, but Mr. Norcross looked amused.

She had decided *against* hitting the guy, but had taken very great pleasure in utterly buckling his knees with a couple of curves, and striking him out three times.

Her mother focused on Mr. Norcross. "I assume you know that she has a scholarship to Stanford?"

Actually, what she had was a guaranteed freshman year, with a *possibility* that the scholarship might be renewed each year after that. But, it wasn't an argument worth having—*again*—especially since her mother was a professor and knew perfectly damn well how it worked.

Mr. Norcross nodded. "Yes. And your daughter could develop very well there. But, given their current roster and their coaching philosophy, she isn't likely to get much playing time until at least her junior year, and that could put her at a disadvantage."

"My primary concern is that she gets the best possible education," her mother said. "And I feel quite strongly about this."

Talk about an understatement. Jill resisted the urge to sigh. *Yes*, she wanted to go to college—but, *no*, she didn't want to roll the dice and hope to be drafted four years from now. Too many things could go wrong, and she might not ever have a chance to—

"And if her baseball scholarship isn't renewed for some reason, the women's basketball coach has already pointed out that her office is right down the hall," her mother said.

Yeah. And she liked basketball, a lot. She was even very *good* at basketball.

But, it wasn't baseball. Had never come close, for her.

"Obviously, this is something only you and your family can decide together," Mr. Norcross said. "But, I can't stress enough how impressed we are by her potential, and—" He stopped, let out his breath, and then looked directly at her mother. "This is something very special, Dr. Cafferty. Your daughter has a chance to make history, and—well, quite frankly, I really hope that the Cincinnati Reds can be part of that."

Her mother looked right back at him. "Do you have children, Mr. Norcross?"

He nodded. "I do. Two little girls."

"Knowing the incredible scrutiny and pressure and expectations they were going to face, and how burdensome and difficult it was almost certainly going to be, would you want one of *them* to be the person to make this particular bit of history?" her mother asked, not sounding terribly friendly.

That was a pretty interesting question, all things considered.

"No," Mr. Norcross said, without hesitating. "I don't think I would."

Wait, he had actually just said something to *further* discourage her mother? Seriously? Jill wanted to point out that maybe *her* opinion mattered more than anyone else's in this situation, and that it was her life—but, she would probably sound peevish, which wouldn't exactly improve the situation.

At least he hadn't made the mistake of saying—incorrectly—that it was "what her father would have wanted," which more than one scout and coach had earnestly told her mother over the years. Unsurprisingly, that never went over well.

"But," he went on, "I can also tell you that when my ten-year-old found out where I was going to be today, she started sobbing hysterically, because my wife and I wouldn't let her miss school to come on the trip and meet Jill in person."

Jill wasn't sure whether to feel flattered—or uncomfortable. Both, maybe.

Mr. Norcross looked at her now. "If you had ignored the child in the pink sneakers to come over and talk to me and the rest of the baseball people, I was going to call the front office and tell them that you're an extraordinary prospect, but that despite your baseball makeup, you don't have the right temperament to be the kind of trailblazer you're going to need to be, and that we should move you quite far down our board."

Their draft board. For the MLB Draft, which was next *week*. When her entire life might utterly and irrevocably change.

Now, he turned to look at her mother again. "This is history that *matters*, Dr. Cafferty. It matters a great deal."

Her mother nodded, but didn't say anything.

It was quiet for a moment, and then he reached out to shake Jill's hand.

"It was a true pleasure to meet you," he said. "I very much hope to see you again."

And she, very definitely, hoped so, too.

CHAPTER 3

After Mr. Norcross gave her mother his card and left, it was silent again.

"I'm going to get drafted," Jill said. As shocking, and overwhelming, and implausible as it felt to say that.

Her mother nodded. "I know. And I'm quite terrified about it."

Jill kind of was, too. Felt a certain amount of dread—but, also, some wild excitement and anticipation. "It's not necessarily going to be the Reds"—although, at the moment, she kind of liked the odds on that—"but, if I get picked in the first ten rounds, and it's a team that's going to take me seriously and not treat me like a novelty act, I'm going to sign," she said.

"Let's just wait and see what happens," her mother said,

"okay? Until we're really forced to—let's please wait."

Fair enough. It was all theoretical, unless and until a team did, in fact, pick her.

"Am I driving you home?" her mother asked.

Jill looked around, and saw that some of her friends were still hanging out on the bleachers, since by now, they were used to her having to spend a lot of time schmoozing after games. "Thanks, but Lauren and everyone are still here, and I haven't even gotten to say hi yet."

Her mother glanced over, too, clearly trying not to be obvious about it. "She's in the wheelchair today."

Yeah. Which was hard to see, since Lauren was mostly only using a cane these days, and usually didn't need the wheelchair anymore—and she had been on the cane, when Jill had last seen her during seventh period. "I know," Jill said. "I hope she's just tired."

"Well, tell her I said hello," her mother said.

"I will," Jill said. "And thanks for coming to the game. Do you mind bringing a bunch of my stuff home?" Since she had her backpack, too, and it was a lot to carry.

Her mother looked a little impatient. "Of course not."

Okay, dumb question. But, it was better than standing around talking about the fact that sometimes, parents *did* have very good reasons to worry that something bad might happen to their children.

And that children needed to worry about their *parents*, too.

Jill carried her gear over to the car and took off her ice wrap, packing it back into the cooler. She quickly changed out of her uniform—which wasn't a big deal, since she was wearing a pair of compression shorts and a shirt underneath it. She put on gym shorts and a grey Under Armour T-shirt, then switched her cleats for a pair of running shoes.

Her mother watched her, her expression very tense. On the whole, Jill *liked* being tall, but her mother nearly always stood in a self-conscious hunch. "You just pitched an entire game," she said.

Jill nodded, and tied the shoes tightly. She did *some* regular weight training, but she spent more time working on plyometrics and flexibility, which meant that the bulk of her strength had to come from her legs.

So, whether current Internet pitching gurus were in favor of the idea or not, she put in a lot of miles running, or on her bike. *A lot* of miles.

"I'm only going to do a few poles, and some sprints, and maybe jog home," Jill said.

Her mother started to say something, but then motioned vaguely at the remaining scouts and coaches, who were watching from a distance.

"After they leave," Jill said. Which they would, once they saw that she was sitting down to have *girl talk*. "So I won't look like I'm showboating."

"Okay," her mother said, and sighed. "Dinner at seven-thirty, all right?" She opened the door on the driver's side. "I wonder where your brother ended up."

Jill pulled her phone out of her bag, and saw that she had a lot of new texts, including one from Theo, which said, "*You looked good out there! But, I had to go find caffeine.*" "He says he needed coffee, so he's probably at Cool Beans." A local place, where she and her friends often went—and pretended they were there to do homework, which, of course, they weren't.

Her mother nodded. "Remind him about dinner, please."

Even though he would still probably forget. But, Jill quickly texted him.

Her mother started to get into the car, but then paused. "Your father would be so incredibly proud of you."

Some days, more so than others. But, today, yes, she was pretty sure he would have been. "Yeah," Jill said. "I hope so."

"I'm very proud of you, too," her mother said, and they both nodded, somewhat uncomfortably.

Which was as good a note to part on as any, probably.

There were still quite a few people around the field, and she had to stop and answer questions, kindly rebuff the *Sports Illustrated* guy again, and be polite to more strangers. But, finally, she managed to excuse herself, and made her way over to the bleachers.

"Fame is a heavy burden," Lauren said.

Jill nodded, and took a seat next to her. There was a great

comfort in having been friends with people since kindergarten. "Where is everyone?"

"Cathy went to get the car, Stephanie had to go to work, and Maureen needed to study for finals," Lauren said.

At the moment, Jill didn't even want to *think* about how much studying she needed to do. "You really didn't have to come to the game," she said, gesturing towards the wheelchair.

Lauren just looked at her. "I wasn't about to skip it."

Okay, last game, senior year—it *had* been kind of a big deal. "You were on the cane all day, though," Jill said.

Lauren shrugged. "So, I got tired, no big deal. Cathy's going to give me a ride home, and I'll take it easy tonight."

She sounded perfunctory—and dismissive, which was entirely reasonable, since Lauren's entire family, and most of her friends, had done nothing but fret over her protectively since the accident. "And I shouldn't bug you, when you have *lots* of other people around to do it, instead," Jill said.

Now, Lauren grinned. "Exactly. I know it's a learning curve for you, but you're doing very well."

Which led to a somewhat troubling thought. "Oh my God," Jill said. "Am I *exactly* like my mother?"

"More or less, yeah," Lauren said.

It came out of genuine concern—but, still. "You can probably make up your own damn mind about when and where and *if* you want to use the wheelchair," Jill said.

Lauren's grin broadened. "So quick. So clever."

Oh, yeah, no doubt. But, it always came as a relief, when Lauren *sounded* like herself again. There had been quite a few weeks—months, even—of monosyllables and near-silence. She was small, and blond, and fine-featured in a way that tended to make people underestimate her, but before the accident, Lauren had been one of the best athletes she knew. Determined, driven, and game savvy, whether it was tennis, basketball, or softball. And now, she spent most of her free time—taking pain medication and doing physical therapy.

"Ready to frighten everyone off?" Lauren asked.

Absolutely. Jill nodded.

Lauren pulled a bottle of nail polish out of her hoodie pocket. Some sort of Eggplant Purple shade.

"That's hideous," Jill said, and held her right hand out.

Lauren nodded, uncapped the bottle, and started carefully applying the polish to Jill's nails. And, indeed, most of the hangers-on looked aghast, and began drifting away.

"Girl stuff," Lauren said. "They just *hate* girl stuff, don't they?"

Jill nodded again. "It's good to have things to count on."

They had figured out, a couple of seasons ago, that sitting down to braid her hair, do her nails, or anything else traditionally feminine cleared out the crowds pretty quickly. Yeah, there was always some jerk around who took photos and put them online, attempting to make a profound statement about gender roles or whatever damn thing—but, it was still their traditional post-game strategy.

"This looks really awful," Lauren said.

Jill nodded. They always made a point of using truly ugly colors, because it was more entertaining that way.

"As far as I could tell, your mother was flipping out," Lauren said.

Yet again. Jill sighed. "I know. I wish she'd have more *fun* with this. I mean, it's pretty exciting stuff."

Lauren glanced up at her. "I wish *you'd* have more fun with this."

She would be annoyed as hell if most other people had said that—but, coming from Lauren, it was probably just the simple truth. "I *am* having fun," Jill said, although she had meant to sound enthusiastic, instead of defensive.

Lauren nodded pleasantly.

"I'm *all about* fun," Jill said. "It's a way of life for me."

"Unh-hunh," Lauren said.

Point taken. "The *Sports Illustrated* guy asked me if there's any way to know whether I'm good enough, and whether I even belong in the conversation, since I haven't faced much serious competition," Jill said.

"They always ask stuff like that," Lauren said, shrugging.

True. And they might be right.

"What did you say?" Lauren asked.

The usual drivel. "That I'm looking forward to getting a

chance to find out, and that I hope there are a lot of interesting opportunities ahead," Jill said.

Lauren laughed. "And if baseball doesn't work out, you can run for office someday."

It was good to have options. "The Reds sent their director of amateur scouting," Jill said.

Lauren's eyebrows went up. "Huge deal," she said.

Very much so, yeah. During the past couple of years, most of her friends had mastered all of the arcane nuances surrounding Major League Baseball scouting and the draft process.

Her right hand was finished, albeit sloppily, and she held out her left hand, instead.

"Think I have backup career potential here?" Lauren asked.

Jill looked at the three spots where the purple had overlapped her nails, so that the polish was on her actual *fingers*. "I don't have high hopes, no," she said.

"Well, the price is right," Lauren said, and kept painting.

When all of her nails were done, Jill waved them slightly in the air, so that the polish would dry and she could go work out.

Their friend Cathy had parked the car as close to the field as possible, and was now walking over to join them. Like so many other people in her class, Jill had known her since elementary school. They had been Brownies together, and learned to ski at Yawgoo Valley, back when they were about seven, among other things.

"Good game, Jill," she said. "You guys all set?"

Jill and Lauren both nodded, and Jill got up to push the wheelchair.

"Watch those perfect nails!" Lauren said.

Watch them smear, mostly.

After making sure Lauren was safely in the car, and then helping Cathy load the wheelchair into the trunk, Jill turned to go back to the field.

"You're not coming with us?" Cathy asked. "We were going to grab some coffee on the way home."

A mocha latte would be entirely awesome right about now. Jill shook her head. "I need to burn off some energy, and run a little, before things stiffen up."

"All work and no play makes you dull as hell," Lauren said.

Unfortunately, dull had kind of become her norm.

She was stretching her hamstrings when she saw Greg come jogging across the outfield.

"I thought you went off with the guys," she said. Thought she was the only person not sensible enough to go enjoy the rest of the afternoon, like a normal carefree, soon-to-graduate senior.

He shrugged. "I had them drop me back here. Figured I'd hang out."

Which was certainly a nice enough idea. "Want to run poles with me?" she asked.

Greg shook his head. "Hell, no. I ate about a thousand Twinkies during the game."

Running poles was enough of a chore so that she probably wouldn't mind skipping it herself. But, she kept stretching, anyway.

Greg reclined on the grass, using his folded hands as a pillow. "One of those scouts is still here. I saw him in the parking lot, in his car, and—I don't know. Seemed like a good idea to stick around, in case he's weird or something."

As strapping, cocky quarterbacks went, Greg was awfully sweet. "Thanks," she said, although she hadn't really felt isolated, since there were people playing tennis on the courts behind them, and a local parks guy cleaning the dugouts. "Which one?"

"Guy in the dark green shirt," he said.

She switched to quad stretches. "What's he doing?"

"On his phone," Greg said. "But, it seemed like he was watching you, too."

Hmmm. "I went to the Reds' home page"—she gestured to her unzipped duffel bag, where her phone was—"and he's their director of amateur scouting, but he's also the assistant director of baseball operations."

Greg sat up halfway. "That means they aren't kidding around."

So it would seem. She switched to a different stretch, for her lower back.

"Well, do the poles, and let's see if he's still here when you're finished," Greg said.

Sounded like a plan.

She was too tired to sprint all out, but she ran hard, starting at the right field foul pole, along the fairly bumpy warning track to the left field pole, and then, back to the right field pole.

After eight repetitions, she was pretty much gassed, but she gutted her way through ten.

"Oh, yeah, dig it out, baby!" Greg yelled. "Show 'em you've got some heart!"

"Watch and learn, son!" she yelled back.

Her legs were shaking from exertion, and she walked across the outfield to cool down—and catch her breath. Almost every book or website about pitching gave different advice—usually some version of "Here is why *everything* you thought you knew is wrong"—about techniques and training and off-season routines and a million other things, so she had long since decided that she would do whatever made her feel healthy and strong, advice be damned. And burning off what she assumed was lactic acid—or maybe just *nerves*—after a game always felt soothing.

Five forty-yard sprints, five interval sprints, some more cooling down, a few extra stretches—and she figured that was enough. Especially since she was entirely worn out.

"You're making me feel like a total slug," Greg said.

A title well-earned.

"He still there?" she asked, bending down to take a water bottle and a small towel out of her bag.

"Yep," Greg said. "Still on the phone, too."

With luck, calling his general manager to ask if they could draft her *really* high. She wiped off her face, neck, and hands with the towel, and then pulled on an old blue New England Patriots windbreaker, zipping it halfway.

She felt *good*. As though her body was humming gently, and the post-game tension was pretty much gone now.

"The *Sports Illustrated* guy is back, too," Greg said, doing ten fast push-ups—probably to remind her that he *could*, effortlessly, and then standing up.

She had no intention of agreeing to a high-profile interview before she was drafted—especially since she might *not* be drafted, and would look like an idiot. People had written a bunch of stories about her in the past few years—which her mother insisted upon keeping as brief and vague as possible—and she'd yet to read one that, in any way, sounded like her, or felt like a decent characterization. Mostly, they went with a "She's a *girl*! And she throws like a boy! Wow!" tone.

There had been a stream of breathless pre-draft articles, and sports website analyses about her prospects, but it was really too stressful to read them, especially since the assessment of her abilities—or, in some pundits' opinions, lack thereof—generally seemed pretty arbitrary. And it was creepy to read judgmental opinions about her size, and what was regularly deemed her "probable lack of projectibility." In other words, she was about as tall as she was likely to get.

Which was pretty damn tall, in her opinion.

"All of this making you crazy?" Greg asked.

She nodded. "Remember when sports were just *fun*? And we could throw the ball around whenever we wanted, and no one cared whether we were any good?"

"Yup," he said. "And then you had to go and screw it up, by not turning out to be mediocre."

Yeah, he was kidding—but, *was* that how it had happened? Maybe it would have been better just to be a perfectly adequate high school baseball player, and leave it at that. She hadn't planned to sigh, but she must have, because Greg looked over at her.

"If you sign, it's only going to get crazier," he said.

That was true, too.

They walked across the infield, Jill automatically stepping over the foul line without touching it. Because everyone knew that that was *very* bad luck.

"Still mad about the bunt?" Greg asked.

Yes. "I was a step slow," she said.

He shrugged. "Maybe. But, Leonard should have been on it before you, anyway. He was late getting out there."

She wasn't going to throw the kid under the bus—but, yeah, it had been his ball.

As they left the field, she saw that Mr. Norcross was leaning against his car, talking on his phone—again? still?—but, he waved her over.

"Let me call you back," he said into the phone, and then slid it into his pocket.

"Mr. Norcross, this is my friend Greg," Jill said.

Mr. Norcross nodded and shook his hand. "Nice to meet you. Are you the quarterback?"

"Thank you for not calling me 'the gay quarterback,'" Greg said, and then paused. "Although I *do* play with quite a lot of joy."

Would it be more effective to punch him—or *kick* him? Jill narrowed her eyes, instead, and he grinned at her.

Although he did get described that way, rather too often. A DII coach, who had been considering recruiting him, had actually asked, "Exactly how gay *are* you, son?" whereupon Greg had said, cheerily, "As gay as a weekend in the country, smelling jasmine, watching little things grow."

To the coach's noticeable consternation.

And later, Greg had said, "Well, guess *that* queered the deal, didn't it?"

In so many ways.

"Where are you playing next fall?" Mr. Norcross asked.

"Amherst," Greg said.

Mr. Norcross nodded. "Decided to go DIII?"

"My *talent* is DIII," Greg said, and gestured towards Jill. "Unlike, you know, Hotshot over here."

Jill wasn't sure about that—in either case—but, with luck, the latter was entirely accurate.

"I'm sure you've had it for the day," Mr. Norcross said. "But, I wanted to ask you one favor." He reached into the front seat of the car, and came out with a baseball, which he handed to her, along with a pen. "Would you mind signing this?"

A brand-new official MLB baseball. Which seemed strange. She glanced over at Greg, who was frowning. "Well, I'm not sure if I—"

"Indulge me," Mr. Norcross said. "Okay?"

It still seemed strange, unless it was another test of some kind—although she couldn't quite imagine what it would be. People often asked her to sign balls, especially when she had a notably good game, but most of the time, it was *little girls*, not MLB directors of scouting. But, she spun the ball in her hand, so that the sweet spot was facing up, and carefully wrote her name on it. Then, she gave it to him.

"Thank you," he said. He examined the signature, and nodded. "That's pretty good. The more clear and legible you can be, the better. You don't want to send someone home with a scribble they can't read."

Okay, so it *was* a test. Or maybe a lesson.

He put the ball back in her hand. "If this all comes to pass, you're going to have a lot of extra demands on your time. And even if you're tired, or in a hurry, or had a bad game, for the person who asked you, it's usually going to be a *big* deal. So, try not to forget to let it be a special moment for them. And use a regular pen, whenever possible, so it won't bleed as much."

Good advice. "What about the ones headed straight for eBay and places like that?" she asked.

Mr. Norcross shrugged. "There's only so much you can control. Focus on kids where you can, and don't stress about the rest. Although if the same guy shows up every single day, asking you to sign, you can assume he's selling them, and maybe run it past the team's PR department. There are going to be a lot of people around who want to help you, so take advantage of that."

Which was making it sound as though he was absolutely *sure* that she was going to be playing professionally.

"This is really going to happen," she said, "isn't it? I mean, that someone or other *is* going to draft me."

He nodded. "Without a doubt," he said.

CHAPTER 4

As soon as Mr. Norcross drove away, Greg snatched the baseball from her, and clasped it reverently.

"Oh, I'm so excited!" he said. "This is a dream come true! I'll treasure it *always*. I think I'll even sleep with it under my pillow."

Being mocked kept a person humble. "You're an idiot," Jill said.

Greg tucked the baseball into the pocket of his shorts. "I'm going to sell it for *a million dollars*."

"Do I get a cut?" Jill asked.

He shook his head. "No, but if you're lucky, maybe I'll spring for a movie ticket or something."

"Always a big spender," she said, and he grinned at her.

Instead of heading straight home, she ran down by the seawall, and sat on a stone bench for a few minutes to look out at the ocean. Normally, she would probably do the beach—a mile down to Narrow River, and then back—but, she was too tired. So, it was nice just to sit, and watch the waves for a while. They were tiny and gentle today, which meant that there weren't any surfers, but there were lots of people—and their dogs—walking by. She liked the beach best on grey winter days, when there was almost no one around, but it was *always* a really beautiful place to be.

When she finally got to her house, it was quiet—although that was pretty *normal* these days. Even six months ago, their setter mix, Maggie, would have rushed to greet her at the door, but she was suddenly aging—rapidly—and it took her longer to get up now—or even hear any of them come in.

Since Maggie had especially been her father's dog, that made it that much sadder, of course.

As she walked inside, Maggie was lying on the orthopedic dog bed in the corner of the kitchen.

Jill put her duffel bag on the nearest chair, and then crouched down.

"Hey there, girl," she said. "How are you?"

Maggie wagged her tail, happily.

"What a pretty girl," Jill said, and kept patting her.

Her mother was sitting at the table, reading the paper.

Actual newsprint, since she was nothing if not old-school. "Are you hungry?" she asked.

Always. Reliably. Constantly. "*Yes*," Jill said, giving Maggie another pat before standing up. "Do I have time to take a shower first?"

Her mother nodded. "We'll eat in about half an hour."

Which seemed like a really long time, and Jill was tempted to bring half the refrigerator upstairs with her as a snack. But, she settled for giving Maggie a biscuit and taking a banana for herself.

"Did I get any messages?" she asked.

Her mother indicated the legal pad on the table, with a pen resting on top of it. "Quite a few. The agents are still swarming, and the networks are remarkably persistent."

ESPN and the MLB Network had both invited her to attend the draft in person, and since she knew she wasn't going to be picked early on the first day, it was easy to say no. And, truthfully, even easier to have her mother do it *for* her.

"You don't have to call any of them back," her mother said. "I told them you would be busy studying." She paused. "Which you will be, right?"

Apparently so, although the idea of streaming something or reading a book sounded a lot more appealing. "Looks that way, yeah," Jill said. She had finished her Senior Project, her AP exams, and the research paper for her ethics class, but the rest of her classes still required finals—mostly to keep the seniors from checking out mentally during their last semester and spending all of their time on the beach.

It would be nice *not* to care about her final exams, since they might not really matter in the overall scheme of things—but, she did. Kind of a lot.

When she went upstairs, she saw Theo on his bed, staring up at the ceiling.

"You collapse from exhaustion from too much texting?" she asked.

He nodded. "My phone's charging."

Oh, the humanity. "How is she?" Jill asked.

"She's *far*," he said glumly. "Far, far away."

It was probably just as well that his summer internship—at a robotics lab in Providence—was going to begin pretty soon, since that would keep him distracted until classes started again.

She *did* study that night. And the next night. And the night after that. And most of the day on Sunday. Which made for an incredibly boring weekend, but at least, she was pretty confident that she would get through the exams in decent shape. Although she also found some time to work out, throw a brief bullpen session over at the university for a last-minute cluster of scouts, and go to the movies with Lauren and a few of their other friends.

The networks were still calling, to try and get her to appear live in the studio during the draft. There were also offers to come to her house and film her *watching* the draft with her family and friends—but, with a very clear image of round after round passing, without her being picked, recorded for posterity and airing *live*, Jill declined.

Much to her mother's relief.

Although—funny thing—all three of her grandparents were *coincidentally* coming to visit, her Aunt Karen was taking Amtrak up from New York, and another aunt and uncle were flying in from Chicago. Theo was even promising less vaguely than usual that he would be around, too.

She had her last two finals on the second day of the draft, so instead of sitting around and watching the early picks the night before, she would be busy—what else?—*studying*.

Of course, she did end up watching some of it, until she got tired of hearing sports pundits speculating about various players' prospects, especially when she was one of the people being discussed. The sportscasters were positively *giddy* about it all, and kept mentioning her constantly, even though there was no chance that she was going to go in the first round. Or the second. Or the competitive balance rounds.

The next day, she had her calculus final in the morning, followed by her Spanish final after lunch. The draft would start up again at one o'clock, but she wasn't really worried about that, since at best, she wouldn't be picked until much later in the day—if at all—so she could relax.

Well, not *relax*, considering that these were final exams, and her entire future also maybe hinged upon whatever was happening in a bunch of MLB draft rooms all over the country—but, close enough.

The second day was rounds three through ten, and then, the last thirty rounds would take place on the third day. She hadn't made her mother a *firm* promise, but they had a general agreement that if she didn't go on the second day, she would head off to Stanford, and wait to see what happened when she graduated.

Probably. Depending. Maybe.

She was in the middle of a translation for her Spanish exam when her cell phone started vibrating, and vibrating, and *vibrating*—which had been happening on and off all day— mostly reporters, she figured. But now, the thing was suddenly going *crazy*, with texts and calls.

Everyone sitting near her noticed, too, and they all looked at her knapsack, and then at their teacher.

"Go ahead and pick up," Mrs. Taveras said.

Didn't have to tell *her* twice. Jill took her phone out, just as another call came in, with an unfamiliar area code. She had been halfway expecting it to be—she hoped—from Cincinnati, but this was a different number.

"Where's four-one-two?" she asked the room in general, and people shrugged.

She was tempted just to let it go to voice mail, and call her mother to find out what was going on, but—well, if it was only a reporter, she could always give him or her a quick brush-off.

"Hello?" she said, cautiously.

"Hello, is this Jill Cafferty?" an older male voice asked.

"Yes, sir," she said.

"This is Ronald Saunders, from the Pittsburgh Pirates," the man said. "I'd like to congratulate you, and welcome you to our organization."

Her heart started beating *considerably* faster, and for a second, she thought she might burst into tears—which surprised the hell out of her. "Yes, sir," she said, and swallowed. "I mean, thank you, sir. Um, what round are we in?"

Mr. Saunders laughed. "Your mother said you were taking a final, but I didn't think—that's great. I love that."

Although it didn't answer her question.

"We're very pleased to have made you our third-round pick," he said, "and are excited to be part of an historic moment for women and sports."

Wow. Third round. Almost certainly putting her in the first one hundred picks. Were they *nuts*? Her heart was pounding even harder, and it was a little bit hard to get her breath. "I see," she said—since her mind was pretty much a complete blank. Nobody would pick a novelty act in the third round—right? "I mean, thank you. That's very nice of you, sir."

She heard warm male chuckles—and realized that she was not only probably on speakerphone, but might also be on live television, sounding like a moron. A moron with good manners, but a moron, regardless.

"Would it be all right, sir, if I call you back after I finish my exam?" she asked.

Mr. Saunders laughed again. "You bet, Jill," he said. "Take your final, and we'll contact you at home later on. And congratulations!"

After he hung up, she stared at her phone for another few seconds.

"So?" Greg asked.

"The Pirates," she said. "Third round."

There was some clapping and cheering, and shouts of "Yeah!" and "All right!" She glanced at Lauren, who made her eyes extra wide, and mouthed the word, *"Pittsburgh?"*

Which was almost certainly the precise reaction her mother had had, too.

And, in all honesty, not too far from her own reaction, which was along the lines of "The *Pirates*?" Other than reading a biography of Roberto Clemente once, she had probably never, in her entire life, given a single thought to the Pittsburgh Pirates, other than being pleased when the Red Sox beat them in interleague games.

"This is wonderful news," Mrs. Taveras said, over the clamor of congratulations, "but, we're in the middle of an exam here. Jill, if you need to be dismissed, it's all right, although—"

Right. They were taking a final. And even if she *wanted* to leave, it would just mean making it up later.

"She's about to be a millionaire," one of the guys in the

back row said. "She doesn't have to pass Spanish anymore."

The money. She hadn't even thought about the third round, and what that meant, in terms of *money*.

A lot. Probably not a million, but—wow.

Mrs. Taveras was trying to get everyone to settle down, and Jill blinked, making an effort to refocus. Exam. Work. Time to concentrate. She looked down at the passage she was supposed to translate from *The House on Mango Street*—or, in this case, *La Casa en Mango Street*.

Spanish. She'd been studying Spanish for years. She was *good* at Spanish. Not quite fluent, but more than comfortable.

Although, at the moment, the words looked entirely foreign, in every way.

Except, if she *was going to be a professional baseball player*, she would need to know how to be able to regain her composure very quickly—and this could be a good exercise.

Being able to speak Spanish was going to be helpful, too.

She churned her way through the rest of the exam—which probably wasn't going to be the best grade she ever got. But, she finished, gave Lauren a "see you later" nod, exchanged high fives with Greg and a few other people, and then handed the exam booklet to Mrs. Taveras.

Her mother, and Theo, and her maternal grandmother were waiting for her out by the main office.

"Oh, it's so exciting!" her grandmother said, and hugged her.

"Oh my *God*, no," Theo said, and grinned at their mother.

Jill turned her head enough to look at her. "Is that what you said?"

"Well, I said, '*Wow*,' after that," her mother said, a little defensively.

Fair enough.

A lot of people—the principal, teachers, people who worked in the office, students—were all coming over to shake her hand and congratulate her, and the hall was very noisy and crowded.

Over near the main doors, she saw Keith, who was a local cop who had served in Afghanistan with her father—and had gone out of his way to keep an extra eye on her family ever since. He came over, and gave her a big hug.

"Third round!" he said.

That part was still fairly shocking to her, too.

He glanced at her mother. "We have a lot of press showing up. So, Vicky"—his partner—"and I are going to give you an escort home. We're assigning at least one car to the house, too."

Which made it all sound far more threatening than it actually was, when they got outside. Yes, some reporters were there, and asked questions, but they were *friendly*, and it was easy enough for her to say that she was excited, and eager to see what happened next, and other bland and benign things. The only question that brought her up short was when someone asked if she wished her father was there to share this with her, but she just told the truth—that she wished that was true *every* day.

They had a big gathering at the house that night, and people from all over town showed up. After a glass—or maybe two or three—of wine, her mother gave a few of the sports and local networks permission to come in and film the party for a little while, and do some brief, fairly raucous interviews with people.

Some of the coverage seemed to be solidly in the "What an exciting day!" camp, while other commentators were more concerned that she had been "a huge reach" as a third rounder, and that the Pirates would regret having wasted such a high pick. It would be the better part of wisdom not to watch any of it—and, mostly, she didn't, although sometimes, the television was hard to avoid. But, it was gratifying to hear one analyst say something to the effect of "She's a six-two lefty, touched ninety-three on the gun last week, and already has the makings of two plus pitches. How is that *reaching*?"

She was getting so many calls and texts—including *dozens* from various agents—that she finally gave up and turned both of her phones off.

Increasingly, the whole day was feeling very overwhelming, and while she totally appreciated that so many people had come over to celebrate, she really kind of wished that they would go home. At this point, she mostly just wanted to escape. Yeah, the party was in her honor and all, but it really wasn't her style.

"I have to get out of here," she said, quietly, to Lauren, after exchanging small talk with yet another well-wisher she barely knew. "Cover for me?"

Lauren nodded. "You're on a call with the White House."

Hilariously, the White House *had* called, earlier—and Theo laughed and took a message, instead of going to find her. They had called back, of course, and she had a short, awkward conversation with the freakin' *President*—and felt like an inarticulate poseur the entire time.

"Exactly," Jill said.

It turned out to be pretty easy to mumble about needing "to go get something" to anyone who asked, and then, slip away.

She ended up in Theo's darkened room. Since Maggie had—very slowly—followed her upstairs, and stretched out on the rug, Jill sat on the floor next to her. Which felt like a good spot, anyway, since she would be out of immediate view, and could have a little privacy. It would be nice, for a few minutes, to be alone, and quiet, and *unobtrusive*. There was something extremely exhausting about a "Me! Me! Me!" day.

She patted Maggie for a while, and then rested her hand on her back, while she closed her eyes and took slow, deep breaths. If a party in her own house seemed like too much exposure, what was professional baseball going to be like? Maybe her mother was right, and this whole thing really *was* a terrible idea. Maybe she should just go to college, like a normal person.

Which would probably come as a rude shock to the Pittsburgh Pirates.

She had almost twenty minutes by herself before Theo showed up.

"Hey," he said. "You all right? Mom wanted me to see if you were okay."

"I'm fine," she said. "Just taking a break."

"Okay, but you're not hiding in *your* room," Theo said.

She shrugged. "First place they'd look."

"Well, yeah," he said. "First place *I* looked." He sat on the floor, too, leaning back against his bureau.

Maggie thumped her tail at him, but didn't get up, and Jill kept patting her.

"You blew off the President," she said. "Were you really being a flake?"

He grinned at her. "Not so much."

Which was what she had suspected. Because he was too damn smart to do anything *that* dumb.

"A little humility here and there is good for world leaders," he said. "Keeps them in touch with their humanity."

No doubt.

They sat there.

"What's up?" he asked. "Big night for you."

Yup. *Too* big. Jill nodded.

"And you pretty much like everyone here," he said.

Also true. In fact, she *loved* more than a few of them.

"So, why are you up here crying?" he asked.

"I'm not crying," she said.

He just looked at her.

Okay, maybe a little. And slightly more so, since he had come into the room. "We're going to lose Maggie soon," she said.

Theo nodded.

"And I'm not going to be able to say good-bye," she said. "I'm going to leave, and the next time I come home, she'll just be *gone*."

He nodded. "Every time I go back to school, I feel that way."

They sat there for a few minutes, listening to the sounds of loud conversations and celebrating downstairs.

"Dad should be here," she said finally.

"Dad should *always* be here," Theo said.

That never stopped being true, but tonight just felt more— *significant*.

"When I got the National Merit Scholarship, I kept thinking, I wish he knew about this," Theo said. "And MIT, and the robotics job, and getting my driver's license, and everything else that's happened."

Yeah, and Stanford, and her scholarship. And getting into Brown, and Columbia, and Middlebury, and Tufts. And winning the state basketball championship.

And being drafted in the third round by a Major League Baseball team.

She noticed that she had pulled her father's dog tag out

of her shirt and was toying with it—and that Theo was doing exactly the same thing with his dog tag, since there had been two, and her mother had given each of them one to wear— which they both did, *always*. And holding it was a habit so ingrained that she generally forgot that she was doing it.

"Think it ever goes away?" she asked.

Theo shook his head. "No."

She didn't, either.

CHAPTER 5

The next couple of days were hectic, and she got almost no sleep. The Pirates flew her down to Pittsburgh, along with her mother and her Aunt Karen—who was a lawyer. Starting in the morning, she was supposed to have a comprehensive physical, meet a bunch of people in the front office, and get started on contract negotiations. Agents were still calling constantly—but, for now, it was convenient to have a high-powered attorney in the family. As ever, the agents were trying too damn hard to *woo* her, which wasn't terribly enticing.

The team sent a town car to meet them at the airport, and they were given a suite at the Fairmont, with a connecting room for her aunt.

The hotel was exceedingly upscale, and it was the first

time Jill had stayed in *any* suite, forget one with floor-to-ceiling windows, and a totally awesome view of the ballpark across the river. The Pirates had a large fruit basket, champagne, and fresh flowers waiting for them, and the hotel had added a batch of fresh cookies, some chocolate-covered strawberries, and a lot of other stuff with too many calories. They had even provided several sets of workout garb, with the hotel logo on them.

There was a telescope set up by one of the windows, and she angled it to focus directly on PNC Park, even though the team was on the road, so it wasn't all lit up.

"Pretty swanky," she said.

Her mother took one of the cookies out of the basket, tasted it, and nodded her approval. "I'd imagine that they're trying to impress us."

"It's *working*," Jill said, and helped herself to a cookie, too.

They were all pretty wired—and hungry—and it was past nine, so they ended up ordering room service and watching a movie in their—fancy—living room.

"I think we made a mistake," her aunt said to her mother, as they polished off most of the chocolate-covered strawberries, "when neither of us ever learned how to pitch."

Her mother nodded. "Clearly."

Well, they both had the *height* for it. "Look, there's exercise gear for all of us," Jill said, pointing at the neatly folded pile of workout clothes. "You guys could get started, first thing tomorrow."

"Oh, yeah, *that's* going to happen," her aunt said, and laughed.

"They look very comfortable, though," her mother said thoughtfully. "They'll be perfect for Netflix."

"*Ideal*," her aunt said.

Jill wasn't sure whether to laugh with them, or *at* them.

Aunt Karen was a partner at a high-end law firm in New York, primarily working in trademark, copyright, advertising and brand management, with a sub-specialty in intellectual property litigation. Although, in Jill's opinion, she was *way* more fun than that made her sound. But, it was a reasonable fit for negotiating a baseball contract, and she had some law school friend who was a sports attorney, with whom she had been consulting for the past couple of days.

"How far above slot do you really want me to negotiate?" her aunt asked, once the movie was over.

Jill shook her head. "Not very. Or maybe even at all. I don't want the other players resenting me, if I get more than my share of the bonus pool." And—although it had only slightly appeased her mother—Major League Baseball had a rock-solid college scholarship plan, which would reimburse her for tuition and living expenses, as long as she started taking classes within two years of retiring or getting released.

Which felt like a thousand years down the road.

She hoped.

"As your attorney, I just want to point out that the

organization is going to make a great deal of money on merchandising because of you, so there's a limit to how much I'm going to be willing to leave on the table," Aunt Karen said. "And you may want to reconsider turning down all of the endorsement offers we have coming in."

"*Punting* endorsement offers," Jill said. "I don't want to cash in, before I actually *do* anything."

Her aunt smiled, which made her look much younger than she normally did in her chic power suits, with her hair up. "I feel like a traitor to my profession—but, okay, I'll take it under advisement."

Once the lights were out, and she was lying in the unfamiliar queen-sized bed, Jill found it impossible to sleep. She decided to read on her iPad for a few minutes, until she was sleepy—but soon, it was two in the morning, and then, *three* in the morning, and she began worrying about looking tired and sluggish, and making a really bad impression on everyone.

At some point, she finally dozed off a little, but was wide-awake again by six-thirty.

So, she swapped her URI T-shirt for some gym clothes and her running shoes, tucked a resistance band into the pocket of her shorts, left her mother a note, drank a glass of water, and went off to find the hotel's fitness center.

Just as she was heading in, a sweat-drenched guy about her age was coming out, and it wasn't until he was already gone that it occurred to her that he was almost certainly one of her fellow draft picks. And although there were a fair number of businesspeople in the gym, she immediately noticed a muscular young brown-haired guy doing lat pulldowns, and was pretty sure that he was the Competitive Balance Round pick. He seemed to recognize her, too, but they didn't do anything other than nod in a friendly way.

She got on a bike for about ten minutes, pedaling at a moderate rate, just to warm up. Then, she spent about fifteen minutes on some gentle static and dynamic stretching, using a mat, a foam roller, and her resistance band. Since she was tired—and tense—she took it easy, just trying to get her blood moving, and her heart rate *steady*. The brown-haired guy was working out *hard*, but she focused on her own plan, instead of giving in to the temptation to be a little competitive. Although it was more of a challenge, when the tall, swaggering first-round pick showed up, frowned at her, and started an ostentatiously intense workout of his own.

A few of the other people using the fitness center clearly recognized her, but only two of them approached to congratulate her on being drafted, and she thanked them, and then went back to stretching. She saw some surreptitious cell phone photos being taken, and hoped they wouldn't be *too* unflattering.

After the stretching session, she got back on one of the bikes, and did twenty-five minutes of intervals, with a five minute cooldown. A trainer brought her a fluffy white towel and offered her a choice between cold water with fresh lemon or cucumber slices—which made her feel a little silly.

"Do you have celery water?" she asked.

He looked startled for a second, but then recovered himself. "Of course. I'll have some sent up."

Wow, this hotel must have a lot of high-maintenance guests. "I'm kidding," she said quickly. "Lemon is fine, but thank you." She had to have a bunch of medical exams later, and wasn't supposed to eat anything, but she was allowed to have water, at least.

When she got back to the suite, her mother was drinking coffee and reading the morning papers—big surprise—and her aunt was on the phone, having what sounded like a somewhat contentious business conversation.

"I don't want to be a lawyer," Jill said.

Her mother nodded. "Thank heavens for small mercies."

"They offered me lemon- or cucumber-flavored water," Jill said.

"Snazzy," her mother said.

And how. "I like the idea of having plenty of money, but I hate the idea of being *rich*," Jill said.

Her mother laughed. "That sounds about right."

Since she wasn't allowed to have breakfast, her mother and aunt held off, too. Then, her aunt headed over to the stadium for a contract meeting, while she and her mother went to Allegheny General Hospital for her exams. They met a group of team doctors there, and she had a full physical, including blood work and drug testing, another eye exam, MRIs on her shoulder and elbow, and any one of a number of other tests. Her regular doctor at home had already sent the team her records, and she felt lucky as hell that her primary injuries had been a broken ankle when she fell while jumping off a rock formation down by the ocean when she was nine, and a broken nose in the tenth grade, when she took an jab to the face during a basketball game. So, there were no shoulder or elbow issues to frighten them.

It was a relief when they told her that the records from her gynecologist would be fine, and that they didn't need to repeat *that* exam. Although, apparently, they were going to check her hormones, to make sure her estrogen and testosterone were within normal gender limits. It really didn't seem like any of their damn business that she was taking the Pill to regulate her period, because it was just *easier* as an athlete, but she confirmed it, when they asked.

Which was all really too weird for words.

She caught glimpses of the three guys she had seen working out, but none of them did anything more than exchange brief nods, since they were all busy having their X-rays and stress tests and so forth.

The doctors finally kicked her loose in the early afternoon, and her mother got a recommendation for a nearby restaurant from one of the nurses. Italian food, low-key, and based upon the photos on the walls, it attracted a sports-friendly crowd. So, she shouldn't have been surprised when she was recognized. There was a good-sized lunch crowd, but they were seated right away, and the owners came over to shake her hand.

Almost before the chef had time to make it back to the kitchen, a basket of just-baked focaccia, seasoned olive oil, an order of mussels, a dish of what was described as greens and beans, and some homemade mozzarella were sent to their table.

"It's a treat," her mother said, "to be dining with a celebrity."

"I didn't expect people to figure it out so easily," Jill said.

Her mother's smile was tense. "You're on a lot of magazine covers lately."

Well, yeah, there was that. But, as celebrities went, she felt like pretty small potatoes. Tiny, little, hard-to-see potatoes.

There was a lot more food than either of them felt like eating—complicated by the fact that quite a few of the other diners came over to say hello, and more than one of them asked her to pose for photos with them. So, there wasn't much time to focus on the actual meal, even though it was delicious. She was also suddenly worried that someone might get terrible photos of her *chewing*, and put them online somewhere.

When the waitress brought them the check, her mother reached for a credit card, looked inside the folder, and then sighed.

"I was afraid of that," she said. "They comped us."

"What, you mean, it was free?" Jill asked.

Her mother nodded. "I'm going to go ahead and try to pay, and failing that, just overtip wildly, I guess."

They had been warned, during the NCAA recruiting period, not to accept *any* gifts from coaches or agents or equipment representatives—and Jill was surprised when she *did* get offered a lot of stuff. Tickets to sporting events, new cleats, gloves, various shirts and hats and sweatshirts, and some truly *prime* sports gear, which were all hard to resist. But, she had been careful never to take anything—even when she *really* wanted it.

Before they left, they stopped to thank the owners profusely—and their waitress thanked her *mother*, since it was a hell of a good tip.

"It was disturbing to watch you have all of those medical tests," her mother said, in the cab on the way back to the hotel.

Jill nodded. The hours at the hospital had made her feel very much like a piece of extremely expensive meat—but, at least it was better than being tested out in the open, at a huge football combine, like a big factory of body parts.

Her mother looked at her seriously. "I want you to do this because you genuinely *want* to play, not because—well, because you feel the weight of historical responsibility."

"Can't both be true?" Jill asked.

"I don't know," her mother said. "Can they?"

She sure *hoped* so.

They rode in silence for a moment, then her mother let out her breath.

"I want you to do what's right for *you*," she said, "but I can't pretend that I'm not afraid."

Jill glanced over. "And you think I'm *not*?"

"Of what?" her mother asked. "Specifically."

Where to begin? "Whether I'll really be good enough," Jill said. Which might be her top concern. "How people are going to treat me—especially the team. I mean, you know what locker rooms are like."

"I don't, actually," her mother said. "But, I've always assumed the worst."

Okay, so maybe she should nip this one in the bud. "They'll probably be fine, but—they think different things are funny," Jill said. To put it mildly. Often, very *gross* things.

Her mother looked worried. "I don't want you to feel as though you have to hide things from me."

"*I* don't want to feel as though your first reaction is going to be 'Quit baseball!' every time I tell you something," Jill said.

Her mother sighed. "So, it's going to be challenging for both of us."

That was about the size of it, yeah.

They were scheduled to go over to the stadium at four-thirty, to talk to people in the front office, and then attend a meet-and-greet cocktail party and buffet supper for high-ranked draft picks and their families. So, that gave them time to go back to the hotel and take it easy for about an hour, before heading over. Her aunt was already sitting at the big table in the suite, with her laptop and a bunch of paperwork.

"How's it going?" Jill asked.

"Right now, I'm pushing for at least two," her aunt said. "But, I think it's going to end up going significantly higher than that."

Jill and her mother stared at her.

"Two *million*?" her mother asked.

Her aunt nodded, not even looking up from her papers.

"But, that's way over slot," Jill said.

Her aunt shrugged. "They can afford it, and frankly, they need to raise the bonus considerably, just for the putting-up-with-media-garbage factor. You're *not* an ordinary slot pick, and I have no intention of pretending otherwise."

Yeah, but—"That's a lot of money," Jill said. And she would have to be *incredibly* good to live up to that amount.

"Well, a huge chunk of it will go to the government, if that makes you feel better," her aunt said, taking rapid notes on a yellow pad.

Not really. "I'm going to want to make some *big* donations," Jill said.

"I don't want you to endanger your financial security, so not *too* big, I hope." Her aunt frowned. "Although it would reduce your tax burden."

Wow, she really *was* a ruthless New York shark. A side of her Jill had rarely seen.

"Jesus, Karen," her mother said. "How about because it's a nice thing to do?"

Her aunt nodded. "Yes, I've heard tell of such things."

Okay, that was a joke. Probably. So, Jill laughed, and her aunt grinned at her, before focusing back on the papers.

Good, she had just been yanking her big sister's chain, then. Mostly, anyway. And successfully, since her mother looked annoyed.

"What do you have in mind?" her mother asked. "For charities, I mean."

"I don't know," Jill said. "Places like Fisher House and TAPS." Charities which helped military families. "Animal rescue groups. Children with cancer. That kind of thing."

"I think it's a *great* idea," her mother said.

"As long as we vet any potential charities, first," her aunt said, jotting a few notes down. "I don't want to see you compromised in any way. I'll also see if I can get the team to match some or all of it. And we'll look for a Pittsburgh-area charity, too." She lowered her pen. "And thank you for not blindsiding them with it at the next press conference. This way, they'll have time to decide how they want to handle it, without any pressure." She looked back down at the legal pad. "Obviously, I'm getting you a basketball waiver, but I'll go for tennis and skiing, too, of course."

Baseball contracts had strict clauses forbidding various activities that were considered physically dangerous, including things like wrestling, hang gliding, racing cars or motorcycles—and, alas, downhill skiing. "If you could get skiing taken out of there, that would be *great*," Jill said. The idea of having to refrain from one of her favorite sports indefinitely, and possibly for many *years*, was pretty awful.

"Working on it," her aunt said, and picked up her phone.

The contract had extensive details and contingencies and addendums and guarantee-exclusion provisions and so forth, and her aunt stayed on the phone almost nonstop for the next hour. It was hard to tell, though, how the negotiations were going, by only hearing one, often terse, side of the conversation.

At her mother's strong behest, Jill had agreed that it made sense to wear a dress to the event, and had spent a little time at home practicing walking in heels. Fairly low heels, but it was still enough of a challenge to make her feel considerably less coordinated than usual. She also went with earrings, her grandmother's pearls, a little bit of makeup, some perfume— the whole nine yards. And she decided to wear her hair down, to look less jock-like, for once.

They got to the ballpark right on time, and she shouldn't have been surprised to see a large crowd of fans and press waiting near the entrance, gathered behind police barricades. Mostly, the people cheered and shouted encouraging things, although there were also quite a few catcalls of the "Go back to softball!" variety, and some exceedingly profane and obscene remarks, along with— yes—people holding protest signs. Because, of course, her very existence on the planet was already *desecrating* baseball.

"I'm not universally beloved?" she said to her mother. "This is terrible."

Her mother's smile was rigid, which maybe wasn't an unreasonable reaction.

"It's always going to be like this," Jill said quietly. Hell, it pretty much always *had* been like this, ever since she started routinely breaking eighty on the gun. "It's easier just to ignore it."

"I don't have to like it," her mother said, sounding very stiff.

No, she definitely didn't.

Hundreds of the fans were closing in, eagerly pushing against the barricades, and she wasn't sure if she was supposed to stop and sign autographs and pose for photos, or what. But, they were quickly ushered inside by a special assistant to the general manager, a couple of people who worked in communications and media relations, and several security guards and Pittsburgh police officers.

"She's *fine*," her aunt said to her mother. "Really."

Which she was, although the visceral anger in some of the shouts had been creepy.

"Well, maybe she shouldn't *be* so fine about it, because it's awful." Her mother shook her head. "If he were here, they wouldn't dare pull that."

Yeah, she was probably right. Jill's father had been a happy-go-lucky type—but, that didn't change the fact that he was a very *large* man, and could be damned intimidating, on the rare occasions when he was so inclined.

And, somehow, her stomach suddenly hurt.

As they moved down a hallway decorated with displays of Pirates memorabilia, Monty, the special assistant to the GM, who was a beefy Caucasian guy in his early thirties, looked over at her curiously. "No pantsuit?" he asked.

What? That was really what he had expected? She blinked. "Uh, no," she said. "We thought—would that have been preferable?"

"Of course not," he said, flushing. "I was just surprised."

That made two of them.

"And you're a clod," Nadine, a slim African-American woman who had introduced herself as the director of media relations, said. "Ignore him, Jill. You look great."

She hoped she looked presentable, at least, and not clunky. Actually, she didn't *own* a pantsuit, and was pretty sure she had never tried one on before, even for a Halloween costume. "Well, I'll be sure to buy some pantsuits," she said, "if that's what the well-dressed ballplayers are wearing these days."

Her mother gave her a sharp look.

"A mannish one, with a ruffled blouse, for an unexpectedly feminine touch," her aunt said.

Her mother sighed. "Don't encourage her, Karen."

"See what you started?" Nadine said to Monty, who looked even more embarrassed.

One of the other assistant general managers came out and brought them to a large conference room, where they met a lot of high-level front office people, from the chairman of the board, to the general manager, the director of baseball operations, the head team physician, and various assistants, coordinators, scouts, and other organization personnel.

It was easy to tell by how friendly people were—or weren't, which ones had been against drafting her so early. Tight smiles, not-very-good eye contact, much briefer handshakes. But, she pretended not to notice, and was equally polite and pleasant to everyone. It was comforting, though, to feel her mother pat her back gently, after they were introduced to one unusually brusque and crotchety scout.

The cocktail party was going to be held on an outdoor picnic deck, overlooking the field. There were supposed to be about three hundred guests, most of whom owned luxury boxes, were corporate sponsors, or were longtime season ticket holders. In some cases, the guests fell into all three categories.

Right before the party started, her mother and aunt were taken off somewhere, while she waited in a hallway with the other three high draft picks. They were all trying to be cool, so she couldn't tell whether any of them were as nervous as she was. As a pitcher, of course, she had learned long ago *never* to let anything resembling anxiety show—since it just gave hitters an advantage. But, right now, her stomach felt so unruly that it was harder than usual to look calm and relaxed. Confident, even.

The first round pick was a big right-handed fireballing pitcher from Texas A&M. Cocky, tall guy, with thick, blondish hair and very broad shoulders. The second round guy was a wiry Latino shortstop from a Florida junior college, who was supposed to be a defensive whiz and speedster, and then, there was the brown-haired slugging outfielder from some high school in California, the Competitive Balance Round pick. Her three fitness center companions.

"You *had* to wear a dress?" the pitcher said.

Yes. "You *had* to wear a jacket and tie?" she said, and heard the outfielder laugh.

The shortstop, who appeared to be suffering from anticipatory stage fright, didn't seem to be listening.

The pitcher looked disgusted. "Why *remind* everyone you're female, you know? And—you're only the third round pick. I don't even know why they invited you to this."

Well, wasn't he an agreeable fellow? "I know," she said. "I shouldn't have begged them to let me come here. That's why I'm standing slightly behind the three of you, as befits my lowly station."

The outfielder laughed again. "You know, you might do all right, Cafferty."

The shortstop still seemed to be caught in his own little anxiety-ridden nightmare. Which maybe didn't bode well for his ability to play baseball in front of large, screaming crowds, down the road. Of course, she probably wasn't one to criticize, when it came to that.

When they were finally summoned, she saw her mother and aunt standing along the side of the big deck, with the other families. It would be really nice to go straight over and join them, but Nadine was already leading her around, pausing to introduce her every few steps. So, she smiled a lot, shook hands, and said things like "Thank you, it's an honor" and "Yes, sir, I certainly hope so."

Being unfailingly charming and approachable was pretty exhausting, and it was a relief when she could finally take a minute to get a glass of ginger ale, stand by a metal railing overlooking the ballpark, and catch her breath. The outfielder, whose name was Scott Bronsky, was doing the same thing, and they nodded at each other. He wasn't handsome, but he was the sort of guy who was still appealing, with a face that was slightly chubby and unformed, as though he hadn't grown into it yet. He was about her height, and just stocky enough to look like a power hitter.

"Hey, Three," he said.

Third round. "Hey, CB," she said. Competitive Balance Round.

"Oh, no, don't turn out to be *fun*," he said. "That would be really disappointing."

"Don't worry," she said. "I'll make an effort to be grouchy and short-tempered and difficult whenever possible."

The outfielder pretended to wipe his arm across his forehead. "Whew."

Catch her on the right day, and it might even be an accurate self-description. "Are you going to sign?" she asked. Although she assumed that all four of them were, or they wouldn't have been invited to this event.

He nodded, his expression brightening. "Definitely. My agent says they should have it wrapped it up by tomorrow. I mean, yeah, I could go spend four years at LSU—but, I'd rather get started, you know?"

She totally knew.

"How about you?" he asked.

She nodded. "They're figuring out contract stuff, but it seems to be going okay. My lawyer is pretty tough." She paused. "She's also my aunt."

"Means you can probably trust her, then. How much you holding out for?" he asked.

"I'd be okay with slot," she said. "But—well, I think"—no, she *knew*—"that she's pushing for more than that."

"What about endorsements?" he asked.

They were definitely getting a lot of *offers*, including products like cars and tablets, which made very little sense. And, along with the usual slew of agents, lot of strangers with merchandising offers were still using every phone number and email address or social media account they could find to try and contact her. "I'd rather see if I'm actually any good at pitching, first," she said.

For the first time, he looked as though he was *really* paying attention to her. "Are you kidding me?" he asked. "You could *go to town.*"

No question, but—"I don't want anyone to give me money for the wrong reasons," she said. "And the bonus pool is only so big, so I don't want to—I'd rather earn it for what I do on the field."

"Hunh." He looked at her thoughtfully. "You're losing jerk points here, Cafferty. This is very upsetting for me."

"You can call me Jill, you know," she said. "Not Cafferty."

"I'm Scott," he said, and they shook hands.

With luck, he was going to be her first professional baseball friend. It would be nice not to go through all of this feeling *quite* so alone. "Am I the only one who's completely nervous about whether I'm really going to be able to play at this level?" she asked.

He grinned at her. "Nope," he said. "You aren't."

Good.

CHAPTER 6

They hung out for a few more minutes, mostly talking about where they might be assigned, both of them agreeing that they hoped they would be sent to the upstate New York–Penn Class A League Short Season affiliate, rather than the raw rookie-level Gulf Coast League in Florida. More of a demanding test competitively—and not as damn *hot*. Then, she noticed that the big pitcher from Texas A&M, whose name was Caleb Kordell, had stopped loudly mingling and preening his way around the party, and was now off in a corner, huddled with his agents, and that everyone was nodding and frowning a lot.

"What's with Number One?" she asked.

Scott shrugged. "I heard his MRI showed a labrum problem. Not sure if the elbow looked perfect, either."

Which was bad news. Major League Baseball mostly considered Tommy John surgery a necessary evil, but shoulder problems made them very leery. With good reason. "Poor guy," she said.

"With his crappy mechanics, I'm surprised he still has any ligaments at all," Scott said.

Jill raised her eyebrows. "Oh, yeah?"

"Hitters watch pitchers," he said. "Want to make something of it?"

Not really. And she'd seen the guy's mechanics, too, on YouTube. Just watching him throw made her own arm hurt in sympathy, although he could bring it up there consistently in the high nineties. "What do you think will happen?" she asked.

"They'll still sign him," he said. "Just for less than he wants. What's the guy going to do, waste a season, maybe play Cape Cod or an independent league or something, and then go into next year's draft?"

Graduating college seniors had—a lot—less leverage than younger players did. They had more experience and, presumably, maturity, and teams had a better sense of how much they were going to grow and develop—but, if they got a bad offer, they *couldn't* say to hell with it and go to college, instead.

Which she and Scott could.

On the other hand, the two of them were giving *up* on regular college lives—so, everything had a downside. And they were jumping into a high-pressure working world *years* before they needed to do so. She could see Nadine looking for her, with a slightly urgent expression—which meant that she had to go smile, and shake hands, and spend some more time being enchanting.

"Tough to be famous," Scott said.

For a guy who had sort of sleepy-looking eyes, he was definitely alert. "Off to jump through hoops," she said, and headed over.

After the cocktail party, there was a smaller, more exclusive dinner, which was held in one of the ballpark's luxury club facilities, with about seventy-five people attending.

Which, just like lunch, didn't really lend itself to *eating*, so she was pretty sure she would have to order room service again when they got back to the hotel.

She and her mother were put at the same table, with a couple of team executives and their spouses, some corporate sponsors and season ticket holders, and the jittery shortstop. The poor kid was on his own, without any family members, and despite having spent a year at a junior college, he spoke very little English.

Jill's Spanish was good enough so that she could talk to him comfortably, to his obvious relief. In fact, she switched seats with one of the season ticket people, so that she could sit next to him, and make sure he wasn't *completely* left out of the dinner conversation.

His name was Jorge, and he was from Mayagüez, Puerto

Rico. His family had sent him up to Florida to live with his aunt and uncle, partially to go to school, but mostly to be in a better baseball program and improve his position for the draft. Which, since he had gone in the second round, had apparently been a smart plan.

His English was *much* better than he thought it was, but he was so nervous that he mumbled a lot and rarely made eye contact.

When they had gone back to the hotel after lunch, she had checked out all three of the other top draft picks online— and Jorge was a shortstop and center fielder. Plus speed and plus-plus throwing arm, great range, with a decent bat, but a low score for potential power, although he was only twenty and might grow enough to increase that. There was lots of online footage of him, and he was one of those guys who just seemed to *glide* to the ball, and was inclined to throw to first in the middle of leaping in the air, even when it might not be necessary. But, it *looked* impressive.

Her aunt was at a different table, and appeared to spend most of the meal conferring intensely with team executives. But, when dinner was over and they returned to the hotel, she assured them that the contract negotiations were moving along very nicely, although there were still a lot of details to pin down.

So, Jill and her mother hung around the city for another day and a half—which was fun, because they both *liked* cities. When they weren't at the ballpark sitting in on meetings, primarily involving lengthy media training sessions, which bored the hell out of her, and security plans, which made her uneasy—they mostly just walked around various neighborhoods, doing some random exploring. They also went to the Carnegie Museum of Art, the Frick Art & Historical Center, and a concert by the Pittsburgh Symphony Orchestra.

The signing ceremony was going to be a huge media deal, and the plan was for her to go home and pack everything she would need for the rest of the summer, since after that, she would be heading directly up to the team's Class A Short Season affiliate in Pomeroy, New York.

They got back to Rhode Island the day *after* graduation, which was a little disappointing, but at least she had been able to avoid making excuses not to drink or anything, at what her friends assured her had been truly *epic* post-ceremony parties. Lauren kindly described the parties as being only *modestly* epic, at best, but the Snapchats Jill had seen indicated otherwise.

Being out of town had thrown off her workouts and throwing schedule. So, it was a relief to go for a run with Greg, as though life was still normal. They did about five miles all around the Pier. It was raining and foggy, so the beach was mostly empty, other than a few dogged surfers.

"I'm really going to miss this," she said, as they ran easily towards Narrow River, where the inlet connected to the ocean. When they were doing *serious* workouts, they plowed through loose sand, but today, they were staying on the hard-packed stuff near the water's edge.

"The beach, or me?" he asked.

Both. "The beach," she said. "Although I might think of you occasionally."

He nodded. "Yeah, I knew all of this was going to go to your head."

Yes, she was very weak.

"A bunch of us were figuring we might road-trip to your first game," he said.

They had reached the river now, and circled back.

"It's probably going to be a madhouse," she said. "It might be better to come when things die down a little, and I can actually spend time with you guys."

"And when you'll be starting to get wicked homesick," he said.

Well, yeah, that, too. She nodded sheepishly.

They had left their gear at Greg's house, so they ran there to get it, and then drove up to the high school. And, just the way they always had, they spent some time playing catch—both baseball and football. With the baseball, they gradually moved from about twenty-five feet apart to maybe a hundred and fifty, and then back in again. Easy tossing, just getting their arms loose. When they switched to the football, they started by throwing it back and forth to warm up. Then, Jill ran a few patterns—slants, crossing routes, posts, and whatever else he wanted—while he threw from three-step and five-step drops. The rain never really let up, but it was warm enough so that it felt pleasant.

"I'm thinking I need some Del's," Greg said.

The absolute best lemonade on the face of the earth, especially when it was prepared with lots of pieces of fresh lemon left behind in the frozen mixture. "Oh, yeah," she said. "We definitely need Del's." Something else she was really going to miss.

When he drove her home, they sat in the car for a while, drinking their Del's. Well, *slurping*, really.

Since there obviously had never been anything romantic between them, she sometimes forgot how good-looking he was. Dark curly hair, bright blue eyes, and one of those rugged jawlines, which pretty much *begged* to be touched.

"You're too handsome for your own damn good," she said.

Greg laughed. "Yeah, those Amherst boys are going to fall for me right and left."

In fact, they probably *would*.

"You really don't want a big send-off?" he asked. "Because people would be up for a total blow-out party or something."

She shook her head. "*Everything* seems too big lately. Lauren's going to come over tonight and help me pack. You can come, too."

"Nah, that sounds like chick stuff to me," he said. "I'm too manly for such things."

She would refrain from mentioning that *he* had been the one who thought they should all go for pedicures during their pre-prom preparations. The prom itself hadn't been much fun, since her date had ended up being Theo's tallest suite mate, a very nice—and *very* boring—guy named Rakesh. They hadn't been at all attracted to each other, although they had tried to pretend otherwise—for about ten minutes—and then, he spent half the night telling her about some EECS—electrical engineering and computer science—major named Maribeth, who he was trying to get up the nerve to ask out.

"When are you leaving for the airport?" Greg asked.

"Around six," she said. "It's a pretty early flight, so I can be there for, you know, the *unveiling*." Otherwise known as a press conference.

He nodded. "Okay. Text me when you're getting ready to head out, and I'll come over to say good-bye."

Greg was a morning person, anyway, so she decided not to feel guilty about him getting up early. "Thanks," she said. She started to climb out of the car, then leaned over to give him a tight hug. "I'm really going to miss you."

"Mutual," he said gruffly.

Which, by his standards, was outrageously sentimental.

Dinner with her mother and Theo was quiet—but, in a good way. Her mother had made a bunch of her favorite foods—baked chicken with a creamy mushroom sauce, rice, roasted beets, carrots with honey and dill, a tomato and fresh mozzarella salad, and a batch of butterscotch brownies from her maternal grandmother's recipe. Theo even made the big sacrifice, and *didn't* bring his phone to the table.

"Oh, someone's cravenly looking for another endorsement offer," he said, when she poured herself a big glass of milk.

"Healthy teeth and strong bones," Jill said.

"Think they would put you in a little milkmaid costume?" Theo asked.

"No, it'll be a baseball uniform, with the cap turned sideways, braids, and freckles drawn on her face," her mother said.

Milk ad campaign, a la Pippi Longstocking. Jill laughed. "That was a joke, Mom. Did you do it on purpose?"

"I think I did," her mother said. "I'll have to try not to let it happen again."

For a moment, they were all amused, but then, there was one of the familiar awful silences, which fell whenever they had a reminder that the three of them were still trying to figure out how to be a normal family again.

Because, before her father died, her mother *had* been funny. Often.

"Dad would have thought this was so cool," Theo said. "He'd *love* the whole baseball thing, and he'd be talking about his plucky little princess and all."

Exactly the phrase he would have goofily used, too. "I *like* this kid, when he's not on his phone," Jill said to no one in particular.

Theo grinned. "He'd be laughing his head off, about a lot of this. And *he* would go through all the online stuff, so the rest of us wouldn't have to."

Yeah, her father had always spent time in the evenings wandering widely around the Internet, and at breakfast the next day, he would be full of unexpected fun facts of various kinds. Sporadic access, except for occasional emails and Skype sessions, had probably been a very frustrating aspect of being deployed for him.

She and Theo both looked at their mother, to see how she was reacting.

"It would certainly be easier," her mother said, after a minute. "But, I think that as long as the three of us stick together, we can muddle through it pretty well."

Versions of which, she had been saying for years now, although most of the time, it felt as though they hadn't made *nearly* enough progress, when it came to moving forward. So, Jill felt herself tensing, even though she wasn't completely sure why.

"I'll tell you what, I am like a *saint* to be going along to Pittsburgh with you guys," Theo said.

Jill let her breath out, and saw her mother do the same.

"Have phone, will travel," he said.

Jill helped herself to another brownie. "So, it'll be *sort of* like having you there with us."

"You can think of me as a portable hologram version of myself," he said.

Probably too true to be funny—but, she still laughed.

"Maybe you can look up briefly, if they take a family photo," her mother said.

Theo thought about that, and then nodded. "*Briefly*. But, that's it."

"We'll take what little we can get, then," their mother said.

When they were finished eating, Jill offered to help with the dishes—but, Lauren showed up with absolutely ideal timing, and they were able to escape upstairs to pack, instead.

"Did I get you out of the dishes?" Lauren asked, taking the stairs very carefully on her crutches.

Impeccably so. Jill nodded. "Yeah, thanks."

They were about two-thirds of the way up, and Lauren paused.

"You don't have to stay right behind me," she said, more than faintly testy.

"*You* don't have to get mad that I'm backing you up, just in case," Jill said, maybe a little testy herself.

Lauren sighed. "Okay. It just gets really old, you know?"

One of the things that had surprised Jill the most about watching her recuperate for so many months was how relentless the ups and downs were. Progress one day, setback the next—over and over again. It was exhausting to watch, and she never wanted to know what it was like to go *through* something like that.

"I also just docked you five points," Lauren said.

Jill grinned. They had a long-standing joke that Lauren—who loved numbers—was keeping track of *everything* Jill did, good or bad, and was, presumably, carrying a running total in her head. Which, Jill sometimes suspected, Lauren actually *was* doing.

Maggie was making *her* careful way up the stairs, too—and didn't seem to mind at all when Jill hovered next to her, and helped her here and there. Then, once they were in her room, Maggie curled up on the rug with a comfortable sigh.

"You're probably going to miss her more than the rest of us put together," Lauren said.

Quite possibly, yeah. Jill nodded, and reached down to pat her.

She had already packed her baseball gear, because it was the easiest to assemble. The Pirates had given her an official team bag, and she had half-filled it with equipment, leaving room for whatever else she was going to be issued along the way. But, the basics were already in there. Cleats, turf shoes, running shoes. Regular glove for practice, her gamer, and a new one she was breaking in. Compression shorts, shirts and sleeves, a Narragansett Mariners cap, some sports bras—and so on. She had also tucked a small, empty knapsack inside, to use on the long bus rides she was already dreading. Her mother had pointed out that she was going to be lugging her stuff around a lot, and that less was absolutely going to be better than more, when it came to packing.

Lauren handed her the drugstore bag she had toted up the stairs, despite the crutches. "Here. These should be a good start."

Jill sat down on the bed next to a pile of clothes and opened the bag to find a little manicure set and three bottles of nail polish—purple glitter, bright neon pink, and a splashy color described as mango. "Well, how fashionable am *I* going to look?" she asked.

"Extremely," Lauren said.

"My mother gave me a bottle of light beige polish, plain mascara, and a very subdued little lipstick," Jill said.

Lauren grinned. "*Zany.*"

That was one interpretation.

She had three basic packing categories—clothes, toiletries, and electronics. And books. Actual books, with pages, to go along with her iPad and Kindle. Shirts, shorts, a pair of khakis, a dress, some black flats, underwear, socks, her Top-Siders, and one light hoodie. Hairbrush, toothbrush, floss, shampoo, some disposable razors, tampons, ibuprofen, a three-month supply of birth control pills, the brand of multivitamins the front office had approved, several pairs of earbuds, some decent headphones, and assorted chargers.

"You look like you're just about set," Lauren said.

Jill nodded. "My mother keeps reminding me that I can actually *buy* things, if I need them." With her new debit card, which had a bank balance her mother had just increased with a good-sized deposit, along with a credit card, for emergencies.

"Yeah, they probably have, you know, *stores* there," Lauren said.

Plus, her new host family might provide things like that, too. Because, on top of everything else, she was going to have to move in with some strangers. Presumably, they were friendly, and nice—but, she didn't know them, and maybe they wouldn't get along, and her teammates were probably going to hate her, and—

"Are you totally losing your nerve?" Lauren asked.

Yes. "I wish there could have been someone else before me," she said.

Lauren nodded. "Sucks to be the first."

And how. It would be much better to be—the third female player. Or the fifth. "I can't be who they want me to be," Jill said. "I'm going to disappoint everyone."

"They probably just want you to be yourself," Lauren said.

No, a trailblazer was supposed to be impressive. *Special.* "I think they're expecting someone—I don't know," Jill said. "Inspirational, and enthusiastic, and—cuddly." Perky. Adorable. The girl next door.

Lauren laughed. "I hate to be the one to break it to you, but I don't think 'cuddly' is ever going to happen."

No, not in a billion years. As far as she knew, she wasn't particularly abrasive—but, she also wasn't exactly—huggable, or—delightful. "They're going to want me to be bubbling over with joy, and—I don't know—*ebullience*," Jill said. Neither of which were in her wheelhouse.

"No one's going to have a problem with it, if you're just polite and gracious," Lauren said.

Well, that would certainly come more naturally. "The media's going to hate that," Jill said. "They want me to have a lively personality and everything. To *sparkle*."

Lauren shrugged. "So, screw them. It's not like you have to pay attention to any of the coverage, anyway."

That was true. She had already—mostly—learned that it was much better *not* to read the articles, or watch the feature reports—or look at *anything at all* on the Internet, since so much of it was unpleasant, and ugly, and misogynistic, and even threatening. So, when it came to social media, for example, she stuck to her *actual* friends and relatives, and didn't really extend it beyond that. Although the Pirates' media relations people had indicated that they were very much hoping that she would evolve into someone considerably more entertaining—and active—on at least some of her accounts.

"You haven't technically signed anything yet," Lauren said. "You can still walk away."

So tempting. Jill shook her head. "No, they've gone to so much trouble, and my aunt worked really hard on the contract, and—I don't know. All of the plans are made."

"You *still* haven't signed anything," Lauren said.

No, but if she backed out, people would be upset, and mad at her, and think she was *weak*, and afraid, and that women weren't up to the task of playing professional baseball, and—"I think it's too late," Jill said. "I mean, they used a really high draft pick on me, and everything."

"If I'm the Pittsburgh Pirates, I don't *want* someone who's ambivalent, and is going to hate playing, when she'd rather be off at college," Lauren said, and paused. "And if I were investing the money, I also wouldn't want America's Sweetheart standing out there on the mound. I'd want a *ferocious*, driven athlete."

Well, she was actually capable of doing *that*, at least. "You would be so much better at this than I'm going to be," Jill said. In fact, Lauren would have been an absolute natural—and cute as a bug's ear, to boot.

Lauren frowned. "Not even close," she said.

"You're tougher, and you're a better competitor," Jill said. "If you hadn't—" No, that wasn't a sentence she wanted to finish. They really *never* talked about the car accident anymore, because Lauren insisted that it was in the past, and that she was moving ahead—although, as far as Jill could tell, it was more that she still got so scared, even thinking about it. "You're better at sports than I am."

"For God's sakes, Jill, I was *adequate*," Lauren said. "Halfway decent, sometimes, but that was about it. Don't god-damn humor me, okay?"

Not the direction she had expected this to go, but Lauren was nothing if not direct—about everything. Which could be intimidating, sometimes, but was, on the whole, one of her best qualities. It was *good* to have a friend who always told the truth. "Well—you're wicked *fierce*," Jill said.

Now, Lauren looked sheepish. "Maybe, yeah. But, you always leave out the part where I looked good on the court, because I was feeding the ball to *you*."

Jill was going to argue—except, that it really would be insulting, because they both knew perfectly well that she had, in fact, been playing at a level that the rest of the basketball team wasn't. Including Lauren. Which had also, of course, been true on the baseball team. On every team she had ever been *on*, for that matter. "Okay, but you usually got the ball somewhere *right near* me," Jill said, "and that was—very helpful."

Lauren's laugh was entirely genuine this time. "You know, that might be an aspect of your personality you don't want to emphasize in public," she said.

Jill grinned. She was usually pretty good at keeping the staggeringly arrogant and patronizing jock side of herself hidden—but, every now and then, under very controlled circumstances, she let it sneak out for a few seconds.

It was quiet in the room, except for Maggie wheezing slightly, as she napped.

"You want to brag a little about your seven-figure contract?" Lauren asked. "While no one else is listening?"

It went without saying that her mother found the staggering amount of money unseemly, while Theo's initial response had been, "Hey, give me a hundred bucks, rich lady." So, she hadn't had an actual "Wow!" moment about the huge bonus yet. "Yeah, that would be fun," Jill said. A treat, even. "Can I whine a lot about the *really* high taxes I'm going to have to pay, too?"

Lauren laughed again. "Knock yourself out," she said.

CHAPTER 7

Leaving the next morning was pretty hectic, with last-minute packing and good-byes, but Jill made a point of getting up early enough to take Maggie for a walk down to the seawall. It was soothing to stand there, and watch the ocean for a while, before heading back. And, right before they left, the last thing she did was to spend a few more minutes alone with her. She didn't want to burst into tears, so she just kept patting her and telling her what a good dog she was, before giving her one last hug.

Except, okay, in the car on the way to the airport, she maybe did cry a little bit, behind her sunglasses.

"Carol"—who was their neighbor—"will take very good care of her, until Theo and I get home," her mother said.

Jill nodded. But, that didn't change the fact that it felt awful to leave her behind.

Their flight was on time, and entirely ordinary. They went to the hotel, first—back to the fancy Fairmont—and had lunch in the main restaurant. All she could manage was part of a club sandwich, while her mother toyed with a grilled chicken salad, but Theo stuffed in a huge meal, including two desserts.

Before heading over to the ballpark, she changed into a blue dress, which was on the preppy side, but also comfortable, and—with luck—somewhat flattering. Her mother's outfit was similar, and Theo—ever himself—was wearing a black fedora, and a bolo tie with a turquoise slide, along with a conventional white oxford shirt, khakis, and loafers.

The day was going to be slightly complicated by the fact that they wanted her to throw a bullpen session after the press conference, so she had to bring along a bag of gear, too. And a hairbrush.

When they arrived at PNC Park this time, there was a much larger crowd of fans—and a lot of security, most of whom immediately swarmed over to lead her inside. Which saved her from the "Do I stop to sign autographs, or not?" problem, since all she had time to do was to smile and lift one hand in a slight wave—and try not to blink at the stream of camera lights and flashes, despite having worn her sunglasses.

First, there was a formal signing ceremony, in a conference room that didn't contain much more than a large table, Pirates logos placed in strategic places, and lots of media, along with front office and MLB personnel.

She signed the contract with the neatest possible penmanship, hearing someone who clearly didn't really follow baseball say, with obvious surprise and pleasure, "She's left-handed!" Which got a pretty big laugh, from most of the room.

There were more camera flashes, and then she shook hands with the commissioner of baseball, the Pirates GM and the CEO, and the scout who had apparently enthusiastically recommended her, even though she only remembered meeting him a couple of times.

From there, they went to the media room for the official press conference. It was mobbed—*jammed*, even—and as she walked out to the podium, she couldn't help worrying that she might trip, even in flats. She also felt pretty damn sick to her stomach, presumably from nerves, and not from the tiny bit of lunch she had been able to get down.

The general manager, Mr. Saunders, handed her a Pirates cap, and she reflexively bent the brim the way she liked it, and then put it on, while people clapped, and camera shutters clicked all over the room. Then, they had to pose, holding up a Pirates jersey, which had CAFFERTY stitched on the back, and was—she was pleased to see—number twenty-eight, which she had requested. Her hands must have been shaking, because after she slipped it on over her dress, it took her a couple of tries to get it buttoned.

More applause, more handshakes, more camera flashes. After the baseball commissioner and Mr. Saunders made opening remarks about what an inspiring day this was for baseball—and for equality—it was her turn to stand at the podium and answer questions. She gave very careful responses—which felt and sounded more rehearsed than they actually were—and said that she was excited to be here, it was an honor, she wanted to do her best to live up to the trust the Pirates organization had put in her, and so forth. Nadine and the other media relations people were probably relieved that she was erring on the side of being benign and pleasant, to preserve her corporate and endorsement viability, and that she was going out of her way not to come even close to offending *anyone, anywhere* about *anything*. But, speaking so cautiously felt like being in a verbal straitjacket.

It helped that most of the reporters seemed to want her to do well, since that made the whole story just that much more heartwarming. In this venue, at least, no one was trying to trick her into anything resembling a gaffe.

"Do you play because of your father?" someone asked. "To honor his memory?"

Which probably wasn't a weird question—but, it *felt* weird, and invasive, and she had to remind herself not to touch the dog tag around her neck. "My father didn't mind baseball, but he was really a football guy," she said. "Although I hope he would have been happy about the way things have turned out so far." And *proud*. "But, because of—everything, for a long time now, my *mother* has been the one helping me play."

Several of the reporters glanced dubiously in her mother's direction—and it was true; she didn't exactly present as an elite athlete. She had been seated next to Theo—who was, of course, texting madly—in a row of chairs lined up near the podium.

"So, um, your mother taught you how to pitch?" the same reporter asked.

Her mother *had* sometimes played catch with her, when she was little, but the last time Jill had thrown to her, when she was about fifteen, her mother missed the first fastball, taking it right off the shoulder—and they both agreed that it would probably be better for her not to act as a receiver anymore.

"She came to my games," Jill said. Mostly didn't enjoy them, but *came*. "Made sure I had healthy meals, and slept enough, and got a new glove or cleats when I needed them." Which was pretty often. "And, to be honest, she put up with me, whenever I was acting completely monomaniacal." Since that was a near *requirement* to succeed at the higher levels of sports. "I'm not always terribly interesting—but, she makes it seem as though I am."

Her mother smiled, her eyes looking a little bright, and Jill knew she was remembering more than a few endless, fretful conversations about grip variations for the changeup, or how to lengthen her stride, or mulling over whether she should drop her arm-slot—and other minutiae, which had probably made her mother feel like taking a nap, instead of listening intently.

When all of the media hoopla was finally over, she had to throw her bullpen session—about which, she was, increasingly, becoming a nervous wreck, although she hoped to hell that it didn't show. Usually, she was pretty good at maintaining a poker face, but today, it was taking *effort*. Too much effort. The breathless "She's a girl! And she can throw a ball! By herself!" stuff was all well and good, but she needed to be able to *pitch*, and to do so impressively, for any of the rest of it to matter.

Nadine had taken her mother and Theo off somewhere—out to the dugout, maybe? In the meantime, Mr. Saunders and Mr. Jarvis, who was the team's CEO, escorted her down to the clubhouse, where she was introduced to a bunch of coaches and trainers and equipment managers, before they left her to get changed. Some of the Pirates were in there already, to work out, get medical treatment for injuries, and whatever else they needed to do before the game started. Most of them appeared to be only mildly interested by her being there, although a few looked irritated or even hostile. But, with the GM and CEO right there, no one said anything—or even approached them.

She was taken to a small room off the trainers' area, and handed uniform pants, an on-field workout shirt, a belt, sanitary socks, and stirrups. She changed quickly, so that she would have time to fix her chignon—and to sit down in a chair and take several deep breaths to try and calm down. For a few terrible seconds, she thought she might actually throw up, but she kept breathing, until she felt under—flimsy—control. Then, she worked on the brim of her new cap a little more to get it just right, put it on, took one more deep breath, and stood up. The shirt fit pretty well, but the pants were too loose, although the belt helped take care of that.

The head trainer, whose last name was Garcia, was waiting for her in the main treatment room.

"I'm going to stretch you out now," he said, "okay?"

She nodded, not sure what she was supposed to do.

He motioned for her to sit on one of the padded tables, so she jumped up there cooperatively. Sometimes, the high school's athletic trainer had helped her learn some flexibility exercises or iced her up after games, and she had done a little work with someone over at the university, and another guy who worked for a local off-season training facility, but the sessions had never been particularly extensive or elaborate.

Garcia reached out, and then hesitated. "Are you comfortable with me putting my hands on your body?"

Oh. Gosh. She frowned. "Well, I was until you said that."

He frowned, too.

"It's probably fine, as long as we decide that we feel a deep and special love for each other," she said.

Now, he stared at her.

Right. Okay. "My humor does not always amuse," she said.

An understatement, apparently, given his expression.

He grunted something she couldn't quite distinguish, and then—cautiously—started stretching her right arm and shoulder, before moving to concentrate on the left arm and shoulder. He had to reach inside her shirt here and there, especially to rub on this really strong heat balm stuff, but she was wearing a sports bra, and it wasn't any big deal. He seemed so tense that she didn't suggest just pulling off the workout T-shirt, to save them some time and trouble.

The stretching took ten or fifteen minutes, and was more like a massage than anything else. When he was finished, her muscles were certainly *loose*, but she was also kind of drowsy— and weirdly keyed-up, which was precisely *not* the way she wanted to feel. The menthol fumes from the heat balm were pretty intense, too.

"Good to go?" he asked.

"Um, yes, sir," she said, and blinked a few times to try and force her energy to come back. "Thank you, sir."

"Good luck out there," he said.

She nodded her thanks, picked up her glove, and then followed him out to the main clubhouse. There were a few more players in there now, mostly in front of their lockers, in various stages of getting dressed—and there were no front office people around. So, it didn't come as a complete shock that two of them were naked, which—since they were parading around, practically *prancing*, as though they had been waiting for her to come out—was clearly intentional.

"Like what you see?" one of them asked.

She had every intention of ignoring them, although she had to concentrate on not flinching when the other one suggested that they come over and check to see if she was wearing her cup—and someone else muttered a crack wondering whether she had been issued any kneepads. Some of the players seemed to think all of that was funny as hell, although it was somewhat heartening that others appeared to be annoyed, and someone barked at them to grow up and knock it off already.

"Hey," she said vaguely to the clubhouse in general, as she passed through, without pausing to wait for any responses.

In the tunnel leading to the dugout, Garcia glanced over at her, but she just shrugged and looked straight ahead, thinking about pitching, and everything she needed to do to try and get into the right mindset.

When they emerged into the dugout, they were joined by the pitching coach, a guy named Durben, who walked to the outfield with her. Her mother and Theo were standing behind the third base coach's box, and she nodded at them, without breaking stride.

It was mortifying—and more than a little hokey—that the public address system came on, and announced her name and number, and described her as tonight's starting pitcher for the Pittsburgh Pirates, accompanied by a massive mock-up photo of her up on the Jumbotron. Most of the players on the field were visibly amused, and she could feel herself blushing—and *hear* Theo laughing on the sidelines. She glanced back, and saw that her mother mostly just looked nonplussed.

"That goes over big, with the country boys," Durben said.

On one level, it *was* kind of neat, but mostly, it made her feel like a total imposter. "Well, I appreciate that they went to the effort," she said.

Durben made a sound that was either a laugh, or a snort.

The trainer had gone over to talk to a balding man who was putting on his shin guards farther down the left field line. The two of them spoke for a minute, glancing in her direction, and then, Garcia came back over to join Durben.

They told her to do what she normally did before she pitched, so she ran a few easy wind sprints, just to get her blood flowing, and then did a series of stretches, uncomfortably aware of how closely she was being watched. By *everyone*.

The man putting on the shin guards was the Pirates backup catcher, and he was now doing his own stretching. He was a longtime veteran, who had played for several major league teams over the years, and she remembered once being very disappointed when he hit a game-winning double down into the left field corner to beat the Red Sox in a crucial game, when she was about eleven.

After he finished stretching, the man came over and put out his hand. He was either growing a beard, or just hadn't shaved for a few days—and most of it was grey hair. "Freddie Morrow," he said. "Nice to meet you."

She shook it. "Hi, I'm Jill Cafferty. It's nice to meet you, too, sir."

He smiled. "That's adorable—but, I'm Freddie, okay?"

Right. And she wasn't blushing again—because that would be entirely not cool.

They threw to each other from about twenty feet apart, and she made a point of hitting his glove precisely, to whatever degree possible. He obviously noticed, because he moved it to different positions as they tossed the ball back and forth—and she damn well hit *those* spots, too.

As they kept throwing, she drifted backwards every so often, until she was about a hundred and twenty feet away from him. Was part of her thinking, "I'm playing catch with a professional baseball player!" the entire time? Totally. But, she was trying to rise above it.

"Far enough," Durben said abruptly, when she started to move back again.

Well, okay. She stayed where she was, and began working her way back in, until they were about twenty feet apart again.

Freddie bent to pick up the rest of his catching gear. "How do you feel?"

Mostly, she still felt like vomiting. Especially because, in addition to people from the front office, quite a few of the players—including members of the visiting team, the Nationals—had wandered out by the bullpens to watch. "Fine, sir—uh, Freddie," she said.

He nodded. "Good. Let's do this."

As they walked towards the home bullpen, right behind the visitors' pen, he glanced over at her. "Garcy told me you got a little static in the clubhouse," he said. "Those idiots shake you up?"

Yes. Sort of, anyway. But, she shook her head. "I've seen it before." Which didn't quite come out right. "Um, I didn't mean—" Wait, she was in danger of making it worse. "Some guys just feel the need to do that, I guess."

He nodded. "Couple of jackasses, though."

Yup.

And frankly, she had been *underwhelmed*—but, she wasn't about to say so.

"Are you going to the GM about it?" he asked.

Thereby changing the dynamics of what had been—so far—a reasonably smooth day? She shook her head. "No. What happens in the"—she was going to say "locker room," but it wasn't the preferred term in baseball—"clubhouse stays in the clubhouse."

Freddie nodded once. "Good answer. But I'm sorry if they embarrassed you."

She had a feeling that if he had been inside, he would, at minimum, have been one of the people telling them to cut it out. Which would have been nice.

If her father had been here, she probably *would* have told him, and he would have taken some quiet, but decisive action.

She would have been happy to let him do it, too. That is, if they had dared to act up at all, knowing that Sergeant First Class Cafferty was someplace nearby.

"You know that you need to signal what you're going to throw," Freddie said, once they were in the bullpen, and he was pulling on his chest protector.

She wasn't sure whether to be insulted—or sympathetic that he was the one who had drawn the assignment of being the first one to catch "the girl."

"I Googled 'how to throw a bullpen,'" she said, "so, we're all set."

He nodded, although she could tell he wasn't entirely sure whether she was kidding. "Okay, then."

One of the best baseball-related things her mother had done over the years was to talk the URI head coach into letting her throw some batting practice for the team, and to work out with them a few times. That had started about six months after her father was killed, and it was the kind of distraction she really *needed*. The Rams had a pretty strong baseball program—Division I—and although she had been too shy to ask many questions, she had made a point of playing close attention to *everything*. Once it was clear that she threw hard enough to make batting practice worthwhile, the guys had been very nice to her, and gave her some tips and advice. In fact, she was still using a version of the changeup grip one of them had taught her.

Anyway, she had also picked up things like how to motion with her glove towards the catcher to indicate she was going to throw a fastball or a curve or whatever during warm-ups and bullpens.

But, wow, there were a lot of people around today. Too many people. It was supposed to be a closed session, so there was no media allowed, but there were a bunch of front office executives, members of the grounds and stadium crews, and at least fifteen players from both teams, who were either curious— or hoping to get a good laugh. So, it was comforting to see her mother and Theo standing with the GM, CEO, and Nadine, although it made her just that much more nervous when she noticed that even Theo was tuned in enough to look a little pensive, while—oh, hell, was the pitching coach talking to her? Quickly, she focused her attention on him.

"This isn't make-or-break, Cafferty," Durben said. "We just want to get a general feel for things."

"Don't listen to him!" some Nationals guy yelled. "Your whole career's riding on this!"

With luck, the ink was dry on her contract, and so, if they decided they wanted to back out, it would be too late.

"Don't pay attention to that clown," Freddie said, his voice good-natured. "The next time he throws a strike will be the first time."

In general, the mood of the onlookers seemed to be pretty cheerful, although there was an anxious edge of anticipation among most of the front office people, to say nothing of her family.

"Just fastballs," Durben said. "Free and easy, maybe seventy-five percent max. We're not looking for you to break the gun here—this is more about mechanics. You have a two-seamer and a four, right?"

Jill nodded, scraping her cleats across the front of the mound to get a feel for it.

"Four-seamers first," he said. "A few down the pike, and then work outside low, outside high. Don't overthrow."

Jill nodded. Could they tell that she was having trouble swallowing? With luck, no.

Time to pretend there was no audience at all. No radar guns. No videographers. No crowd of kibitzing major league baseball players. That she was at home in the backyard, throwing to Greg, who would generally shout things like "Don't hurt me!" and pretend to scream in pain every time the ball cracked into his glove.

The mound was perfectly manicured, but she smoothed her landing spot with her cleats, anyway. Which felt good. Familiar.

The challenge now, was to make the world very *small*. Focus on hitting the glove—and nothing else.

She had never thrown to a catcher who looked so calm, and still, and relaxed. A massive target. A *man*, not a boy.

Her first three pitches felt terrible coming out of her hand, and went at least a foot away from where she had planned.

There was maybe a little discontented rumble from the many bystanders—which, of course, she *absolutely did not hear.* Nope. Not even faintly.

She took a deep breath to focus—and the next three hit his glove *and* generated enough pop to get people's attention. Which changed the rumble to something more like a small buzz of low-voiced conversations.

"Outside corner," Durben said.

She went low with two pitches, and then high, with two more.

"Too much plate," he said. "Barely kiss the black."

Kiss the black. Okay. She put the next several pitches about two inches off the plate.

"Inside, now," he said. "Low, then high."

She felt strong. In control. In *command.*

Durben grunted with what she hoped was approval, although it was hard to be sure. "Go to the two-seam. Same pattern."

She was perspiring enough now so that her arm was nice and loose, and the two-seam fastball had good movement today. Lots of sink, lots of tail. She moved it up and down, in and out.

"Let's see the change," Durben said.

It was easy to overthink a changeup. But, she needed to keep it all about the grip, and stay with her normal arm action. Take advantage of having big hands, and let the ball sit deep in there.

The glove. All that mattered was hitting the glove. Nothing else even existed.

After she threw about half a dozen, Durben made the same grunting sound. "Okay, make the people happy," he said. "Show me the hook."

Curveballs were fun. She'd only been throwing one for a couple of years now—before that, she'd worked off the changeup—but, right from the start, the curve had been a really good fit. Nothing made her feel more confident than throwing a true hammer that pretty much fell off a table, especially when batters completely *froze* at the plate. She snapped off a few, with good sharp breaks, reminding herself to stay low in the zone— and heard corresponding murmurs, and even a soft whistle, in response.

"Okay, that'll do it," Durben said. "Go with Garcia, have him set you up with some ice and a cooldown."

Jill nodded. "Yes, sir. Thank you, sir."

The Pirates manager said something unintelligible, and Durben said, "Oh, hell, yeah. Love the long stride, too."

While the two of them conferred with Mr. Saunders, glancing at her every so often, Freddie took off his mask and came over with a big grin on his face.

"Nice work, Jill," he said. "Stay focused, and someday, you're going to be back here for real."

How excellent would that be? She grinned back at him— because she couldn't resist.

Had it been a perfect session? No. One of the curveballs spun a little, and her location was shakier than she would have liked—and if she thought about it long enough, she could probably come up with a long list of other self-criticisms.

But, as far as her potential career was concerned, it had been a damned good start.

CHAPTER 8

As she left the bullpen, front office guys were practically tripping over themselves to shake her hand—even the ones who had been unfriendly the first time she met them. And she noticed people congratulating the area scout who had recommended her. The *players* were more friendly now, too, teasing her and goofing around as she walked across the outfield—but, that was a *good* sign.

Theo gave her a thumbs-up, and her mother was trying to hide a very broad smile, probably because she didn't want to seem *too* obviously proud.

Jill winked at her as she walked by with the trainer. Then, she gestured towards the dugout, and her mother nodded.

It hadn't been that many pitches, but now that it was over, she was *worn out*.

A player fell into step with them, and she wasn't sure who it was. One of the bullpen guys, maybe. But, even though she had made a point of *not* looking too closely, he was definitely one of the—for lack of a better phrase—weenie-waggers from the clubhouse. Garcia narrowed his eyes, but didn't say anything.

"Here to check my cup?" she asked, stiffly.

He shrugged, not meeting her eyes.

They were about the same height, which gave her some extra confidence. She—in no way whatsoever—had to look *up* at him.

"You've got some good late movement there," he said.

She nodded, not in the mood to be even marginally friendly.

"Good location, too," he said.

She nodded.

They crossed the foul line, heading towards the dugout, and the clubhouse beyond.

The guy let out his breath. "Look. I'm sorry. Okay? Jay and I were being assholes."

"Damn right you were," Garcia said, very grim. "She's a *kid*."

"I'm trying to fucking apologize, man," the guy said, and then looked at her. "You're going to catch a lot of shit, you know? Lot of people don't *want* you to succeed."

She glanced over. "Are you one of them?"

"Fuck, yeah," he said. "But, you know, I gotta say, you threw great. Where they sending you?"

"Pomeroy," she said.

He nodded. "Hang tough. Don't let any of us scare you off." Then, he turned and jogged back onto the field.

"Is he a pitcher?" Jill asked.

Garcia nodded. "Mop-up, mostly. He's not a bad guy. I would've told them to lay off, but I guess I wanted to see how you would react. The way I figure it, if you can't handle *that*, you'll be gone in a week, anyway."

True enough. So, she nodded.

"I'm not crazy about this whole thing with you playing, either," he said, "if you want me to be honest. Not too many guys *are*, probably. But, if it turns out you're for real, and can hold your own, and help the ball club someday? Hard to be against *that*. And I liked what I just saw out there."

With luck, most of the rest of the baseball people she ran across were going to feel about the same way.

When they got back to the clubhouse, she was strapped up with an astonishing amount of ice, to a degree which made her feel either ridiculous—or very frail. Garcia explained, at length, the post-pitching routine they were going to want her to adopt, and talked about her overall diet, nutrition, sleeping patterns, and a bunch of other practical, if somewhat mind-numbing, stuff.

After he took the ice off, he did some more stretching of

her arm and shoulder. Then, she followed him to a weight room where various players were working out. They noticed her— but, none of them seemed very interested. Lifting weights was, in this particular environment, serious business.

Garcia showed her some cooldown exercises and stretches, and put her on a stationary bike for twenty five minutes. Then, she was issued a fresh T-shirt, a batting practice jersey, and another pair of baseball pants. She changed in the same small room, and one of the assistant general managers appeared to walk her back out to the field, where she was supposed to shag fly balls during batting practice, and then have an informal meeting with the media.

Well, informal in the sense of being totally structured and planned.

When they got outside, her mother was sitting at the far end of the dugout, reading a book, with a cup of Gatorade by her side—which seemed hilariously odd. Theo was talking to some of the guys on the grounds crew, hanging out near a huge, rolled-up tarp.

There were a bunch of players spread around in the outfield, vaguely catching flies and fielding outfield grounders, but it was all pretty desultory, and a lot of the guys seemed to be goofing around. She joined them, standing apart, without making a point of avoiding anyone.

No one struck up a conversation with her, but most of them gave her a nod, or said, "Hey" in a reasonably collegial way. The mop-up relief pitcher kept his distance, which was fine with her.

There was music playing on the ballpark's public address system, to help keep batting practice entertaining, presumably. High-energy rock and roll, for the most part, with some rap thrown in. She had heard that when a team didn't like the visiting team, they would sometimes play things like Gregorian chants or children's songs during their BP and warm-ups. Passive-aggressive, but kind of funny.

The brim of her cap still wasn't quite right, and she bent it some more. Plus, it was a good way to kill time. She caught a couple of easy fly balls, when they came in her direction, but was careful not to do anything that might look like showboating or false hustle.

One of the pitchers came over to stand next to her. She recognized him right away—an ace right-hander, who had been on the All-Star team more than once.

"Watched your bullpen," he said.

She had made a point of *not* noticing whether any star players had been among the spectators. "It was a new experience," she said, since she didn't quite have the nerve to ask him what he had *thought*.

He nodded, reaching out casually to snag a fly ball. "Don't get cute," he said, as he tossed the ball back in the general direction of the infield.

"I'm not sure what you mean," she said.

He shrugged. "You got a foundation. Build on it, tweak it, make adjustments, whatever, but don't tear it down."

Which made sense.

"Everyone'll be giving you advice," he said. "*Everyone*. Some of it might be okay, but you're gonna work off that curve and the change. Don't screw around with sliders, or cutters, or a knuckler, or whatever the fuck else. *Maybe* a sinker, get those ground balls. But, don't let 'em monkey with you. Yeah, you'll make your adjustments, but if it ain't broken, keep it that way, you know?"

She nodded. She had been getting unsolicited—and, very occasionally, requested—advice for *years*, but most of it conflicted, and wasn't terribly helpful. The information she was going to hear now would often come from people who were experts—but, yeah, she didn't like the idea of having someone take her mechanics completely apart, and then try to put them back together again. "Thanks," she said. "That will really help. It's all pretty confusing sometimes."

"Gotta say, that never changes," he said, and went back to where he had been standing before.

She had to give significant points to a veteran who was willing to share some wisdom, without making a big deal about any of the rest of it.

After a while, the gates must have opened, because a bunch of fans started to come into the ballpark, and she could tell that the more savvy ones were looking for her among the other players in the outfield. Sometimes, she could hear shouting, or see people pointing, and it looked as though a lot of them were taking cell phone photos and the like.

"You aren't going to wave?" one of the players nearby asked.

"I think that would make me an even more annoying rookie than I already am," she said.

The guy laughed. "Good call."

She was saved from having to worry about it, as batting practice abruptly ended, and everyone started trotting off the field. Some of the players paused along the stands to sign autographs, and since a bunch of fans were calling her name, she decided that she would, too.

When she approached the box seats on the third base side, a startlingly large number of people rushed over, and there were what looked like hundreds of baseballs and caps and scorecards and other items being held out for her to sign.

No matter how many things she autographed—very neatly—and then handed back, the crowd never seemed to get any smaller, and she smiled and signed and said things like "Hello" and "Thank you" and "Good to see you" over and over. Increasingly, though, they seemed to press closer, making noisy requests, and thrusting cell phones and cameras practically into her face.

It was a relief to see Nadine come striding briskly in her direction. There was nothing remotely athletic about her, but she was chic as hell and moved with confidence. The kind of woman who was never without dramatic dangly earrings.

"I'm afraid we need Miss Cafferty inside now," she said, projecting her voice with no apparent effort. "But, thank you for coming out today and enjoy the game!"

There was some grumbling, and a lot of disappointed looks, and then Jill saw one little boy whose eyes had filled with tears, so she went back.

"Okay if I sign your hat?" she asked.

He gave her a big grin, even as the tears spilled over.

It was extremely disconcerting to make children cry. "There you go," she said, and put it back on his head, before joining Nadine again.

"Pomeroy is going to have someone from media relations on the field before and after every home game," Nadine said. "They're bringing on extra security, too."

Jill looked at her uneasily. "Do you think I'm going to *need* it?"

Nadine hesitated a second longer than Jill would have liked. "We'd rather play it safe. No one is really quite sure what to expect, but there are similar arrangements in place when the team is on the road."

Expect the best, prepare for the worst. And it would probably be a good idea *not* to imagine any versions of what the worst could be.

As they approached the dugout, she could see that Mr.

Saunders was surrounded by a large pool of reporters, and he waved them over.

"You're okay with this?" Nadine asked.

Well, she had damned well *better* be, given that it was her reality—both now, and going forward. So, Jill nodded.

"I'm going to stick around," Nadine said. "Bail you out, or redirect, if it seems necessary. Back them off, if they get difficult, that sort of thing."

Jill nodded. "This might sound stupid, but do I have to be bland?"

Nadine tilted her head. "What do you mean?"

"I'm not *colorful*, exactly," Jill said. Except, maybe, somewhere deep down inside, she possibly was. Or, anyway, *wanted* to be. "But, it's boring to talk about staying within myself, and taking it one day at a time, and all. And the shtick of 'Isn't it amazing that I'm a *girl*' gets really old."

"Well, you should just be yourself, of course, but—" Nadine looked worried. "You might want to avoid making promises about your performance levels, or—"

"Oh, I would never do that," Jill said quickly. Not only was it braggadocio, but it would also be a really good way to put the whammy on herself. *No one* with any sense *ever* messed with the Sports Gods. "I just—well, if possible, maybe I don't want to iron out all of the quirks."

Without seeming to be aware that she was doing so, Nadine glanced at the corner of the dugout, where her mother was turning a page in her book, while sipping her orange Gatorade, looking refined, academic—and out of place.

"Wait until she pulls out her dip, and starts spewing tobacco juice," Jill said. "It's pretty jarring."

Nadine looked startled, and then, amused. "Is that quirk?"

Not her A-game quirk, but it would suffice. "A little bit," Jill said.

With luck, Theo wasn't doing anything too weird at the moment. She looked around, and saw that he was still being distracted by the grounds crew, who seemed to be showing him every single tool and gadget they had—which was good, because otherwise, he would probably be lying underneath the scoreboard or something, examining how it worked, and possibly—if no one was watching closely—*tinkering* with things.

For a moment, she missed her father so intensely—he had played football at Holy Cross, and would have been so *relaxed* here with a bunch of jocks, and also made everything feel really fun—that she couldn't think at all. Then, she realized that Nadine was saying something to her, and gave her head a small shake to try and focus.

"Would you rather go inside and freshen up, first?" Nadine asked.

Which would, no doubt, involve another parade of genitals. "No, I'm fine," she said. Albeit, probably, quite disheveled. "Good to go."

Nadine looked relieved—and slightly concerned.

As it turned out, the reporters had boring questions, and she reflexively said that it was exciting to be here, and that she was looking forward to reporting to Pomeroy and learning as much as she could—and on and on. One of them stumped her when he asked where she was going to shower—and she had to concede that she had no idea. Fortunately, Mr. Saunders jumped in, and said that the team would be setting up a specifically designated area, and that a newly hired trainer up there was a woman, who would ensure that there were always proper facilities at visiting stadiums—which was welcome news, as far as Jill was concerned.

Of course, it was entirely possible that her Aunt Karen had negotiated all of these points. She hadn't read all of the fine print yet, but her contract was full of atypical and complex details, including a clause mandating that her uniforms would be tailored to fit properly—which had led her maternal grandmother to say, "Thank goodness she won't look boxy!"

But, considering how loose her uniform pants were at the moment, the Pirates were already in breach of *that* part.

"Will they be making other special arrangements?" one of the reporters asked, and the whole group looked at her attentively.

Time for some quirk, maybe. "Well, I'm not sure how it's going to be received," Jill said, "but, there's something of a comfort factor knowing that on the days I pitch, the mound is going to be moved in to fifty feet, five inches."

So many of the reporters—and team officials—looked aghast, that she had some immediate concerns about her comic timing.

Fortunately, Nadine laughed, which gave everyone else a cue that she was playing around with them.

"I heard you had some problems in the locker room," a reporter said. "Do you want to talk to us about that?"

She wasn't sure who gave her the sharpest look—Nadine, Mr. Saunders, or her mother—who actually put her book down. But, it probably wasn't surprising that someone had told someone who told someone else—and that the reporter had caught wind of it.

She immediately felt panicked, since all hell might break loose, if she was honest. But, she made herself pause, and take a sip from the bottle of water a team official had handed her earlier, to give herself a few extra seconds to think. She didn't like to lie—but, that didn't mean that she had to tell the exact truth, either. "I didn't see anything particularly notable," she said. Which *was* true. "Maybe it was before or after I was in there. I really couldn't say."

"Well," the reporter said, "I heard that—"

Nope, she wasn't going there. "I iced up, did some stretching, put in time on a bike—it was pretty routine," she said.

The reporter clearly wanted to pursue it further, but got hard looks from Nadine and Mr. Saunders, so he subsided and jotted something down on his notepad.

There were a few more questions, which she answered cautiously and conservatively. Which was tedious, but seemed like the best strategy.

When the interview was finally over, Nadine, Mr. Saunders, *and* her mother followed her down the dugout tunnel.

"What happened in the clubhouse?" Mr. Saunders asked.

There was really no point in going into what had, unfortunately, been pretty run-of-the-mill stuff. "Just boys being boys," she said.

He looked suspicious, and her mother's expression was downright *stormy*, but Jill didn't feel like getting into it with either of them.

"Mom, I'm going to go change. I'll meet you and Theo upstairs in about twenty minutes, okay?" she said—and didn't wait for an answer.

When she went into the clubhouse, there were guys everywhere, in various stages of undress, but it was *always* going to be like that. And, this time, she didn't get the sense that anyone was trying to harass her. At the end of the day, they were really all just getting ready for work—in an extremely peculiar profession—and it shouldn't be much more complicated than that.

After another formal dinner with corporate sponsors and local politicians and so forth, the front office wanted her to watch that night's game from the owner's box—which predictably turned out to involve more meeting and greeting than actual watching. But, it was pretty funny to see her mother and Theo pretending to be captivated by baseball.

She was sent over to the television announcers' booth during the fifth inning, to answer questions and be introduced to the Pirates' viewing audience. The play-by-play guy and color commentator were nice, although she was more ill at ease than she had expected to be. But, she was getting better—which might not be a good thing—at answering questions on autopilot, while looking far more engaged than she really was.

When the color commentator asked her whether she thought that, at that very moment, millions of little girls all over the country were practicing their pitching motions, she was caught off guard, and said that she hoped millions of little girls were currently reading books and doing their homework.

They didn't seem to like that answer, because both announcers frowned.

"You don't want girls to play baseball?" the color commentator asked.

She would have assumed that being pro-education was a very safe position. "Of course I do," she said. "I hope that any kid in the country who wants to play baseball *can*." And she should have left it at that, but it had been a long day, and she was very tired, and she couldn't resist going a little further. "But, I think the path to total world domination by women will be much easier, if we're all extremely well educated."

They stared at her, and the play-by-play guy's gum actually fell out of his mouth, so it was a struggle not to laugh.

"Well, gosh, Jill," the color commentator said. "That is a very interesting remark. You've given our viewers a lot to think about."

She was *damned* if she was going to say that she had been kidding.

Because, after all, maybe she *wasn't*. So, she just nodded, and smiled, and said something about looking forward to having girls and young women find more opportunities to play competitive sports like baseball, professionally and otherwise.

But, she had a feeling that they weren't sorry when the inning was over, and they could wish her luck and send her on her way.

"World domination?" Nadine said, as they walked back to the owner's box.

And how. "You bet," Jill said.

Nadine smiled. "Well, you're preaching to the choir." She started to say something, and then stopped.

"It's okay," Jill said. "I'll try not to be flippant anymore."

Nadine shook her head. "No, do whatever you need to do to handle the pressure. Just"—she hesitated—"please pitch well."

Meaning—what? Jill looked at her with some confusion.

"What you're doing matters to *so* many people," Nadine said. "It's good to blow off steam, and I know you've been given a hard time today, but you're going to take the game itself seriously, right?"

She couldn't even imagine clowning around on the mound. "*Very* seriously," Jill said.

And then some.

CHAPTER 9

They were going to fly from Pittsburgh to Albany—by way of Philadelphia—and then rent a car and drive to Pomeroy from there. Before they left, at the team's request, she was interviewed from the living room of the suite by all of the major national morning shows, as well as a couple of local ones, and she went out of her way *not* to be controversial. And to look wide-awake. And not to feel like an utter idiot.

It was almost two-thirty when they drove up to the stadium, which had that old-fashioned minor league look, with a red-brick façade and a quaint, small-town atmosphere. There was a large statue of a beaming dog dressed in a team uniform out in front, which was probably a likeness of the Pomeroy Retrievers mascot.

"That's a big dog," Theo said.

"They use an actual golden retriever to fetch bats, I think," Jill said.

Her mother paused in the act of parking to turn and look at her. "Seriously?"

Jill nodded. "As far as I know."

"Do the hitters get upset about the teeth marks?" her mother asked.

Good question. "I hope so," Jill said. Since, after all, what made a pitcher happier than fretful hitters?

There were ESPN and other television trucks parked out in front, but luckily, they weren't prepared for her to arrive, because she was barely filmed as they walked by. In fact, an amusingly high number of them didn't even notice her.

When they went inside the entrance to the main offices, there was the usual round of introductions, and she forgot most of the names within seconds. The GM said to call him Richard—he was one of those crewneck sweater went-to-law-school-instead-of-playing-baseball guys—although she stuck with "sir" or "Mr. Brayton." The assistant GM, a very friendly woman in her late forties or early fifties, introduced herself as "Indira," but Jill was, of course, more comfortable with "ma'am" or "Mrs. Doshi." In rapid succession, she met a series of other front office people, stadium employees, and an interchangeable group of interns. To her relief, all of this was closed to the press, but a team photographer clicked away pretty much nonstop, standing closer than she wanted, while she gamely smiled through a stream of grip-and-grin photos.

Once it was time for actual *baseball* stuff, her mother and Theo left to go check into the motel, although they were planning to come back for the game. She would stay at the motel with them as long as they were in town, before moving in with her host family, to whom she was going to be introduced later, according to Mrs. Doshi, who also seemed to run the travel and logistics aspects of the team's operations.

Mr. Brayton—*Richard*—brought her downstairs, through several corridors that felt more like musty tunnels, where the clubhouse, coaches' offices, equipment room, training area, and weight room were. Since she was with the general manager, people were polite, if not wildly enthusiastic, about meeting her.

The clubhouse was mostly deserted, except for two young guys, one of whom was hanging clean uniforms in players' open wooden lockers, while the other was putting sandwich makings, snacks, and drinks on a large folding table set up along the far wall. They both looked like they were in their early twenties, and one was pudgy with glasses and dark hair, while the other was a skinny pale guy with too many tattoos and an ineffective attempt at a mustache.

"These are our clubbies," Mr. Brayton said. More formally known as clubhouse attendants, but she had never heard anyone refer to them that way. "Anything you need, they'll get for you. Nicky, Terence, meet Jill."

It developed that Nicky was the one with glasses, and Terence was the tattooed guy.

"Hi," she said. "Just let me know how you handle clubhouse dues and everything." As far as she knew, each player had to pay about ten dollars a day for food and other supplies, and then add hefty weekly tips on top of that.

They both nodded, without really looking at her, and she was relieved to have Mr. Brayton motion for her to follow him into the training area. There were only a couple of players around, getting worked on by the trainers—a very muscular man named Louis and a stocky woman named Sofia—and she assumed that most of the others were out on the field, taking BP or something. The two players nodded briefly at her, and she nodded back.

Out in the corridor, the franchise had converted a nearby small room—maybe a former office, or storage space—into a dressing room for her, although they hadn't finished the tiny shower stall and bathroom she would be using. So, for a few days, they would either have to figure out a way for her to shower in the main locker room—privately—or she would just have to get cleaned up in the restroom the women who worked in the front office used. At most of the ballparks on the road, it was likely that she would have to use civilian restrooms.

"Well, let's go see Benny, get you settled," Mr. Brayton said.

Benny was Mr. Adler, the manager. She didn't know much about him, other than that he had played for a couple of years in the majors, and had worked as a coach or manager at various levels of the minor leagues ever since.

"Benny has been in the game for a *long* time," Mr. Brayton said, as they walked down the hallway. "You may find him abrupt, but he's a good baseball man."

Gruff, but lovable, ideally.

"Not a chatty person," Mr. Brayton said. "Don't take it personally."

Which was good, because otherwise, she probably would have.

"We'd like you to have your first start here in Pomeroy, before the team heads out on the road," he said. "The front office is going to be flying in for it in the morning. Will you be ready for that?"

So, she could be pitching as soon as *tomorrow*? Whose bright idea was *that*? But, she nodded, trying to project confidence. At the moment, she felt ready for absolutely nothing whatsoever—except, possibly, blowing all of this off and heading straight to college as fast as her little legs could carry her.

A door just ahead of them was ajar, and Mr. Brayton knocked, getting a grunt in response. As they went in, the manager stood up from behind a desk covered with paperwork, folders, and a somewhat outdated laptop. He looked like he was in his mid-fifties, and had smoked at least seven trillion cigarettes in his life, and never once, even for a second, used sunscreen. There was a strong reek of tobacco in the office, with a slight overlay of beer and Big Macs.

"Benny, this is Jill Cafferty," Mr. Brayton said. "I think you're going to enjoy having her here."

Mr. Adler maybe twitched, but at least he didn't outright laugh. "Pleasure," he said, and shook her hand.

They all stood there.

"The team's really shaping up," Mr. Brayton said heartily. "I think it's going to be an exciting season."

Jill and Mr. Adler both nodded, although she was pretty sure she was the only one who smiled.

"I know you have a lot to do to get ready for the game," Mr. Brayton said, "so I'll leave you to it. Jill, remember, my door is *always* open to you. Everyone here wants all of this to go as smoothly as possible, and for you to succeed. So, don't ever forget that."

Jill nodded. "Yes, sir. Thank you, sir."

Once the GM was gone, Adler sat down, and gestured abruptly for her to sit in the folding chair on the other side of the desk.

"You got pristine little lungs?" he asked.

Well, she certainly *hoped* so.

"Brace yourself," he said, and lit up a cigarette.

She coughed, ever so delicately, and he did something that was sort of like smiling.

"Ready to quit and go home yet?" he asked.

"I'm going to try and stick it out for another hour, sir," she said. Possibly more true than funny. "But, after that, all bets are off."

His mouth moved again. "ESPN and whatnot showing up already."

"Sounds like a hootenanny," she said.

He nodded, exhaling a big enough cloud of smoke to obscure what she suspected might be an amused expression. "I can throw you tomorrow, or Wednesday. Your call."

"Actually, it's *your* call, sir," she said.

"I'd rather run you out there this weekend, on the road, give you a chance to get your sea legs," he said. "But, not much we can do, with the circus in town."

She maybe didn't want to think about how big the circus was going to be.

"You'd have time to take a couple deep breaths, be able to get on the same page with the staff, and all of that," he said. "Although the Power People are showing up in the morning, so—you get the drift?"

Yes. She was pitching tomorrow. So, she nodded.

Adler shrugged. "Hand we were dealt."

Pretty much. And it wasn't—remotely—ideal, but she would have to make it work. "Just for the record, sir?" she said. "I want to pitch, not be a dog and pony show."

"I'll keep that in mind," he said, and paused. "Got a good report on your bullpen."

That was a step in the right direction, then.

"You met Sawyer and Bannigan yet?" he asked.

She shook her head.

"Pitching coach, and strength and conditioning guy," he said. "You'll sit down with them and the trainers, set up the program we want you doing, try to get you kicked off right."

She nodded. "Thank you, sir."

It wasn't clear whether the conversation was over, and she started to get up, but then had the sense that he wasn't finished yet and she sat back down.

He inhaled deeply on his cigarette, then exhaled. "Think you'll go to pieces, if I ask you a personal question?"

"Presbyterian," she said.

His right eye maybe flickered, but that appeared to be the extent of his reaction.

It was entirely possible that levity was not his favorite thing—and that he was also weak on pop culture. "I'm sorry, sir," she said. "Please ask whatever you want."

He looked at her for a minute, and then nodded. "Okay. Are you gay?"

Well, *that* was direct. She blinked. "Excuse me, sir?"

"I guess the proper term is lesbian," he said. "Are you a lesbian?"

She was going to have to spend an entire summer being coached by this prehistoric guy? Who was, in fact, corrupting her raised-on-fresh-sea-air lungs? "Is there a correct answer?" she asked.

He shook his head.

In which case, why ask such an invasive question? "As it happens, sir, I am not," she said—possibly through her teeth. "But, I'm not sure why it would be relevant, either way."

"I was hoping that you *were*," he said.

"To adhere to a traditional cultural stereotype about female athletes?" she asked, trying very hard not to clench either fist.

He frowned, but then shook his head. "If you were gay, the boys would *understand* that. To be honest, it'd make them relax. Different energy."

"Well, I'm terribly sorry that my heterosexual status is going to be inconvenient for everyone," she said. "With luck, they'll be able to cope."

This time, Adler smiled. "You have a little bit of an edge, don't you, Cafferty?"

Apparently so.

"*Good*," he said—again, unexpectedly. "You're going to need it." He stubbed the cigarette out. "Let's take a walk."

She followed him to the clubhouse, where batting practice had just ended, and players—some fully clothed, some not—were gathered around, making sandwiches from the pre-game spread, playing cards, bent over their phones, and just generally hanging out.

Adler let out a sharp whistle, and everyone who didn't have on headphones or earbuds looked up, with the others reacting more slowly.

"This is Cafferty," he said. "Act right, or I'll bounce your heads like Ping-Pong balls. Got it?"

Some of the guys looked agreeable, some unfriendly—and some had blank expressions, so she could tell that quite a few of the players on the team spoke very limited English.

"Be nice to me, or he will dribble your heads," she said—at least, she *hoped* that was what she said—in Spanish, moving her hand as though she was bouncing a basketball. "Very hard."

Several of the Latino guys laughed, and exchanged muttered remarks.

"You're full of surprises, Cafferty," Adler said, and looked at Sofia and an older Hispanic guy—maybe a coach? "How'd she do?"

Sofia shrugged affirmatively, and the older guy pursed his lips, and she could tell he wasn't even close to being on the "it's so great to have a female player here!" bandwagon. "Not bad," he said finally.

"That'll be useful," Adler said, and motioned towards the overweight clubbie. "Nicky, get her set up with gear."

And with that, pretty much everyone went back to whatever they had been doing, although it was a relief to recognize Scott, the Competitive Balance Round pick, putting together a thick sandwich.

"See you out there, Caffy!" he said cheerfully.

"You bet, CB," she said. With luck, she was going to have one friend here, at least.

Nicky waved shyly for her to follow him to a room where equipment was stored.

"Um, they had us set aside stuff for you," he said. "But, they're bringing in, like, a tailor tomorrow?"

Fittings and alterations. "Great, thank you," she said, glad to see that, once again, she had been given number twenty-eight. "Did anyone else want the number?"

"One guy, yeah. Schwartzman," he said, avoiding her eyes.

And probably already not a fan of hers, if he'd had to give up his favorite number.

"Senior sign," he said. "So, um, you know."

No clout, in other words. Some animals were more equal than other animals. Well, she would figure out a way to make it up to him. Buy him a steak when they were on the road, or something.

There was a surprising amount of gear. First, he handed out home and road uniforms, as well as a batting practice version, and three different caps. Sometimes, there would be one-time-only jerseys for theme nights at the ballpark, which would usually get auctioned off after the game. She was also given two pairs of long shorts—which were going to be much too baggy—a couple of high-tech, moisture-wicking, dri-FIT, hypercool workout shirts, two more on-field team T-shirts, sanitary socks, stirrups, a belt, a pair of shower shoes, a light windbreaker/warm-up jacket, a thicker jacket, and a Pirates fleece, as well as a Pirates hoodie. Everything else, except for one of the T-shirts, was Pomeroy-specific issue, with PR and cartoon dog logos.

Once Nicky had checked through the entire pile, he handed her an inventory sheet to sign, since everything would ultimately be returned whenever she left the team—for whatever reasons—and reissued to another player.

A player who probably wasn't going to be thrilled about the alterations.

"We, um, have extras stocked," Nicky said, still not making eye contact. "Because I think the Hall of Fame, and like, the big club, will be taking some of it after you play. But, I have to keep track on the sheet, okay?"

She nodded. "Absolutely. I'll be careful not to lose anything."

"Do you have—cleats?" he asked.

That was a serious question? Wow. She nodded.

"And—turf shoes?" he asked.

She nodded.

"You only wear team stuff at the ballpark," he said. "Or you get fined?"

She nodded a fourth time. She had been surprised to hear that they weren't even supposed to wear their *caps* when they were out in the world, but she assumed that it was to help players keep a lower profile—and maybe not disgrace the team if they did anything stupid in public.

"Well, so, um, yeah," Nicky said, and looked in the direction of the clubhouse.

Eager to leave, then. "Thanks. I'll see you later," she said.

He gestured towards the gear. "Unless you, uh, need me to carry this stuff for you?"

Because—lugging a small pile of clothes all the way across the hall was going to be hard. "Well, it *does* look very heavy," she said.

He looked at her uncertainly, but then moved to pick the stack up.

She had always thought that baseball people were a happy, lighthearted lot—but, it really wasn't seeming that way. "Sorry. I'm kidding," she said.

"Oh." He stepped back. "Okay. It's cool. This is all just, you know, *different.*"

That, it was.

CHAPTER 10

Her new dressing room was very small, with a regular wooden locker—exactly like the ones in the clubhouse—a folding chair, and a small wooden stool. There was a shelf above the locker, to use for personal items, she assumed, since there was a small box on the left that could be locked—although, since she didn't know the combination, that was kind of moot. The shelf had a neatly arranged supply of new travel-sized toiletries, including a bar of soap, some shampoo, two plastic razors, and a small can of shaving cream.

There were also two cubbyholes at the bottom of the locker, for things like cleats and street shoes. And, very sweetly, there were several bouquets of flowers on the floor in the corner, two of which turned out to be from her grandparents, plus one from her mother, and some from a couple of family friends.

The door didn't lock—which might not bode well for potential pranks, but at least, it closed tightly. So, she changed into compression gear, and then put on the home uniform, which had *Retrievers* blazed across the front in royal blue. It didn't fit quite right, and she was probably going to need to swap the pants out for the next smaller size. The tailor was going to come in handy, since she was pretty sure that the jersey made her look like a beefy rectangle, but the dressing room didn't have a mirror, so she couldn't tell for sure.

She put up her hair in the usual chignon, making sure that her new cap—with the smiling cartoon dog—would fit comfortably above it. Then, she hung up the road and BP uniforms, and unpacked enough of her baseball stuff so that she could put on her cleats and have a glove ready for warm-ups.

When she was done, she wasn't sure if she should venture bravely out, wait for someone to come and get her—or just sit there quietly in the folding chair, take a few calming breaths, and mull over the degree to which her stomach was upset again. For lack of a better idea, sitting in the chair seemed like the least stressful choice.

Then, it occurred to her that it had been an *eternity* since she had checked her phone. Maybe the most soothing thing to do would be to text people like Lauren and Greg, see what was going on at home, and what she was missing.

She was retrieving the phone from her bag when there was a knock on the door, so she went over to answer it and saw a guy standing there in full uniform. A teammate, she assumed, as opposed to a *very* young coach. She had no intention of noticing whether any of the other players were attractive—but, this guy was, in an understated sort of way. African-American, hair closely cropped, but not shaved, carried himself well.

"Hi, I'm Marcus Grimes," he said, with a soft Southern accent, although there was a distinct note in his voice that commanded attention.

"Hi, Marcus," she said. "I'm Jill Cafferty."

They shook hands, quite formally.

"So," he said. "Welcome."

She nodded, trying not to look as anxious as she was feeling. "Thanks. I'm guessing"—based upon his build, which was similar to a defensive lineman—"that you're a catcher or first baseman?"

He smiled slightly. "Catcher."

Ergo, they would be spending a lot of time together this season.

"I was wondering," he said. "Did they do it of their own volition, or did you request a private room like this?"

She didn't want to say that the grown-ups had decided—since she was supposed to *be* one. "I think the front office presented the idea," she said. Possibly, her aunt had worked on it during negotiations, too. "Although I'm sure my mother would have *strongly* advocated for it, if they hadn't."

"But, you've spent time in male locker rooms," he said.

Most notably, yesterday. "Not much," she said. "Usually just for team meetings, and things like that."

He leaned against the doorjamb and folded his arms. Not quite as tall as she was, but *way* more muscular, with wide shoulders. "Are you squeamish?" he asked.

Strange question. "I don't know," she said. She wasn't big on cinematic gore, but that probably wasn't what he meant. "I guess it depends."

He nodded gravely. "Will being around male genitalia be something that would unnerve you?"

Did *everyone* think she was gay? She frowned at him. "Is that a trick question?"

"Clubhouses are rowdy," he said. "And often crass. Will that be a problem?"

Points to him, for being up-front. "I could probably do without the homoerotic hijinks," she said, "but, no, as long as I don't have to take group showers, I don't really care. I mean, female reporters have been in locker rooms for *decades*."

"Many of whom have been harassed, and hazed," he said.

He had extremely bookish diction, for a jock. "Where'd you go to school?" she asked.

"Vanderbilt," he said, somewhat impatiently. "But, right now, I'm trying to figure out your position on this."

"Well, I assume most people are here to play baseball," she said. "And that there's a difference between harassment and practical jokes."

He nodded. "Okay. Although there are plenty of guys who can't necessarily *tell* the difference."

Good point. "If they're just burning off energy, that's one thing," she said. "If they're intentionally trying to make my life difficult, that would be another. I kind of figure that most of them probably usually know which one they're doing."

He nodded again.

"Are you saying I should have a regular clubhouse locker?" she asked.

"It makes sense for you to shower and change in here," he said. "But, sitting by yourself constantly doesn't seem like a good idea. I mean, in the minors, there probably isn't going to be a lot of team cohesion. Too much competition for too few slots. So, that's isolating in and of itself. If you're going to be spending most of your time alone, it's going to be even tougher than it needs to be."

All of which made perfect sense. "Yeah," she said. "Only, what if—"

He pushed away from the doorjamb. "Come on. Let's go talk to the guys."

Well, okay, then. She put on her cap—except, it was the away cap, so she swapped it for the home version, and tucked her glove under her arm.

"Bring your fleece," Marcus said. "It got pretty chilly last night."

If she knew him better, she would have saluted, and said, "Yes, sir!" or something otherwise obnoxious, but instead, she pulled her fleece out of her locker, and followed him out to the hall.

Marcus glanced at her sideways. "'Homoerotic hijinks'?"

She grinned at him. "Just registering that one?"

"A little slow on the uptake, maybe," he said.

Not very often, she was guessing.

Adler was standing a few feet away in the hall, conferring with a coach she hadn't met yet, and he looked surprised to see them coming out of her dressing room, although he didn't do anything other than raise an eyebrow.

"Are you okay with it, Skip, if we have a quick players-only meeting before stretch?" Marcus asked.

Adler paused, before answering. "We've only lost the one game, son."

Marcus smiled. "Well, let's try to keep it from getting worse."

Adler looked at them, then nodded. "Carry on."

When they walked into the clubhouse, almost everyone was in the middle of changing into game uniforms and getting ready to head out to the field.

"Chick in the house!" someone yelled, although she wasn't sure who it was, and a few guys laughed when someone else screamed in mock terror and covered himself with towels.

"All right, listen up," Marcus said, once they had settled down a little.

"Shhh," Scott said loudly to the guy sitting next to him. "Mother is speaking."

Jill looked at Marcus. "They call you Mother? Already?" With the season only a couple of days old?

"I can be a mite bossy," he said, rather stiffly.

Yes, she had already caught on to that.

"Here's the law, guys," Marcus said to the room in general. "I know there's been some yapping and complaining, but we're not going to have a member of the team off by herself all season. So, we need to figure out a way for Jill to be able to spend most of her time in here, and to make sure she feels comfortable."

"Well, it's not like we can't take turns *visiting* her," a guy with a seedy-looking light brown mustache said.

It got really quiet, although some of the ballplayers were still speaking Spanish among themselves. She felt her face get very hot, but she wasn't sure if it was embarrassment, or fury, or—more likely—both.

"We've already figured out that you're a dick, Owen," a tall, lanky guy with dark hair said. "You don't have to keep proving it."

"What?" Owen said defensively. "It's what a lot of you were *thinking*."

Oh, she hoped not. "Obviously, at least one of you is going to be an idiot," she said, just as Marcus started to say something. "But, with luck, most of you *aren't*. Either way, I'm here to play, and if anyone acts like a jerk, I'm *still* here to play."

"Cafferty, we'll get the clubbies to set you up with a locker," the lanky guy said. "Mother's right—you need to be able to hang out with us, or there's no way this is going to work."

"Yeah, go ahead and change clothes in here," Owen said. "Give us a show every day."

Really? "Shut up, Owen," she said, as several other players said versions of the same thing, although "shut the *fuck* up, Owen" was the most popular choice.

A guy who was clearly bilingual was filling in the rest of the Latino players, although she couldn't help contributing that one of their teammates was *un imbécil*—among other things. She managed to rise above using the word *pendejo*—but, it took some concentrated effort.

There were three loud knocks, and then one of the clubhouse doors was pushed open by a guy in black Under Armour sweatpants and a gold Pirates polo shirt.

"Time for stretch," he said. "Let's get out there, guys."

That broke—although didn't *erase*—the tension, and people were grabbing their caps, and gloves, and whatever else they were going to need during the game—including, she saw, more than one tin of chewing tobacco. Which was supposed to be illegal in the minors, but she had assumed that there were still people who did it, since it was a baseball thing. A *stupid* thing, but pretty popular, even on the AAU team she'd played on.

"Thanks for backing me up," she said to the lanky guy. *More* than lanky, she could see, now that she was up close—he was at least six-six.

"No problem," he said, and put his hand out. "Dimitri."

"Jill," she said.

After they shook, she followed him out to the tunnel leading to the dugout, and the field.

She'd always liked the sound of cleats on cement. It was a "Play ball!" sound.

There was enough crowd noise outside, so that it was probably a full house. She was trying not to be conspicuous, but as soon as she left the dugout, there was a surge of energy in the stands, and people were calling her name from a lot of different directions.

She lifted her hand in a wave, but didn't stray from the team, as they headed out to the right field foul line to stretch. Marcus was off with that night's starting pitcher, but it probably would have looked dumb if she had clung to him like some insecure little shadow, anyway. So, she found an open spot, and followed along as the guy in the Pirates shirt—a man, actually, in his early thirties, maybe—led them through a series of organized stretches. Shoulder shrugs, arm circles, hamstrings, quads, and so forth.

Of course, being baseball players, more than a few of her

teammates didn't exactly overexert themselves, although there was a noticeable lack of chatter and joking around.

"How those groin stretches feel for you, Cafferty?" someone asked.

She didn't even have to look up to know who it was. "Shut up, Owen," she said, which was echoed by Dimitri and Scott and at least two other players.

Owen just kind of leered at her. "You wearing your—"

"*Don't* say it," she said, before he could get the word "cup" out. Christ, guys were obsessed with their damn athletic supporters.

"Let's see some *focus*," the man leading the stretches said, sounding grim.

This did not lighten the atmosphere.

When it was time to break off into pairs to play catch, she had a "What if no one picks me?" moment of panic, the likes of which she hadn't felt—well, *ever*—in her entire life, when it came to sports.

"Who's Schwartzman?" she asked, hoping that it wasn't Owen.

No one said anything right away, but since they were all looking at the same guy, he sighed and lifted his hand briefly.

"Me," he said. "Why?"

"Thank you for the number," she said. "I think I owe you a steak dinner or something."

"Get him a *car*," someone said.

Okay, *all* high draft picks probably got grief about their bonuses. She saw Owen start to open his mouth, and pointed at him. "Shut up, Owen," she said, before he could even let out one syllable—and several of the guys laughed.

There was a big canvas Pirates bag full of baseballs, and people were helping themselves, to use for the pre-game throwing routine.

"Are you really okay with it?" she asked Schwartzman.

He shrugged. "It's just a number."

Yeah, but baseball players were superstitious, so she definitely appreciated it. "Want to warm up with me?" she asked, before he could slip away.

He hesitated, but his better angels must have won out, because he nodded. "Sure."

Guys were already throwing back and forth, but baseball teams were usually loose, and this group wasn't—at all. So, for the hell of it, when Schwartzman tossed her the ball, she sent it back underhand, in a reasonable facsimile of a fast-pitch softball pitcher.

He stared at her with such horror that the ball—which was already wild, because her release point was way off—zipped right past him.

The rest of the team had also stopped playing catch, and most of them looked equally dismayed.

"Just fulfilled all of your worst expectations, didn't I," she said.

Pretty much everyone nodded vigorously.

"Did I even do it right?" she asked, since softball pitching mechanics were complex, with a lot of moving parts, and she had never really tried to do it before.

"No," a guy with a crewcut said. "My sister's a DI pitcher, and—well, that was terrible."

At least half of the guys were now throwing to each other underhand, and the mood was suddenly much lighter.

"Knock it off, bozos!" Louis, the male trainer, said grumpily. "We have a game, remember?"

So, they went back to normal throwing, but people were joking around now, and she felt less like an unwelcome interloper.

"You know this is just for position players, right?" Dimitri said.

Oh. Hunh. News to her. She'd assumed that all pre-game warm-ups were mandatory. "I do," she said. "But, I wanted you all to see that I'm open-minded, and willing to mix with you, sometimes."

Which amused at least some of them.

She and Schwartzman threw easily back and forth, as he moved deeper into the outfield every few tosses, and then gradually in again.

"What position?" she asked.

"Corner outfield, mostly," he said. "I think they might give me some time at third, too."

Which made sense, because he certainly had a strong arm.

Once the warm-ups were finished, people headed back to the dugout, except for the starting players, who began to do some jogging or sprints, or get stretched out by the strength coach and the trainers.

"You can run, too," Dimitri said, from the ground, wincing slightly as Sofia worked on his hamstrings and lower back. "For solidarity."

"I'm very fast," Jill said. "I don't want to show anyone up."

He nodded, even though he was wincing more visibly. "That's a good story. Stick to it."

Yep. Because she totally and completely knew what she was doing.

And she had *intended* to stand here, by herself, for no reason, with nothing to do. She was not at all embarrassed, or self-conscious.

Nope. Not even a little bit.

CHAPTER 11

A black guy in chinos and a Lacoste shirt came over, with his hand out. He was one of the people to whom she'd been introduced when she first arrived, but at this point, that was all a blur.

"I'm Jeremiah," he said. "Media relations. We met earlier."

Right. "Hi," she said. "I'm sorry, I've been introduced to so many people today that I'm having a little trouble remembering names."

"Understandable," he said, and gestured towards a younger white guy wearing beige cargo pants and a Retrievers T-shirt. "This is Paul, my intern."

"Hi," Paul said, seeming to think that he was being quite covert about checking her out—except for the part where it was hard to miss.

Jeremiah had an ex-jock build, whereas Paul had unkempt brown hair and glasses, and looked like a college guy who probably never did anything more athletic than play the occasional intramural Frisbee game with a beer in his free hand.

"We should sit down when you can, to talk about our overall approach, your social media presence, and any concerns you have," Jeremiah said.

This probably wasn't going to be the right time to say that her primary goal on social media was to keep as low a profile as possible. "My mother might want to join us for that," she said.

"We've actually *already* met with your mother," he said, very blandly.

"Were you bowled over by her uncontrollable excitement?" Jill asked.

Jeremiah smiled, without elaborating.

That was a big no.

"At least one of us is always going to be with you, when you're interacting with fans," he said. "We're hoping to keep things from getting out of hand."

"I'm supposed to sign autographs, right?" she said.

Jeremiah looked puzzled. "Do you mind signing?"

"No," she said quickly. "But, that's *a lot* of people over there, and—well, the game starts pretty soon."

Jeremiah nodded. "Got it. Don't worry about it. Just sign until one of us intercedes, so that you can get to where you need to be. You can let us know when to step in."

Jesus, she had *handlers* now. What was next, an actual entourage?

Most of the kids in the stands seemed to be extremely excited to see her, but others were only chirping mindlessly for her to give them a ball. Which made her flash on being at a Pawtucket Red Sox game with her father, when she was about seven, and him giving her a "Don't be *that* kid" speech, since he wasn't a fan of what he called "ball grubbing."

Over the years, she had been at minor league games where she saw quite a few children—and some adults—eagerly amassing a *stack* of baseballs, most of which she assumed they never looked at again, once they brought them home. Her father had always said that getting a ball in the stands should be *special*, and the one she kept on her desk at home was a foul ball he'd snagged one-handed for her at Fenway Park once, when she was maybe ten years old.

Although, of course, she also had a milk crate full of baseballs from important games she'd pitched over the years, starting in Little League, to AAU, to high school and the local travel teams, which she'd saved and carefully marked, if she'd pitched a no-hitter or had an unusually high number of strikeouts or something. She had actually thrown two perfect games in her life—one in Little League, and one in AAU— although several others had been spoiled by things like errors, or passed balls on strikeouts, with the batter ending up safe at first. Which, even in Little League, was a pretty freakish achievement, so she was going to have to keep those two baseballs as nice amateur memories, because a pitcher throwing a perfect game in the *pros* was considerably less likely than getting struck by lightning. No-hitters weren't exactly common, either, but perfect games—twenty-seven up, twenty-seven down, not a single mistake—were kind of the Holy Grail of pitching. In fact, as far as she knew, in the entire *history* of Major League Baseball, it had only happened a couple of dozen times, out of more than *two hundred thousand* games. It happened even less frequently in the minors.

When she went over to the stands, too many of the people wanted autographs *and* selfies, and since the latter was entirely not her thing, she had to remind herself to smile graciously and—with luck—convincingly. There were also professional photographers and videographers all over the place, but she did her best not to let them make her feel self-conscious—even when they were right on top of her.

Some of the fans were pushing and shoving, which made a few security guards move closer, and she was aware that Jeremiah and Paul had, too. People were probably only being enthusiastic—but, it was disturbing, especially when adults elbowed children out of the way—or when their damn hands flailed out violently in her direction, and came close to hitting her.

"Game time, everyone, sorry," Jeremiah said, and then he deftly guided her away.

She was probably supposed to be *embracing* this fame thing—but, the whole scene had made her dizzy, and it was hard to catch her breath. Christ, was she really going have to deal with this kind of thing for the rest of her life? Was there anything *smart* about doing that? Especially, on purpose.

"We're going to work on some strategies," Jeremiah said, watching her. "Figure out a sort of hit-and-run technique, so you can have more control."

She nodded. "Yes, that would be good. Thank you."

The dugout felt like a haven, albeit one filled with strangers. But, she had barely stepped inside, when it was time to turn around and line up on the first base side for the national anthem.

She took her cap off, and gripped her father's dog tag with her right hand, holding it over her heart. Paying respect to the flag, and all that it meant, was not a challenge for her—ever. Once the performance was over—the singer wasn't half bad, although he was shaky on the high notes—she gave the dog tag one last squeeze, and then put it back inside the compression shirt she was wearing under her jersey.

Most of the guys who weren't playing were already standing on the top step of the dugout, leaning against the railing, but she didn't feel quite ready to do that yet, and picked a spot in the middle of the bench instead, which wasn't blatantly isolated, but wasn't really close to anyone else, either.

Of course, now that she was sitting down, she wanted some Gatorade, but felt shy about getting up to help herself to a cup from the big orange dispenser. So, she stayed where she was, trying to look relaxed. Which would have been easier, if she hadn't left her sunglasses inside.

There was a baseball game going on. She could watch it. Except that she was so tense that it was hard to focus.

A small white plastic bucket full of bubble gum was resting on the concrete shelf above the bench, and even though she wasn't a gum chewer, she helped herself to a couple of pieces. She could blow some bubbles, maybe. But, for now, she just held the pieces in her hand, finding even the decision about whether to unwrap them kind of overwhelming.

After a few minutes—there seemed to be at least one runner on base, although she wasn't sure how he had gotten there—someone sat down about a foot away from her. She looked over to see Sofia, the trainer. She was probably in her late twenties, and at least ten inches shorter than Jill was, with short black hair, and a body type that was somewhere between athletic and chunky.

"Oh," Jill said, and shoved the gum into one of her back pockets. "Are you my designated friend?"

Sofia scowled. "I am an extremely competent trainer. I *hate* it that they hired me because I'm a woman."

That was reasonable. "I hate it that there's all this fuss about *me* being a woman, when I really just want to go and"—she gestured towards the visiting team's dugout—"strike all of the sons of bitches out."

"*Can* you strike all of the sons of bitches out?" Sofia asked, sounding more curious than anything else.

Well, that was the crux of the entire matter, wasn't it. "I'm pretty sure I can strike *some* of them out," Jill said. "But, I think there's also probably going to be a considerable learning curve."

Now, Sofia looked at her with what appeared to be genuine interest. "Well, okay," she said, and then turned her attention to the field.

They watched the rest of the inning in friendly silence, and then, as the team came off the field, Sofia got up to meet the starting pitcher at the other end of the dugout. The energy in the dugout was more of a "Don't worry, we'll get 'em back" mood, than an "All right!" celebratory one.

So, she checked the scoreboard, and saw that they were down 2–0. She had no idea how that had happened, but it was only the first, and two runs was no big deal.

The center fielder sat down near her, setting his glove on the bench with a thump. He was quite good-looking, in a sleek, polished way, with black hair and improbably gorgeous teeth. He nodded at her, before gulping down some Gatorade.

Okay, she would be brave, and try to engage him in conversation. He was her teammate, right? "*Hola!*" she said.

He grinned at her with those beautiful teeth. "90272," he said.

She looked at him blankly.

"I'm from the Palisades," he said.

Which meant absolutely nothing to her.

"California," he said.

Well, it wasn't as though there weren't plenty of people in California who spoke Spanish. "Okay," she said. "Hello, then."

He grinned again. "Hi, I'm Hector." He indicated the cooler. "May I get you some Gatorade?"

She would love some—but, she could certainly pour it herself. "No, thanks, I'm fine," she said. There would be few things more awkward than having guys on the team *wait* on her.

"Well, let me know," he said, and focused out at the field.

At the next half inning, the pitching coach, Sawyer, walked down to the section of the bench where she was sitting. So far, she hadn't done anything more than say hello to him, but she remembered his being a journeyman middle reliever in the big leagues for quite a few years. Now, he was bald, in his late forties, and appeared to have gimpy knees.

"Are you watching their hitters?" he asked.

It hadn't even occurred to her to do that—which was embarrassing. Especially since she was starting tomorrow, God help her. "You're right," she said. "I'm sorry that I wasn't."

He frowned. "I shouldn't have to tell you to do it. You should *want* to."

She had now officially established herself as someone who wasn't willing to do the *work*. She nodded. "I apologize. I think I'm kind of—disoriented." She looked at him uncertainly. "Should I be charting pitches?" Which starters usually did the day before their next outing—partially as a way to learn the other team's tendencies at the plate, but also to help stay focused. Writing down what every pitch was, *where* it was—and what the outcome was. Sometimes, they charted from the stands, and sometimes, from the dugout.

"Not tonight," he said. "Suarez is doing it. Where you're concerned, the routine is all fu—screwed up. So, we'll just have to roll with things."

About which, the man did not sound happy.

She felt like a tourist in a staggeringly foreign country. "I really am sorry, sir, but where would be the best place for me to be?" she asked.

For the first time, he looked more sympathetic than irritated. "It's still *baseball*, Cafferty," he said. "And we're supposed to treat you like—look, you have to tune out all of the static. Focus on *baseball*."

That might be the best advice she got all season—from anyone. Possibly the best advice she would get in her entire career.

"Yes, sir," she said. "I'll do that, sir."

She located an open section and ventured up to the dugout railing, which was padded, and therefore, a nice place to lean. The guys on either side of her nodded, and she nodded back. Unfortunately, when people in the stands saw her, a bunch of them started yelling her name and taking pictures and all, and she *really* wanted to go back to the comparative safety of the bench.

"Don't do that," a guy she'd heard people call Nathan, who was further down the railing, said. "They'll lose interest soon enough."

"Or, at least, they'll lose their *voices*," someone else said, and most of them laughed.

There were a lot of "Can I have a ball?" and "Jill, throw me a ball!" requests being shouted in her direction, and she shrugged apologetically at them, without turning all of the way around. They actually weren't supposed to toss baseballs into the stands during the game, which made it easier to refuse.

"You're a mean girl," Owen said, also along the railing.

She was going to tell him to shut up—except, that remark had been kind of funny, so she shrugged at him, too.

The guy to her left nodded to her, and she returned the nod. He was about six-four and appeared to be biracial, with the thick sort of lower body that usually indicated a power pitcher.

"Pitcher?" she asked.

He nodded again, and held out his hand. "I'm Jonesy."

"Jill," she said, and shook it.

"Do my best to remember that," he said, and then winked at her. "Although the guys will probably call you Caffy or Jilly or something."

Since baseball nicknames were often pretty basic. The truly delightful names, like a guy who had once played in the Red Sox farm system who had been known as "Pork Chop" Pough, weren't nearly common enough. That had been her father's all-time favorite baseball name, although he'd liked Harry "The Hat" Walker, too. But, she could live with "Caffy," since it was almost certainly better than some of the other likely possibilities.

If he was a bullpen guy, he would be down there already, unless— "Closer or starter?" she asked.

"Starter," he said. "I went last night."

Good, that meant she could maybe pick his brain.

"Can't believe they're making you pitch *tomorrow*," he said. "It's like throwing a baby into the water to see if it can swim."

She didn't entirely disagree, but she shrugged.

"It's probably better than Wednesday, though," he said. "That's getaway night, and we'd be stuck waiting for you to finish up with ESPN and all."

She couldn't hear any rancor in his voice—probably because he was just stating the simple, *accurate* truth.

The other downside to pitching on Wednesday, it occurred to her, would have been a rushed, possibly tearful, farewell to her family—while the team sat around waiting for her to get on the bus already.

"How are they?" she asked, indicating the hitter at the plate, but meaning the entire team.

He glanced over. "What have you picked up?"

She could stutter and fumble—or be honest. "Not much," she said. "I was too busy being incapacitated by anxiety."

He was either going to laugh—or give her an odd look, and she was relieved when he went with the former. "That kid Scott," he gestured towards left field, "kept saying that you weren't really a diva princess, and that you were pretty fun in Pittsburgh—but, not too many of us were buying it."

She had a terrible feeling that either Diva or Princess were potential nicknames. So, maybe she should redirect, although this was going to be based more on the rhythm of the game, than any savvy observations. "They're swinging at a lot of first pitches," she said.

"You got that right. That kid"—Jonesy waved vaguely at the mound—"has had trouble finding the plate all night, and they're *still* swinging." He shook his head. "Every pitcher in the world is lucky that hitters are as dumb as rocks."

Well, yeah, that was pretty much the gospel, among pitchers.

"No idea what you've really got," he said. "But, except for one or two guys, you can be pretty far off the black, and they'll still bite at it."

It was a hell of a lot easier to get hitters out, if they were *helping* with the process. "Thanks," she said.

Jonesy shrugged. "Mother'll take good care of you. That guy was *born* to sit behind the dish. Too bad he can't hit worth a damn."

For Marcus's sake, she hoped that that wasn't true.

She spent the next few innings at the railing, with Jonesy making the occasional "Walked right up the ladder with that guy" or "That one doesn't like you coming inside" remarks, all of which she carefully filed away.

The third baseman on her team, some guy named Geoff, hit a solo shot in the fifth, and she high-fived him along with everyone else. It was his first home run as a pro, and he was very excited. So much so that he high-fived her right back without missing a beat.

She finally located her mother and Theo sitting in two box seats behind home plate, when she turned around to look at the crowded stands between innings. Theo was using his phone, of course, but he gave her a thumbs-up, and nudged her mother, who waved. She tipped her cap ever so slightly at them, and then went back to leaning against the railing.

They were losing, eight to three, but no one seemed to be terribly devastated about it, except for that night's starting pitcher, who had left the game during the fourth, and returned from the clubhouse in the seventh. He was sitting by himself, unhappily expressionless, with a big ice pack strapped to his shoulder.

Hector, who was lounging against the railing on her right side, shook his head. "I may not speak Spanish," he said, "but most of our gardeners are Japanese, so at least I can say a few things to *that* poor guy."

She glanced back at the miserable pitcher, who was staring straight ahead at nothing. "Can you teach me a couple of phrases? And what's his name?"

"Shosuke," Hector said. "I would have figured he would know *some* English, but he can barely say hello."

So, he was probably feeling even more lost and off-kilter

than she was. Especially after giving up six runs, in what was probably his first start. And he looked really *young*, too. "That must be"—She stopped. "You have *multiple* gardeners?"

Hector nodded cheerfully.

So, he came from extreme wealth—in a zip code that must be near the famous 90210. "That explains the fabulous dental work," she said.

Hector nodded again, and smiled a very toothy smile.

"Anyway," she said. "About Shosuke?"

"I don't know much," he said, "but I can teach you a couple of things. *Kon'nichiwa* is hello."

She pronounced the word quietly to herself a few times, to try and commit it to memory.

"And *sayonara* is good-bye," he said.

That one, she already knew.

"*Arigatō* is 'thank you,'" he said. "But, sometimes they say *dōmo arigatō*, which could be for emphasis? I'm not sure."

She repeated those words, too.

"And, well, that's about it, sorry," Hector said. "Mother Grimes"—he gestured towards Marcus, who was down at the far end of the dugout, conferring with a relief pitcher, who had come into the game the inning before—"has been using some apps to try and learn enough to communicate with the guy. So, he'll probably end up being the expert around here."

Somehow, that didn't surprise her at all.

When the half inning was over, and they had all gone back

out to the field for the top of the eighth, she moved to sit near Shosuke, who was quite skinny, and looked to be maybe twenty years old.

"*Kon'nichiwa*," she said, tentatively.

His eyes lit up, and he rattled off a couple of rapid sentences.

She felt guilty about having to shake her head. "I'm sorry, but I don't speak Japanese. I just—*dōmo arigatō*? And—*sayonara*?" She wouldn't insult him by saying words like *sushi* and *teriyaki*.

He made a small bow in her direction. "Hel-lo," he said, sounding very shy.

"*Kon'nichiwa*," she said again.

He smiled. "*Konbanwa*," he said, and pointed up at the sky.

So, that meant—night? Or maybe—good night? Or—the sky itself? She would have to look it up later—or ask Marcus. "*Konbanwa*," she said, doing her best to mimic his pronunciation perfectly.

He nodded, and bowed again.

She held up a baseball glove, then raised her hands questioningly.

"*Gurōbu*," he said.

She repeated that, and then said, "Glove," which *he* repeated, with enough confidence to make her assume that it was a word he already knew.

By the end of the inning, they had moved up to the railing,

so she could watch the hitters, and gone through "baseball," "pitcher," "foul ball," "ground out" and "strikeout." She wasn't sure if she would remember any of the words, but he looked more at ease, and ironically enough, she felt as though she was really *communicating* with one of her teammates—even though they spoke different languages.

By the end of the game, almost the whole team was up at the railing, rooting for an unlikely comeback, but they ended up losing nine to six.

Jeremiah intercepted her as she was heading towards the clubhouse and her dressing room, and she ended up doing several brief stand-up interviews on the field, with local news affiliates, and a few national networks. A group of fans was clustered by the edge of the stands, and she signed at least fifty autographs before making her way down the tunnel.

It was frustrating that she didn't have a shower yet, but since she hadn't played, she could get away without taking one until she got to the motel. But, she did stop by the employee ladies' room to wash up, before going to her dressing room to change. There was a small laundry bag neatly folded on her chair, which she assumed had been left by one of the clubbies. She wasn't sure what to put in there, so she decided to leave them only her uniform, her sanitary socks, and her stirrup socks. She could hand-wash everything else easily enough in the motel sink. She also didn't know what gear she could safely leave behind in her dressing room, but decided to bring everything but her turf shoes with her.

She hadn't been able to look at either of her phones for *hours*, and dozens of messages had come in, most of which she ignored—especially the six or eight from just one agent, a very smarmy and persistent guy named Aaron Marshak, who had been trying to land her for about two years now. He had even once—rather creepily—sent flowers to her *mother* on Valentine's Day, with the apparent assumption that the entire family would be charmed by his doing so.

Since it would only take a few minutes, she went ahead and sent quick texts back to people like Lauren and Greg and her relatives.

There was a hesitant knock on the door, and she opened it to find Terence, the clubbie with all of the tattoos.

"You all set?" he asked. "You need anything?"

"No, thanks," she said. "I'm supposed to put my uniform in the bag, right?"

"Yeah. Put everything in there, after you hook it on to this laundry loop," he said, handing her a white cloth contraption. "We mark the shirts and all with your number, to make sure you get back the right stuff." He glanced in her locker. "Where are your cleats?"

She pointed to her gear bag.

"You need to leave those," he said. "Nicky and I clean them."

God, they had a terrible job.

"Stinks that you don't have a shower yet," Terence said.

"But, there was a problem with the pipes. They're supposed to have guys coming in here tonight, to work overtime on it."

She nodded.

"There's a tailor showing up tomorrow, too," he said. "For, you know, alterations, I guess."

She hoped it would be someone who worked quickly, since she really didn't want to pitch in a baggy uniform. "I'd maybe like to go down one size in the pants," she said. "If you have any smaller ones?"

He nodded. "You bet. We'll take care of it."

"Thanks," she said. "And maybe tomorrow, you can walk me through how the dues work, and stuff like that."

"Sure thing," he said. "We have, um, you know, a post-game spread, if you're hungry—but, I told Mr. Brayton I'd bring you up to see him right now. Since he's with your family."

In which case, details could wait. "That would be great, thank you," she said.

Because, the truth was, she was not only very tired and ready to go crash out at the motel, but she could *really* use a hug.

CHAPTER 12

Once Terence brought her upstairs, she only got to say a fast hello to her mother and Theo before she was introduced to another series of strangers—including the friendly looking retired couple who were going to serve as her host family. After that, she had to do a few more interviews with print and online reporters, and by the time they were able to leave the ballpark, it was so late that the only place they could find that was still open was an all-night diner.

Her father had always ordered whatever a diner was offering as the daily special, and she had gotten into the habit, too. Which, tonight, meant meatloaf with mushroom gravy, mashed potatoes, carrots and peas, fresh cornbread, and Jell-O or pudding for dessert. All she had to do was add a dinner salad and a glass of milk, and she was reasonably good to go. Also, Theo gave her his coleslaw, and her mother shared some of the roast turkey from her open-faced sandwich.

"You think they're ever just going to let you, you know, *play baseball*?" Theo asked.

It didn't seem that way, did it? Jill shrugged. "They *have* to give me some space tomorrow. You can't mess with someone when they're pitching." Although she had already been warned that an MLB camera crew was going to be following her around all day for a documentary or some damn thing.

"They're fairly convincing about *wanting* you to succeed," her mother said. "But, I guess it's going to take a little while for them to figure out how to do that."

And no, her mother had *not* been happy about the lack of a working shower or bathroom in her changing room.

When they got to the motel, she was tired enough to want to flop facedown onto the bed, without even changing into a sleeping T-shirt or anything. But, she took a shower, and hand-washed her compression shorts and shirt and underwear, first. *Then*, she let herself fall onto her bed, already half-asleep, barely managing to grunt her assent when her mother asked if it would be okay if she read for a while before turning out the light.

A light she never noticed, once she closed her eyes, and for all she knew, her mother read until dawn.

In the morning, they had breakfast at a nearby Denny's,

before driving over to the stadium, where she was going to have a fitting with the tailor at eleven-thirty.

Once the word had got out that she would be starting that night, they began to get messages from people who were going to drive up for the game, including her father's sister and husband, and their family friend Keith, who had been deployed with her father, and was planning to show up with people from their National Guard unit. Her maternal grandmother lived in Chicago, but was going to fly in to see her play later in the season, maybe when the team went to play Staten Island or Brooklyn in New York City, and her paternal grandparents, who had retired to Arizona, had similar plans. Greg immediately offered to drive Lauren and some of their other friends up, but since she knew it would mean Lauren would have to miss physical therapy, and that she wouldn't be able to spend any time with them at all, she asked if they could come when the team played the Connecticut Tigers or the Lowell Spinners, later in the season.

Having so many people in the stands was going to add some pressure, but it would also be nice to have extra support. Among other things, the damn game was going to be televised on ESPN—which ranked much higher on the pressure scale.

Her dressing room was still a work in progress, but when she walked in, a plumber and a couple of carpenters were in the shower area, toiling away.

"A few more hours," one of them said. "Should be done by then."

She nodded, gathering up the uniforms and issued gear in her locker to take to her fitting session. No one seemed to know where to do it, and finally, she ended up in a small conference room, where someone or other pushed the table against the wall, to make more room.

The tailor was a burly older man, who was unshaven and had an unlit cigar in his mouth. He was introduced as Russo, with no further elaboration, so she decided to fall back on her traditional strategy, and call him "sir." He mumbled to himself, as he pinned and taped various seams in place, starting with the home and road uniforms. For a man with thick hands, he had a deft touch, pausing every so often to say "Throw" or "Field," and she would pantomime the motions, and he would reposition some of the pins, to adjust the fit.

And she possibly did a *triple* take, when she realized that he was using the cigar as a pin cushion.

Since the Hall of Fame was going to whisk away tonight's jersey, as soon as she took it off, Nicky brought out an extra one for him to alter.

"How 'bout the fleeces and workout clothes?" Russo asked. "And the BP jersey?"

She hesitated, not wanting him to have to do *crazy* amounts of work.

"Spit it out, girlie," he said.

"The hoodie's fine," she said. "But, maybe the fleece could be a little more fitted. Mostly, people won't see the BP jersey, but maybe we could do one of the T-shirts, and those incredibly baggy shorts? I look like a yahoo in them."

He lifted a scruffy eyebrow. *"We?"*

"You," she said. "Sir."

He nodded, and motioned for her to put on the workout clothes. So, she stepped behind the open door to a storage closet they were using as a changing room.

"Not exactly one of those skirts who's gonna be walking 'round in a sports bra all day," he said.

No, it wasn't who she was. She might put on a tank top, now and then, when it was hot, maybe, but she had always erred on the side of being reserved. She had private moments of being vain about her body—she was, after all, pretty damn fit—but, that didn't necessarily mean that she wanted to waltz around for one and all to see. "No, sir," she said. "I think that's a safe assumption on your part."

"Ain't no harm in it, but I don't think it's no more respectful than players goin' shirtless on the field," he said. "The ballfield's a *temple*."

She was a charter member of the Church of Baseball herself. "Yes, sir," she said. "It is."

Somewhat to her surprise, he smiled. "You got those military kid manners, don't you?"

She *never* thought of herself as being a "military kid"—her father had had an active business restoring old houses, and only served in the Guard part-time—but, in certain ways, it was true. "Yes, sir," she said. "I probably do."

"I'm really sorry about your dad," he said.

She nodded. "Thank you, sir. It's—well, we never stop missing him."

"He'd be *mighty* proud of you," Russo said, around a mouthful of straight pins, as he worked on the shorts.

"I hope so, sir," she said. Assumed so—but, at some level, it was all just theory now. "My mother says a lot of people from his unit are driving up tonight."

Russo nodded. "Good for them. Doesn't surprise me none, though. Did some time in the service myself, back in the day."

Which didn't surprise *her*. People in the military had a certain way of holding themselves, even years later.

He studied her T-shirt. "You want 'em sleeveless, or capped sleeves?"

She had no idea. "What do you think?" she asked.

"You got pretty nice guns," he said. "But, capped'll be aces for you."

"Okay, then. Rock on, sir," she said.

He didn't seem to know what to make of that, but began measuring and pinning the sleeves.

"Are you coming to the game tonight, Mr. Russo?" she asked.

He shrugged. "Well, I don't rightly know. Have to admit,

the wife and me don't mosey on out to the yard too much."

There was something very charming about his rough edges. "I'd like it, if you came," she said. "Could I ask them to put aside a couple of tickets for you?"

"Think we could probably spring for 'em," he said.

True, minor league prices weren't exactly through the roof, but— "I'd rather have them be comps from me," she said.

"Okay," he said, and half-smiled. "Give me a chance to see how the uniform hangs."

As good a reason as any.

Once the fittings were finished, she went down to her dressing room—and the work crew left long enough for her to gather up a BP cap and non-gamer glove, and change into the right clothes for team stretch. After which, Jeremiah and his intern—whatever his name was—brought her down to the GM's office, where the MLB documentary team was waiting. Having two cameramen, a producer, and a stand-up reporter follow her around was probably a necessary evil—and it wasn't as though she had been given the option to *decline*, so she nodded and smiled as though she thought it was a *great* idea.

They were harder to ignore during PFP—Pitchers' Fielding Practice—because she was awkward and clumsy on a few of the plays, and got more than one coaching criticism of her footwork and approach to the ball. A downside of teaching *herself* how to do so many aspects of baseball was that she had picked up some bad habits.

She heard one of the other pitchers say, "Man, she *sucks*," and someone else—Jonesy, maybe?—said, "Give it a rest already." She could only hope that the directional microphones weren't sensitive enough to have picked that up.

She wasn't sensitive enough for it to have bothered her, of course. She had barely even *noticed*.

When PFP was over, she was supposed to meet inside with Sawyer and Marcus about tonight's game. The TV people started to follow them into the clubhouse, but Marcus raised his hand.

"I'm sorry, you have to leave my pitcher alone now," he said. "We have game prep to do."

The producer held up the media pass hanging from a lanyard around his neck. "We're All-Access."

"I appreciate that," Marcus said, "but the clubhouse is closed to the media right now. We need to get our work done."

"I'll just shoot for a few minutes," one of the cameramen said. "Then, we'll get out of your hair."

Marcus shook his head. "No. Take it up with media relations. My pitcher needs to focus."

The MLB producer looked at her, as though she might overrule him.

"I'm sorry," she said. "I don't argue with my catcher."

So, they were able to escape into the clubhouse, unescorted.

"Thank you, Mother," she said—and meant it.

He frowned. "I really don't like being called 'Mother.'"

"What do you prefer?" she asked.

"*Marcus*," he said.

Duly noted. "Thank you for running interference, Marcus," she said.

He waved that off. "Come on, we'll pull some chairs over to your locker."

Except for Nicky, who was cleaning someone's cleats, the room was deserted, since BP had started and everyone else was out on the field.

Overnight, she had been set up with a locker—complete with a "Cafferty" nameplate—three down from Marcus, with Shosuke on her left and a pitcher named Suarez on her right.

The clubbies were earning their tip money, because they had put new toiletries on the top shelf, and tonight's game jersey was already hanging up. She glanced at it, and saw that Russo was a speedy seamstress—or whatever the male form of the word was—because it had already been altered with neat, gently curved seams.

She would do most of her changing in her dressing room, but there was no reason why she couldn't finish up with the top layers in here. If any of the guys had a problem with that, so be it.

Sawyer turned out to be a stats guy, and had detailed notes and spray charts for her to examine, as well as videos of hitters on his iPad.

"It's so early in the season that we don't have much

information yet, but this is a start," he said.

It looked comprehensive to her—which was another reminder of how little she knew.

"I haven't gotten to see you throw yet," Sawyer said. "You feel good about your two-seamer and your four-seamer?"

Her fastballs. She nodded, since that seemed to be the right answer.

"We're going to think long-term, and build you up, brick by brick. So, I don't want to see anything but fastballs in the first inning," he said. "Maybe the entire outing."

She tried not to look utterly appalled.

"Yeah, yeah," he said. "I know you work off the change and the hook, but we're starting a process here, you get what I'm saying?"

She wasn't at all on board with this, but nodding still felt like the smartest option.

"This isn't high school," he said. "You won't be overmatching anyone, sitting around eighty-nine, ninety-one. What I'm looking for is movement, and how you change speeds."

She nodded yet again—since it was the only thing she seemed to know how to do.

Marcus mostly listened, and took notes on *his* iPad, while Sawyer talked about pitching mostly being about real estate, wherein all that really mattered was location, location, and *more* location.

"If you've got command, you don't *need* anything else," Sawyer said. "Capisce?"

She nodded. "Yes, sir."

When the strategy session was over and Sawyer went off to the coaches' communal office, she looked at Marcus.

"Is this really a good idea?" she asked. "I feel like I'm going to be going out there with my hands tied."

"We'll move the ball around, and switch up the two and the four, so we can throw off their timing," he said. "And then, every inning, we'll reevaluate. But, he's right—it'll give him the purest view of your pitching, and he'll know where we need to work the most."

Going on national television without her two best weapons made her feel sick with despair, but yes, in the big picture, it probably made sense. It was still hard not to be afraid that her first matchup with professional hitters, using a pedestrian set of fastballs, could lead to disaster.

Terence was putting out the pre-game spread now, which looked like fruit, a big cooler filled with bottles of water and Gatorade, potato chips, granola bars, several loaves of bread, and other stuff. She was going to need to eat at some point—for the fuel—but, she wasn't hungry.

"What would you usually be doing, a few hours before game time, on days you start?" Marcus asked. "Do you have a routine?"

"Sixth and seventh period, and then *homework*," she said.

He laughed. "Right." Then, he shook his head. "Why on earth didn't you go to college? Be in a hard-core program, and work against solid DI hitters?"

A question that never became any easier to answer. "I didn't think I was going to go in the *third* round," she said. "I assumed someone would take me much later than that, and then I could just turn it down."

He looked at her curiously. "You mean, you did it for the money?"

God, no. She shook her head. "Of course not. It seemed like—a window of opportunity, and I guess I'd rather find out if I'm any good sooner, rather than later."

He nodded.

"What about you?" she asked. "I mean, I know you went to Vanderbilt. Did you like it?"

"Very much," he said. "I'm supposed to start med school in the fall, so I'm just going to see how the summer goes."

"Where?" she asked.

"Johns Hopkins," he said. "I almost went with Duke, but changed my mind."

Top schools, which was precisely what she would have expected, although she might not have guessed that he wanted to be a doctor. She could probably do regular college on an extended schedule, even if it meant only attending fall sessions, and maybe some online credits. But, medical school would be less flexible, especially the very *best* medical schools. "Will they let you defer?" she asked. "If you decide to—"

A guy she didn't know—Vince, maybe?—opened the main

door. "Last group's about to go in the cage, Mother," he said. "You'd better come out, if you want to hit."

"On my way." Marcus glanced at her as he stood up. "Take some time to do whatever it is that you need to do to focus. And be sure to eat something, and stay hydrated. Don't let the adrenaline make you think it'll be enough to carry you through the game. Some guys crash out for an hour or two, so go for it, if that works for you."

"Mother" was such a good nickname for him, that it was a shame not to be able to use it.

When in doubt, it always made sense to spend some time checking her phones. She went down to her changing room, where the plumber was still working. So, she sat on the floor in the hall, and found dozens of texts on the business phone, most of them from people she either barely knew, or had never met—all of which she decided to ignore. On her private phone, there were mostly good luck messages, and she quickly sent texts back to a bunch of the people. Her mother had texted to let her know that she and Theo would be in the same seats at tonight's game—which would make it much easier to find them, if she needed as much reassurance as she was afraid she might.

Since Lauren would be home from physical therapy—she still had to go three days a week—Jill texted her to ask if she was up for Skyping, and within seconds, Lauren had already initiated a call.

"Hey," she said.

"Big night," Lauren said. "Are you ready?"

Not so much. "I don't think so," Jill said. "They only want me to throw fastballs tonight. It's like—I don't know. One of those Food Network challenges, where you're supposed to cook a great meal, but they only give you ridiculous ingredients."

"They want you to win, though," Lauren said, "right?"

Whoa, she hadn't even thought of that. "What if they *don't?*" she asked. "They could totally be setting me up to fail."

Lauren looked dubious. "How likely is that?"

She didn't know Sawyer at all—but, couldn't imagine Marcus doing anything other than what he thought was best for his pitchers. "Yeah, you're right," Jill said. "It doesn't matter so much if you win here, because they're just trying to teach you how to *play*. But, God, I really don't want to be awful on television."

"You can't let yourself think about *that* part," Lauren said.

No, not if she wanted to succeed. Jill sighed. "Yeah, I know. How was PT?"

"Sitting here with my good friends Advil and ice," Lauren said.

Status quo, then. "I'm sorry," Jill said. "That stinks."

"My left hip is getting stronger, they think. If I can just make it back to where I only use the cane, I'd be okay with that," Lauren said. "I still have time, before orientation."

Because she didn't want to go off to Wesleyan in the wheelchair, if at all possible.

So, bitching about fastballs was pretty damn shortsighted, and—just maybe—selfish.

When they finally hung up, about twenty minutes later, she headed back to the clubhouse, since Marcus was right—she needed to make sure she ate something. What she really wanted was some yogurt, but the spread only had things like white bread, peanut butter, grape jelly, some bologna, sliced American cheese, condiments, oranges, and bananas. So, she went with Gatorade, peanut butter and jelly on a slice of bread that she folded in half, and a banana. She wasn't even remotely hungry, but she managed to force it down—while the rest of the team pretty much swarmed the food table like locusts.

No one ever bothered a starting pitcher before a game, so she didn't worry when none of them spoke to her. They were all too busy eating and checking their own phones, anyway.

She did say "*Kon'nichiwa*" to Shosuke, and introduced herself to her other neighbor, Suarez, whose first name turned out to be Javy, and whose English was rudimentary, and was really more Spanglish than anything else, but they could understand each other, and that was all that mattered.

The media was allowed in for a while, and they surrounded her locker with even more enthusiasm than the guys had attacked the pre-game spread. She tried very hard to be receptive—and not at all newsworthy.

It was a relief when she could escape down to the changing room, to start putting on her uniform. The workmen were gone, and the shower now appeared to be functional, but the lavatory and sink were still works in progress.

She dressed more carefully than she ever had for a game before, smoothing her socks in place, switching her red compression shirt for a dark blue one, and so on. Russo had done a beautiful job, and her uniform pants now *fit*, without being confining in any way. She fixed her hair last, making sure that the chignon was securely in place, and then putting on a little bit of mascara and lip gloss.

She was supposed to meet Sofia in the training room at six o'clock to get stretched out, and was startled to realize that she was about to be late. The afternoon had dragged, but now, time seemed to be moving all too quickly.

There were a few other players getting treatments— Louis was working on Dimitri's lower back, Harvey Schwartzman was waiting to get his right ankle taped, and a backup outfielder named Nathan seemed to have a gimpy wrist. But, the atmosphere in the room was professional enough so that she didn't mind lying on a table in her sports bra, while Sofia massaged and manipulated her left shoulder and arm.

"Excellent range of motion," Sofia said.

Jill nodded, since she had spent *many* hours working on her flexibility.

After the stretching session, she pulled the compression shirt back on and went out to add her game jersey to the ensemble, tucking it in neatly and fastening her belt. She bounced a few times in her cleats, and then retied them, a bit more tightly.

Marcus was waiting near her locker, holding his catching gear. "Ready to head out?" he asked.

Jill nodded.

Game on.

CHAPTER 13

When they stepped out of the dugout, she couldn't help being flustered by the extent of the massive media contingent, with cameras and reporters everywhere, as well as hundreds of fans taking pictures of their own. The stadium was *packed*, including at least a couple of thousand extra people who were standing room only.

"Just another game," Marcus said.

Yeah, sure. "Is the Pope in town?" Jill asked.

He laughed. "That might actually draw slightly *less* attention."

At the moment, it definitely seemed that way.

Sawyer joined them on their slow walk down the foul line to the outfield. The clicks and whirrs of the cameras seemed almost deafening, and it was hard to tune them out. Especially, of course, the MLB documentary team, which was right on their heels, with the videographers sometimes running ahead of them to catch a different angle. People were shouting questions—or requests—or jeers—in her direction, and she did her best to tune them all out.

So, she, naturally, didn't notice things like the "Go Back to Softball!" and "Don't Destroy America!" signs some people were holding.

"Poor America," she said to Marcus, who looked amused.

"Normal warm-up," Sawyer said, all business. "Assume we'll refine it next time."

So, she did pretty much what she had been doing before every start since ninth grade—jogging along the warning track, followed by some relaxed sprints, and then moving into a series of active stretches, trying to keep a smooth flow going.

Thousands of fans seemed to be screaming at her at once, and while a lot of them sounded supportive, it was hard not to zone in on the ones who were yelling things like "Go home, you bitch!" and "You don't belong here!" But, she made a point of *not* looking at any of them, and kept her expression as blank and unconcerned as humanly possible.

Although she was so damn tense and self-conscious, that every move she made felt stiff and awkward.

"You okay, Jill?" Marcus asked.

Oh, yeah, she was *awesome*. But, she just nodded, and put on her glove, punching her fist into the pocket harder than was probably necessary.

After he strapped on his shin guards, they played catch, with him on the foul line, and her working her way out to about a hundred and fifty feet, and then back in.

"Ready?" he asked.

"Is it going to look bad if I pass out?" she asked.

Marcus smiled. "Do you want me to be gallant, and catch you—or let you slump gracefully into the grass?"

She wouldn't have thought that anything could make her laugh right now—but, that actually did. "Just leave me there in a little heap," she said. "The grounds crew can scoop me up later."

As they walked into the bullpen, so many fans and photographers were leaning over the grandstand railings that she was afraid that a fair number of them might tumble right in on top of her. One scowling guy tossed a beer in her direction, and she had to jump back to keep from being splashed. Some security guards roughly hustled him away, and she wasn't sorry to see even more security moving in to take positions by the railing.

The bullpen itself was crowded, with a few of their relief pitchers standing around to watch, along with Mr. Brayton, Mrs. Doshi, the Pittsburgh GM, the director of the Pirates' minor league system, the minor league pitching coordinator, a video guy, and a couple of other people with radar guns.

Normally, she didn't have much trouble locking in, but today, she was too damn aware of her heart beating, and it was hard to get her breath down past her upper chest. She closed her eyes for a few seconds, and then started with easy fastballs, slowly heating up, and as the ball really started cracking into Marcus's glove, there were lots of oohs and aahs.

Sawyer stood next to her, his arms folded across his chest. Every so often, he would say something like "Keep it down" or "Paint the corners," and she would nod and respond accordingly. He asked her to throw a few changeups, and moved away from her, watching her arm action intently. Then, he wrote something on his clipboard.

Somewhere up above them, a man yelled, "You suck, you—," but it was cut off by the sound of a grunt, and what might have been a scuffle, and more security people and police officers showed up.

"Cafferty, focus!" Sawyer said. "Show me Uncle Charlie."

She threw a god-damn *beautiful* curve—and Sawyer's posture straightened. Just like in Pittsburgh, when she had her bullpen session, the observers who really understood baseball—which was a much smaller subset of the group than she would have expected—either looked startled, very alert, or a combination of both.

"A couple more," Sawyer said. "Then, wrap it up with a few heaters."

When she finished, a lot of the front office people patted her on the back or said complimentary things, none of which she was able to process, since she was just trying to get her heart rate down.

"Stick with the plan," Sawyer said. "But, okay, now I get it about the curve. It's all still a process, though, right?"

"Yes, sir," she said.

Hundreds of fans were crowding along the grandstand by the field, shouting encouragement, or calling her name, or expressing—loudly—their general disgust about her being on the field at all, but she just walked straight ahead, taking steady, powerful steps.

She was still holding the baseball she had used to warm up, and right before they got to the dugout, she veered over to the sidelines and handed it to an excited girl about nine years old, who was wearing a red cap and a softball jersey.

"Here you go," she said, smiled at her, and then kept walking.

"You are a marketing department's dream," Marcus said softly.

Which made her laugh again—which, in turn, helped release some more tension.

Inside the dugout, her teammates seemed to be pretty charged up about having such a massive crowd on hand, as well as the game being nationally televised, but she concentrated on the way her hand felt inside her glove—familiar, comfortable, warm, *safe*—to the exclusion of pretty much everything else.

"Remember something, okay?" Marcus said in a low voice.

She looked over at him.

"You are *absolutely* for real," he said. "Don't ever let anyone tell you otherwise."

She hadn't known that that was what she needed to hear—but, it must have been, because she suddenly felt at ease—and *eager*. Ready to go out there and set them down.

The public address system was giving out the starting lineups, and when the announcer finished up with, "And our starting pitcher tonight, number twenty-eight, Jill Cafferty," the crowd's response was so loud that it seemed to echo inside her chest, and make the entire ballpark shake.

As they took the field, she was so nervous that her hands were shaking, but Scott gave her a thumbs-up as he trotted past her on his way out to left field, which helped. She headed to the mound in a crisp jog, reminding herself to *breathe*. Deeply, if possible.

And her stomach was jumbled enough so that she was glad she had barely eaten half of a sandwich earlier.

She looked down, trying to orient herself. Freshly raked dirt, the rubber, a plastic cleat cleaner, and a rosin bag. These were all soothingly familiar things, and of a much higher quality than she had ever used during a game. In high school, she had always brought along her own rosin bag and a supply of tongue depressors to clean mud and dirt from her cleats. The opposing pitchers would often sneer at her—and then, ask to borrow them.

The mound seemed *high*. Very exposed. Granted, pitchers were inherently the center of attention, but it usually felt less overwhelming.

No one seemed to be warming up, which was—oh, because they hadn't done the national anthem yet.

And it looked like the Retrievers were going to make a big production out of it, because a veritable *flock* of small children was running onto the field. They joined each player in groups of two or three—except that at least *eight*—no, more like *ten*—little girls were racing towards her.

The children seemed to be from about four to eight years old, and based upon the wide range of ethnicities, Pomeroy was clearly aiming for diversity tonight. The little girls were *very* excited, all of them shouting her name and trying to stand next to her simultaneously. So, it was a challenge to corral them into a relatively orderly clump.

The public address announcer was saying that the anthem was going to be sung by a Sergeant Pollard from the 10th Mountain Division, and asked for everyone to rise and remove their hats.

"Okay," Jill said to the little girls, who were still awfully agitated. "We all have to stand up straight and salute the flag."

Which led to a stream of "What flag?" and "Where is it?" questions, and she pointed out towards center field, above the wall. It seemed to take forever to get the girls lined up—she really needed a *wrangler* of some kind.

Jill's plan was to hold her glove in her left hand, and put her right hand near her heart, but a very small girl with pink-ribboned ponytails was reaching up to hold her hand—and at least three of the other girls said that they wanted to have *their* hands held, too, but unless she grew several more arms instantaneously, that wasn't going to work.

"Here," Jill said, and arranged three of the girls on the rubber, well aware that her teammates were restless, and maybe even annoyed. "You guys stand here, and"—she looked to see which of the remaining children appeared to be the most uncontrollably eager—"maybe *you* could hold my glove," she said to a tiny fidgety girl. Then, she scanned the others to check who looked disappointed. "And *you*," she said to another little girl, "can hold my hat. And the rest of us will stand up nice and tall, and pay attention to the flag, while the sergeant sings."

The sergeant had a *beautiful* voice, and Jill was horrified to feel herself choking up a little.

Or, okay, more than a little, as she got slammed with a wave of emotion she hadn't expected, and was afraid she might burst into tears. So, it was a relief to be able to hold on to a small, hot hand. Clutch it, even.

When the anthem was over, one girl wanted a hug, which made the other little girls decide that *they* wanted hugs, too— and it was a chaotic flurry of embraces. Some of the children who had been standing with other players also came over for hugs, and the mound was getting *damn* crowded.

"Is it okay if I keep this?" the child who was holding her cap asked, before receiving her hug.

Jill panicked for a second. "I'm sorry, I need it to pitch," she said. "It's a rule. But, maybe you could put it on my head for me, for good luck?"

The little girl liked the sound of *that*, and Jill had to bend way down for her to be able to reach, and the girl gave her an enthusiastic hug—which made two of the other girls each want *another* hug. On top of which, she had to retrieve her glove from the girl who was proudly carrying it off the field, holding it like a prized possession.

It was a relief to see Jeremiah, a couple of interns, and the staff sergeant coming over to hustle the remaining little girls and boys away.

The field was finally clear of children, and she could see her teammates warming up, most of them looking amused as hell by everything that had just gone on.

"Is there a game tonight?" Dimitri asked, from first base.

Jill wasn't sure whether to laugh—or cry already exhausted tears, but she went with a laugh. Christ almighty, she hadn't even thrown a pitch yet, and she was wrecked.

Marcus was waiting for her by the mound, holding a brand-new New York Penn League baseball. "You don't see that every day," he said.

"Can I go home now?" she asked. "I've had it."

He smiled, but then looked serious. "You need to snap back in, okay? Just hit my glove, and make everything else go away."

She nodded.

"Give me a few fastballs," he said. "Nice and easy, let's not show them that you have much."

She nodded again, and glanced down at the mound, which was *covered* with small sneaker and sandal prints. "My God, look at that," she said.

He looked down, too, and his smile widened. "Okay, but it's still just me and my glove," he said. "Let's get the game started."

Yes. They were supposed to play baseball sometime this week.

Her eight warm-up pitches were shaky and erratic, and not even *close* to the stuff she had had in the bullpen. Throwing felt—foreign. Was she going to turn out to be one of those poor sods who dazzled during practice, but fell apart once the game started?

Marcus tossed the warm-up ball to the bat boy, who carefully put it in a yellow bucket, instead of the regular big white plastic one. Almost everything she touched tonight was going to be carefully collected, catalogued, and authenticated for charity auctions and the Hall of Fame and so forth. Then, he accepted a new ball from the grumpy umpire and threw it down to second base, where the shortstop—a wiry guy named Raffy—caught it, and went around the horn.

Marcus came out to the mound, motioned for Geoff, the third baseman, to flip him the ball, and then put it in her hand. "That other one wasn't any good," he said. "But, *this* one is perfect."

She managed a faint smile.

"Shut it all out, Jill," he said. "You and me, playing catch."

Be nice, if it were that easy. But, she nodded.

The home plate umpire came out halfway to the mound. "We going to play ball anytime soon?"

Annoying an umpire did not tend to work out well for pitchers.

"We're ready to go, sir," she said.

"Took you long enough," the umpire said, and went back to the plate, with Marcus right behind him.

Jill pulled in a deep breath, trying to center herself somehow. None of this even *resembled* any start she could ever remember, and she felt as though her mind was bouncing in at least ten directions at once. But, if she was going to try to be a professional baseball player, she was going to have to do a lot better than that.

The huge crowd, the noise, the yellowish tint of the stadium lights, the ESPN cameras, the large groups of people crammed into the photographers' wells—none of that should matter at all. It was still just baseball. Sixty feet, six inches, with a catcher's mitt facing her.

Which meant that there was no good reason to feel *quite* so sick to her stomach.

The guy stepping up to the plate turned out to be one of those jittery types, with grating tics, and a bat that was never still, which annoyed her more than it normally would.

It was strange to be throwing to a catcher who wasn't familiar yet, but he was set up in a solid and reassuring way. And she already knew that he was a nice guy—and probably the closest thing she had to a friend on this team of near-strangers. So, it was stupid that she was standing here, feeling shy about throwing to him.

But, the mound really *did* seem high. Had it been poorly constructed, maybe, or—she dragged in another deep breath.

Should she get more rosin? No, she should *throw the ball*. That thing that pitchers were supposed to do.

Marcus wanted a low, outside four-seamer. Okay. She certainly didn't have the wherewithal to shake him off, or suggest something different. Besides, it seemed like a good call.

She knew how to pitch. Had been practicing for *years*. She just had to do it. And, perhaps, sometime before midnight?

Low and outside. Okay.

Her set position didn't feel quite right, but it was too late to start over—and just as she released the ball, she had the sinking certainty that it was slower and flatter than usual—and right down the middle.

The batter must have been *overjoyed* to see that—and he smoked a violent line drive right back at her, so hard that she didn't even have time to be scared before—thank God—her reflexes kicked in, and she got her glove up in time to snag it—a split second before it would have hit her in the face.

Jesus!

She stared at the ball for a second, her heart slamming around inside her chest, and then quickly whirled and threw it to Dimitri—who was walking towards the mound.

He looked bemused, but caught the ball easily and tossed it back to her. "He's already out," he said, grinning.

Oh. Right. It had been a line drive. "Well, I know that," she said. "I just wanted to be sure that *you* did."

He laughed, and went back to his position.

Her heart was still pounding, and she felt shaky, and scared, and—now, she saw Marcus heading out to talk to her.

Ideally, the first words out of his mouth weren't going to be, "Wow, you're *terrible*."

"That was interesting," he said.

She could think of stronger words to describe it.

"You throw a cookie like that to a *good* hitter," he said, "and it's going to end up somewhere in Canada."

Now, she felt even more anxious. "He's not a good hitter?"

Marcus shook his head. "Punch-and-Judy."

Even though he'd nearly taken her head off? This was a total disaster. She was way out of her league—in every sense.

"Come on, Jill, calm down," he said. "Try to get a breath past your bronchial tubes."

Her chest *did* feel constricted.

He reached over to take the baseball out of her glove. "This ball has very bad mojo," he said, and rolled it towards the bat boy. "Let's get a better one."

Well, it couldn't hurt. But, it was starting to feel as though it was going to be hard to find a baseball with *good* energy in it tonight.

He turned towards the home plate umpire, motioned for a new baseball, and then handed it to her. "Ignore the carnival," he said. "Just pitch. I saw you in the pen, so I *know* you know how."

All right. Okay. Right. Yeah. She nodded, took another too shallow breath, and stuck her glove under her arm, so she could rub a little of the shine off the new ball. It felt sort of like—a rock, or—an ice cube.

Why in the hell hadn't she just decided to go to college?

CHAPTER 14

The good news was that she had gotten the first out, at least.

She was still shaky, but worked the next batter somewhat more competently. Low outside four-seamer, high inside two-seamer, in on the fists, out at the edge of the zone. But, he walked on four pitches—two of which she would have *sworn* were strikes. Damn good strikes, even. But, glaring at the umpire wasn't going to help—and since Marcus had taken a few seconds to adjust one of his shin guards—with his lips moving—she assumed that he was expressing a strong opinion about the strike zone to the guy.

The next batter looked supremely cocky, and when her first pitch was called a ball, he grinned out at her.

"Move in a few steps," he said. "Might be easier for you."

Which she found far more infuriating than she should. And she had also forgotten to check the runner, who stole second so effortlessly that it was downright embarrassing.

Her next pitch skidded into the dirt. Marcus was able to block it, so the damn runner didn't take third—but, it was a close call. Too close.

Marcus wanted the next one in on the hands, but it got away from her and hit the batter in the thigh.

"Ow," the guy said, and laughed. "That tickles."

She knew he was just trying to get a rise out of her—and, damn it, he was *succeeding*.

The cleanup hitter was so eager to face her that he practically *ran* to the batter's box. Could hardly wait to hit a three-run homer off her, apparently.

Which seemed all too likely to happen.

It was tempting to look up at the owner's box, to see if the GMs had their heads in their hands, or anything similarly demoralizing—and even more tempting to scan the crowd for her mother and Theo. At the moment, she *really* wanted her mommy.

Marcus trudged back out to the mound with yet another new baseball.

Because the bad mojo was *everywhere*.

"Is that son of a bitch ever going to call a strike?" she asked.

Marcus shrugged. "He's squeezing you, so what? Start *pitching*, Jill."

Which pissed her off enough so that her first pitch to the cleanup hitter was *definitely* at least ninety-three miles an hour, and she put it right on the black, where Marcus perfectly framed it—and the god-damn umpire called it a ball.

She wasn't going to get mad. It wasn't going to help, if she got mad.

And she wasn't paying attention to anything other than the task at hand, of course, so she absolutely did not notice that most of the crowd sounded unhappy, frustrated, and *disappointed*. Or that the guys in the visiting dugout were laughing and taunting and catcalling.

The two-seamer had some good late movement tonight, and the guy fouled it down the third base side. Marcus and Geoff both raced over there, and Geoff almost fell into the stands, but made a great, off-balance catch.

"Two down," he said, and flipped the ball to her. "Piece of cake, Cafferty."

Yep. She was almost out of the inning. Could go sit in the dugout, and put a towel over her head—or maybe dunk said head into the Gatorade container for a while.

Except for the part where she walked the next hitter on five pitches—three of which looked *perfect* to her. But, the bases were loaded now, and this was all on the verge of getting even uglier.

What a totally awesome debut. A dream come true. Women everywhere must be feeling so proud and empowered.

And here came Marcus again, starting to look a little weary.

She bent to pick up the rosin bag, bounced it on the back of her right forearm a few times, and then—to her own amazement—spit violently into the dirt.

Marcus blinked. "Did you just spit?"

On national television, no less. "Weak moment," she said grimly. And her mother must be *cringing*.

"Nothing personal," he said, "but it's really not a good look for you, Jill."

Maybe not, but the urge had been *truly* irresistible. "Just give me the damn ball," she said.

Now—oh, hell—her *manager* was strolling out of the dugout. Not the pitching coach. The manager. Was he going to yank her out of the game, in the first inning? Jesus, what a debacle.

She turned enough to glance at the bullpen, and no one was warming up yet—but, a couple of them had started moving around, and one guy was even stretching.

Not a good sign.

"This isn't exactly a made-for-TV movie, is it?" Adler asked, once he had gotten to the mound.

More like a horror show. She shook her head. "No, sir, I'm afraid not."

"Wouldn't have pegged you to crack under the pressure, though," he said.

Neither would she—indicating that they had both severely

misjudged her psyche. The infielders had all wandered over now, and were standing in a little cluster behind them. The second baseman, Diaz, spoke almost no English, but Raffy seemed to be translating for him.

"You want me to pull the plug?" Adler asked. "You can hit the showers, call it a night, rethink your entire life?"

God, no. She shook her head.

"Well, then, maybe you should throw some strikes," he said mildly.

Easy for *him* to say. "I *am* throwing strikes," she said. "That—" She couldn't think of a non-profane word to use. "That *person* isn't calling them."

And, right on cue, the umpire showed up.

"You all plan on breaking up this little tea party anytime soon?" he asked.

"Not until someone serves the cucumber sandwiches," Dimitri said.

The umpire, however, was not amused. "Did you see her spit?" he asked her manager.

Adler nodded. "I did. It was pretty awful."

"*Disgusting*," Geoff said, and grinned.

"I damn near ran her, right then and there," the umpire said.

He couldn't throw her out of the game for *spitting*, could he? At least, not as long as she didn't spit *on* him.

Which, at the moment, she was considering.

Now, the infield umpire came over. "Was the game called, and nobody told me?"

Everyone was just hilarious tonight. She gritted her teeth.

"We were talking about her spitting," the home plate umpire said.

"Oh, that was gross," the other umpire said, looking very amused. "Never expected to see that. I almost lost my dinner."

Were they kidding? "I'm a professional baseball player," Jill said. *Was* she? "Or, anyway, *theoretically*. And spitting is a time-honored tradition."

"Please be quiet, Cafferty," Adler said, and then turned to the home plate umpire with a bland smile. "Calling things pretty tight this evening, Joseph."

The home plate umpire shrugged. "Not my fault. Tell her to throw strikes."

She wasn't going to spit again, but it was *so* tempting.

Adler nodded. "I suggested that, but maybe it would be nice to have a zone bigger than a postage stamp."

"Tell her to throw strikes," the umpire said gruffly, and scowled at her. "Spit again, and you're out of here."

Yeah, fine, whatever. She gave him a very terse nod.

"Throw strikes," Adler said, and went back to the dugout.

Well, what incredibly helpful advice. If only *she* had thought of that.

Bases loaded. In the very first inning, of her very first game.

And the front office was probably trying to figure out

whether they could nullify her contract somehow. Maybe a morals clause—or a decorum clause, if there was such a thing.

The next batter was looking quite happy to be facing a rattled and sublimely incompetent pitcher. It was hard to be offended, since she would feel exactly the same way, if she were in his position.

She paused to check the bases—the *loaded* bases—and several of her teammates promptly spit, and laughed. Because baseball players were nothing, if not reliably goofy.

She managed to throw a strike—a *good* one, sneaky fast, right on the inside corner—so, the batter swung at the next pitch, and sent a sharp grounder up the middle, which she didn't manage to get anywhere near.

Terrific. That meant two runs, and she was a complete— except the shy second baseman streaked over, flicked it backhanded from his glove to Raffy without missing a beat— and that was the third out.

What a great play! And he'd made it look *easy*.

She was so relieved that she intercepted him on his way off the field and couldn't stop herself from giving him a truly heartfelt hug.

He looked horrified, and extricated himself, speaking so rapidly in Spanish that she only managed to catch a few phrases, most of which were along the lines of "Holy Mother of God!"

So, she backed away from him, raising her hands

apologetically—but, still, that had been a *big league* play. She was practically in love with him, for making that play. *Deeply* in love.

It felt as though a huge weight had lifted from her shoulders, and she suddenly felt so cheerful, that she almost wanted to *bounce* into the dugout.

She paused in front of Adler, waiting for his reaction.

He looked at her for a few seconds, with about eight expressions moving across his face, before settling on a small frown.

"Don't hug the infielders," he said. "They hate that."

Seemed that way, yeah. "I won't, sir," she said. "Thank you, sir."

"Good." He motioned towards Sawyer. "See if you can teach her something, Dave, before she has to go back out there."

Was it her imagination, or did Sawyer look pessimistic about that?

The dugout was pretty boisterous, with a lot of guys giving Diaz high fives and fist bumps, but since she hadn't exactly earned any of her own, there was something of an awkward silence as she made her way to the bench. But, really, what *could* any of them say after a debut inning like that?

Looked like she was going to need to set the tone. "So," she said, as she picked up a towel to wipe off her face. "I have a no-hitter going. How about *that?*"

Most of them laughed—even some of the ones who *really*

didn't want her here—and she felt a little more weight leave her shoulders.

Then, in almost perfect unison, at least eight of them spit on the dugout floor.

"It was a glorious moment," she said. "Play of the Day, no doubt."

There were some more laughs, and then, guys started going about the business of getting Gatorade, putting on batting helmets, and the like.

She sat down next to Marcus, who looked a lot more hot and tired than players usually did after half an inning.

"I got four grey hairs during that," she said. "How about you?"

"More like *forty*," he said.

Usually, she just slipped a jacket over her left arm between innings, but Sofia came over with a moist hot pack, swiftly strapping it around her shoulder with a thick ACE bandage.

"How's the arm feel?" she asked.

"Inept," Jill said. "Confused. Uncertain."

Sofia looked taken aback. "Are any of those things painful?" she asked, after a pause.

"It's a little death of the soul—but, physically, no," Jill said.

Now, Sofia was the one who looked tired. "I think you would have been a lot happier at Stanford."

No doubt. "I'm incredibly happy," Jill said, and gestured towards Marcus. "I'm sitting here with my new bestest pal in the entire world, and I'm on *television*, and—really, could I ask for anything more?"

"Unh-hunh," Sofia said, and went to lean against the dugout railing and watch the game.

Some of the manic energy was fading away, and she looked at Marcus. "That inning was pretty abysmal."

He nodded. "I would have said putrid—but, abysmal works."

That was about the size of it, yeah.

Sawyer was, indeed, an avid details guy and sabermetrician, because he sat down on her other side with spray charts and diagrams and statistical models. He started giving her extensive advice, some of which she actually managed to take in.

Although, in the end, didn't it all really come down to "throw some damn strikes"?

In their half of the first, the guys scored three runs— maybe the over-the-top hoopla was making the other pitcher nervous, too—and so, she went back out to the mound with a cushion, and the ability to breathe almost all the way down to her diaphragm.

A lazy pop-up to left, and then another walk, but a quick double play took care of that, and she did not hug Diaz, even though he caught Raffy's toss, spun, leaped over the sliding runner, and threw to first with astonishing grace. The third inning was also relatively smooth—including her first strikeout, on the curve Sawyer had promised she could throw, if she had two outs and two strikes on a hitter. Then, since she was at sixty-three pitches, she was done for the night.

She went back to the quiet clubhouse with Sofia, where she was stretched and massaged and bundled up with ice, and then pedaled a stationary bike for a little while, before returning to the dugout to watch the rest of the game.

Which they won, six to four. She hadn't helped much, but at least she hadn't *hurt* the team, either.

She went out to the infield and lined up to high-five her teammates, including quite a few whose names she still didn't know—and several of them, including Owen and two relief pitchers, made a point of avoiding her hand entirely. Which was disappointing, but not exactly shocking.

At least half of the crowd was still in the stadium, and a line of police officers, security guards, and ushers had moved into a ring around home plate and up past the dugouts on either side. She couldn't see her mother or Theo, or her aunt and uncle, but she was pretty sure that Keith and some of the other National Guard members were in a group up by the third base concourse.

The grounds crew had assembled a stand, with several chairs and a rectangular table—which was being covered by a cloth with the ESPN logo all over it, and television techies were snaking thick wires all over the place, and setting up lights and microphones. Jeremiah—and the intern sidekick whose name kept slipping her mind—were standing nearby, watching the preparations, and when Jeremiah looked over at her, she nodded, so he would know she was aware that she had Media Responsibilities.

"I was two for four," Scott said, coming up next to her. "Think they're waiting for me?"

If only. "Well, if you want, you can go out there and talk about how *fabulous* you think I am," she said. "They would probably eat it up."

He shrugged. "Fork over ten dollars, Three, and you have a deal."

That would be pretty good bang for her buck.

Most of her teammates had escaped to the clubhouse, and there were only a few guys left in the dugout, including Hector and Dimitri—who both seemed to be enjoying the hell out of what was unfolding on the field, and Marcus, who was packing his catching gear into a Pirates bag.

It occurred to her that she probably looked a little bedraggled, so she used her hands to smooth her hair, put her cap on more neatly, and swiped on some lipstick from the tube in her back left pocket.

"Oh, no, you did *not* just do that," Dimitri said.

Yes, she had, and *yes*, she carried it in her back pocket during games, so that it would be handy. Lip gloss, too, which she was now applying. "Television lights are tough," she said. "I really don't want to look *too* terrible."

He studied her briefly. "You look all right. I mean, I've certainly seen *worse*."

A tepid assessment—which about matched the way she had pitched tonight.

Scott laughed. "Really, dude? Way to go! That's going to be a nice boost of confidence for her."

"I didn't mean it that way," Dimitri said defensively. "She looks *fine*. I mean, are you all bent out of shape, Cafferty?"

"Well, I'm maybe feeling weepy," she said, and gulped. "But, I'm trying to hold it together."

Dimitri smiled nervously.

"Hey, if you ask me, you look *hot*," Hector said. "Go get 'em, tiger!"

Okay, she liked that assessment much better.

The interview area seemed to be just about set up now, and Jeremiah came over.

"The networks want you first," he said. "And both GMs are going to be up there with you. Then, we've agreed to a small presser with the rest of them, down in the main conference room."

It sounded like all of that was going to take forever, but she nodded cooperatively.

"We'll try to wrap it up pretty quickly, so you can go see your family," he said, "but it's a big night, you know?"

That was the rumor, yeah. So, she nodded again. "Sure, no problem," she said. "But, this'll die down soon, right? I mean, we're not going to need a press conference after *every* game, are we?"

Jeremiah shrugged. "I honestly have no idea—we're just feeling our way along. I assume it'll mostly be on nights you pitch, and at every new venue, when the team is on the road."

She had *chosen* this career, so it didn't make sense to complain—even though she was tired, and hungry, and *really* wanted a shower.

But, yeah, the damn circus was in town—and the animals needed to be fed.

CHAPTER 15

Once the first live interview started, the GMs mostly held forth, while she sat there like a decorative plant, wearing a hat with a silly-looking dog on it. She started to slip it off her head, but Mr. Brayton looked alarmed, and she remembered that her presence here was very much about merchandising.

There was a lot of talk about the historical significance of the game, and she contributed the requisite "Yes, it was a very exciting evening" sorts of remarks when it seemed to be indicated.

"So," the sports network host said heartily. "You had a few hiccups out there tonight, Jill."

Really? *That* was his take on the game? "I was trying to heighten the drama," she said. "Everyone likes a redemption story."

"You have a reputation for excellent command," he said. "What happened?"

Well, *someone* wasn't a fan, was he? "Just one of those nights, I guess," she said. "I'm hoping for better results next time." Although, all things being equal, she could live with no hits and no runs, any day of the week.

"Do you think it's possible that you're simply not going to be able to compete at this level?" he asked.

If people were hate-watching this, he was giving them a lot of material. "It probably makes sense to try one or two more starts, before I throw in the towel," she said.

"Yes, but—" he said.

"We'll have to see what happens," she said. Was it always going to be like this? Because it was very tiresome. "In the meantime, the team won, and that's what matters in the end, right?"

Both GMs were already jumping in to defend the results of her—admittedly rocky—start, but it was a relief when the interview ended. Right after that, the tablecloth with the ESPN logo was removed, and replaced by one that featured MLB Network—and she had to go through the same song and dance again. And then again, with another network. And another. And *another*.

When the television interviews were finally over, there were still so many people waiting for autographs, that it was going to seem *really* rude if she did nothing but wave and disappear into the dugout.

She glanced at Jeremiah, who nodded, with one quick tap on his watch, to indicate that they would be on the clock. So, she walked over to the railing where a rambunctious crowd was holding things for her to sign, and taking photos with so many unexpected flashes that she could barely see well enough to be able to tell exactly where—or what—she was autographing.

"Hi," she said. "Thanks for coming out tonight. We really appreciate it."

Once again, it was too crowded for her to make it *at all* personal. Just swift encounters, where she signed her name, and added her uniform number—and then tried not to smear the fresh autographs when she handed the items back to the people who thrust them at her.

Off to one side, Jeremiah gave her a small "wrap it up" signal with his right hand.

"I'm sorry, but they need me downstairs," she said to the still too-big crowd, and motioned towards a little clump of hesitant children. "So, could you all maybe let these guys through, before I have to go?"

Once she had signed about fifteen more autographs, Jeremiah began to usher her away to the dugout tunnel—and more interviews.

God, she was tired. And grimy. And *starving*.

But, once they were inside the makeshift media room, she was gracious and cheerful, and fielded questions for another forty-five minutes or so. For years, she had been annoyed when she saw athletes be abrupt and surly in post-game interviews—but now, she was starting to understand why it happened so often. In most cases, they were probably just too worn out to think clearly.

The shower in her dressing room finally *was* working, although the water temperature didn't get past tepid. It was still nice to get cleaned up and put on regular clothes, and go find her mother and everyone.

There were lots of hugs, and handshakes, and solid claps on the back from the more gruff members of her father's unit. Keith and one of the other guys had convinced a nearby Applebee's to stay open much later than usual—and since the manager had put in four years in the Air Force, she was very pro-veteran, and her staff also seemed perfectly happy to work longer shifts for one night.

When they finally got back to the motel, it was very late, and she was nearly staggering. Her phones had an exhausting number of messages, and she ignored almost all of them—although the GIF Greg had sent of her spitting was pretty funny. Horrible, but funny.

Her mother must have been as tired as she was, because she turned out the light *without* reading first, which was pretty much unprecedented.

"Quite a night," her mother said, as they lay in the two double beds, in the dark.

"There were a lot of people," Jill said.

"There certainly were," her mother agreed.

It was quiet for a moment.

"Want to hear a secret?" her mother asked.

For sure, because secrets were *fun*. Jill sat up partway. "Definitely, yeah."

"I told your grandmother that, yes, the spitting was awful," her mother said. "But, to be honest, it made me proud."

Jill sat up all the way. "Did someone put something in your drink?"

"You looked like a *baseball player*," her mother said. "You looked—it was suddenly so real. And—I was incredibly proud."

She had known her mother, obviously, for her entire life—but, sometimes, she felt as though she didn't know her at all. "Whoa, head trip," Jill said. "So, you want me to *keep* spitting."

"I want you never to do that again, ever in your life, for any reason," her mother said without hesitating. "But, frankly, in that situation, it was quite cool."

So, wonders did not, in fact, ever cease. "I sort of feel like we're living in a really bizarre alternate dimension," Jill said.

Her mother laughed. "Believe me, I do, too," she said.

In the morning, they had continental breakfast in the wan little motel dining room. The food wasn't anything special, but Jill had never been picky, and had no trouble at all filling up on muffins and cereal and orange juice and hot chocolate.

The plan was to check out, and then drive over to her

host family's house. Her mother wanted to make sure that she was settled in, before she and Theo drove back to Rhode Island. None of them really spoke, and Jill was already feeling homesick—and hoping like hell that she wasn't going to cry.

It was a little white ranch house, with dark green shutters, and a small, well-kept yard. Mrs. Wilkins must have been waiting eagerly, because she came out to the front stoop to greet them before they had even gotten out of the car. She seemed to be an effusive sort, because she had a forceful embrace for each of them—and it was faintly embarrassing that they all flinched.

"Come in, come in," Mrs. Wilkins said, using two hands to drag Jill's gear bag out of the car—she was short, and quite round, with grey hair—and lugging it towards the house. "I have coffee and snacks waiting."

Jill and Theo carried the other bags, while her mother brought in the groceries they had picked up at a nearby Hannaford supermarket—lots of Greek yogurt, apples, a few boxes of Chex cereal, and some Gatorade, among other things. Mrs. Wilkins bustled about, packing everything away in what appeared to be about thirty seconds, and then ushered them around the house.

"I'm so sorry my hubby isn't here," she said. "You just can't get that man off the golf course!"

Jill and Theo and her mother all nodded and smiled. Which

they did a lot during the next fifteen minutes, because Mrs. Wilkins was—chatty.

It was the sort of house that had lots of tchotchkes on tables and shelves, scented candles everywhere, and wall hangings and plaques with inspirational sayings—including words like "Love" and "Joy" and "Sunshine" and "Blessings"—stitched or painted on them. There were more than a few crosses and devotional items, too.

"They *really* love the *Lord*," Theo whispered to her at one point.

Jill nodded. It certainly seemed that way.

After showing them the kitchen, the dining room, and a combination living room and den, Mrs. Wilkins led them downstairs to a finished basement, which had a bedroom with two twin beds, and a small bathroom—which included a shower. There was also a laundry room, and a room full of tools and supplies, which seemed to be used for woodworking and crafts. Then, she hustled them back up to the dining room, where tea, coffee, and homemade cookies were waiting. Delicious cookies, as it turned out, and really top-notch coffee.

"Horace and I are so excited about having Jill here," Mrs. Wilkins said, passing around cream and sugar. "We've had other ballplayers stay with us, of course, but this is really something special."

"You have a lovely home," Jill's mother said. "And I can't

tell you how much I appreciate that she'll have such a supportive place to stay this season."

Jill could tell that Theo was *dying* to check his phone, but he seemed to be sublimating the urge by putting away cookie after cookie.

Even though the conversation was stilted, Jill was in no hurry to have it end. But, she was supposed to be at the stadium early, to meet with Sawyer to assess last night's start, to sit down with the trainers to set up her workout regimen, and then with Jeremiah, to talk about whether the team really *did* want her to start being active on Twitter and such.

Mrs. Wilkins stayed inside—tactfully, no doubt—while Jill walked out to the car with her mother and Theo. She was feeling tearful, and could tell that her mother was, too.

"She seems like a very nice woman," her mother said. "I think you're going to do fine there."

Jill nodded, because, really, what else could she do?

"Anything you need," her mother said, "*anything* at all, you just let me know."

Jill nodded, feeling an extremely large lump in her throat.

"Enjoy this," her mother whispered, when they hugged good-bye. "It's a good and exciting thing."

Theo's hug was surprisingly intense, too, albeit clumsy. "If anyone bothers you, *tell* me," he said, quietly enough so that their mother wouldn't hear. "I'll happily come back and take care of them."

She thought of Theo as being his mother's child, for the most part—but, some of her father was in there, too.

"And keep on spitting," he said, more loudly. "I'm counting on you!"

The last thing she had said to him, when they dropped him off at MIT for the first time—all of them standing there, blinking hard—was "Don't blow up the lab!" Jill nodded. "Every single game. Without fail."

"That's right, make us proud," he said, and gave her a light smack on the head as he stepped away.

She watched them pull out of the driveway, her arms folded tightly across her chest. The same sort of parting would have happened if she'd gone away to Stanford, too. It was probably *normal*, even if it didn't feel that way.

But, okay. She was officially on her own now, and even if she wanted to run down to the dark little basement bedroom and sob, that might not be the best way to start off being an adult. So, she took a deep breath, and made sure that she was smiling when she walked into the kitchen.

"Did they get off all right?" Mrs. Wilkins asked.

Jill nodded.

"How long a drive is it for them?" Mrs. Wilkins asked.

She actually wasn't sure. "Maybe five hours? It depends on traffic, I guess," she said.

"Well, they should do well, at this time of day," Mrs. Wilkins said, and motioned towards the refrigerator. "The groceries are helpful. It gives me a sense of what you like to eat. But, it would be good if you made a list for me, too."

Jill nodded. "Yes, ma'am, although I'm sure anything you have will be fine." This all felt very awkward, and she shifted her weight. "Um, thank you, ma'am, for allowing me to stay here."

Mrs. Wilkins beamed. "It's our tenth year as a host family. We *love* having players in our home. What time do you need to be at the ballpark today?"

Logistics. Okay, that would be an easy topic. "One o'clock, although I'd like to get there just after twelve, if possible, to play it safe," Jill said. In baseball, arriving on time was considered being *late*. "And we're leaving on the bus right after the game. So, I guess I'll be back here on—Wednesday, I think."

It was mind-blowing that trips like that were going to be her new normal.

They stood there, smiling at each other—uncomfortably, in Jill's case.

"Why don't you get settled downstairs, and packed for the trip, and then I'll fix a quick lunch and give you a ride over," Mrs. Wilkins said.

The stadium was about two miles away—so, while she could walk, it would be kind of arduous, carrying her knapsack and travel gear bag. "If it isn't any—" she started.

"No trouble at all," Mrs. Wilkins said.

The basement steps were wooden, and she tried not to clomp too noisily as she walked down. Something she would need to keep in mind, on nights when she got back late from games, so that she wouldn't wake them up.

The bedroom was simple, and very plain. Two extra-long twin beds, a dresser, two small bedside tables, a student-sized desk and chair, and a medium flat-screen television on top of the dresser, with a remote control next to it. There was also a dorm-sized refrigerator, which would come in handy, and an Xbox setup, which she was unlikely ever even to turn on.

The house had Wi-Fi, and she had already been given the password, which was a relief. It would make Skype and FaceTime—both of which she expected to use constantly—a lot easier, for one thing. There was a closet, which was empty, except for a row of white plastic hangers. The desk and bedside tables each had a lamp, and the floor was covered with thick, greenish-blue carpet. The windows had what looked like homemade white curtains, and while there wasn't *a lot* of light, it wasn't impossibly gloomy.

The walls had an inexpensively framed poster of PNC Park, a large map of the greater Albany/Troy area, and a poster that had yellow flowers and a Scripture quote on it: "Whatever you do, work at it with all your heart, as working for the Lord, Colossians 3:23."

There was also a Bible with a plain black cover on the bedside table. She wanted to put it away in a drawer, but was afraid of offending Mrs. Wilkins. Were she and her husband proselytizing, or did they think that baseball players were routinely observant Christians?

Which, probably, a fair number of them were. She had heard that lots of major league teams had Sunday chapel meetings—and there were plenty of athletes who started off every single interview by thanking God. Minor league teams were probably similar.

She peeked inside a drawer, and found a copy of the New Testament and a paperback of *Daily Devotions for Athletes*. So, she stuck the Bible in there, too, and closed it.

So far, her first official hour of adulthood was kind of *weird*.

CHAPTER 16

Lunch turned out to be grilled cheese sandwiches, a small salad—which included fresh vegetables from Mrs. Wilkins's garden—tomato soup, and iced tea. Jill was too edgy to have much appetite, but it all looked good.

Before they ate, Mrs. Wilkins said grace—a long grace—during which Jill bowed her head.

"I gather your family isn't very religious?" Mrs. Wilkins said.

That was putting it mildly. Jill tried to think of an inoffensive way to respond. "Well, it's not that we—" She stopped. "I mean, generally, uh—"

Mrs. Wilkins smiled. "There's no rule that says you have to be a believer, too."

Sounded like good news for both of them.

After attempting to eat, Jill went downstairs to make sure she had packed everything she would need for a six-day road trip. Right before they left, Mrs. Wilkins sweetly provided her with a little zipped cooler bag, which she said was a care package.

Once she got to the park, she left her main gear bag and knapsack in the clubhouse, because Terence and Nicky were going to be packing the bus for getaway day that night, and she wasn't entirely sure when they would get started. Then, she went to her dressing room to change into workout clothes, before sitting down with Sawyer and Marcus to discuss her pitching performance, and things she would need to work on. Like, say, a much better pickoff move—although it would help, in the future, if she remembered to check the damn runners. There was also talk of adjusting her position on the rubber, depending upon whether she was pitching to someone left-handed or right-handed, and Sawyer gave her a lecture about working on her focus and concentration—which she knew full well that she deserved. Her next start was going to be in Williamsport on Monday night, so she would have her first real five-day routine to follow.

After stretch and PFP—Pitchers' Fielding Practice—drills, she met with Bannigan, the strength and conditioning guy, along with Louis and Sofia, and he explained the specific exercise and pre- and post-pitching programs they had designed for her. She mostly just nodded and listened, but occasionally interjected things like the importance, for her, of doing extra work on her legs, hips, back, and core, to offset any biological upper body deficiencies, since she counted on her lower body to help her power through pitches. It seemed as though she was a bigger proponent of long toss than the organization was, but she got a sense that they were willing to compromise. They were also okay with her scheduling time to throw a football on non-bullpen days, since she had being doing that with Greg for *years*, and was convinced that it helped maintain her arm-slot. Apparently, one of the bullpen guys, someone named Danny, had been a high school quarterback and had also asked permission to do the same thing, so she would have a partner—if he was so inclined.

The discussion didn't exactly feel free-flowing, but it was going to be a *long* and unproductive summer if she couldn't figure out a way to have less guarded conversations with these people.

She might as well go for the jugular, and see if that changed the dynamics. "So," she said, brightly. "I guess we need to talk about my cycle, and how it's going to affect my pitching."

There was a painful silence, and then Sofia let out a short bark of a laugh. Bannigan and Louis did not join in.

Bannigan coughed a few times, and then ran his hand back through what little hair he had. "Are you, um, able to pitch during your, um, menstrual period?"

Yes, he really had just asked that. Although, okay, she had maybe set him up. "I'll be fine," she said, making sure to sound brave, "as long as I can lie down between innings."

The sound Sofia made this time was closer to a guffaw, while Bannigan and Louis exchanged—queasy—glances.

"The good news is that I almost always pitch better than usual, because it makes me really *mean*," Jill said. There was even a little truth to that, on a given day, if the ibuprofen didn't kick in.

The silence lingered extensively this time.

"For God's sake," Sofia said. "She's teasing you."

"We knew that," Bannigan said, after looking at Louis. "Yeah, we absolutely—why don't we go down to the weight room, and we'll walk through some exercises?"

The general principle was low weight, high repetitions. Maintain what she had, and use the off-season to rebuild. She was a fan of doing shoulder and arm exercises with resistance bands—and it was agreed to add that to her regular workouts, as well. The weight room was—to put it politely—*compact*, and erred on the side of being bare bones, but there was enough equipment for players to get their work in, as long as they took turns.

A position player whose name she didn't know asked Bannigan a question about his deadlifts, and Louis was quick to go over and join *that* conversation.

Jill looked at Sofia. "Do I sense palpable relief on their part?"

Sofia shook her head. "It may take them *hours* to recover," she said. "Let's go to the training room, and I'll give you your fluff job."

Jill wasn't sure what that meant—but, it sounded odd.

Sofia let out a long-suffering breath. "We work out the kinks from your start last night. Then, you'll do at least twenty minutes on the bike."

A fluff job turned out to be yet another extensive massage, and Sofia found tiny little sore sports in her arm, shoulder, and back that Jill hadn't even known were there. It was a whole new world to be *coddled* like this, and she could already see how easy it would be to get used to being considered so very damn *special*—and to turn into an insufferable person.

After her session on the stationary bike, she got out to the field just in time for batting practice. It was pretty hot, and it was hard not to be *languid* about shagging fly balls, many of which her fellow pitchers sort of waved at, or caught on a couple of bounces. But, they were all more alert than they looked, especially when they were collecting stray balls to dump into the bucket behind second base. Which was mostly her responsibility today, since she had pitched the night before.

She stood near Shosuke in right center, and they taught each other the words for *cap, fly ball, grass, clouds,* and *sun.* At least, she was *pretty* sure those were the right words. Either way, they did a lot of pantomiming, and it helped pass the time.

A new hitter stepped into the cage, and hit a line drive in

their direction, and the unusually sharp crack got *every* pitcher's attention. It was Scott, whose second swing produced an almost identical shot.

"Wow," Jill said.

Jonesy, who was standing off to her left, nodded. "I'm not sure that kid has any idea how good he is."

Two more shots came out to right, followed by several seemingly effortless liners to deep center and left.

She glanced at Jonesy. "It's a different level, isn't it?"

Jonesy nodded again. "Yeah, you can't teach that."

Scott stepped out, and Hector replaced him. Hector was a decent hitter—but, it wasn't the same. His hits were scattered, and much less authoritative. And she couldn't help thinking that even though every player on the field was a superb athlete, most of them were never going to get anywhere near the majors, and quite a few weren't even likely to go anywhere further than this level. It was hard to ignore the fact that, in a very basic way, baseball was inescapably sad.

Jonesy locked eyes with her for a second, and she could tell that he was thinking something very similar.

"Some of them are going to grow into their bodies," he said. "And some of the ones you won't expect will suddenly put it together, three, four years from now, and go rocketing up."

She nodded. And some of them were going to get hurt, and some were going to flame out—and a tiny lucky few were going to prosper, and progress, and end up in the big leagues.

"Day at a time," Jonesy said.

It was the only way to do it—because any other outlook would just lead to madness.

In the meantime, she could see Scott goofing around and holding Schwartzman in a headlock, and Geoff was in the batter's box, hitting fly balls, two of which went over the left field wall. Lots of power, less authority.

Once BP had ended, she decided to run a few poles, to work off a little energy—and some remaining stiffness in her legs and hips. Her guys had gone off to the clubhouse, and the visiting team filed out to take their place. A couple of them shouted somewhat friendly, and somewhat barbed, remarks at her, but she just waved and kept running. When she left the field, several of the players said a casual hello, which felt nice, because it was a reminder that—national sportscasters' opinions aside—she *hadn't* embarrassed herself last night, and so, maybe they could react to her as a fellow baseball player.

She was supposed to have a meeting with Jeremiah at five o'clock, but even though he was obviously accustomed to being around athletes, she decided she would really rather put on a fresh T-shirt before going upstairs.

There seemed to be some kind of commotion inside the clubhouse, and she could hear yelling and swearing coming from Adler's office, too. So, she decided to avoid all of that—whatever it was—and go directly to her dressing room.

But, as she turned down the corridor to get there, she saw

that the door was open, and that several people were standing out in the hall. Mr. Brayton, Mrs. Doshi, Terence, and the head of security, whose name she couldn't remember—all of whom looked grim.

That couldn't be good.

"What's going on?" she asked.

The others exchanged looks.

"A small disturbance, that's all," Mr. Brayton said. "If you want to go up and wait in my office, I'll come and talk to you in a little while."

This was weird. "Am I in trouble?" Jill asked.

"*No,*" Mrs. Doshi said. "You're not. We just want to take care of a situation."

"Please head up to my office," Mr. Brayton said, "okay?"

She wasn't about to argue with the GM, but—Terence looked downright ill, and now she wondered if *he* was the one in trouble.

"Yeah, well, fuck you!" someone yelled, inside Mr. Adler's office.

Then, Adler's door smashed open, and although the head of security and Mrs. Doshi immediately moved in front of her, she caught a glimpse of some player storming out—who they apparently didn't want her to see.

"Go pack up," Mr. Brayton said to Terence, who nodded and headed for the clubhouse.

So, he *was* in trouble? She wondered what he had—except

then, she saw words scribbled in thick black Magic Marker across the wall in her changing room: "Go home," followed by a denigrating profanity about women that she never even allowed herself to *think*, forget say. A word she utterly despised—and had heard far too many times over the years, usually in angry hisses, when she walked by people on the sidelines, or past opposing players.

She leaned against the doorjamb, staring at the jagged scrawl.

"Why would Terence do that?" she asked. She had been under the impression that he *liked* her.

"It wasn't Terence," Mr. Brayton said. "He just happened to walk in, and—well—" He stopped, looking very uncomfortable.

Okay, now it made more sense. Some guy on the *team* had come in, and Terence must have caught him in the act. "Well, it's unpleasant," she said, "but, it isn't—" She stopped, realizing that she smelled something familiar, something— "Is that *urine*?"

Mr. Brayton, Mrs. Doshi, and the head of security all nodded.

Stupidly, her legs felt weak, and she reached back with one hand to keep her balance.

"Was it Owen?" she asked. Since he was the most obvious suspect.

"No," Mrs. Doshi said. "But, are you having a problem with him?"

Not *this* serious a problem, so she shook her head. "No, I—" She was feeling fuzzy enough to need to shake her head. "I'm sorry, I wasn't—is all my stuff wrecked?"

"We're assessing that right now," Mr. Brayton said. "We'll have one of the clubbies do an inventory."

She remembered, now, that because it was getaway day, her gear bag was in the clubhouse, and she had her gamer glove and caps and jerseys in there, so unless the guy had messed around with her main locker, too, all of that was probably safe.

But, it was still hard to take in the fact that *one of her teammates had urinated in her dressing room.* What kind of person would *do* that?

Mr. Adler came in to join them, silent, but exuding fury— and no one seemed to know what to say, including her.

"Is he going to go quietly?" Mr. Brayton asked.

"He'd *better*," Adler said.

"If not, I have some of my people standing by," the head of security said.

Jill still couldn't figure out how she was supposed to be reacting, so she just stared at the furious writing on the wall— and the visible damage to her shower slides, turf shoes, uniform pants, T-shirts, and the care package Mrs. Wilkins had so nicely given her earlier.

"Do you want to press charges?" the head of security asked her. "Because we can—"

Did she? Was it a crime, or just an ugly prank? And did she want the big media fuss that would kick up, if the police came barreling in, and whatever else? So, she shook her head, and then glanced at Adler, whose expression was harder to read than usual.

"Who was it, sir?" she asked.

"Nelson," he said.

Who in the hell was *that*? "Bullpen guy?" she asked.

He nodded.

Probably the sullen one who had made nasty cracks every time she screwed up at PFP, trying to cover first base or whatever. "I've never even *talked* to him," she said.

"He's already been released," Mr. Brayton said. "He'll be off the premises permanently within the hour."

It was startling that they had taken such swift and decisive action—but, she wasn't going to argue.

Mr. Brayton cleared his throat. "Jill, I want to apologize to you, on behalf of the entire—"

She raised her hand to cut him off. "Thanks, sir," she said—probably more abruptly than was wise, but she wasn't ready to have any kind of conversation about it yet. "I really don't want to make a big deal out of this. It's, um, it's just—well—"

Mrs. Doshi stepped forward. "I think we're going to open the gates about half an hour early tonight, and do an autographing session up on the concourse," she said. "Benny, we'd like to have two players up there, so maybe you could pull someone out of the clubhouse, and have him meet Jill and me in my office?"

They all frowned at her. Maybe there was some kind of method to her madness, but Jill had no idea what it might be.

"Benny?" Mrs. Doshi said, sounding very no-nonsense.

Adler looked at Jill briefly, then nodded. "Okay. I'll send Bronsky up."

Scott. Yeah, she wouldn't mind getting a chance to talk to Scott—and the sooner, the better.

"Great, thank you," Mrs. Doshi said, and took Jill's arm. "Please have one of the clubbies bring a fresh jersey and pants for Jill, also. Come on, let's go upstairs."

Jill went with her, since she couldn't think of a way to escape.

They walked very quickly past the clubhouse, where there was still a lot of yelling going on, and Jill found herself reaching inside her shirt to take out her father's dog tag, and hold it tightly in her right hand for a moment.

"We are *so* sorry about this," Mrs. Doshi said, once they were out of everyone else's earshot. "I mean, I assumed there would be a few malcontents, but—well, I just don't know what's the matter with some people."

Jill nodded, trying to separate the unwieldy mix of rage and embarrassment roiling around somewhere inside.

Mrs. Doshi gave her a concerned, motherly look. "Are you all right?"

Yeah, she was *nifty*. Jill shrugged, and gently tucked the dog tag away, instead of answering. Mrs. Doshi had the sense not to push it any further—which she appreciated.

On their way upstairs, they ran into Jeremiah, who was rushing down, but stopped when he saw them.

"I was just coming to look for you," he said. "I heard."

Yeah, rumors—and exaggerations—were probably already flying around like crazy. And the press was going to go to town, and her mother would be *really* upset. "Can we keep it, you know, in-house?" Jill asked.

Jeremiah frowned. "Do you *want* to?"

God, yes. The last damn thing she wanted was for the media—and the Internet—to start pontificating and screeching about bullying or something—because that would make her a *victim*.

A role she had no intention of ever playing.

"It'll probably get out"—since too many people *already* knew—"but I'm pretty much going to deny the whole thing," Jill said, "and I don't want to answer any questions about it. Ever."

Jeremiah looked dubious, but he nodded. "Okay. I'll see what I can do."

"Thanks," Jill said, and kept walking.

Mrs. Doshi had stayed behind to talk to Jeremiah, but Jill just wanted to go somewhere and absorb things, without anyone else looking at her. So, she went into Mrs. Doshi's office, out of sight of the doorway. It would be good if she had her phone—but, she wasn't sure who she should—or would—call, and—what if it was covered with urine now, and she would never be able to touch it again? Although both of her phones had been up on the top shelf of the locker, in a little box, so maybe they were okay?

She had forgotten that the team's bat dog belonged to Mrs. Doshi, and apparently, he spent the day in her office, because he got up from the carpet by the desk and wagged his tail.

A dog was *exactly* what she needed right now, and Jill sat on the floor to pat him, happy to have him wag his tail even harder and lick her face playfully. He was a young golden retriever, who seemed to be unusually sweet and affable, and during every game, he was sent out during the third or fourth inning to retrieve bats—before, she assumed, going back to his owner's office to nap.

When Mrs. Doshi came in a few minutes later, Jill started to get up, but Mrs. Doshi motioned for her to keep patting the dog.

"His name is Batty?" Jill asked, since that's how he had been introduced by the public address announcer the night before.

Mrs. Doshi shook her head. "No, that's just to be cute for the fans. He's actually Oscar."

Which was a much better name.

"You don't have to do any autographing," Mrs. Doshi said. "But I thought a quick change of scene was a good idea."

And, it probably had been. "I don't mind signing, if you think people would like it," Jill said. Although she really would rather spend the evening—or maybe the entire season--sitting in here with the dog.

"I think they would *love* it," Mrs. Doshi said. "But, if you don't feel up to—"

"I'm fine," Jill said. "No problem."

Mrs. Doshi leaned back against the crowded desk and gave her a long look. A *parent* look.

"Do you have children?" Jill asked.

Mrs. Doshi nodded. "My son is going to be a sophomore at Northwestern, and I have a daughter who will be starting at Wharton in the fall, and my oldest girl is working in publishing."

Not at all surprising, since she had that unmistakable motherly quality.

There was a tentative knock on the door, and they turned to see Scott standing in the hallway.

"Um, hi," he said. "They told me to come up here?"

Mrs. Doshi straightened up from the desk. "Yes, thank you, Scott," she said. "Come on in."

Scott walked into the office, looking ill at ease and surprisingly uncoordinated. "Yeah," he said, and then handed the cap, jersey, and uniform pants he was carrying to Jill. "Uh, here."

He wasn't even coming close to meeting her eyes, which made her wonder whether she maybe wanted to gather up her non-destroyed stuff—if there was any—and then call and ask her mother to drive all the way back to pick her up, and get the hell out of here.

"Thanks," she said, also avoiding eye contact.

He glanced at Mrs. Doshi. "Um, I'll go out into the waiting room, and—well, *wait*, I guess."

He left the room without giving either of them a chance to answer, and now, Jill didn't feel like putting the uniform on—or having anything to do with this damn team ever again. She hadn't expected *Scott* to be such a—then, suddenly, he was back in the doorway.

"We all feel really *bad* about this, Jill," he said. "I don't even know what to—yeah, I knew there were some jerks, but not like this. I mean—I just—are you okay?"

In the past five seconds, she had started feeling about a hundred times better. "Yeah, I'm fine," she said. "But—well, it was really disgusting, and—are other guys going to do stuff like that?"

"*Fuck,* no," Scott said, and then looked guiltily at Mrs. Doshi, who was now sitting behind her desk, and either actually reading some paperwork—or pretending to do so. "Um, sorry, ma'am." He looked back at Jill. "You really think guys like me and Mother and Hector and all won't *totally* have your back? But, we'll get it, if you don't want to have to deal with crap like this and you're leaving."

Is that how they thought she was going to react? That she was just going to walk away?

The fact that she suddenly had an out-clause didn't mean that she had to *take* it.

Even if she kind of wished that she could.

They both glanced at Mrs. Doshi, who appeared to be engrossed in her paperwork.

"You know Andrew?" Scott asked.

Their quiet closer—*so* quiet that she had never spoken to him, or even seen him have a conversation with anyone else—who was a sixth round pick out of the University of Virginia.

"He *whaled* on that guy," Scott said. "I mean, *took him down*. A bunch of us broke it up, but—well, we didn't exactly hurry, if you know what I mean."

That was gratifying—and embarrassing, somehow—to hear.

"Adler was pissed, but he didn't yell right off, either, you know? Because—well." Scott shifted his weight a couple of times. "Anyway. I'm really sorry, and I hope you're okay, and—I guess I'll go back now and let you hang out up here."

She would have to be made of pretty flimsy stuff if anything that had happened today made her *quit*. Not that she was going to let go of it anytime soon—but, she wasn't going home, either. "I was just waiting for you to come up with my uniform, so we could go out there and sign," she said.

He looked surprised. "Oh. I mean, oh! Yeah. Okay."

Mrs. Doshi pushed her papers aside, and motioned for him to follow her. "Scott, why don't you and I go sit out in the reception area, and let Jill get changed," she said.

"May I use your phone for a minute, ma'am?" Jill asked.

The fact that hers was—downstairs—was best left unsaid right now.

"Of course," Mrs. Doshi said. "Help yourself."

Once they were gone, Jill changed into the uniform pants, and put the jersey on over her T-shirt without buttoning it. Her mother should probably be her first call—but, she found herself dialing Greg, instead.

He answered right before it went to voice mail, sounding out of breath.

"It's me," she said.

"Sorry, didn't recognize the number," he said, still breathing hard. "What's up?"

"What am I interrupting?" she asked.

"Crazy, exciting, *scandalous* things," he said. "Or maybe me at the gym, working out. Don't you have a game?"

All too soon, yeah. Good thing she wasn't pitching tonight. "Some guy urinated in my locker while I was out at BP," she said.

There was a short pause—and then, a loud clank, as he apparently set down some weights. "Those *fuckers*," he said.

"I think there was just *one*," she said, "but, yeah, for all I know, some of the others were egging him on."

"Want me to get in my car?" he asked.

Which was exactly what she had expected him to say—and

what she wanted to hear, even though she wouldn't take him up on it. "No, I'm okay," she said. *Was* she? More or less, probably.

After she had brought him up-to-date on the whole story—including the vicious invective scrawled on the wall, she checked the door to be sure that no one could hear.

"Part of me wants to say screw this and walk away," she said. "But, that would be dumb, right?"

"There are guys there you're pretty sure you can trust?" he asked.

Scott. Marcus. So, that was two. And probably Dimitri, and Hector. Shosuke. Jonesy, as far as she could tell. Diaz, as long as she didn't hug him. From what Scott had said, Andrew—a total stranger—could be on the list, too. "Yeah," she said. "Most of them seem to be fine. *Nice*, even."

"How sick do you feel?" he asked.

Very god-damn sick. And grossed out. "I don't know how much of my stuff is ruined," she said. "I mean, we're supposed to go on the road tonight, and I'm not sure what I still *have*, and—the truth is, I want to go pretty berserk."

There was a pause.

"Hang on, I have to take this outside for a minute," he said.

She had no idea why, but she listened, while he left the gym, and went out to the parking lot, or into an alcove, or whatever he was doing.

"Okay, I'm back," Greg said, and then paused again. "Did Theo ever tell you what happened to me? Freshman year?"

That could be almost anything, and a lot of her freshman year was a blur, anyway, after her father died, right before Thanksgiving. "I'm not sure," she said.

"Then, he didn't tell you," Greg said.

It was quiet again.

"If it's private," she said, "you don't have to——"

"It's just humiliating," Greg said. "It was that fall, right after I came out, and some of the seniors——" He stopped. "It was all my stuff, too, but it was more than urine."

Oh, God. "How come you never told me?" she asked.

"I don't know," he said. "I was *ashamed*. My sneakers, my clothes—I had to throw away everything, while a bunch of those guys stood there, and——" He stopped. "And then, I had to walk home in my cleats, and my mother got mad when I said I lost my sneakers somewhere, and—it was terrible."

He had been pretty tall when he was fourteen, but really skinny, to the point of being almost *frail*.

"I didn't cry in front of them, because—well, fuck *that*, right?" he said. "But, I never wanted to go back there again."

She wanted to cry *for* him, remembering how generally difficult it had been for him for a while, right after he had come out. But, she hadn't known that it was *that* hard. "Where does Theo come in?" she asked.

"I needed to talk to a *guy*," he said. "And my father wasn't cool with me yet, and *your* father had already deployed—and one day, I went over to your house when I knew you wouldn't be home, and—I don't know." He paused. "He was *really* cool—and I'll always love the guy for it. I think he and some of his friends even went and yelled at them—but, I'm not sure. Seemed that way later, from the way they acted, but I took care of it on the field, anyway. Because after Peter got hurt, I was going to be their damn *quarterback*."

And threw three touchdown passes, as well as scoring two on the ground himself, in his very first game. It wasn't the size of the dog in the fight, it was the size of the fight in the *dog*. "How'd you take care of it?" she asked.

He didn't answer right away. "Football's a pretty rough game, Jill. And the quarterback has some *control* over what happens out there."

When he didn't elaborate, she knew that was all she was going to get—and, probably, all she wanted to know right now.

"I was going to tell you, but then, everything happened with your father, and you and Theo were like zombies, and—I guess the right time never came up," he said.

Until she needed to hear about it. "Do you think I should make a big deal about *this*, or shut up and play the game?" she asked.

Greg sighed. "Jill, if you told me you wanted to rob a bank, I'd say, 'You go, girl!' and—I don't know—drive the getaway car. So, *anything* you decide to do will be cool, as far as I'm concerned."

It was comforting to know that he meant every word of

that. "Including moping, and complaining, and obsessing about it for a while?" she asked.

"Yup," he said.

She sighed. "Sometimes, don't you just really hate jocks?"

Greg laughed, quite bitterly. "*Lots* of times," he said.

CHAPTER 17

Even though she knew she was supposed to go out there for the signing, she called home next, because if her mother—or, far more likely, Theo—heard about it on the Internet before she told them herself, they would be even more upset. They had just gotten back to Narragansett, and she only gave them the bare outlines of the story, and assured them that she was fine, and the guy was gone, and that she had to go sign autographs. They *were*, unsurprisingly, upset—but, she promised that she would call them after the game, to let them know she was okay.

After hanging up, she wanted to call Lauren, too, but the autographing was scheduled to start, so she buttoned her jersey and tucked it in. She looked sloppy without a belt, but under these specific circumstances, she assumed no one was going to give her grief about it.

She and Scott ended up at a folding table on the concourse, up behind home plate, where they signed autographs for about twenty minutes. The line of fans was *really* long, but Jill concentrated on smiling, signing, and thanking each person one at a time. Jeremiah, his intern, and several security people were stationed nearby, but the fans just seemed overjoyed to have arrived at the ballpark, and unexpectedly have two high draft picks right there to greet them.

Promptly at six-fifteen, Jeremiah shut the signing down, explaining that she and Scott needed to go and get ready for the game. There were still at least a hundred people in line—all of whom were noisily disappointed, but she and Scott were guided so quickly off the concourse and into the front office area that there wasn't much they could do, other than wave as they left.

Mr. Brayton intercepted them as they came into the main reception room, but Jill spoke up before he could say anything.

"We need to go downstairs and suit up, sir," she said. "It's almost game time."

He hesitated, but then nodded and stepped back.

She was dreading having to walk into the clubhouse—but, at least, she didn't have to do it by herself. As they entered the room, all of the chaotic pre-game activity seemed to freeze into instant suspended animation—and Jill had a moment of wanting to spin around and walk right back out again.

The silence felt so painful that she knew *someone* had to break it.

"What, no slow clap?" she asked.

A few people smiled, but the tension was still pretty damn excruciating.

"You all right?" Dimitri asked.

"Well, I think he's off the family holiday card list," she said.

That hung in the air, too—but, much more lightly.

"I'm fine," she said, in Spanish, to make sure everyone in the room got the message. "Let's play some baseball." Then, she headed for her locker, while almost everyone else went back to whatever they had been doing.

Marcus and Javy—who was tonight's starting pitcher— were having a last-minute huddle before going out to the field to warm up, but Marcus took just enough time to give her a quick, intense look, which she returned with a "What can you do?" shrug.

Shosuke was sitting on his stool at the locker next to hers, and he turned, clasped both hands over his heart, and shook his head sadly.

She nodded. "*Dōmo arigatō*," she said, and he smiled— sadly.

It was a tremendous relief to see that most of her personal stuff was here in her clubhouse locker—and, therefore, unharmed. Thank God for getaway day. But, she should probably get her nerve up and go back to the changing room and find out what the situation really was in there.

When she went down the hallway, she saw a security guard posted near the open door. She nodded self-consciously at him, and he nodded back. Inside the room, poor Terence was scrubbing away with big wads of paper towels and some bleach spray.

"God, Terence, you don't have to do that," she said.

He looked up. "Actually, I do. It's my job."

Well, yeah, come to think of it, since he was a clubbie, that was true. But, still.

"I'm not going nuts with it," he said, "because Mr. Brayton is going to have everything repainted, and a new locker brought in, while the team's out of town. I think he wants to put a lock on the door, too. With keys for you, and me and Nicky, and no one else."

Which, at the moment, was fine with her. "What actually happened?" she said.

"I was coming in with another box of fan mail for you, and he was, you know, just starting to take a leak," Terence said.

"Where?" she asked.

He tilted his head in confusion. "Well—in your locker. I mean, you knew that, right?"

"*Where* in the locker," she said.

"Oh." He pointed. "Down here, on the right side."

"So, anything on the shelf should be okay?" she asked. Her

phones, her hairbrush, and so forth.

Terence nodded. "Nicky and me already did an inventory, and during the game, we'll put new shirts and shower shoes and stuff in the clubhouse for you. And Mr. Brayton said for us to buy you some new turf shoes, too."

"Probably not much you can do about the brownies and all my host family made me for the trip," she said.

He looked embarrassed. "No. Sorry."

She'd been joking, but she understood why Greg said he'd felt ashamed, because she did, too—even though she knew perfectly well that none of this was her fault. "What did he do when he saw you?" she asked.

"He was like, oh, shit, and then, he asked me how much I wanted not to tell anyone," Terence said.

Well, yeah, after getting caught doing something wrong, a player's first thought would be to pay off the clubbie. "I should give you money," she said, "right? I mean, for having to do something so awful?"

"Are you kidding?" he asked. "No way. I have *sisters*. I'm not taking money for, you know, *not* being a dick."

She would still be sure to overtip him with her regular dues. Nicky, too. "Thank you," she said. "I appreciate it."

And, she very much did.

When she went back to the clubhouse to put on a belt and her cleats, most of the team was already out on the field. Sofia saw her coming in, and headed right over.

"How are you?" she asked.

"Filled with joy, and goodwill towards all men," Jill said. Emphasis on *men*.

Sofia's brief smile was mostly a grimace. "You need anything?" she asked.

Plane fare to Palo Alto, maybe? "Do you have any alcohol wipes?" Jill asked. "Terence says my phones are okay, but I'd rather be sure."

Sofia nodded. "Let me get you a full dispenser."

Even *two* dispensers might not be enough.

Once she was out in the dugout, she really didn't feel like interacting with *anyone*, so she sat by herself on the bench and kept her sunglasses on. Shosuke sat about two feet away, and they nodded at each other, but then, he had the sense to face forward and watch the game. Which she did, too.

Javy had a good outing—two runs on three hits, in five innings of work—but, unfortunately, the second guy out of the bullpen, whose name was Burney or Barney or something, got *lit up*, and seven runs scored in only two-thirds of an inning, and they lost.

Jeremiah fell into step with her, in the dugout tunnel— which came in handy, since a national magazine reporter intercepted them before she could escape to the clubhouse.

"Do you have time to talk, Jill?" he asked. "We've had some reports that—"

Oh, she was *so* not in the mood. "I'm sorry, not tonight,"

she said—before Jeremiah could do it for her. "We have a bus to catch, and I can't be late."

"Yes," the reporter said, "but I heard there was an incident—"

"I'm really sorry, I need to get ready to go, so that I don't hold them up," she said, cutting him off a second time. "Maybe we can sit down when the team's back in town."

The guy frowned, but raised his hands in surrender. "Okay, thanks," he said. "Jeremiah, can we set something up?"

"You bet, Mark," Jeremiah said. "Give me a call tomorrow."

It was gratifying to see a "Closed to Media" sign on the clubhouse doors, but before she could go inside, Jeremiah put his hand on her arm.

"How come you know how to do that?" he asked. "Dismiss them so easily?"

Because—her family had a television, and she occasionally *watched* it? "Nadine Cameron had me do some media training when I was in Pittsburgh," she said.

"I know, but you actually *learned how*," Jeremiah said.

It wasn't his fault that she was feeling testy, so she *didn't* say, "It's called 'paying attention.'" Instead, she just shrugged.

"We have a pretty good lid on it, but it *will* get out," he said. "I'll be working with Nadine's people to keep it minimized to whatever degree possible. Tell anyone who asks to call me, instead."

That would unquestionably be easier. Jill nodded. "Thanks. I'll do that."

Inside the clubhouse, people were quiet and grumpy, as they filled paper plates with the post-game spread, which was ziti in two big foil pans, cooked with tomato sauce and hamburger, along with a few loaves of Italian bread, and some wilted salad. Jill wasn't sure whether the clubbies had cooked the meal, or had it sent in—but, it was clear that the unknown chef was not a big fan of seasonings.

She wasn't at all hungry, but forced down a few bites before going to the female employees' restroom to change into chinos, her Top-Siders, and a royal blue cotton V-neck T-shirt with three-quarter sleeves. She would rather have showered, but there was something skin-crawling about the idea of using the one in her dressing room, even with a guard still standing outside, so she decided to wait until they got to the motel in State College.

The bus ride was supposed to be about five hours, if everything went on schedule, and they would probably arrive around dawn. She assumed they would check right in, and get to sleep a little, before reporting to the ballpark. Or, anyway, she *hoped* so.

After calling her mother and Theo and Lauren and Greg, for brief "I'm fine, no problem, it's all good" chats, she went through her knapsack more than once, to make sure her iPad, iPod, Kindle, and phones were all charged and safely packed, along with her streaming stick for the motel televisions. Her gear bag was gone, which made her nervous, but Jonesy must have seen how alarmed she looked, because he told her that the clubbies had already packed all of their luggage under the bus.

Nicky came over with a small zipped-up cooler bag. "From, um, Mrs. Wilkins?" he said.

"Thanks," she said, and looked inside to see a fresh care package—which almost made her cry. Someone—her mother? Mrs. Doshi, maybe?—must have called her and told her what had happened.

She was one of the last players to emerge outside—and was delayed further by a cluster of waiting fans who wanted autographs. Some of the other players were signing, too, which made her feel less conspicuous.

"Ooh-la-*la*," Scott said, when she finally made her way over to the bus. "Look at your hair!"

Yes. Her hair was down. No ponytail, no chignon, no *anything*—because she bloody well didn't feel like it—and she had thrown away the damn hairbrush, just in case it was contaminated. "I'm a fashion plate," she said—and resisted the urge to peek inside her knapsack one more time, to make sure everything was there.

Most of the team seemed to be exchanging glances, and she stopped walking.

"What's wrong?" she asked. Were they *that* freaked out about her hair? She reached up to touch it, but everything felt normal. So, she gripped the knapsack with both hands, not sure what to do.

"I'm very sorry, Cafferty," Adler said, "but I'm not going to be able to let you on the bus like that."

Okay, it must be a damn joke, but she had no idea what it was. She looked down at herself. "I don't understand, sir." As far as she could tell, she looked fine. "Is it the Top-Siders?" Because people from New England *liked* to wear Top-Siders. They might not be dressy, but they were certainly presentable.

Except, most of the rest of them were wearing sneakers, other than Marcus, who had on a pair of loafers, and a couple of guys who had gone with cowboy boots.

Adler indicated her shirt. "I'm sorry, but that's against the dress code."

Seriously? But, it was one of the brand-new shirts she had bought with her mother, and she was wearing a nice silver necklace—with, okay, a black-and-gold Phiten necklace, plus her father's dog tag—and she had even put on the blue beaded earrings her friend Cathy had made for her birthday in May. "I'm confused, sir," she said, not sure whether to panic, or get mad as hell. "This is a very nice blouse. I mean, it's as close as I *come* to being cute."

"You really didn't play much travel ball, did you?" Schwartzman asked.

No, but—she was still missing the point. Adler was standing with his arms folded, blocking the bus door, and she stayed uncertainly on the sidewalk.

"Jill, we're going on the road," Marcus said. "We wear collared shirts on the road."

Her V-neck did not, in fact, have a collar. She looked around and saw that almost everyone else was wearing a polo shirt—with a collar. Marcus, unsurprisingly, had on a button-down oxford shirt.

Damn. She had only brought one polo shirt to Pomeroy—and it was back in the dresser at her host family's house. Was she going to have to stay behind? Or call Mrs. Wilkins—who had already gone above and beyond today—and reluctantly ask her to bring the shirt over to the stadium?

"I'm sorry," she said. "I didn't know." She glanced at Adler. "Is there a team handbook I didn't get issued? Maybe you could give me a copy, to review?"

Marcus had already gone over to the baggage compartment, where he poked around briefly, and then unzipped what must be his travel bag, and handed her a black polo shirt with a Vanderbilt Commodores logo.

"Thank you," she said. "Excuse me, I'll be right back."

"Hurry up, Ladybug," Dimitri said—in his red designer polo shirt. "We have a pretty long ride tonight."

She went back to the restroom and changed, trying to stay calm, but feeling her temper rising with every passing second. The shirt was at least two sizes too big—but, it had a collar.

Like it really mattered, one way or the other? Adler was

clearly just a son of a bitch who was on a power trip—and an ill-timed one, at that.

Instead of heading back outside, she yanked out her phone and called Lauren again.

"Are you on the bus?" Lauren asked, when she picked up.

"Adler wouldn't *let* me get on," Jill said. "I mean, he's out there *bullying* me, right in front of everyone, and I think they all think it's funny, and—I so *totally* don't need this garbage."

"That doesn't make sense," Lauren said.

Maybe, maybe not. And it might not have hurt for her to say *hello*, first—but, too late now. "They all hate me," Jill said. "Why am I wasting my time? This is just *stupid*. I think I should call Mom, and my aunt, and have them get me *out* of this."

Lauren paused, before answering. "What actually happened?"

Hadn't she just *told* her? Jill took a deep breath, trying not to let her temper completely explode. "I started to get on the damn bus, and he said no, and stood in front of the door, and—I can't *believe* how much I hate it here."

"What are you leaving out?" Lauren asked.

Nothing. "I came outside, he said there was something wrong with my shirt, and everyone laughed like hell," Jill said. Or, anyway, they all *looked* at each other. "What's confusing about *that?*"

There was another pause.

"Don't yell at me, because *you're* having a bad day, how about?" Lauren said stiffly.

"Right," Jill said, and took another deep breath, in an attempt to ramp down. Also, not to burst into tears. "I'm sorry. I just—things really *suck*, and I don't understand what's happening."

"What are you wearing?" Lauren asked.

"One of the shirts Mom and I got up in Warwick," Jill said. "The blue one."

"Yeah, that's a nice shirt," Lauren said.

It *was* nice. Both feminine and professional.

"It doesn't have a collar," Lauren said.

Jesus, why was everyone so hyped up about the god-damn collars? "So?" Jill said, struggling not to sound as pugnacious as she was feeling.

"Come on, even I know that professional athletes have to wear shirts with collars when they travel," Lauren said. "And when you're not tired and upset, you do, too."

Jill frowned, not saying anything.

"He was doing you a favor," Lauren said.

"Oh, the hell he is," Jill said. "He's just piling on."

"No, he's treating you like a regular baseball player, Jill," Lauren said. "And he's giving *them* permission to do that, too. You're not the only person on the team who doesn't like what happened today. So, he's reminding *all* of you that you can still act like baseball players."

Jill thought about that, but still wasn't convinced. It seemed too—devious.

"What are you going to do about the shirt?" Lauren asked.

"Marcus gave me one of his," Jill said. "I'm supposed to be in here changing, and coming right back."

"So, go out there, and then call or text me, once you're on the road," Lauren said.

"And yell at you some more?" Jill asked.

"Yeah," Lauren said. "That'll be good. I'm looking forward to that."

After tucking the phone away, she took a few minutes to wash her face, and otherwise compose herself, and then went back out to the parking lot.

"Is this okay, sir?" she asked, trying not to clench her teeth—or, at least, not to be *obvious* about it.

"Yes, you may board the bus, Cafferty," he said.

She nodded stiffly, and then climbed up the metal steps with her small knapsack, saying hello to the driver, Stan, as she passed him.

Most of the seats were already taken, and she hesitated, not sure what to do, but then, Sofia—who was sitting up near the front—motioned to the empty seat next to her.

"You want the window?" Sofia asked.

Yes—but, only on the other side of the bus, where the cold metal wouldn't vibrate directly against her pitching elbow. "I'm fine, thanks," Jill said, and then sat down, pulling out her iPod and her private phone.

Sofia lowered her voice. "Did you take all of that personally?"

Jill nodded, scrolling through the iPod for something that might be *soothing*.

"He looks like a dinosaur, but he's a smart man," Sofia said.

Yeah, sure. "Treating me like just another ballplayer, right?" Jill said.

"Yes," Sofia said. "Exactly. I'm glad you already knew that."

Be nice if she *had* known. On top of everything else that had happened today, she had also become very stupid, apparently.

Some of the guys—longtime travel and college ball veterans, probably—were all set up with neck pillows, and tablets, and laptops, and snacks, and one of the utility guys, Reilly, even had a guitar—which could end up being tedious, if he spent the next several hours playing it.

Because it was the first road trip of the year, Adler gave a speech about bus protocol—phone calls should be brief and quiet, headphones were required for personal music or movies, so other people could hear if they wanted to watch whatever movie the bus driver put on, and that sort of thing. There were even instructions about using the restroom, and what they should, and shouldn't, do in there, if at all possible.

A bunch of the guys laughed, and she was a little grossed out—but, well, they were all going to be spending a lot of time together in close quarters, so there was no reason for him not to be blunt.

It would be nice if she could read, but that always made

her feel carsick in moving vehicles, so she would listen to music, and—if she was lucky—get a few hours of sleep.

"Do you mind if I text?" she asked Sofia.

Sofia already looked half-asleep, and peered at her through mostly closed eyes. "You have a free pass tonight," she said. "But, are you one of those people who makes a lot of exclamations about every single response she gets?"

"I'll try to subdue my chortling," Jill said.

Sofia gave her a strange look, but then seemed to decide to find that funny, before moving back into a more comfortable sleeping position.

For the first part of the ride, there was a fair amount of conversation and excitement. Would they all still feel energized by road trips a few weeks from now? Probably not, but if she were in a better mood, she would admit that it was pretty cool to be with a bunch of fellow professional baseball players, on their way off to play a series of three games in one town in Pennsylvania, and then three more in another Pennsylvania town, before heading home.

She texted with Lauren for quite a while, and by the time she finally tucked her phone away, Sofia had long since fallen asleep—which Jill envied. Her father had always been able to sack out absolutely anywhere, whenever he wanted, which he said was an army thing. She and her mother and Theo tended to be a lot more restless, and *much* more nocturnal.

But, if she started thinking too much, she was going to

feel even more homesick, and unhappy—and trying to sleep seemed like a smarter idea. Some of the guys were zonked out, although there were still a few conversations going on, and Reilly was plucking away. There was a lot of shifting around, though, because almost all of them were *tall*, and the seats were designed for much smaller people. Dimitri was stretched out on the aisle floor, with his head on a travel pillow, and mostly, people were managing *not* to step on him.

She dozed on and off, and listened to music, and felt the highway rumbling under the bus wheels. With luck, Stan was a good driver.

The bus smelled like a locker room, with overtones of very strong aftershave, muscle-relaxing liniment, and just general guy smells, not all of which were pleasant.

At one point, she looked around, and saw Marcus, across the aisle and a couple of rows back, staring at his tablet, and moving his lips every so often. She would have bet at least a thousand dollars that he was sitting there, trying to learn Japanese, while the rest of them were just doing their best to sleep.

It was about two in the morning when Stan pulled up at a roadside McDonald's and almost everyone got out, and used the restrooms, and bought an astonishing amount of food, especially considering that they had recently eaten a hell of a lot of ziti.

"Growing boys," Sofia mumbled, and promptly went back to sleep.

Once they got on the road, the bus *reeked* of Big Macs and french fries. She wasn't really hungry, but found herself eating a granola bar, anyway—and mentally thanking Mrs. Wilkins from the bottom of her heart for bringing the new care package over.

Every so often, she would hear someone spit rhythmically into a cup, and wondered how anyone could possibly enjoy chewing tobacco. A couple of the coaches and several of the players were addicted to the stuff, even though it had been outlawed for years in the minors, and any player who got caught would be fined.

At about four in the morning, the bus pulled over at another rest stop, and most of the guys didn't even wake up. The rest of them stumbled outside, and she was amazed to see several people buying even more burgers and fries.

For her part, she went in to use the restroom, and then stood under the dark sky for a few minutes, taking deep breaths of fresh air—and wasn't the only one doing so.

Stan finished a cigarette, slugged down some coffee, and then warned all of the stragglers to get back on the bus, before he "up 'n left 'em to fend for themselves in the forest."

This wasn't even a particularly long ride—but, it felt endless. As though she had trapped herself into a nightmarishly long summer.

A really long *career*, for that matter.

Damn. Why in the hell hadn't she just gone to Stanford?

CHAPTER 18

They got to their motel around six in the morning. Everyone, including Adler and the coaches, was groggy and a little short-tempered, and there wasn't much conversation. People mostly just wanted their room keys, so they could go in and get some more sleep. Louis was also handing out their per diem meal money—twenty-five dollars each—and checking their names off on a sheet of paper.

Jill had been assigned to share a room with Sofia, since they were all doubled up, except for Adler, as far as she knew.

"Which bed you want?" Sofia asked, sounding half-asleep.

"I don't care," Jill said.

Sofia grunted assent, dumped her travel duffel on the bed closest to the door, and then lurched off to the bathroom.

Except for sleepovers with people like Lauren, she had never shared a room with anyone before, other than her family, when they went on trips. Her family tended to be—private—about pretty much *everything*, and give each other a lot of space. But, before she got too anxious and homesick, it was probably worth remembering that going away to college would have meant having a stranger as a roommate, too.

Sofia came out in nothing but a baggy T-shirt and underpants, and got into bed, pausing only to set an alarm on her phone, and to call the front desk and leave a wake-up call for nine-thirty.

"Try not to make noise," she said—and then, conked out with no apparent effort.

Jill took a Star Wars T-shirt, some sweatpants, and her toothbrush out of her bag, and went into the bathroom to get ready for bed. It was really weird to be going to sleep at six-thirty in the morning.

She would have liked to stream a Buffy episode or something, but even with earbuds, she was afraid of disturbing Sofia with the flickering light of the show. So, she decided to read on her iPad for ten minutes—which turned into an hour. Right now, she was working on *War and Peace*, which was a slog, but she was churning her way along—and whenever it seemed just too damn ponderous, she would switch off to a mystery or a beach book for a while.

Their wake-up call seemed to come about thirty seconds

after she finally managed to close her eyes. Sofia wasn't exactly the perky type—but, she was alert and efficient, and almost out the door by the time Jill had managed to get from sitting on the edge of the bed, to considering standing up.

"Don't forget to be there for the bus at twelve-fifteen," Sofia said, already on her way out. "It *will* leave without you."

It wasn't quite "Good morning! What a wonderful day!"— but it was helpful information.

Sofia paused, one hand on the door. "Was it just because yesterday was awful, or does it happen every night?" she asked.

That didn't sound good at all. Jill looked at her nervously. "What do you mean?"

"The nightmares," Sofia said.

Well, she knew she had nightmares—it had been happening regularly for several years, but didn't know that they were *noisy*. At least, not every night. "I have no idea," Jill said.

Sofia frowned, then nodded, and left the room.

With luck, they had just been gasping and thrashing-around nightmares, and not *screaming* ones.

She kept sitting on the bed, taking in the fact that she was all by herself, in a motel room, somewhere in Pennsylvania— and couldn't quite remember ever feeling *this* lonely. So, she put through a video call to her mother, who must have been expecting that, because she picked up right away.

"How are you today?" her mother asked.

"Okay," Jill said. More or less, anyway. "I wanted to say hi, that's all."

"Did you sleep?" her mother asked. "You look exhausted."

She wasn't about to admit that she'd had audible nightmares. "Well, it was a long ride, but I'm in the motel in State College, and it's—well, fine, I guess. Is Maggie okay?"

"Yeah, she just came inside," her mother said, and pointed the screen at Maggie, who was napping comfortably on her orthopedic bed.

God, she missed Maggie. And she was pretty sure she didn't have nearly as many nightmares when Maggie was keeping her company.

"Did you know they call that part of Pennsylvania 'Happy Valley'?" her mother asked.

News to her. "I haven't seen any signs of that," Jill said, "but I kind of haven't left the room yet."

"What about breakfast?" her mother asked.

Well, there was the whole problem of not leaving the room. "Mrs. Wilkins gave me some granola bars," Jill said. "And the room has one of those little coffeemakers, so I'm good."

Her mother did a poor job of *not* looking worried. "What about your teammates?" she asked. "Do they all have breakfast together?"

Probably, yeah. "I don't know," Jill said. "No one really tells you anything, and—" Which reminded her of something. "Oh, could you maybe mail me a couple of shirts? Like, maybe the green Lacoste one, and the red NHS one?"

"Sure," her mother said. "But, what's wrong with the shirts we just got you?"

"Mr. Adler wouldn't let me on the *bus*," she said, noticing that she was still damn angry about it. "You're supposed to have a collar, but no one told me, and—they were all laughing, until Marcus let me borrow one of his. Except it's *huge*, and it looks stupid."

Her mother sighed. "I'm sorry. It's such a strange new world you're in. What's the motel address? I'll get a package together right now, but I'm not sure if they'll deliver on Sunday."

Good point. "I don't know," Jill said. "Maybe the Wilkinses' house? Because I only have one there, and I guess we need to wear them a lot."

"Okay, I'll send them right off," her mother said. "I'm sorry they laughed. It seems very unkind."

"Lauren thinks that was just them acting like normal players, and *not* picking on me—but, I don't know," Jill said. "Maybe she's right." And maybe they hadn't actually been laughing that much—although it had certainly *felt* that way.

They talked for a while longer, with her mother expressing sympathy—repeatedly, and reassuring her that Maggie truly was fine, and then trying to cajole her into considering *venturing out of the room.*

There was a sudden pounding on the door.

"Hey, Ladybug!" a voice yelled, and there was more

pounding. "Come on, Mother found a diner."

"Who's that?" her mother asked.

"Probably Scott," Jill said. "Maybe he wants me to go to breakfast with them."

"Okay, that's good," her mother said. "I like Scott. Go do that."

It probably made more sense than hiding in her room for the next couple of hours, until it was time to get on the bus to the ballpark.

When she opened the door, it *was* Scott, standing with Marcus and Hector and Jonesy.

"Come on, Ladybug," Scott said. "Get suited up, we're waiting for you."

Apparently, she had a nickname now. "Can I meet you out front in ten minutes?" she asked.

"We're very hungry," Hector said, "so it's cruel. But, if you *must*."

She glanced at Marcus. "I think I need to wear your shirt again, until my mother can send me some of mine."

He nodded patiently. "That's fine, Jill. Hustle up, okay?"

Yes, *sir*. "Be right out," she said.

"There's no such thing as a girl, and 'right out,'" Jonesy was saying to the others, as she closed the door.

She wasn't exactly high-maintenance, but she *did* need to take a fast shower and everything. It took her about twelve minutes to join them outside, but Marcus was the only one she saw check his watch. Dimitri and a bullpen guy named Danny, who looked about thirteen years old, had joined the group, and they ended up at a diner that was about three blocks away, crowded into two adjacent booths.

Everyone was carefully budgeting their per diem, although she had looked up "The Palisades," and found out that Hector really was from one of the very most exclusive parts of Los Angeles, and was probably not hurting for pocket change. And she and Scott were in pretty damn good shape, too, given their contracts—but, that didn't mean that anyone else at the table was, and she decided that it would be tactful to stay within her per diem, too.

Hector—who guys were calling "Mr. Health," because he kept a prized jar of raw Manuka honey in his locker, from which he would have one spoonful before each game as "a tonic"—ordered an egg white omelet, with a side of fruit and some cottage cheese, but almost everyone else went with things like pancakes and waffles, and Jonesy got something called The Lion's Feast, which cost almost eleven dollars, but had a large array of eggs, pancakes, and breakfast meats, including scrapple. Marcus ordered poached eggs on toast, bacon, sliced tomatoes, and a glass of milk—and muttered to her when she chose French toast and fruit salad that she needed to have some *protein*. So, she added a side of fried ham and a dish of yogurt, and he seemed to be appeased. Or, anyway, he shut up about it.

Scott was more chirpy than the rest of them put together,

and kept stealing food from people's plates, even after putting away a huge stack of pancakes and four pieces of bacon. Everyone else looked tired, and when they got up, she noticed that Dimitri, in particular, was very stiff. There was no way he could possibly have been comfortable on the bus, even lying in the aisle. During team and pre-game stretches, Louis and Sofia *always* seemed to do extra trainer-assisted stretching with him, and she assumed that he had a significant injury history.

When they were walking back to the motel, Marcus fell into step with her.

"I wish I could have been more overtly chivalrous yesterday," he said. "But, I was afraid that would only make things worse."

It probably would have, yeah, since she didn't want to look as though she *needed* protecting. "Scott told me Andrew"—to whom she had still never really spoken—"had a very—strong—reaction," she said.

Marcus nodded. "Still waters there."

Apparently so. Someday, she and Andrew might even exchange words. "Should I have picked up the check?" she asked. "I mean, to be nice?"

He shook his head. "No, you don't want to throw it in guys' faces. But, pay for a really good post-game spread some night, and you'll win quite a few fans."

That sounded like wise advice, and she nodded.

Because it was the second day after her start, this would just be a workout day for her. Lots of stretching, time in whatever weight room the visiting team got to use—lower body and core work, predominantly, playing a little catch, and either long toss or throwing a football with Scott's road roommate, Danny. She would also probably run some stadium steps, and do a series of sprints. Plus, they would have team stretch, and maybe some PFP, too, depending on the home team's schedule.

The stadium turned out to be unusually nice, with huge weight room and exercise facilities, a large indoor hitting cage and pitching mounds, and even a dedicated media room. Penn State's varsity baseball team used the same field during their season, so there were actually *three* clubhouses, and she would have the Penn State one all to herself, for changing and showering, while they were in town.

Visiting teams were always assigned shorter batting practice sessions than home teams were, and she stood in the outfield with Shosuke and Danny. He was a high school pitcher from Louisiana, who had a mighty thick Cajun accent, and relied heavily on a good sinker and getting people to ground out.

The gates must have opened very early, because there were already fans in the stands when they were leaving the field. The State College public relations person, a curly haired woman in her forties, asked if she would mind stopping to sign autographs, and whether she would be willing to be interviewed by the local press, and since she had quite a lot of time to kill before the game started, she was happy to agree.

The whole thing took longer than she expected, but she and

the PR woman both were mostly able to deflect any questions she didn't feel like answering—and gradually, the reporters shifted into less stressful topics. By the time she got down to the clubhouse, the pre-game spread had been pretty well picked over, although it didn't appear to have been at all lavish in the first place. So, she fixed herself a peanut butter and jelly sandwich—which was going to get boring, sooner rather than later, helped herself to a bottle of water and an orange, and sat in front of her locker to read, until it was time to change into her game uniform. Christ, being a baseball player was *so* much more monotonous than she ever would have guessed.

The clubhouse was pretty rowdy, with a series of highly competitive Ping-Pong games going on nonstop, and Raffy and a couple of other guys were dancing around to some very loud salsa music. But, she was really only interested in her too-late lunch and her Kindle, and paid no attention whatsoever. Maybe they'd all had one too many Red Bulls or Monster Energy drinks or something. Rip It was another brand she had noticed around the clubhouse—and around National Guardsmen, for that matter. As far as she knew, team officials didn't really want them abusing energy drinks, but they weren't outright banned, either. Especially since they could accomplish pretty much the same thing by getting a few shots of espresso somewhere and adding a bunch of sugar to it.

On her way to the cavernous, empty Penn State locker room, she passed Adler in the hallway, and he stopped.

"You get why I gave you a hard time last night, right?" he asked.

Maybe, but she still wasn't *in favor* of it. "After two different people explained it to me," she said.

"Good," he said. "When you didn't come back out, I started to worry that you might be in there crying."

Yes, she was the most delicate of tiny flowers. But, there was no reason not to be as direct as he was. "I was on the phone with my best friend, yelling about how mean you were being," she said.

"Glad to hear it." He started down the hall, then stopped again. "Are you hanging in, Cafferty?"

Was she? "More or less," she said.

"Good enough," he said, and continued on his way.

The game that night was one of those wandering, lead-changing ones, with a lot of pitching substitutions, and an unsatisfying rhythm. Jill spent most of it up at the railing with Shosuke, both of them watching, while Shosuke kept the chart, but they also showed each other the grips they used for their pitches. He threw lots of cutters and sliders, neither of which had ever really intrigued her, because—well—she was kind of in love with her hammer. Their mostly speech-free friendship had progressed to the degree that they could amuse each other by making incredulous or judgmental expressions, upon seeing the other person's changeup grip and the like.

In the eighth, their third baseman, Geoff, went into second

base hard, trying to stretch a single—his fourth hit of the day— into a double. Somehow, one of his spikes caught on the bag, and he flipped over awkwardly, landing with most of his lower leg pointing in the wrong direction.

Louis and Sofia ran out there, along with the Spikes' trainer—since the fact that Geoff had *screamed* when he hit the ground made it clear that it was a serious injury. In the end, he was taken off the field on a gurney, and left in an ambulance.

The dugout was *really* quiet after that, and players on both teams were swinging at first pitches, trying to end the game as quickly as possible. The early word was that Geoff had a compound fracture of both bones in his lower leg, and was gone for the rest of the season, at a bare minimum.

The post-game spread was somewhat-cold meatball and chicken parmigiana subs, and people ate without much conversation, before filing out to the bus. A few of the guys were planning to go out to some bar, but no one invited her—and it really wasn't something she wanted to do, anyway, especially since searching for eager local female companionship was the primary goal. She was fine with going back to her room, making a few calls, and then working on *War and Peace*.

She was in bed reading, when Sofia came dragging in a couple of hours later, looking very tired.

"How's he doing?" Jill asked.

Sofia shook her head. "He's having surgery to stabilize the fractures, and it looks like he did some serious knee ligament damage, too. He has a long rehab ahead. With luck—I don't know. They're trying to figure out how soon he can travel, so they can get him home to Oregon."

Somehow, it felt like an extra bitter pill, on a night when the poor guy had gone four for four, and had to have been feeling on top of the Short Season world. "It can happen that fast, can't it," Jill said. "One minute, everything's great, and then, just like that—" She snapped her fingers, and winced at the thought of his bones making a similar sound.

"It's true of life in general," Sofia said.

Yes, she knew that all too well. In fact, she and Lauren had talked for quite a while tonight about the randomness of everything, and how—frankly—scary it was.

Sofia disappeared into the bathroom to take a shower, coming out in black mesh shorts and an Ithaca College T-shirt.

"Is that where you went to school?" Jill asked.

Sofia nodded, rubbing her hair with a towel to dry it. "Yeah. And then, I got a master's in kinesiology at Michigan."

"Did you always want to be a trainer?" Jill asked.

Sofia peered under the towel at her. "Do we have Twenty Questions going tonight?"

"Sure, why not," Jill said.

"Well, I'll do ten, maybe," Sofia said, and carried her towel into the bathroom to hang it up. "I was aiming towards being a physical therapist, but I love sports, and played a lot of softball, and I ended up going for athletic training." She looked over.

"You never played any softball at all?"

Jill shook her head.

"Do you *hate* softball?" Sofia asked.

"No, I really like watching it," Jill said. Especially since almost every female friend she'd ever had had been a player. "But, for me, it's sort of like comparing crew and kayaking. They're *similar* sports, but also totally different."

Sofia nodded. "Okay, I can see that."

"Would you rather have been a softball trainer?" Jill asked.

Sofia shrugged. "Softball or baseball. Or—anything, really. Except for football. I did some work as an assistant when I was in school, and those guys really get *hurt*. I mean, I hate what happened to Geoff tonight, but if everything goes okay, he should be able to come back, and it isn't going to endanger his *life* or well-being. Football is just madness."

Jill had often felt guilty about *enjoying* watching the NFL, especially when players got carted off the field right and left during every game. "My father was totally into football," she said. "He was an outside linebacker at Holy Cross, and sometimes, he got some snaps at tight end, too."

"Pro-level talent?" Sofia asked.

Jill shook her head. "He always said he was at least two steps too slow." She noticed that she was holding his dog tag— her usual reflex—and dropped it back into her T-shirt.

"You don't talk about him much," Sofia said.

"No," Jill said. Except, maybe that sounded too abrupt.

"It's still too hard. So—well, I try to keep it from coming up."

Sofia nodded. "I'd love to tell you that it goes away, but my mother died when I was a junior in college, and it really doesn't. It gets *easier*, over time, but it never leaves you."

No, grief hadn't been at all what she would have expected it to be. There were *still* days when it felt as though it had just happened, seconds before, and she had the same chilling sense of utter shock. "I'm sorry about your mother," Jill said.

"I'm sorry about your father," Sofia said.

It was quiet for a minute.

"Well," Sofia said, and picked up the room phone to request another wake-up call. She started to climb into bed, and then paused. "I don't know if I should bring this up, but you know I'm a lesbian, right?"

She hadn't, actually, so she just shrugged.

"Is that going to create problems for you?" Sofia asked.

And what would give her that impression? Jill frowned at her. "In what way?"

"We'll obviously be spending a great deal of time together," Sofia said. "A lot of people are going to think that you're gay, too."

Oh, please. "People *already* think that," Jill said. Routinely. *Constantly*. They always had, and probably always would. Except, of course, for people who thought she was unusually promiscuous, and sleeping with half the guys on whatever team she was on. Old news, in her life. "What do I care?"

"Okay, but—" Sofia frowned, too. "Well, yes, I suppose they do."

"I don't think the notion of women playing sports should lead to *any* assumption of sexuality," Jill said. "But, we both know it does. Especially when you play at a high level, and you're *tall.*"

"Can't argue with you there," Sofia said. "But, I didn't want to make things even harder on you than they already are."

Which she appreciated.

"You're a lot less irritating than I was afraid you'd be," Sofia said.

Jill had to laugh. "Yeah, yeah, yeah," she said. "That's what they all say."

With luck.

CHAPTER 19

The next day was her bullpen day. They had her throw to the backup catcher, a guy named Ramón, who was in his third year, after spending his first two seasons in the Dominican Summer League and the Gulf Coast League. His English was pretty comprehensible, when it came to baseball terms, but he wasn't very comfortable with regular conversations.

Marcus hovered nearby the entire time, leaning against the fence with his arms folded, even though Ramón grinned and said, "*Mamá!*" while making a waving-away motion with his hand.

"Stay around sixty percent, seventy-five percent max," Sawyer said, standing close by and holding his clipboard. "We're going to work from the stretch today, get you on a better footing. No slide-steps, though—we'll save that for down the road."

Jill nodded. "I'm definitely weaker from the stretch."

"Most of you guys are," Sawyer said. "You're not used to having people on *base*, the way you will here. It's why your pickoff move isn't anywhere close to where it needs to be."

He was talking to her like a *pitcher*. It felt good.

The session went pretty well, although he stopped her a few times, to give instructions, or adjust her position, but she actually *learned* things—which was great.

"Okay, nice work, Cafferty," he said, when she was finished. "Go get fluffed, and iced, and be sure to get some cardio in." He turned to Marcus. "We'll sit down with Jonesy after stretch."

During their post-BP downtime, it occurred to her that there was an easy solution to her collared shirt problem. So, she grabbed her debit card, went up to the concourse, and walked around until she found the team store. It wasn't officially open yet, but when she knocked on the door, they were quick to let her in—and even seemed excited to do so.

They sold Penn State gear, as well as Spikes' team items, and she left with a navy blue women's Nittany Lions polo shirt. They had wanted to *give* it to her, but that didn't seem appropriate, even though she appreciated the offer. They ended up steering her to a shirt that had been on a clearance rack, and she was fine with that.

It was probably silly, but as she left the store with her

bag, she was kind of proud of herself for solving the collar problem. It was a small thing, but somehow, it felt like an *adult* accomplishment. In fact, she wanted to call her mother immediately, and say, "Guess what I did!"

"Hello, Jill!" a too-hearty voice said. "How are you? I was hoping to run into you. *Great* to see you."

It was Aaron Marshak, a man who was so damn determined to be her agent that he didn't seem to grasp that that made it even more unlikely ever to happen. She had gotten used to him popping up unexpectedly for the past couple of years, although it usually felt more like he was *pouncing*.

"Nice to see you, too, sir," she said, and then moved past him.

"What do you have there?" he asked.

Was it any of his business? "It's for my stuffed animal collection," she said. Of course, she didn't have a stuffed animal collection, but for a few seconds, she wondered if she *wanted* one, and she could maybe collect mascots from every ballpark the team visited, and—then what? Give them personalities? Play imaginary games with them? Cuddle them in the dark of night?

Aaron did a double take, but then seemed to try and hide that reaction. "I wish you had let me buy that for you, Jill. It would have been my pleasure."

"Thank you, but I'm all set," she said.

"I hope they didn't make you pay for it," he said. "I can go in there and speak to them about it, if you'd like."

"I'm fine, thank you," she said.

"You really shouldn't be paying for much of anything *anywhere*," he said. "You don't have to anymore."

Jill repressed a shudder—since that was surely not a world where she wanted to live.

Aaron was the kind of guy who always wore an ostentatious gold watch, and would probably *love* telling her how much it had cost. In fact, from his casually draped sunglasses to his polished leather shoes, she was pretty sure he could itemize the price of every single thing he had on without a second thought.

"So, are you finally ready to sit down and do the paperwork?" he asked.

The man was a walking self-delusion.

"Come on, you're not a little girl anymore, Jill," he said. "It's time to step up, and get down to business."

"Mr. Marshak—" she started.

"Aaron," he said.

"Mr. Marshak," she said, again. "I have a legal advisor, and that's all I need right now."

Aaron shook his head, and she was afraid he might be going to sling his arm around her, so she took two steps backward, out of reach.

"You only say that because you don't fully understand what I can do for you," he said.

"I'm really not looking to cash in, sir," she said.

He moved his hand dismissively. "Don't be a fool. You have

stratospheric earning potential. In fact, I have a *global* strategy to monetize your career, and I'd like to lay it out for you."

"I appreciate your interest, Mr. Marshak," she said, "but I'm really not—"

"You always say that, but *this* is the time for us to bring all of this to fruition," he said. "Not tomorrow, not next year, not five years from now. *Today*. You can't just be a child and stick your head in the sand and pretend it isn't there."

She wanted to look around and see if there were any nearby security guards or ballpark personnel to run interference—but, she could take care of this herself, right? Even though it was stressful. "Sir, I don't know how to put this," she said, "but I really don't want an agent, and if I *did*, I'm afraid that I wouldn't be picking you."

He stared at her. "What?"

How would it be possible to be more clear than that? "I'm sorry, but if I decide, at any point, that I want representation, it'll be someone else," she said. *Anyone* else—up to, and including, Batty-Oscar, the bat-fetching dog.

His expression darkened so much that it was an effort not to back up a few more steps. But, instead, she folded her arms and held her ground.

"You unbelievable bitch," he said through his teeth. "Don't you have any idea how much work I've *already* done for you? I've been laying the groundwork for your future for months now. *Years*, really."

Without ever noticing that she hadn't actually hired him? And didn't take his calls? "I'm sorry if you went to any unnecessary effort, sir," she said.

He scowled at her. "Your fastball's nothing special, you know. I would have been wasting my time, anyway. Your only hope is to cash in *now*, before everyone else figures it out."

Nice guy. A prince, even. "Well, let's hope no one catches on," she said, and headed towards the clubhouse.

The next two games were uneventful, other than her spending the second one leaning against the railing—with her very own clipboard—and charting pitches. It was harder than she expected, and she had to ask Jonesy for advice a few times, and also switch from a pen to a pencil, because she kept making tiny mistakes. Since she would be pitching against an entirely different team, it wasn't going to help her learn much about the hitters, but she could see that it was a good way to improve her concentration—and quietly absorb the way other pitchers worked, and what was, and wasn't, successful.

They were back at the motel just before ten o'clock, and most of the team seemed to be planning to go out and take advantage of being in a college town, where potentially dateable young women were easy to find. She assumed that the availability of said women was why several players had seemed more than slightly hungover during the past couple of days.

It was easy enough to slip out of sight, and go to her room, without anyone really noticing. Hector did shout, "Come on, Ladybug, come paint the town with us!", but she just smiled and said, "Thanks, maybe next time."

If nothing else, she was making excellent progress with *War and Peace* lately.

Before settling down, she went out to the hall to get ice, where she found Scott buying a couple of drinks from a soda machine.

"What are you doing here?" she asked. "I thought everyone went out."

Scott shrugged. "It wasn't that fun last night, and besides, I'm trying *not* to break up with my girlfriend—and being around those guys could make it really hard."

She had known that he often texted with a girl who was going to USC in the fall, and had assumed it was pretty serious.

"Did you not go, because you're pitching tomorrow?" he asked.

That, too. So, she nodded. "Is it hard, keeping things up long-distance?"

"Yeah," he said, and fed money into the machine, until two more Cokes popped out. "I think we're already maybe broken up, but I'm trying to keep it going." He shrugged again, looking far more pensive than she had ever seen him. "Anyway, Danny and I are bored. You want to hang out?"

Very much so, actually. "Sure. We could watch a movie," she said.

Their room was something of a pigsty, so since Sofia had gone out somewhere, they ended up in her room, watching—for unknown reasons—*The Lego Movie.* And *enjoying* it.

At first, they all sat on the edge of her mattress, but that wasn't really relaxing, and after a while, they ended up lying on the bed in a row, propped up on pillows, the way she generally watched things with Theo and Greg. There were still some snacks in the bag Mrs. Wilkins had packed for her, so they ate candy and granola bars, and drank Cokes—and it was nicer than anything she had done so far as a professional baseball player.

Which was how Sofia found them, when she came into the room, stopping short in surprise.

"My God, you look like children," she said.

Scott nudged both of them. "Hit it!" he said, and they sang a rousing, mostly on-key version of "Everything Is Awesome!" together.

Sofia shook her head. "You all *are* children."

Since they were three of the youngest players on the team—yeah, the description probably fit.

Jill thought she might get grouchy about the room having been hijacked, but after a perplexed moment of staring at them, Sofia helped herself to a package of Reese's Peanut Butter Cups, lay down on *her* bed, and watched the end of the movie with them.

"*Frozen?*" Danny said, when it was over.

Sofia groaned. "God, no. I need some sleep, we have an early bus tomorrow."

"We sing good, though," Danny said.

Sofia shook her head. "Go away, boys, and leave me in peace."

It was late enough now, so that Jill really did want to get some sleep, so she would be in good shape for her start. They agreed that they would watch *Frozen* in Williamsport—and try very hard not to let any of their teammates find out. Except, possibly, for Shosuke, who she now realized was equally unlikely to have gone out drinking tonight.

In the morning, Adler's lone comment before she boarded the bus in her new polo shirt was "Go, Lions!"

They got to Williamsport right before noon, so they went straight to the stadium, instead of checking in to their new motel. It was one of the oldest minor league stadiums in the country, so not nearly as fancy as the one in State College had been. But, it was neat, the way it was right in the middle of a regular neighborhood, with houses visible over the outfield walls. Old-fashioned ballparks were her *preference*.

The stadium didn't have a special area set aside for her, so she changed in an alcove off the trainers' room. Showering at the motel wasn't ideal, but it wouldn't be the end of the world, either. The clubhouse was pretty nice, and must have been renovated in the not-too-distant past, because the lockers and carpet were in very good shape.

During team stretch, some of the guys were full of tales about their adventures in State College, which she tuned out. It got pretty raunchy, and at one point, Dimitri said, "Knock it off, you frackin' morons!", before Marcus had a chance to say anything similar, albeit probably more formal.

On her way inside for a pre-game pitching meeting, the Crosscutters' public relations guy came over and introduced himself. He gave her details about the post-game press conference they were going to hold, and asked if she might be willing to meet with a Crosscutters personality known as the "Director of Smiles," and a few groups of Little Leaguers and some youth softball teams the next day, and possibly a similar event with local veterans the following day. She agreed— because, really, what else was she going to say?—and she didn't mind, anyway.

This was the first game the Retrievers would be playing against this team, so they really didn't have any solid information about the lineup. But Sawyer was a damned hard worker, and he had come up with high school or college film on quite a few of their hitters, so she was able to see which guy she would work high, because of his uppercut, a guy who bailed out too quickly on inside pitches, and other helpful tendencies. Marcus was going to be her catcher tonight, but Ramón was going to catch the next night, so he joined them in a small circle of padded folded chairs to go over everything. Of course, it didn't hurt that she could translate in both directions. Marcus did pretty well with baseball-related Spanish, but not in a way which captured nuances.

She was *determined* to do a better job of mental preparation and focusing tonight, and hoped that the media circus would be less elaborate. So, she fixed a Swiss cheese and mustard sandwich from the pre-game spread, grabbed a banana and a bottle of water—God, she was tired of bland, predictable food; no wonder she was never hungry anymore—and sat down at her locker, facing away from the rest of the room.

Earbuds didn't shut out enough sound, and she wished she had thought to bring a pair of good headphones with her, but they were back at the Wilkinses' house or had maybe been trashed during her "locker inventory"—she wasn't sure which. Regardless, she didn't have them. People were smart enough to know not to bother a starter before a game, but it was still too easy to hear almost everything else that was going on in the room.

When it was closer to game time, she would switch to get-pumped-up rock and roll—and, *especially*, movie soundtracks—but for now, she picked classical. Supposedly, they had done studies that found that students who listened to Mozart before tests scored higher than people who didn't, and maybe it would help her pitching? It certainly couldn't *hurt*.

When Sofia indicated that it was time to have her active stretching session, Jill nodded, turned off the music, and headed for the trainers' room. They were increasingly relaxed with each other, and Sofia had already figured out that she liked to have some work done on her wrist—the better to snap off curves—and that extra time on her hips was a good idea, too. Jill was also finding that she really maybe didn't like to talk much at all before starting, so when the session was over, she nodded her thanks, and Sofia nodded back, and held up an encouraging "You go!" fist.

One last trip to the restroom, and she returned to her locker, touched the dog tag, and then put on her game jersey and belt, and made sure that her cleats were tied in precisely the most supportive, yet comfortable, way. Last of all, she checked that her hair was secure, then put on her cap and tilted the brim ever so slightly to the left. Routine. It was all supposed to be about the routine.

When she picked up her glove and jacket, Marcus appeared in front of her locker, also ready to go. It had been easy to hear increasing rumbles from the fans for the past hour or so, and she assumed that it was going to be another standing-room-only crowd, along with a heavy press contingent.

Which it was, to the degree that she lost a step on her way out of the dugout, and damn near tripped.

"Just a walk in the park," Marcus said.

Which wasn't at all how she felt, but Jill nodded.

The dugout was completely open, with a small raised concrete ledge out front, while the bullpen was an exposed area along the left-field line, adjacent to a picnic deck, which was *crammed* with fans. They were excited, and noisy, and—mostly—happy to see her.

Even with security people and police officers posted in the general area, the crowd felt *so close*. Much *too* close.

She tipped her cap—camera shutters clicking everywhere—and then set her glove and jacket down on the grass just inside the foul line, before starting her regimen of jogging, sprints, and stretches. Bannigan had modified her routine since the first game she pitched, adding stretches that included more hip and torso rotation, and some high leg kicks.

He and Sawyer were standing nearby, watching, and Bannigan came out a couple of times to assist with some of the dynamic stretches, and to say things like "Nice and slow" and "Keep it easy."

The very fact that she was worried about her focus meant that her focus wasn't good enough. But, her warm-up went pretty well, even though her curveball felt less sharp than usual. Once she was finished, she looked for a little girl, tossed the baseball up to her, made sure she caught it safely, and then walked to the dugout with two security people and Sawyer on one side, and Marcus on the other.

Sawyer wanted her to stay with the four-seamer, two-seamer strategy, to whatever degree possible, and her primary goals were first-pitch strikes, showing enough command to keep tonight's umpire from jerking her around, and setting a good tempo. She *liked* to work fast, and last time out, she'd done far too much dithering.

The guys scored a run in the top of the first—mostly driven by Hector's hit-and-run single into right, which let Diaz advance to third and score on Scott's liner up the middle. It might be a *slim* lead, but it was nice to have, regardless, as she walked out to the mound.

The crowd reaction wasn't entirely positive, but it was damned good, considering that she was pitching for the visiting team. She felt a flash of nerves, and touched the dog tag chain for a second, to ground herself.

Since poor Geoff was presumably at home in Oregon, looking at months of rehab, Owen was playing third. After the ball went around the infield, he walked towards the mound, and then flipped it gently to her underhand.

He probably didn't mean anything by that—but it pissed her off, and she caught the ball with an impatient snap of her glove. Being annoyed overrode the nerves, and her first pitch—a low, inside two-seamer for strike one—had some serious *bite*, and late movement. Enough so that the batter stepped out of the box, and made a bit of a production of knocking dirt from his spikes, before digging in again.

And *zing*, went the strings of her heart, whenever she saw a hitter show some anxiety.

He was gone in four pitches, the last one intentionally in the dirt—but, he swung, and Marcus blocked it, and then tagged him smoothly, before throwing down to third.

The ball went around the horn, and Owen underhanded it to her *again*.

Which bugged her—again, and she got the next guy on an easy grounder to short.

She changed speeds enough on the third guy, so that while he got his bat on the ball, it was a little pop fly—which unfortunately fell into no-man's-land, in front of a hustling Schwartzman in right field.

Which meant that she had given up her first hit as a professional pitcher, and she spent enough time internally berating herself so that she stupidly left a ball up in the zone to the cleanup hitter, who pounded it into left-center.

She ran into foul territory, ready to back up third or the plate—but, Scott ran it down deep in the gap, making one of those catches that looked effortless, but were actually very difficult.

Whew, okay. She closed her eyes for a second, relieved to be out of the inning, and waited, so that she could smack her glove against his, on their way off the field.

"What happens when you leave the ball up like that?" Sawyer asked, as she came into the dugout.

"Your left fielder makes a highlight-reel catch!" Scott said cheerfully.

Hector laughed. "You didn't even leave your feet, dude. It doesn't count, if you don't get some air."

Scott stopped, and pointed up at the sky. "That sound you

hear? Angels singing. Because they can't believe what a *beautiful* line I took to the ball."

As far as Jill was concerned, she was one of the converted to whom he was preaching, when it came to that.

Sofia was strapping on her heat pack—she wasn't crazy about the heat pack; they might need to come up with something different for next time—while Sawyer talked to her about not letting her front shoulder fly open, maintaining her focus, and staying aggressive.

She gave up a ground ball single in the bottom of the second, but otherwise escaped unscathed, getting a double play, and then a nice called third strike on a changeup, which caught the hitter off balance.

As she walked towards the dugout, two frat-boy types came rushing up through the stands and threw a bunch of small white objects at her. She ducked, but also reflexively raised her glove to try and catch them.

Some of the objects pelted her, and she looked inside her glove to see—several tampons.

Tampons? *Really?*

Dimitri, Raffy, and Marcus were within a few feet of her, and looked equally startled.

Owen, who was jogging past them to the dugout, glanced at her glove and smirked. "Good hands," he said, and kept going.

"Those *assholes*," Dimitri said, and it looked like he might leap into the stands to go after them. But, security people were already on it and waved him off, while they escorted the two guys away—and she assumed that they were going to be thrown out of the ballpark.

There were about a dozen tampons scattered on the ground, and she started to bend down, but Marcus's hand closed around her arm.

"Leave them," he said, his voice even—but angry. "Someone else can take care of it."

He was right—it would not be dignified to scrabble around after a bunch of damn tampons.

Once she was in the dugout, she dumped the detritus in her glove into a big plastic trash can, resisting the urge to kick the can—or anything else she could find—as hard as she could.

"It was kind of funny," someone—she wasn't sure who—said tentatively.

"Yeah," she said. "It was a scream."

She still wanted to kick something, but instead, she slammed her glove and cap onto the bench, and then sat down.

Marcus took a seat next to her, and she could tell that his simmering was almost as close to a boil as hers was, but he didn't say anything.

Hector and Scott and Shosuke came over and sat on her other side—which she absolutely appreciated.

Sofia approached with a heat pack, and she was going to dismiss her, but Marcus shook his head. So, Jill let her wrap the thing on with the usual ACE bandage. When she was finished,

Sofia patted her on the *other* shoulder, and then went to check the hand—maybe he'd jammed a finger, when he got taken out during the double play—Diaz was holding in her direction.

The dugout, in general, was quieter than usual, but the team must have been fired up, because they scored six runs, and she went back out for the bottom of the third with a solid lead.

And, since *she* was pretty charged up herself, she set the side down easily, working off the changeup—which had *great* separation today, getting two easy grounders and a pop-up.

"Hey, Cafferty," the Crosscutters third base coach said, as she strode towards the dugout without looking at the stands.

She paused.

"*We* all thought that was bush-league, too," he said.

Which was good to hear, because it damn well *had* been.

CHAPTER 20

Her pitch count was low—she'd been very efficient—so, she was able to complete five innings, and left with an eight-run lead.

"Still pretty steamed?" Sofia asked, as they went back to the visiting clubhouse.

Jill nodded.

"Had a good effect on your pitching," Sofia said.

Probably, but that didn't mean that she wanted it to happen ever again.

Massage, ice, a flush ride on the stationary bike—and she was back out to the dugout in the bottom half of the seventh inning. Brumley—not Burney or Barney, as she'd thought—was pitching, and having another rough night, because five runs were in, and there were guys on first and third. But, he was able to get through the inning without any more damage, and the back end of the bullpen—including the ever-silent Andrew—finished out the game, which gave her first professional victory.

Yay.

The local GM and public relations person both apologized, at length, for the tampon thing, and she assured them that it was no big deal, and that she wasn't at all disturbed. A bunch of fans were gathered in the box seats, shouting things like, "We love you, Jill!" and she made a point of being approachable and agreeable, and signed autographs until she was summoned to the media room for a crowded press conference.

To her surprise, she saw Adler standing at the back of the room, with his arms folded, which seemed like an unexpectedly supportive thing for him to do. The GM gave a detailed statement during which he formally apologized for the behavior of the two fans, and said that he hoped she would not hold it against a baseball town with such a storied history, and she said, no, of course not, these things happen—and it all felt like a degrading waste of time, when she would much rather be inside the clubhouse, getting something mediocre from the post-game spread.

She knew the media people weren't going to ask much about the way she had actually *pitched*—and they didn't. But, when one of them wanted to know if she was going to file a criminal complaint against the two idiots, she was caught off guard, since that hadn't crossed her mind.

"Um, well, you know, it was just *paper products*," she said, and a few people laughed. "If I flip out every time I run across a couple of antediluvian"—Could she say "schmucks" to reporters? Probably not—"cretins, it could get pretty tedious."

"Would you like to describe some of the gender harassment and abuse you've experienced," someone asked. "For example, when your locker—"

Nope, she wasn't going there. "I'd rather focus on the fact that almost everyone has been extremely welcoming," she said. Should she throw Williamsport a Valentine? "I thought we had a great crowd here tonight, and I'm grateful for their support. I loved being able to play in a beautiful old stadium like this."

"Does anyone have a baseball question?" Adler asked, from the back of the room. "If not, I think it's time to call it a night."

There was a brief silence, a few murmurs, and then a couple of people managed to come up with questions that involved the *game*. Then, the PR guy took over, and she was able to escape.

Adler waited for her at the door, and they walked towards the clubhouse together.

"You doing okay, Cafferty?" he asked.

She nodded.

"Liked what I saw out there tonight," he said. "It's good to see *grit* in a ballplayer."

"Thank you, sir," she said.

The corner of his mouth noticeably jerked up for a second. "Sorry about the shower situation, but the boys are going to be antsy to get on the bus, anyway."

Since it had been an even longer press conference than usual.

The post-game spread had been pretty much demolished, which didn't thrill her, because by now, she was *hungry*. But, when she got on the bus, wearing her Penn State polo, Marcus motioned for her to sit next to him, and handed her a Gatorade and a Styrofoam takeout box with two pieces of now-cold pizza inside, as well as some napkins and an apple.

"No juice box?" she asked.

He just looked at her.

Sometimes, he really was humor-challenged. "Thank you, Marcus," she said.

He nodded. "That's better."

The first thing she did when she got back to the motel room was to take a very long and hot shower. She felt sweaty, and tired, and a lot achier than she usually was after a start. So, before she dug into her now-much-*more*-cold pizza, she took a couple of Advil.

Sofia, who was lying down on her bed and skimming through a thick file folder, noticed immediately. "Are you all right?"

"I threw *hard* tonight," Jill said. "I can feel it."

Sofia looked alert. "Are your shoulder and elbow okay?"

"Yeah," Jill said. "My muscles are just tired, in general." And achy as hell.

"We'll work on that tomorrow," Sofia said. "Try not to read half the night, for once, okay? You don't get enough sleep."

Not lately, no. But, she was hoping that the more worn-out she was, the less likely she would be to have violent nightmares on any given night. She had bad dreams at home, too, but it wasn't nearly as dislocating, when she was in her own bed, and she could pat Maggie until she felt better.

She *missed* Maggie. She missed everyone, of course—but it was too quiet and lonely, without Maggie.

People who knew her well had sent texts and left voice mails with some version of "Antediluvian cretins?!" in it. She was too exhausted to call anyone—even her family, but sent a number of reassuring texts back, before putting her phone away.

It was harder to fall asleep than she expected—and even more difficult to *stay* asleep. So, she ended up streaming three *Gilmore Girls* episodes on her iPad, under the covers and with earbuds on, to try and disturb Sofia as little as possible.

When it was time to get up, she felt very lethargic, but made it down to the motel's free hot breakfast buffet, before they shut down. Most of her teammates were already in there, and judging from the huge piles of food on their plates, they had been keeping the kitchen staff very busy.

Once she was at the ballpark, she got extensive treatment from Sofia, including about fifteen minutes of ultrasound on her shoulder and elbow. After that, she did a light workout with free weights and a medicine ball, and then some jogging in the outfield, as well as running up and down the steps in every single section of the stadium. Some of the guys were bitching that they had had much better facilities in college than they now had as pros, and it was probably true, but everything seemed fine to her.

She did a meet-and-greet on the concourse, with about a hundred Little Leaguers and softball players, almost all of whom wanted autographs and to have their photos taken with her. Since the guys were milling around, waiting to take BP, she waved at Scott to come join her, and he brought Hector and Diaz and Schwartzman with him.

Hector surprised her by being especially at ease with the kids—relaxed and funny, and so unruffled by the general clamor, that she wondered if he might end up as a *really* good middle school teacher someday. Scott was mostly goofy, and made faces in front of the cameras, which cracked the kids up, while Schwartzman was more inclined to be brusque and say, "Here, kid," after signing each autograph, and quickly turning to the next one. Diaz was as shy and quiet as ever, and responded to each child with nothing more than a soft "*Gracias*," no matter what they said to him.

During BP, Brumley—who had something of a lantern jaw, anyway, but looked even more hangdog than usual—slunk up next to her in the outfield.

"Sorry I almost fucked up your W last night," he said.

She shook her head—even though it was true. "You got out of the inning just fine," she said.

"Yeah," he said, sounding grim. "I'm real proud of myself."

The poor guy's ERA was in double-digits—and she had no idea what to say. He was a late-round senior sign out of Oklahoma, and so far, he seemed to be in *way* over his head. "It's baseball," she said. "There are always going to be ups and downs, right?"

He shrugged, looked glum, and went back to where he'd been standing before.

The next day, there was a luncheon for local veterans on the picnic deck, and after working out—which often felt like a *grind*, lately—she was more than happy to be brought up to meet them. It was mostly Vietnam-era veterans, with some from Desert Storm, Iraq, and Afghanistan sprinkled in, too. They might not all have been thrilled about the idea of a woman playing in the minors, but because of her father— she assumed—they were friendly and respectful and seemed to be pleased to meet her. And at least she knew enough to say "Thank you" and "Welcome home," although there were actually veterans who got annoyed by being thanked, and would only give a gruff "Just doing my job, ma'am" response.

She was particularly drawn to the four female veterans in the group, but she talked to each person individually, spending enough time with them so that Martinez, the hitting coach, finally came over as visitors' BP was about to start, and said, "Hey, Cafferty, do you still play for us?"

It wasn't as though she was lounging around in front of video games or something—but, he had a point. "I do, sir," she said. "I'll be right there, sir."

So, after some quick good-byes and more handshaking, she hustled to the clubhouse to get her glove, and joined the other pitchers in the outfield. She stood between Shosuke—who gave her his customary smile and small bow—and Andrew, who was about six-five, and had a distinctly courtly way about him. And he threw some *impressive* heat.

"Line drive?" Shosuke asked her, his pronunciation somewhat halting, as he pointed to a ball Scott had just hammered into right field.

She grinned at him. "A *smoking* line drive," she said, and made a whooshing movement with her arm, to indicate speed.

He grinned back. "*Smoking*," he said, and then ranged off to his left to catch a fly ball.

She glanced over at Andrew, who she could tell *wanted* to move elsewhere, but was much too polite to do so. "So. I gather that I owe you a thank you," she said.

Andrew looked anywhere *but* at her. "I got three outs against the bottom part of the order," he said, finally. "Nothing special. You did the heavy lifting."

"I'm glad you closed the game out, but I was actually

thanking you for taking my side in the clubhouse the other day," she said.

He had such short, light blond hair that it was easy to see his blush go all the way up into it.

"It was really nice of you," she said. Not necessary—but, *nice*.

He shrugged, looking as though he might jump out of his skin any second now.

"Don't worry, I won't keep bringing it up," she said. "I just wanted to thank you once."

"I didn't want to"—he frowned—"diminish your agency, but I was raised to believe that a gentleman doesn't stand by, when a woman is treated with disrespect."

Agency? Golly. "Did you major in women's studies?" she asked.

Instead of blushing this time, he went pale. "*No*," he said. "Economics. But, my cousin did, and she's—talkative—during the holidays."

And Andrew must have been *listening*. "I hope you didn't get hurt, when you—you know," she said.

Andrew's smile was—not to her surprise—bashful. "I was very angry," he said. "But, that didn't make me forget to protect my arm."

Second nature for pitchers, of course.

"I'm sorry about what those guys did during the game," he said.

The feminine protection shower. "If that's the worst thing fans do this season, I'll count myself lucky," she said.

"Well, the way you're handling it is impressive. I know *I* couldn't do it." He glanced over. "I've heard people say some terrible things."

She had learned an astonishing number of words used to describe—and denigrate—female genitalia, starting back when it had first become clear that she really *did* know how to pitch. The words were rarely shouted; more often, a person muttered, or even loudly whispered, them when she was in earshot. And, of course, sometimes they were written on her damn *wall*. It went without saying that almost all of the offenders were male. But, sometimes, women—or other high school girls—were the ones calling her a slut or whatever, which was always extra disturbing.

"I'm sorry they do that," he said. "It must hurt your feelings."

Actually, it did. She nodded, reaching out to catch a bouncing drive and flick it back towards the infield. "It makes me sad, that people feel as though they need to act that way. I don't really see the point."

He nodded, too—and possibly even shuddered. "I don't understand it, either."

Shosuke came loping cheerfully back with Javy—they'd been wrestling a little—and she taught both Andrew and Javy "*Kon'nichiwa*," and they all passed the rest of batting practice trying to teach one another simple phrases in three languages, while occasionally ambling off a few steps to field a ball.

There were worse ways to spend an hour on a summer day.

Around six o'clock, it started raining, and the tarp was pulled onto the field. This was the last time they were going to be in Williamsport this season, and so, it was a game the league *really* wanted them to play, if possible. They sat around in the dugout for a while, waiting, and then ended up going back to the clubhouse—to sit around some more. None of the starting players—especially Eduardo, who was pitching—were sure how much to eat, or *when* to eat, and there was a fair amount of grumbling and complaining.

Left to her own devices, she would have been fine with sitting at her locker and reading, but it felt antisocial. Scott waved her over to the table where he and Hector and a few other guys were playing cards, so she joined in. Except that she didn't know how to play Hearts, their current game, or Crazy Eights, or Spades—and when they tried to explain the various rules, she was almost immediately lost.

"Did you have a deprived childhood?" Scott asked.

"Well, we gambled heavily on poker, of course," she said, "but that was about it."

Dimitri shook his head. "No poker before a game—it's too hardcore, and people get pissed off."

Since he had been in the minors for about seven years, as a rule, they all took just about everything he said as baseball gospel.

"I bet you and your family spent a lot of time reciting poetry, and admiring art," Hector said.

This, coming from Mr. Privileged Palisades himself? "We rarely *recited* it," she said. "Mostly, we read the poems quietly to ourselves."

Hector grinned at her, and she couldn't help thinking that if he used hair product, he used it damn *well*. "'What do the simple folk do?'" he asked.

A Hollywood kid, with parents in the business, *would* be reliably good with musical references, wouldn't he? "We dance," she said. "We sing. We feel a deep connection with Mother Earth."

Hector was amused, and she could see Marcus smiling, as he stared down at film of opposing hitters on his tablet.

"C'mon already, what are we gonna play?" Danny asked impatiently.

"What do you know?" Scott asked her.

She had never cared for cards *or* board games. "Not much," she said. "War. Old Maid. Go Fish. That kind of thing."

None of her teammates who were listening seemed to know whether to laugh—or be deeply embarrassed for her.

"Go Fish, it is," Scott said, shuffled the cards, and began dealing.

Six of them played several hands, with increasing numbers of players gathering around to make unsolicited—and snarky— comments. Somewhere along the way, she motioned for

Shosuke to pull an extra chair over next to hers, so she could teach him how to play—which was easy, since he knew most of the English words for numbers, and really only had to memorize the words for aces, kings, queens, and jacks. Learning "Go Fish!" was no challenge at all, since half the team yelled it out every time someone requested a particular set of cards and was turned down. She got Diaz and Ramón to join the throng, and she and Raffy took turns teaching them the game, too.

"You're going down, Pretty Boy," she said to Hector, who was sitting across the table from her.

"I'm not pretty, Ladybug," Hector said. "I'm *dashing*. Crisp, black hair, dazzling smile—a classic Lothario."

Hunh. Sounded like a direct quote. "Are you writing a screenplay in your spare time?" she asked.

He hesitated. "No," he said, a beat too late.

Which was very funny.

"We got too many smart fuckers on this team," Danny said to Nathan, who was standing next to him. "We need a lot more dumb sonsabitches."

Scott looked up from his cards. "I'm a meathead, if that helps."

"A little, I guess," Danny said.

"Not enough," Nathan said.

It was her turn, and Jill looked at her cards—and the most likely opponent to query.

"Not the fours!" Dimitri said, as she got ready to make her

move. "You're doomed, if you ask for fours!"

She laughed, and asked Scott for fours, anyway—because she felt like it.

He didn't have any, of course, and most of the team shouted, "Go Fish!"

This was a room full of people who played a game for a living. A high silliness quotient was to be expected.

Bannigan—who had watched the card game for a while, before shaking his head and leaving the clubhouse—came back in. "Tarp's coming off," he said.

And with that, the card game was over, as Scott declared himself the Supreme Winner—an unearned honor—and everyone who was starting tonight headed for their lockers to get their gear and go outside to warm up, or into the training room to get re-taped or whatever.

Jill was surprised, when she got out to the dugout, right before the national anthem, that several hundred fans had waited around, even though the starting time had been delayed by almost two hours.

"Getting their money's worth," Jonesy said.

She nodded, although they might also just be die-hard baseball fans. But, the concession stands must have done some solid business during the delay.

By the end of the second inning, the game showed every sign of being a blowout—in their favor—and Eduardo was having a reasonably solid night, giving up three runs on five hits and a couple of walks. Unfortunately, poor old Brumley came in with a purely mop-up role—and gave up another six runs, which made her feel awful for the guy. Danny was the next reliever up, and managed to calm things down, and Andrew blew fastballs past every single hitter he faced—the guy routinely sat around ninety-nine miles an hour—and they came away with the victory.

At which point, it was almost midnight, and they had a *long* bus ride home to Pomeroy.

The post-game spread was mostly unsold items from the concession stands—hot dogs, hamburgers, and tired-looking french fries. The food was barely lukewarm, and she only got down about half a burger before giving up.

"Hop aboard, Lion," Adler said, when she went out to the bus, wearing her Penn State polo.

Louis and Sofia were bent over some reports, and Jill looked around the bus, trying to decide where to sit. Luckily, the seat next to Marcus was open, and he lifted his messenger bag from it to make room.

"Thanks," she said.

"I'm not a good bus sleeper," he said. "Will the iPad keep you awake?"

She shook her head. "I'm going to *try* to sleep, but I don't do very well, either."

Which put them in the minority, because before they even pulled out of the parking lot, it seemed as though at least half of the team and coaches were already out cold. Small screens flickered in some seats, but it was a safe bet that this was going to be a quiet ride.

She wasn't even *drowsy*, so she did some texting, and then popped onto Facebook for a while—where she used her mother's maiden name, instead of Cafferty, and wasn't friending *anyone* these days, other than people like Scott and Hector.

It didn't take long for the reading to bother her eyes, and she put her phone away. Jeremiah had been gently encouraging her to be more active on social media, and was hoping that she would start posting wry and charming things on Twitter or Instagram or whatever—but, it felt too much like invading her *own* privacy. He'd suggested that media relations could post things *for* her—and she had maybe been a tiny bit snappish when she indicated that *nothing* was ever to go out with her name on it, unless it came from her directly.

Marcus was staring at his screen, but she could feel from his rigid posture that he was frustrated.

"How's it going?" she asked, keeping her voice quiet, so she wouldn't bother anyone. She could hear the low, indistinct hum of a couple of other conversations nearby—along with a lot of snoring, and someone humming in a tuneless and annoying way. But, at least Reilly wasn't playing his damn guitar.

Marcus sighed. "It doesn't come naturally." He closed out the app, clicked off the iPad, and stuck it next to his armrest. "You seem to be very good at them."

"I have to work at it, but yeah," she said. "I like languages. And I want to work for an NGO someday, so it might come in handy."

"Doing what?" he asked.

Good question. "I'm not sure," she said. "For my Senior Project, I designed an organization that was supposed to help a small community become self-sustaining. So, I had to figure out things like clean water, food production, access to health care, a literacy program, products and services that could create income, and"— She must sound incredibly naïve and idealistic, and she felt her face flushing in the darkness. "Well, you know, stuff like that. I made up a Third World country, but I might rather work here somewhere, in a city, or a rural area, or something."

He laughed softly. "Would I be wrong if I said you sound more enthusiastic about *that*, than you ever do about baseball?"

No. He would not be. "It was fun," she said. "My friend Lauren is really into science, and the environmental impact of things, so she did her project about my community, too, but she was the one who was creating the technology we would use for the water supply and our crops and sanitation and all of that."

"I hope you got As," he said.

A *pluses*, in fact. "You know, we're going to need a good primary care doctor to open a practice there," she said.

Marcus laughed. "I'm sure you are. Seriously, though. What about baseball?"

Was she ever going to find a satisfactory answer to that question? "I don't know," she said. "I guess I'll play, until I don't play."

"Meaning *what*?" he asked.

She tried to think of an explanation that would make sense—to both of them. "When I'm actually *pitching*, I love it," she said. "And I like the practicing, and the thinking, and trying to perfect things, and the *team*, but—"

"But, if you were a guy, you wouldn't be here right now; you'd be getting ready to go away to school," he said.

She nodded.

Marcus glanced over at her. "Uneasy lies the head."

Maybe Danny was right, and they *did* need fewer intellectuals on the team. "Something like that, yeah," she said.

Or, maybe, *precisely* like that.

CHAPTER 21

"What about you?" she asked. "What are you going to do about med school?"

"I can't hit," Marcus said.

Jill didn't want to say the wrong thing, so she stopped for a moment to think. During BP, she and the other pitchers always got tense when he was in the batting cage, because they *wanted* his hitting to sound the way Scott's did. "Well," she said, "I think—"

He raised a hand to cut her off. "Please don't insult my intelligence by telling me that you disagree."

"You never have *time* to work on hitting, because you're so focused on us," she said. "I mean, when you're having meetings with Sawyer and a pitcher, Scott and the other guys are somewhere hitting off a tee."

He shook his head. "I couldn't hit in the SEC, either. Couldn't catch up to the good fastballs, and forget about breaking stuff. But, most of our pitchers were head cases, and I could handle *that*, so they kept me busy."

"You wouldn't have gotten drafted, if you weren't a great player," she said.

"I was a great player in *high school*," he said. "But, I'm a solid catcher, and I can work with"—he glanced sideways at her—"complicated pitchers, so I'm a nice organizational guy for them. And for me, it's an interesting summer, before I have to buckle down and focus on school again."

Organizational guy. Roster filler. Marginal prospect. The terrible descriptions no minor league player ever wanted to hear—even though the overwhelming majority of them fell *into* the category. "I'd be happy to throw you curveballs all day long, if you think it would help," she said.

He laughed quietly. "First of all, I'm not about to let you throw your arm out. But, the truth is, I don't think I can hit *Avila's*, so believe me, I wouldn't be able to get anywhere *near* yours."

Avila was a rarely used bullpen guy, whose knuckle curve didn't have much more than a little wrinkle.

"But thank you," he said.

They rode in silence for a few minutes. It was raining now, and Jill found herself hoping that Stan, the driver, was super alert, and that the bus tires were in good shape.

"I figured out freshman year that I wasn't the player I'd hoped I was, so it was a good surprise when the Pirates took me, but—" He let out his breath. "My girlfriend has made it clear that she *wants* me to fail, and—well, I have to say that that's really been bothering me lately."

Jill was determined not to feel a private twinge of disappointment that he had a girlfriend, since it wasn't as though they were ever going to date, or that she'd even vaguely considered the idea—but, okay, she felt a small painful jolt inside. "What makes you think that?" she asked.

"She didn't want me to sign," he said. "My plan was to go home and spend the summer working as an EMT, and then head up to Johns Hopkins in the fall. But, when I got drafted, I guess I couldn't resist trying. So, there's been a stream of 'I can't wait until you get this ridiculous baseball stuff out of your system' and oh, my favorite one, 'Why are you wasting your time?'"

The girlfriend certainly sounded like a treat. "Is she a hometown person, or did you meet her at college?" she asked.

"Vanderbilt," he said. "We got together sophomore year. I mean, she's great—she's brilliant, she's beautiful, she's *interesting*. But, baseball has always been a real sore point for her."

Even though it was something her boyfriend *loved* to do? "Is she going to come and see you play?" Jill asked.

Marcus shook his head. "I don't think so. She got a

fellowship to go to Italy on an archeological dig, so she's over there right now. Then, she'll be going to Yale to grad school."

"Not medicine?" she asked.

"A doctorate in medieval studies," he said.

So, she probably *was* brilliant.

The bus was pulling off the highway now, into a rest stop. Not everyone on the bus woke up, but the people who did—as ever—fumbled their way outside to go to the restrooms, get some food at Burger King, or both.

Jill wasn't really hungry—*again*—but, seeing a Dunkin' Donuts franchise inside gave her a happy little pang of familiarity, and she ordered a regular decaf and a couple of plain donuts. Donuts were *big* in Rhode Island. Allie's was the best place in the state, but they were all pretty fond of Dunkin' Donuts, too. *Any* donuts, for that matter.

They were still a few hours away from Pomeroy, so she downloaded the same Japanese language app Marcus was using, and they spent about an hour going over basic conversational phrases—as quietly as possible. Somewhere along the line, she gave him one of the doughnuts, and then, she managed to doze off for most of the last ninety minutes of the drive.

When she opened her eyes, she was mortified to realize that she had fallen asleep on his shoulder, and that it felt—cozy. Quickly, she sat up, hoping that no one—including Marcus— had noticed. He *seemed* to be asleep, but she couldn't tell for sure.

In any case, she rubbed her face to try and wake up, and

then started checking texts on her phone, being careful to keep a respectful few inches of space between them for the rest of the ride.

When they got to the stadium, it occurred to her that she had no idea how she was going to get to her host family's house. Some of the guys on the team had cars, and she thought Sofia did, too, so maybe she could get a ride from someone.

But, it was a pleasant surprise to see Mrs. Wilkins standing in the parking lot, waiting for the bus to arrive, even though it was barely six-thirty in the morning. There were other host families there, too, and she wondered if it was a requirement, when people took players in for the summer. Since the base pay was so low in the minor leagues, the front office had to assume that almost none of them had personal transportation.

Nicky, the clubbie, was there to unload the bus, which made her feel horribly pampered, but no one else seemed to be giving it a second thought.

"It's okay that we don't help you do this?" she asked, just to be sure.

He nodded, piling gear bags onto a metal cart with wheels. "When you come back to the field later, find me or Terence, and we'll give you your key," he said.

"What key?" she asked.

"The door to your, um, you know, *room* has a new lock," he said.

Which brought her right back to a reality she had managed

to put aside, mostly, while they were on the road. But, okay, now she had a lock. It was what it was, right?

"Stretch at two o'clock," Adler said, to the team in general. "Go home and grab some rest."

That was good, since everyone looked damn tired.

"Over here, Jill!" Mrs. Wilkins said.

Jill nodded, and waved back. "Anyone else need a ride?" she asked.

"Don't worry about it," Dimitri said. "I've got plenty of room in my car, and Mother can take a few people, too."

So, she headed over to where Mrs. Wilkins and her husband were waiting. She had only met him once in passing, so Mrs. Wilkins reintroduced her. They wanted her to call them Connie and Horace—but, that probably wasn't going to come easily for her.

Mrs. Wilkins seemed to be perpetually chatty and outgoing, but she had no sense whatsoever of Mr. Wilkins, other than that he golfed, and that her mother liked it that he was a retired police officer, since she thought that upped the safety aspects of the host home considerably. So far, Jill hadn't seen any evidence that fans—or reporters—were eager to find out where she was living and plague her—but, if they did, Mr. Wilkins would probably know how to handle it.

When they got to the house, Mr. Wilkins went back to bed, and Jill stood in the kitchen, holding her knapsack and the small plastic laundry bag she'd gotten at one of the motels, where she had packed—unsurprisingly—her laundry.

"Would you like some breakfast?" Mrs. Wilkins asked. "Or just to go to sleep?"

She was kind of hungry, but—"I'll do that, if you don't mind," Jill said. "I'm pretty tired."

"What time do you have to be back at the field?" Mrs. Wilkins asked.

"I'd like to get there around one, if that's okay," Jill said.

"Of course," Mrs. Wilkins said. "I can have some lunch ready to go, if you want. Is there anything you don't like?"

"No, I'm sure whatever you have will be—" Jill stopped, since that wasn't true. "Well, actually, I don't care for tuna fish."

Mrs. Wilkins nodded, and pretended to write that down. "Got it!" she said, sounding very jolly.

After thanking her profusely for the replacement road trip care package, Jill made her way downstairs. There was some mail on one of the twin beds, including a priority package from her mother, which would be her polo shirts. It would be a relief to wear ones she liked, and maybe retire the Penn State shirt, although she could always keep it as a spare. Then again, it reminded her of that jerk Aaron Marshak—so, maybe she would just toss it.

There were some yogurts in the mini-fridge in her room, but she had to go upstairs to get a spoon.

Mrs. Wilkins was sitting at the table, drinking coffee—and reading what looked like a Bible. "It's no trouble at all to fix you something," she said.

Probably, but she would feel shy sitting there, and what if they didn't have anything to talk about? It might just be painful and awkward. "Oh, I'm fine, thank you," she said. "But, it's very nice of you."

Feeling lonely, sitting on a twin bed, eating a yogurt, wasn't ideal, of course—but, it seemed better than feeling shy and self-conscious in front of someone she didn't know.

Somehow, she felt more out of place and unfamiliar in someone's *home*, than she had felt in the motels on the road trip. She was technically supposed to *live* here, and everything seemed so strange.

And God, did she miss Maggie. Daily. Nightly. *Endlessly.* Maggie almost always slept on Jill's bed, and these days, Jill had to lift her up gently, since it was hard for her to jump up there by herself. Sometimes, Maggie was restless or had bad dreams, and once in a while, she seemed to be afraid of being up so high, even though she'd slept on their beds her entire life. When that happened, Jill would ease her onto a specially padded arthritis dog bed on the floor, and bring down a couple of pillows and a blanket, so she could sleep next to her.

Thinking about Maggie was just going to make her sad. In fact, thinking about *anything* related to home might make her cry, so she carefully set the priority mail box and a few cards from relatives on the desk, to open later. Besides, she had been up almost all night—she needed to try to get some sleep, if she wanted to be functional at the ballpark. At least she wasn't pitching tonight, but she *was* scheduled to throw a side session and would need to have enough energy to do a good job.

So, she rinsed the spoon and the yogurt cup in the bathroom sink, and changed into a URI T-shirt and shorts. She would have to pretend that it was *normal* to go to bed in the morning—and it wasn't like she hadn't stayed up late lots of times. So, maybe all of this wasn't as different as it seemed.

Maybe.

The bed was pretty comfortable, but the pillows were way too soft. They smelled different, too. Not bad, just—different.

She was really tired, but couldn't seem to fall asleep, no matter how hard she tried. Everything felt too—foreign. Sounds, scents, the way the light came in around the edge of the curtains.

Not to belabor the point, but at home, she almost *never* had trouble falling asleep, and if she did, she could pat Maggie, or go downstairs and get a snack, or sit on the porch for a while or something. So, being here—and *not* being there—really sucked.

She closed her eyes and took some slow, deep breaths— which accomplished nothing whatsoever. Hector was such a California boy, that he was big on meditating, so she might need to get him to teach her how. For now, maybe she should give up on sleeping, and just read? And try to grab a pre-game nap somewhere?

She reached over to check her phone, and saw that it was

almost eight, and her mother would definitely be up. So, she texted, "Is Maggie okay? I'm worried about her." Within about five minutes, her mother had texted back a video of Maggie in the kitchen, her head in her bowl, and her tail waving, as she ate some breakfast.

Jill was relieved, but it made her miss home even more. Which her mother must have figured out, because her phone promptly rang.

"Just getting up?" her mother asked.

"No, we were on the bus all night, so I'm trying to sleep now, but—" She lowered her voice. "They're really nice and all, but I don't like it here."

Her mother didn't answer right away. "Is it them, specifically, or being with a host family, in general?"

"I don't know," Jill said. "Both, maybe? I don't know."

"They seem like awfully nice people," her mother said. "And I'm sure they're used to hosting players who feel a little shy."

A *little* shy? "What if I decide I just hate all of this too much?" Jill said. "How long do I have to give it?"

There was another pause. "Longer than this," her mother said.

"Yeah, but—" Except that her mother rarely spent *that* much time choosing her words, so it was fishy. "Have you been reading articles, about what to do when your kid calls up, and is all homesick and everything?" Jill asked.

Her mother laughed. "Yes, actually. In fact, I'm not supposed to share how much I miss *you*, so I am going to make a point of not doing that."

Okay, maybe that was funny. "Oh, well played," Jill said.

"I'm going to try to help guide you towards creating problem-solving strategies, *without* telling you what to do in any way, even though it goes against the grain," her mother said.

Yeah, that was funny, too. Jill smiled, in spite of herself. "So that I can feel the pride of, you know, making my own decisions, and being independent?"

"Yes," her mother said. "Have you been reading articles, too?"

Just maybe, yeah. She felt better, until she hung up, and was sitting there again, by herself, looking around the empty room. Should she call back? Or call someone else? Or read until she fell asleep?

She picked the latter, and alternated between reading and nodding off, until it was time to get up, take a shower, and head over to the stadium.

Mrs. Wilkins had made roast beef sandwiches on homemade bread, served with chips that were also made by hand, and pickles and fresh lemonade—which were all delicious. Mr. Wilkins had just gotten home from a round of golf, and Jill bowed her head, while he said grace.

She said, "Yes, sir," when he asked her if she had slept well—and pretty much told brief, stilted lies in response to any questions either of them asked, although she was telling the truth when she said that the sandwiches were really good. And those still-warm homemade potato chips had been fantastic.

It was a relief to get to the ballpark, except for the part where she had to deal with going into her dressing room. But, Terence appeared with her key, and went in with her, showing her the new locker, freshly issued workout and other gear, new Pirates shower shoes, a pair of pristine—and unfamiliar—turf shoes in her size, a row of unused toiletries lined up on the top shelf, and so on. The room had even been repainted, and was now light blue, and everything had been rearranged slightly, too.

"Um, looks good," she said, when she realized that he was waiting for her reaction. "I mean, thank you. Great job!"

Terence grinned with one side of his mouth, with a rakish quality she hadn't noticed before. "I'm totally embarrassed, too," he said. "You don't have to pretend you're not."

Good. Because she sure as hell was. With luck, none of it would ever have to be mentioned again. According to Lauren and Greg, it had been getting some attention on the Internet, but the reporters had pretty much given up, once it was clear that they couldn't get her to answer any questions.

Mr. Russo must have been summoned while they were out of town, too, because when she changed into a new T-shirt and shorts, she could tell that they had already been altered. He was, once again, very good, because they no longer flapped foolishly, but still felt loose enough to move in.

There were several large plastic bins stacked in the corner of the room, each of them full of new fan mail. Was she supposed to answer *all* of them? By herself? What an exhausting prospect.

She picked up a random envelope, and saw that it had already been opened, which she assumed Jeremiah and the interns had done, so that they could check them first, and make sure that there wasn't anything—disturbing.

Which she might ask him about—or she might *not*. It might be better to remain oblivious.

When she walked into the clubhouse, it was noisier than usual, and the energy felt—different, somehow. Charged up, and a little ragged. Someone seemed to be holding court, and she wasn't thrilled when she recognized Caleb Kordell, the number one pick. She'd heard that he had stepped up negotiations and was on the verge of signing, right after Texas A&M got knocked out of the College World Series, but she had foolishly been hoping that he would be assigned to the Gulf Coast League— even though she knew better. They were probably bringing him along slowly, though, because of the labrum, she assumed.

She looked around until she caught Scott's eyes, and he pantomimed dropping a noose around his neck and hanging himself.

Yeah, that's about how where she was, too.

Now, Caleb noticed her. "Hey, Cafferty," he said. "You haven't been released yet?"

Well, the day wasn't over. "Nice to see you again," she said, dropping her knapsack into her locker.

"Just be ready to step up your game," Caleb said. "Don't want to be left in my dust."

Yeah, she would be sure to get right on that. At least his locker wasn't next to hers. As she was saying hello to Shosuke and Javy, Scott came over and commandeered her folding chair.

"Number One finally signed," he said.

She nodded. "Lucky us."

"And Brumley got cut, and Nathan got sent down to the GCL," Scott said.

Whoa. "Cut, like *gone*?" she said.

Scott nodded.

Wow. Just like that? She knew baseball was a ruthless business, but seeing it in action was still kind of shocking. Nathan hadn't gotten much playing time, so they probably had wanted him to go to a team where he would get more work in. But, poor Brumley.

She saw that Nathan's locker had been cleaned out, Eduardo had been moved over to Brumley's former locker, and Caleb had taken over Eduardo's spot, between Jonesy and Marcus.

"Did Eduardo get bumped to the bullpen?" she asked.

Scott shrugged. "Looks that way. I'm not sure."

She asked Javy in Spanish, and he nodded.

It was awful, but she had a "Thank God it wasn't me!" thought, and based on their expressions, as they all covertly looked at Eduardo, she was pretty sure that Javy and Shosuke felt the same way.

Caleb was loud during team stretch, too, bragging about this and that, although she made a concerted effort not to pay attention. At one point, a couple of people glanced at her, and she tuned in just enough to hear that he was going on about some "chick" he had "nailed," and how he pitched better when he "got some"—and so on and so forth. A few guys joined in, and the whole conversation was considerably more crass than usual, although Bannigan yelled at them to focus on the *work*.

Caleb wasn't the first jerk she was going to have to play with—and he wouldn't be the last—but, she definitely wasn't looking forward having him be here.

At all.

CHAPTER 22

Naturally, Caleb was very vocal during PFP, too—and quick to shout, "Way to go, Cafferty!" when she managed to drop the ball *and* stumble over the bag, while trying to cover first on one play.

Jonesy was similarly inept on the next play—and grinned at her when he got back in line, so she knew he had done it on purpose.

"Thank you," she said.

"Be a duck, Ladybug," he said. "Let the rain roll right off your back."

That was good advice, and she tried very hard to concentrate solely on the drills—and *not* to notice that Caleb mocked her mistakes much more harshly than he did anyone else's.

When it was time for her bullpen, she walked out there with Marcus. Ramón would be catching her, but as far as she could tell, Marcus was incapable of letting any of the pitchers on the staff do anything without him either helping directly, or closely observing.

"Poor Brumley," she said.

Marcus nodded. "I think Adler did it this morning, after everyone else took off from the bus. At least, it was easier on the guy's pride."

The rumor was that when someone got released, a coach came into the clubhouse and said, "The manager wants to see you," and the player would have to go and get the ax right then and there, with everyone else trying to avoid making eye contact. If it ever happened to her, she hoped like hell that she wouldn't instantly burst into tears.

Even if they turned out to be tears of gratitude.

"So, they just give you a ticket home, and that's it?" she said.

"More or less," Marcus said. "Some guys get picked up by other organizations, or maybe give independent ball a try. But, I think most people go home and try to figure out what their new lives are going to be."

It would be hard for anyone, but especially the players who truly lived and breathed baseball, and didn't have any backup plans. She was pretty sure that Brumley had been one of those guys.

When it was time for her side session, she had been

hoping that Caleb would be busy down in the weight room or something, but no such luck—he was hanging out by the bullpen to watch, while blowing obnoxiously large bubbles with his gum.

The best idea was probably to think of him as a garden-variety heckler in the stands—and go out of her way to ignore him. But, it was hard, with him snapping the damn gum every other second, as though he was *trying* to throw her off.

Sawyer had her working from the stretch again, and today, they were spending part of the time incorporating a slide-step, too. Which felt awkward, and noticeably threw off her command.

"No, here, try it this way," Sawyer said, and moved her position.

She'd never needed a slide-step in high school, and it felt more like playing catch, than *pitching*. It was hard to maintain her regular velocity, and Sawyer had to keep suggesting adjustments and refinements—which amused the hell out of Caleb, and seemed to unnerve the organization's minor league pitching coordinator, who was observing today, presumably having come to Pomeroy to see Caleb's session later on.

"She seriously doesn't know how to do a fuckin' slide-step?" Caleb said, to no one in particular, although the pitching coordinator looked tense.

"Your bullpen's at four, Kordell," Sawyer said, without even looking up. "Until then, I don't want to see your face."

Caleb laughed. "Yeah, I can tell that she's sensitive," he said, and jogged off into the outfield.

Jill didn't let out an actual sigh of relief—but, it was tempting. And she pitched a hell of a lot better during the rest of her session, so the pitching coordinator was probably relieved, too. In any case, he looked more relaxed, and was taking fewer notes.

When she finished up, nobody commented on her obvious inability to concentrate, in front of a certain draft pick, although Ramón touched his ear, and shook his head at her. She nodded, since she didn't want to get a reputation for having rabbit ears. She was a professional; she needed to be able *not* to hear things.

Sofia was down in the weight room, helping Dimitri with some back rehab exercises—the poor guy had some issues there that just wouldn't quit. So, Louis did her post-session stretch and massage, and then packed her up with ice. The two of them weren't exactly pals yet, but they were learning how to work with each other in a productive and businesslike way, and she really couldn't ask for more than that.

When she went back outside to do some running, it was almost time for Caleb's first bullpen, and Adler and Mr. Brayton and Mrs. Doshi and some other front office people had joined the pitching coordinator to observe the session. She was damned if she was going to stand there and watch, too—but, she maybe lingered nearby, and she wasn't the only pitcher to do so. Several of the others were outright leaning on the side of the bullpen, not trying to hide their interest.

Caleb had the ideal big power pitcher body—he was about six-four, and at least two hundred and twenty pounds, and he moved with *supreme* confidence. The ball was really popping every time it hit Marcus's glove—and she could see Sawyer and the coordinator guy nodding with approval, and maybe even *excitement*.

She didn't like looking at his mechanics—the idea of using her elbow that way made her cringe—and his leg kick looked constricted, but the pitches were *great*. Speed, movement, location. A slider, instead of a curve, and he seemed to be throwing a cutter, in lieu of a two-seamer.

Except, of course, she wasn't paying close attention.

When she saw him wrapping up, she made sure that she was running in the outfield—and away from his probable preening range. He swaggered off, deep in conversation with Sawyer and the pitching development coordinator, while Marcus, Ramón, and the third-string catcher, Jackson, trailed behind. Once they were all down by the dugout, she jogged over to Andrew, who had been one of the bullpen onlookers.

"How good is he?" she asked.

Andrew looked surprised, as always, to have someone engage him in direct conversation. "He's a legitimate first rounder," he said. "Some giddy-up on the heater." He shrugged. "I saw him in the Super Regionals when we were both sophomores, and he's a lot better now."

Damn. It was going to be annoying if he backed up all of the talk with his performances. Hard to miss how happy the front office people looked, though.

And she did not, in fact, know how to do a slide-step properly.

Before changing into her home uniform, she took the time to call both Lauren and Greg—who were nice enough to commiserate about the Arrival of Caleb, and just generally be sympathetic and supportive. And Lauren complained about how much she hated physical therapy, and Greg was moping about some URI guy at the gym who he had finally gotten up the nerve to ask out—after they had been flirting for *weeks*— only to get abruptly and unkindly shot down.

So, they were possibly the three most glum eighteen-year-olds who had ever lived—but, it was still nice to talk to them.

She had no game responsibilities that night—she would be charting tomorrow—so she hung out up at the railing with Javy and Ramón and an infielder named Juan who rarely got to play, all of them speaking in an idiosyncratic mix of English and Spanish. Mostly, they talked about food, which made her hope that the post-game spread would be something remotely enticing.

She did pay attention to the Aberdeen hitters, since she would be starting against them on Friday. The lineup seemed to be a pretty polished group—more so than usual—and Dimitri, who wasn't playing, told her that a lot of them were holdovers from the previous season and, accordingly, very comfortable with life in the New York–Penn League. Her team had some second-year players, too—Eduardo, Jonesy, Vincent, Jackson, and Owen, among others—but, Aberdeen seemed to have at least twice as many.

Dimitri hated to talk about anything involving his injuries, but it didn't seem right not to mention it at all.

"How's the back?" she asked, able to see that he was favoring it, even though he *seemed* just to be relaxing against the railing.

"It's all right," he said, staring straight ahead. "Long bus ride last night, that's all."

She had been pretty stiff herself this morning, so being crammed into a small seat for hours must have been even harder on him. But, it was obvious that he didn't want to discuss it, so she just made a sympathetic sound and turned her attention to the field.

After the game, a lot of fans were waiting for autographs, so she stopped to sign as many as possible. There were Pirates hats, and T-shirts and jerseys with the number twenty-eight on them everywhere—and *so many* of the people wearing them were little girls, which was cool. The merchandising and licensing were still being worked out, according to her aunt and the new associate at her firm who was going to be handling most of that, but MLB had already created a line of clothing with female baseball player silhouettes—although they had ponytails or long hair hanging down, so it was considered a *generic* player. The fact that she was the only one currently active professionally was, no doubt, an absolute and complete coincidence, and not relevant in any way, especially financially. This situation was displeasing her aunt a great deal, but Jill, personally, found it more irritating that far too many of the shirts she'd seen during the past few weeks were *pink*.

Signing was always tiring, but she was learning how to drift along the stands, keeping a slight distance away, moving closer when she saw kids, and making an effort just to glide past, if it was a crowd dominated by adults.

When she was the only player left on the field, she kept signing for the group closest to the dugout, but glanced at Jeremiah's intern, Paul, for a second.

"Jill, they need you down in the clubhouse," he said, too loudly.

Not really subtle, but with luck, no one had noticed. "Okay, thank you," she said, and smiled at the people for whom she was signing. "Let me finish up here, and I'll be right down."

She autographed a very beat-up Little League baseball, and then someone handed her a business card.

To sign? No, maybe it was yet another agent, or—she glanced at the person, who was a very tan woman in her twenties, with spiky blonde hair. Her name was unfamiliar, and her listed job seemed to be at an IT company. The woman pantomimed for her to turn the card over, and Jill was puzzled to see a phone number written there.

The woman winked at her.

Whoa. *Now*, she got it. She tried to hand the card back, feeling a little panicky, and the woman just smiled, waved it away, and winked again before fading back into the crowd.

For lack of a better idea, she handed the card to Paul—who didn't seem to know what to do with it any more than she did.

She signed another baseball and a scorecard, then waved politely, and slipped into the dugout.

Once they were in the tunnel, Paul held out the card.

"Here," he said.

"Keep it," she said.

He grinned. "Giving me your castoffs?"

Was that really what he thought? She shook her head, and moved past him.

"Do you get a lot of propositions?" he asked.

Usually, it was older men, being smugly insinuating, and she would pretend not to see or hear them. In high school, she had sometimes been too innocent, and the first time a man offered to give her some "private help," she thought he actually meant with her *pitching*. Luckily, a couple of her older teammates had overheard—and roughly sent him on his way, and she had gotten much better at avoiding situations like that. Women had sometimes been flirtatious, too, but since tonight's approach had caught her so off guard, it was entirely possible that she got other come-ons—and didn't always pick up on it.

"I'm not sure," she said. "Sometimes, maybe?"

He frowned at her. "You can't tell?"

Did she have to be an expert on *everything*? "Well, when people are overt, I guess," she said. "I don't know."

"Go out and have a drink with her or something," he said. "She might be nice."

Jill tilted her head, not sure whether he was kidding. "Um, I think her intent was to get together with a fellow lesbian."

"Yeah," he said. "And—?"

"So, it might have been disappointing to spend time with *me*," Jill said.

"Oh," he said, and looked startled. "Okay."

Yet another person who didn't think she was straight? Supposedly, Princeton was hard to get into—but, maybe he was a legacy. "Sorry if that ruins your day," she said.

"No, not at all," he said, and grinned. "That means I still have a shot."

Which wasn't the response she had expected, and she turned to look at him curiously, as Jeremiah came down the tunnel.

"There you are, Jill," he said. "I have a couple of local affiliates waiting for you, if you don't mind giving them a few words?"

She was tired, and didn't feel as though she would have anything interesting to say, but she nodded and followed him down to the media room.

And tried *not* to think about whatever her mother and Theo

had had for supper tonight, and how nice it would have been to be *there*, instead of here.

No, that never even crossed her mind.

By the time she was finished, the post-game spread had been entirely ravaged, and the leftovers did not look appealing. It appeared to have been some kind of taco casserole, served with mixed vegetables, and Fritos. All of which had probably tasted fine, but the remaining scraps weren't worth the trouble.

The glitz and glamour of professional baseball, rearing its head yet again.

Mr. and Mrs. Wilkins were kindly waiting outside the players' entrance to drive her back to their house. As far as she could tell, being a host family included some fairly arduous demands—especially because they had to wait even *longer*, when another group of fans gathered around for autographs.

When she finally made it over to the car, she wasn't sure she had enough energy even to open the door to the backseat.

"I'm sorry it took so long. I didn't expect to be in the media room tonight," she said.

Mrs. Wilkins gave her a happy smile. "Jeremiah sent that nice young intern out to let us know."

"I should probably text you," Jill said, "when I'm running late. I know this is pretty inconvenient."

"We're happy to wait," Mrs. Wilkins said. "We *love* being at the ballpark."

Mr. Wilkins grunted his agreement, as he pulled out of the parking lot.

Even so. "It seems like a lot of work, though," Jill said. "And isn't it hard, not having privacy?"

"We've been doing it for *years*," Mrs. Wilkins said. "Ever since our kids left home. We like having young people around. During the school year, we usually host exchange students, too."

There was no question that they were generous people who enjoyed helping others. "What if the person staying with you is, I don't know, surly?" Jill asked.

"Oh, they're always great," Mrs. Wilkins said. "Some of them are a little quiet, especially the youngsters from other countries, but we enjoy each and every one of you."

She didn't seem like the kind of person who would give a dishonest answer, so Jill decided to take her word on that.

"There was that one kid," Mr. Wilkins said.

Mrs. Wilkins winced. "Oh, yes. But, that poor thing didn't adjust very well, and it didn't last long."

That sounded ominous. "You mean, you kicked him out?" Jill asked.

Now, Mrs. Wilkins chuckled. "Of course not. But, baseball really wasn't a good fit for him, and he got released."

Without even knowing who he was, Jill felt sorry for him. "They cut one of the other pitchers this morning," she said. "He was a nice guy."

Mrs. Wilkins turned in her seat to look at her. "I'm so sorry! Was he a good friend?"

Not exactly, but— "Well, I *knew* him, and—I don't know," Jill said. "It was sad. He rode home on the bus with us last night, and today, he was just *gone*."

"Part of baseball," Mr. Wilkins said. "Had a season in the Cubs organization myself."

She hadn't known that—and might not have guessed, since he was, um, substantial, and it was hard to see the ex-athlete in him. "What position did you play?" she asked.

"First base, and corner outfield," he said, and glanced at her in the rearview mirror. "I was much thinner then."

"Yes, sir," she said, hoping that he hadn't read her mind.

"I made it through the first season, but they cut me early on in spring training the next year," he said.

"I'm sorry," she said. "That must have been disappointing."

He shrugged. "It's okay. I liked being a cop."

"How did you two meet?" Jill asked.

"He arrested me," Mrs. Wilkins said.

That was a joke, right? She checked Mrs. Wilkins's expression, to be sure, and then relaxed. "Well, that's a good story for your grandchildren," she said.

Mrs. Wilkins laughed. "And don't we tell it to them that way, every single time!"

"I met her in the ER one night, when we came over with some MVA victims," Mr. Wilkins said. "Connie was the best nurse they ever had over there."

"Oh, hush," Mrs. Wilkins said fondly.

"You *were*," he said. "That place has never been the same, since you retired."

"You do go on, Horace," Mrs. Wilkins said, and they smiled at each other.

They were extremely nice people. She wasn't sure how much common ground they were going to be able to find, or if she would ever really feel comfortable living in someone else's house, but her mother was right—as host families went, she could definitely have done worse.

A lot worse.

CHAPTER 23

Her next start was two days later, and she tried very hard to keep to the game-day routine she was developing—even though she still wasn't completely sure what she wanted her routine to *be*. So far, it was mostly trial and error. When to eat, when to relax quietly, when to start getting psyched up. The pre-game strategy session went fine, and so did her stretching with Sofia, and her on-field warm-ups.

But, for some reason, once she was in the bullpen, she didn't feel right. Her fastballs weren't crisp, her location was terrible, and when she tried to throw a curve, it spun ineptly, instead of breaking.

"You're pressing," Sawyer said. "Just throw easy, stay with your delivery."

Jill nodded, focusing on her arm-slot, with the hope that if she got that right, everything else would fall into place. By the time her warm-up was over, she felt a *little* more smooth, but still not like her normal self.

"Forget about it," Marcus said, once she had put her jacket on, and they were walking towards the dugout. "What happens in the bullpen doesn't have anything to do with the game. You'll be fine once you get out there."

Maybe. "I feel—off," she said.

Sawyer looked at her sharply. "You have any injuries you're not telling me about?"

She shook her head. "No. I just—I don't know. I'm off-kilter, somehow."

"Mother's right, you'll be okay," Sawyer said. "Bear down when you get out there."

She nodded and looked around for a little girl in a convenient spot next to the field. But, she couldn't find one, so she handed her warm-up baseball to an eager small boy, instead. Just as she did it, she wondered whether she was putting the whammy on herself, by changing her routine—but, no, that was stupid, and she smiled at the boy, before continuing on her way.

The national anthem was sung by a local school choir, and once again, a cluster of children joined her on the mound, although this time, there were five girls, and two boys—all of whom were vociferously excited. But, she did a decent job of keeping them under control, and Jeremiah and Paul were quick to guide them off the field once the anthem was over.

Her warm-up tosses were somewhat better, so maybe it had just been a lousy bullpen. And with the game starting, she had an utterly clean slate.

Which almost immediately turned into an ugly slate. The first batter hit a sharp single on a fastball with almost no movement, and the next guy doubled to the gap, followed by a very deep sacrifice fly to Schwartzman, so she had given up her first damn run—and the guy on second advanced to third on the throw.

Where he was promptly driven in by *another* double, on a two-seamer that moved like a wounded bird.

And, here came the second run.

There was a lot of rumbling from the crowd, and she distinctly heard Caleb laughing, and saying something to the effect of "Oh, yeah, *that's* what I'm talking about!"

Marcus walked out to the mound with a new baseball. "Take a couple of deep breaths, Jill," he said. "Relax."

Relax? What game was *he* watching? She stared at him.

"Look at my glove, and hit it," he said. "Nothing else exists."

Well, except for the damn runner on second. "Do I do a slide-step?" she asked.

He shook his head. "No, just pitch. We've done some work on the stretch, and you're solid there. Start fresh with this guy, and you'll be fine."

She glanced at the plate, where a muscular Latino guy was grinning at her, and waggling his bat with great anticipation.

"Just hit my glove," Marcus said.

Except, the truth was, the batter was *huge*, and she was afraid he might hit her crummy fastball about a thousand miles, so she tried to aim off the plate—and walked him on five pitches. She was able to get a ground ball from the next batter, but Raffy double-clutched on the throw, and Diaz barely managed to keep it from sailing into the outfield, so the bases were loaded. That was followed by *another* damn double, and it was five to nothing, with only one down.

None of her pitches were working. The four-seamer was slow, the two-seamer was flat, the changeup was completely out of control, and the curveball had only a vague, forlorn spin. Hell, her *grandmothers* could probably hit doubles off her tonight.

She wanted to look at the bullpen, to see if anyone was warming up—but, no point in broadcasting the degree to which she was totally overwhelmed right now. She was damned if she would look over at the dugout, either, but she had definitely heard Caleb laughing again.

Marcus trudged back out to the mound. "Keep the ball down," he said. "Let's get out of the inning."

How were they going to do that? "Why can I suddenly not throw?" she asked.

"You *can*," he said. "Put the dog tag away, okay?"

She frowned at him, then looked down and saw that she was, in fact, clutching it tightly.

"It's a tell," he said. "You play with it whenever you get nervous."

She was going to argue—but, since it was in her hand, the only sensible thing to do was to tuck it back into her jersey.

"We're going to work this guy low," he said. "Get him to ground out. You're fine. Just *focus*."

Low. Outside. She could do that. And the guy wouldn't be able to put a good swing on the ball.

Once Marcus was behind the plate, she sucked in a breath and tried to tune out *everything* except for his glove.

It was a perfectly good plan, but she left the ball up again, and the guy smashed a line drive single up the middle, and the guy on second scored—and her stomach was starting to ache.

Now, she was facing the number nine hitter—a scrawny little middle infielder, who looked about fifteen—and her first pitch skidded into the dirt, and skipped towards the backstop. The runner on first took second, and after three more lousy pitches—two of which Marcus had to lunge to snag—she had walked the tiny banjo hitter.

Great. Just great.

And she *did* want to clutch the dog tag.

Jesus Christ, this was a nightmare. An unmitigated disaster. She looked in at Marcus, who still wanted her to keep the ball low, which she actually managed to do—but, the guy at the plate golfed a scorcher of a line drive, which Owen dove and caught.

Dimitri came over partway from first. "Pitch to contact, Jill," he said. "We'll get the last out for you."

The sooner, the better. She couldn't remember *ever* getting smacked around like this, not even in Little League.

And her stomach was hurting badly enough to make her want to double over.

She threw a two-seamer so far outside that Marcus barely managed to corral it. Maybe her curveball would work? God knows nothing else was. She shook him off—more than once—until he gave up and signaled for the curve.

Good. Her curve was her best damn pitch. She could *throw* a curve.

But, as it left her hand, she knew there was almost nothing on it—and the batter turned on the pitch with obvious delight, sending the ball deep into the sky, and *way* over the left field wall.

One run crossed the plate, and then another, and the two guys waited to exchange high fives with the happy kid who had hit the homer.

9–0. Freaking *nine* to nothing.

Marcus had started to come out, but she waved him off, threw her first decent two-seamer of the night, and the hitter swung and missed.

Of all things! A strike. Would the world stop spinning on its axis?

So, she threw another, but took a little off it, and the guy was so overeager that he popped up to Diaz, and the god-damn inning was finally over.

Nine to nothing.

She *sucked*.

As she walked off the mound, there were so many boos that she was disconcerted, and almost stopped right she was.

"Is this a home game?" she asked Marcus.

"Well, at least you'll have fewer autographs to sign later," he said.

Mr. Silver Lining.

The closer they got to the dugout, the more the boos intensified, and it sounded as though the whole stadium was joining in, but surely, they couldn't *all* have decided to start hating her. There were a lot of insults and jeers, which drowned out the stray "It's okay, Jill!" and "We still love you!" shouts here and there. One guy yelled, "Hey, how's that world domination working out for you?"—and since that was legitimately funny, she almost laughed.

Although she was also seriously considering throwing up.

"This is what happens to fans in fair weather," Dimitri said, off to her left.

Apparently so.

The boos weren't letting up at all, and without thinking about it, she lifted her hands in a mea culpa shrug—which diffused some of the negative reception. But, she was damn glad to be able to step inside the dugout.

Adler was waiting for her, completely expressionless, with his arms folded across his chest—and she shrugged at him, too.

"You want to hit the showers?" he asked.

More than she could possibly express.

Up at the railing, Caleb laughed. "*We* all sure want her out of there. Man, that was pathetic."

"Shut up, Kordell," someone said—and she was surprised to see that it was, of all people, Owen.

"Hey, at least I'm not charting tonight," Caleb said, and gestured towards Javy, who was holding the clipboard. "That poor tool's hand is cramping up."

Christ, he was really a piece of work. But, she looked at Adler, who was watching her closely. "That was a very bad inning, sir," she said. "A disgrace, even. I certainly *earned* being yanked, but I'd like another shot at them, if that's okay."

He looked at her some more, then moved his jaw. "Give me one good reason."

Well, *that* was going to be a challenge. "Because I haven't pitched yet tonight," she said.

"No, you haven't," he said, then nodded. "Okay. I'll give you fifteen pitches, and then I'm pulling you."

Fair enough. "Yes, sir," she said. "Thank you, sir."

Hector held up a raised solidarity fist as he walked past her on his way to the on-deck circle—for which she felt pitifully grateful.

Her throat was tight with tension—she hoped it wasn't *tears* threatening—and she paused to half-fill a cup of Gatorade before heading towards the bench to sit down.

"Man, with the shit she throws," Caleb said to Jonesy, "she's going to get hurt out there. I mean, they are *teeing off.*"

Before Jonesy even had time to respond, Marcus spun around. "One more word," he said softly, "and I'm going to hit you so hard that your head will land in Connecticut."

Caleb laughed. "Staking out your turf there, Grimes?"

It only took a split second for the dugout to go absolutely silent—including the guys who didn't speak nearly enough English to know what he had said, but who had picked up on the *tone.*

"After he's finished," Dimitri said through his teeth, "I'm going to go up to Connecticut, and kick that fucking head all the way to *Europe.*"

"Ooh," Caleb said, and turned to give Jill a big wink. "You've been putting out, haven't you, you naughty girl?"

"All right, that's it," Adler said, with such crackling authority that everyone in the dugout froze even more. "Kordell, you seem to have a lot of energy tonight. Go inside and get on the damn bike until I send someone in to tell you to get *off* the damn bike."

"Sure thing, Skip," Caleb said, and patted Javy on the back. "Good luck, man. Try not to let your hand get tired."

"Bronsky, you're on deck," Adler said, as Caleb headed

down the tunnel. "Katsaros, you're in the hole. Get your damn heads in the game!"

Scott put on a helmet and grabbed his bat, while Dimitri began pulling on his batting gloves, and slowly, the dugout eased back into its normal flow, which was a relief, although there was still some tension in the air.

As Jill sat down, Shosuke reached over to pat her hand lightly and then withdrew, and she said, "*Arigatō*," and he nodded sympathetically.

From the end of the dugout, Sofia held up the heat pack, and she shook her head. Sofia nodded, and set it aside, and Sawyer came over, instead.

"Okay, then," he said, his voice as calm as if it had been an entirely routine inning. "A lot of the work we've been doing has been geared towards getting you through nights like this. So, tell me what your approach is going to be out there."

Her mind was a total god-damn blank. "Um," she said. "Well, I—throw strikes?"

"*Think*, Cafferty," he said. "The curve isn't there tonight, and you're not locating the changeup. So, what's your plan?"

She still had no clue. "Well, I guess—I mean—" Wait, she *did* know the answer. Or, anyway, *an* answer. "I work the black with my two-seamer, change speeds as much as I can, and keep them honest with the four-seamer, but I try to make sure *that's* off the plate or up in their eyes," she said.

Sawyer nodded. "All right, then. That sounds very much like a plan, doesn't it?"

In fact, it did.

"So, let's see you execute it," Sawyer said, then paused. "And *do not* shake off Mother again. Your curve is horseshit tonight, and he was trying to help you, but you threw it, anyway—and now, it's sitting out there in the trees somewhere."

Halfway to Connecticut, even. "No, sir," she said. "I won't, sir."

Ramón, who had been listening, straining to follow the conversation, came over and patted his own left shoulder, violently. "Open," he said. "No good."

Sawyer and Marcus both nodded.

"He's right," Sawyer said. "You were flying all over the place out there. Remember to finish your pitches."

She was pretty sure that, during that inning, she hadn't even been capable of remembering her *name*.

It would have been nice to slump down and drape a towel over her head, but the game was being televised regionally, and running on MiLB.com, too. Which meant that the camera was probably lingering on the dugout, trying to capture her looking as though she had plummeted into total despair—or was maybe even weeping. So, she just sat calmly, staring straight ahead, taking slow, regular breaths through her nose, and releasing them through her mouth.

She had a long wait, because the guys—in a methodical,

determined way—scored five runs. Nine to five was assuredly not as awful as nine to nothing.

"They did a good job for you. Return the favor," Adler said in a low voice, as she moved purposefully past him.

She nodded, and strode out to the mound. Most of the fans were not happy to see her back out there—but, the fans were not her problem. Marcus threw down to second, the ball went around the infield, and then Owen tossed it to her with an exaggerated underhand motion.

"The hell's the matter with you?" she asked.

Owen pointed defensively at home plate. "Yell at him, not me."

Well, that figured. "He told you to piss me off?" she asked.

Owen shrugged, and went back to his position. "Hey, lady, I'm just here to play baseball."

And so, god-damn it, was *she*.

Fifteen pitches would be plenty. The batters were going to be cocky, after the disaster of the first inning, and she knew they would come out *hacking*.

No need for strikeouts, even though it would be emotionally satisfying. But, economy and precision would be much more helpful.

The first batter swung at a ball out of the zone, and she knew she didn't have to be too perfect—it would be enough to give him pitches that *looked* more tempting than they actually were.

He grounded to short, and the next guy hit a fly ball that Hector caught without having to move more than a step or two, and it had only taken her six pitches to get two outs.

If *she* had been hitting, she would have assumed that the pitcher was feeling shaky, and let a few go by. But, instead, the third guy swung right away and fouled the pitch straight back—which meant that he was on the baseball a lot more than she wanted him to be. He let the next one go by, but it caught enough of the outside corner for the umpire to call it a strike.

Marcus wanted her to put a four-seamer up at eye level, and the guy checked his swing, but not quite enough, and the infield umpire rang him up for strike three.

Nine pitches. That was fine.

She walked off the mound, noticing more cheers than boos this time—but, it still felt like the bloom was very much off the rose, insofar as the fans were concerned.

"Good work," Marcus said.

"Did you tell Owen to annoy me?" she asked.

He nodded.

"It was effective," she said.

He nodded again.

"That's more like it," Adler said, when she came into the dugout.

"I still have six pitches to go, sir," she said.

He looked amused, but shook his head. "Nope, you're done. Chavez, send Kordell back out here, when you get down there."

Sofia nodded, and motioned for Jill to follow her.

When they walked into the clubhouse, Caleb was pedaling the bike without much energy, and staring at his phone. He grinned when he saw them.

"How many more runs you give up?" he asked.

Jill ignored him, heading straight for her locker, unbuttoning her game jersey along the way.

"Adler wants you back in the dugout," Sofia said.

"So, I don't get to stay for the striptease?" Caleb asked. "And I mean *tease*."

Sofia didn't even look at him, already getting out the massage supplies and ice.

"Whatever," Caleb said, got off the bike, put his phone on the top shelf of his locker, and headed for the door.

"Wipe that bike down," Sofia said. Snapped, really.

"Isn't that your job?" he asked.

She shook her head, not smiling.

"Whatever," he said, and smacked a towel over the seat and handlebars, then dropped it on the floor and left.

"He's something else, isn't he," Sofia said.

That was for sure. Jill reached for some alcohol wipes and cleaned the bike much more aggressively, then tossed the wipes in the trash, and picked up the discarded towel, putting it in the laundry cart.

After which, she went into the training room, and washed her hands—at length.

"Think you got rid of all the cooties?" Sofia asked.

"Well, he was breathing the oxygen in here, unfortunately," Jill said.

Sofia nodded, and picked up a can of air freshener, spraying some around. "Better?"

"Maybe a little," Jill said.

But, so far, this had been one *hell* of a bad night.

CHAPTER 24

By the time she got back out to the dugout, it was the seventh, and they had eleven runs—and Aberdeen had twelve. But, Scott homered with two on in the bottom of the eighth, Andrew slammed the door in the top of the ninth—and they, improbably, won the game, fourteen to twelve.

She had no interest in signing autographs, but there were enough children waiting so that she had to stop, after exchanging some low-energy high fives with her teammates out on the field. If the kids had sat through that entire marathon of a game, they *deserved* autographs. But, she signed as quickly as possible, being careful to take the time to smile at each child, since it wasn't *their* fault she had been so terrible out there.

"Hey, Ladybug, you want to come out with us tonight?"

Dimitri asked, when she was finally able to escape into the dugout. "Blow off a little steam?"

Boy, would she ever. And it was nice to be invited. "I think I have to go let the media savage me for a while, first," she said. "I don't want to hold you guys up."

He shrugged. "Between eating, and showering, most of us will probably still be here. And if people want to go ahead, I'll wait and give you a ride."

"Okay, thanks. Where are we going?" she asked.

"Moynihan's," he said. "Sound good?"

A bar in town, which she had heard was kind of a dive, but the place usually attracted a lot of players, so it must be halfway decent. "Sure," she said. "Thank you."

Jeremiah was waiting for her in the corridor, looking concerned.

"We have a pretty full house down in the media room," he said. "Do you want me to get you out of it?"

Yes, and *double* yes. "I stunk up the joint tonight," Jill said, and pulled out her lip gloss. "I might as well own it. Let me just go brush my hair, and I'll be right there."

"You sure?" Jeremiah asked. "It's easy enough to say you're getting treatment in the trainers' room or something."

It would be *very* easy—but, also, cowardly. "No, it's okay." She put the lip gloss away, then felt to make sure her hair was reasonably well in place. "I'll get cleaned up, and then come right back."

She went down to unlock her dressing room, wishing she

could take the time to shower and change—but, that could wait. She sent a quick "I'm going to go out for a late supper with some of the guys" text to Mrs. Wilkins, adding that one of them would give her a ride home, afterward, and Mrs. Wilkins wrote back, "Okay, have fun."

Would they wait up for her to get in? Probably. So, she texted that she would probably be quite late, and not to worry. Mrs. Wilkins's response was, again, to have fun, and be safe.

Her phones were exploding with even more messages than usual, but the "Buck up, little princess!" text from Theo was the only one that made her smile. She answered the tiny few from people who really would *care* about whether she was okay, and then went back to where Jeremiah was—patiently— waiting.

The media room was, indeed, packed—to the degree that she wondered whether a bunch of reporters who hadn't originally planned to come to the game had headed over to the park after hearing about how badly she'd been rocked in the first inning. Sharks in the water.

And the questions were *harsh*. What had gone wrong, why had she pitched so badly, whether tonight was the *reality* of her as a pitcher, with everything else she had done so far just being a fluke, and so on. Someone even asked if she was ashamed by her performance.

What kind of question was *that*? She saw that Jeremiah was about to intercede, but shook her head. Adler and Mr. Brayton were both standing in the back of the room, and she shook her head at them, too.

"All that happened here is that I did a lousy job of pitching," she said. "So, I'm disappointed that I didn't have better results, but, no, sir, *shame* is definitely not part of the equation."

The guy was squirming a little, but he was from one of the major sports networks, and didn't seem to want to go away quietly. "Do you think tonight has shown that even the most talented female baseball players can't compete with men?" he asked.

The *second* inning had been pretty damn good, as far as she was concerned. "If you want to spin it that way, you can," she said, "but, it would be"—stupid—"facile."

"Okay," the guy said, "but—"

No, she wasn't in the mood for yet another follow-up. "I think people have been missing the point for weeks now," she said. *Years*, even. "I don't actually represent *all* women. I'm *one* athlete with, you know, a certain skill set, and whether I end up succeeding is going to be a combination of all sorts of factors, and gender really doesn't have anything to do with it."

"So, do you think—" a different reporter started.

She decided to cut *him* off, too. "The whole idea of women wanting to take over professional baseball is—" Cliché might not be the right word, but it was the right *concept*. "It's a complete trope. Anyone who ever picked up a bat and glove has probably had a fantasy of playing major league baseball, but it's a combination of hard work, luck, and an—I don't know—accident of genetics. I mean, if I were precisely the same pitcher, but a foot shorter, even *this* outcome would be unlikely." Oh, hell, was she going to crush the dreams of millions of diminutive children by saying that? "It's possible, of course," she said, "but I would need to have been born with considerably more talent to make up for it."

Some of the reporters looked befuddled, and some looked intrigued, but all of the cameras were, for damn sure, still running.

People were jumping in with follow-ups, but she raised a hand to wave them off, because, damn it, she was on kind of a roll here.

"It's about getting to play baseball, *period*," she said. "There are little girls out there, who would rather play baseball, instead of softball, and they're either discouraged— or outright not allowed to do it. People just want to be able to have fun, and play the game, without it being such a ridiculously big deal."

"What if the girl players aren't good enough?" someone asked.

Yeah, because every guy who had ever lived was an *innately* gifted baseball player. "Well, a lot more of them are going to be good, if they get a chance to play for *years*, instead of being locked out by the time they hit junior high," she said. "So, maybe it would be helpful to—I don't know—reframe the entire discussion, and just talk about having more opportunities for *everyone*, instead of this stupid"—okay, she'd gone ahead and said it—"idea that women are only interested in sticking it to the guys, and keeping some of *them* from being able to play."

Some of the reporters' eyes seemed to be glazed over, but others were listening with obvious interest.

"It's supposed to be the American pastime," she said. "Maybe it's time to let the other fifty percent of the population actually get a chance to *play*, if they want. And the fact that I was terrible out there tonight has nothing to do with what any other female player might do on some different night."

It was slightly embarrassing to have gone off in such an impassioned way, and she took a sip from the water bottle on the table.

"Do you want to elaborate?" someone asked.

Isn't that what she had just been doing? At considerable, tendentious length? "Let's call it food for thought, and leave it at that," she said.

"Yes," one of the magazine reporters said, "but I'd love to hear—"

"I think poor Mr. Brayton has been wanting to contribute to the discussion, and it's his team," she said, motioning towards the GM. "So, instead of having me monopolize the conversation, why don't we let him take it from here."

Mr. Brayton nodded, and came up to the podium table, pausing to shake her hand as she passed him on her way out.

Adler felt into step with her as she left the room. "Are you a Democrat, Cafferty?" he asked.

Such a peculiar man. "Yes, sir," she said. "Although I want to keep, you know, an open mind, depending on the issue."

"Too bad," he said. "That's going to make it a lot harder for me to vote for you someday."

What? "I'm not going to go into politics, sir," she said.

He smiled. "Check back with me in fifteen or twenty years, let's see where you are then."

Maybe they should bet a significant amount of money on that one, because he was *definitely* going to lose.

After she had showered and changed, she found Dimitri waiting in the clubhouse, along with Scott and Danny.

"There you are," Dimitri said, standing up. "Were they tough on you?"

She nodded. "Yeah. It wasn't much fun. But, it's not like they were *wrong* about the way I played."

"Yo, man, everyone has off nights," Danny said.

With luck, that was all it had been—but, it was hard not to have doubts.

Nicky was busy cleaning up the remnants of the post-game spread. "Sorry," he said apologetically. "You ate before, right?"

No, but no point in making the guy feel as though he'd screwed up, even though she seemed to be missing out on meals *constantly*. "I'm fine, thanks," she said, and helped herself to a banana from the counter where the fruit was kept. Also, presumably, she could order some food at the bar.

"You ready to head out?" Scott asked.

She nodded. "Who else is coming?"

Dimitri was checking his pockets, to make sure he had his keys, his wallet, and his phone. "Mother drove a bunch of them over already. I'm not sure how many of them ended up going."

That was surprising. "Marcus hangs out at Moynihan's?" she said.

Dimitri laughed. "God, no. But, you know how he is—he wants to keep an eye on people." He looked at the three of them, and shook his head wryly. "Hell, I feel like a chaperone myself tonight. This is just going to be fun, right, guys? Don't any of you get too blasted."

Scott, at least, looked like he *might* be old enough to drink, but she wasn't sure if she and Danny would even get served. It would still be nice to hang out for a while, instead of going to the Wilkinses' house, and sitting around alone downstairs for the rest of the night.

The place lived up to its reputation—crowded, noisy, dimly lit, cheap pitchers of beer, somewhat sticky sawdust on the floors, and free bowls of peanuts and popcorn. There seemed to be a higher percentage of comely young women than one might expect—which made sense, for a bar that also attracted baseball players. Or, maybe it was a chicken and egg situation.

The other guys had already taken over three big booths in

the back, near the pool table. As they walked over, she could see Hector, Eduardo, Schwartzman, Jackson, Raffy, Jonesy, Ramón, Owen, a new reliever up from the GCL named Mike, and—oh, swell—*Caleb*. Marcus was sitting with them, but managing to make it seem as though he was staying slightly apart. He also appeared to be the only one who had gotten a soda.

When the waitress came over to take their orders, she and Danny drifted over in the direction of the pool table, to avoid having to show their IDs.

Not that the waitress didn't know, Jill assumed. In fact, when she casually ordered a club soda, the woman just gave her a look, and said, "Unh-hunh."

Jill *did* drink the club soda, but she also let the guys pour her a beer, and was perfectly fine with it when they kept topping off everyone's glasses, including hers.

"Dude, you *know* you hate this," Jackson said to Marcus. "Why do you put yourself through it?"

"I want to make sure everyone gets home in one piece," Marcus said, not even looking up from his iPad.

"Den mother!" Owen shouted, and clinked glasses with everyone within reach.

The beer supply kept coming—and when the waitress wasn't around, Jill made sure to drop more than her share of money on the table, noticing that all of the highest draft picks—with big bonuses—did the same. Even Caleb, to give him a tiny amount of credit.

Maybe she wasn't supposed to be out drinking—but, she was having a good time. The conversation was loud, and energetic—and maybe kind of rambling and pointless—but, still fun.

Young women joined them frequently, but since, luckily, none of them came on to *her*, Jill didn't care one way or the other. More than one of her teammates was clearly making a special new friend—at least, for the evening—and since it all seemed very consensual, what was the harm? Besides, it wasn't any of her damn business.

The beer didn't seem to be having much effect on her— probably because she was, you know, *tall*. She did go to the ladies' room at one point, and maybe stumbled a little—and was vaguely aware of Marcus focusing on her. But, she ignored him, because it wasn't like he was *in charge*. She could have a couple of beers, if she wanted, damn it.

When she found her way back to the table, the guys were talking and laughing about the game.

"You really *sucked* tonight, Cafferty!" Caleb said. "It was embarrassing. Good thing Eddie and Mikey bailed your ass out."

The bullpen had been great—although the hitters were the ones who had pretty much saved the day by scoring so many runs.

"Do you even know *how* to throw a curveball?" Caleb asked.

"Doesn't look that way," she said, and this time, she topped off her own glass.

Caleb laughed. "Next stop, GCL! And it's *hot* down there."

She did not want to spend the rest of the summer roasting in Florida. "Maybe, yeah," she said, and took several gulps of beer.

"They've gotta be *slamming* you on ESPN tonight," Caleb said.

The Internet was almost certainly destroying her, too.

"The WNBA must be looking mighty tempting right about now," he said.

"Hey, come on, Kordell," Hector said. "She just had an off night. Give her a break already."

"But, she seriously *sucked*," Caleb said. "I mean—"

"Zip it," Marcus said, his voice quiet, but still managing to cut through the noise. "Don't talk about a teammate that way."

"What, she can't take it?" Caleb asked, slugging down half the beer in his glass. "She better toughen up, then. I'm just busting on her a little. I'd do it to any of the guys." He paused. "I mean, if they sucked as bad as *she* did tonight."

On second thought, maybe being here was less fun than it had seemed to be at first.

"Hey, Kordell," Dimitri said. "That one over there in the sundress keeps checking you out. You should go over and say hi."

Caleb squinted towards the bar, where a group of three young women *did* seem to be pretty interested in what was going on at their table. "Yeah, they're not bad," he said. "Think I like the redhead better." He stood up, managing to bump into the table and tip over a couple of beer glasses. "Come on, Jonesy, be my wingman."

"Yeah, why not," Jonesy said, finishing off his beer. "Right behind you."

"Want another?" Raffy asked, once Caleb and Jonesy were out of earshot.

Very definitely. She nodded and held out her glass.

Someone ordered some nachos and cheese fries, and the personnel at the table fluctuated, as girls joined them on and off, and a few of their other teammates wandered over to the bar, and guys went off to play pool, or go to the men's room, or go fool around with—new friends—in the parking lot, or whatever.

Hector put his arm around her shoulders. "Want to sign up for the next game?"

"Sure," she said, since it probably didn't matter that she wasn't very *good* at pool. Wicked sucked, even. As she did, at *all* games and sports. She got up, using the edge of the table to help herself balance.

And, predictably, Marcus looked over—and she pretended not to see him. The dance of masked drunkenness they had been doing all night.

There were other people lined up to play ahead of them, and she and Hector sat at a small table off to the side.

"Wait a second," he said, and went back to their former

table to liberate a pitcher of beer, and then refilled both of their glasses.

"Thanks," she said, and drank some. Drank quite *a lot*.

Hector sat down in the chair next to hers, instead of the one across the table. "Caleb's a blowhard idiot," he said. "I'm really sorry about the way he's been acting."

"Good pitcher," she said.

Hector shrugged. "Million-dollar arm, maybe, but he's got a fourteen-cent head."

Wait, that wasn't quite right. "Don't you mean ten-cent head?" she asked.

"No," Hector said. "I've known guys dumber than him. Fourteen cents is about right."

Which struck her funny, and she laughed. "So, tell me about your screenplay," she said.

"How do you even know I'm writing one?" he asked.

Right now, she couldn't quite remember. "I just do," she said. "Tell me about it."

He ducked his head. "No, it'll sound stupid."

His hair—such nice, thick black hair—was flopping so perfectly over his forehead, that she wanted to touch it. Smooth it back, maybe. "No, I really want to hear about it," she said.

"It's about a guy who isn't as good a baseball player as he thought he was," he said. "And how he deals with that."

Really? "Come on, no, it isn't," she said, although she wasn't sure.

Hector grinned, with those teeth that never *stopped* being glorious. "Okay," he said. "It's, um—well, it's a thriller. It's about an exchange student doing his junior year abroad—but, he's actually a spy. And he gets caught up in the middle of a big terrorist plot, and, of course, there's a *girl*, and—well, it's high concept, and exciting." He frowned. "At least, I *hope* it is."

"Tell me more," she said.

Which he did, and it was so noisy, that she had to lean closer to hear. They talked about his script, and then, about what movies they liked, and he refilled their glasses—and when he shifted his position, suddenly, his knee was touching hers, and neither of them moved. Except, possibly, a few fractions of an inch closer.

He looked at her; she looked at him.

And neither of them said anything.

He was so *handsome*. And he was lean, in a speedy gap hitter way, not like a slugger. And his *mouth*. Such a nice mouth. She really liked his mouth.

They looked at each other, and she could tell that he was possibly noticing her mouth, too. And that maybe he thought her breasts were a little less—nondescript—than she had always considered them.

He reached out and rested his hand on her leg, and she let it stay there. Considered covering it with hers.

Was he going to lean over and kiss her? Was she going to kiss *back*?

Hell, yes.

Did she want him to do it right away, or was it kind of *exquisite* to draw it out?

Either.

Both.

Yeah.

There was a lot of tension. Good tension. The *best* tension.

This was *awesome*.

CHAPTER 25

She and Hector kept staring at each other, and she wasn't sure if she had ever looked into *anyone's* eyes quite so intently.

Should she touch *his* leg now? Yeah. It was going to be warm, and strong, and once she did that, maybe they could—

"Last call, guys," someone said.

They both looked up, Jill feeling more than a little confused, her hand in midair.

"Time to call it a night," the person said.

Marcus. Naturally.

"You want to give us a little space?" Hector said, through his teeth. "We're—"

"We have a game tomorrow," Marcus said. "Come on, let's get moving."

She already *had* a big brother; she didn't need a second, self-appointed one. "Everything's fine, Marcus," she said. "If you want to head home, you should—"

"You've both had enough," Marcus said. "Come on, we're out of here." He turned. "Scott? Danny? Harvey? Anyone else need a ride?"

Jill was going to argue—and it looked like Hector was ready to *slug* him—but, everyone who wasn't already paired off and in some stage or other of a hookup, was getting up, settling the tab, and about to head out.

Fine. Whatever. She reached into her pocket for money, and dropped a few more bills on one of the tables, not even looking to see how much it was.

Marcus sighed, picked a couple of the bills up—twenties, maybe?—and gave them back to her.

"I'm *tipping*," she said.

He ignored that, just ushering her towards the door.

She was aware, walking outside, that she was pretty damn drunk—and it was *fine*. Fun, even.

Although maybe she wanted to be careful not to fall down or anything, because that would be a dumb way to get injured.

"Is anyone drunk driving?" she asked.

"*No*," Marcus said. "Why do you think I sat in a crummy bar all night, when I'd rather be home getting some sleep? The others are all within walking distance."

Okay, whatever. She tripped over the curb—but, didn't go all the way down, at least.

Four of her teammates were crammed into the car, which smelled like spilled beer. There was some kind of rowdy conversation going on, but she was tired enough just to sit in the back, half on Scott's lap, leaning against the door, dozing slightly.

Marcus dropped everyone else off first, but she stayed where she was, in the backseat.

"Is that really necessary?" he asked, instead of pulling away from the curb.

Damn right. She texted Lauren, sharing the information that Marcus was a self-righteous, power-mad jerk.

"I am not your chauffeur," he said through his teeth. "Please sit up front like a normal person."

Since when was she allowed to *be* a normal person? Besides, he was treating her like she was a disappointing child—which was bugging her.

"Try *not* acting your age," he said. "This is incredibly tiresome."

Lauren had texted back, but her phone was kind of smeared, and it was hard to read the screen. So, Jill just sent her another message about how annoying Marcus was.

"Are you trying to make me feel like *Driving Miss Daisy*?" he asked.

That one penetrated, and she felt insulted, but was damned if he was going to berate her into moving. "You are such a prig," she said.

He whirled around. "I'm going out of my way to help you, and you just called me a *prick*?"

"Prig," she said. "With a *g*. Open your damn ears."

Now, he sighed. "Come on, I'm really tired, Jill. Give me a break and sit up here."

She lurched grumpily out of the car, and made her way into the front passenger's seat. The seat belt was unnecessarily complicated, and she fumbled with the catch, trying to fasten it correctly.

Marcus sighed again, and reached over to connect it for her, like it was totally *easy* or something.

Her phone rang, and her eyes weren't focusing quite right, but it looked like Lauren, so she answered. "Hey, whassup?" she asked.

"Did you pocket-text me?" Lauren asked.

Jill laughed. "No. I *texted* texted you."

There was a pause.

"Are you all right?" Lauren asked.

"I am fine," Jill said, making sure to pronounce each word correctly. "Even though I *suck*."

"What's going on?" Lauren asked. "You sound weird."

"Well, I'm being kidnapped by a total *jerk*," Jill said, "but—"

Lauren had such an anxious—and loud—reaction, that Jill had to move the phone away from her ear.

Marcus shook his head, pulled the car over, and then plucked the phone out of her hand. "Hello?" he said. "Is this Lauren?" He listened briefly. "Okay, this is Marcus." He laughed. "Yeah, that Marcus. Did you see anything about the game tonight?" He listened. "Well, some of the guys talked her into going to a bar, and she had a *very* good time, so I'm driving her home to make sure she gets there safely." He paused again. "I had a couple of Cokes, actually. Why don't you talk to her now, while I'm driving." He listened. "Okay. Have a good night." He passed Jill the phone. "Here."

So, Jill talked to Lauren for the rest of the ride, allowing as how Marcus *wasn't* a kidnapper, but *was* controlling, and mean, and very patriarchal—a word she couldn't quite get out of her mouth right—and that giving up nine runs had *sucked*, and that *she* sucked, and that maybe she should quit and go to college, except she would probably suck *there*, too, and flunk out—and on and on, along those general lines. She also promised that she was okay, and that she would drink a lot of water before she went to bed, and that she would, in fact, *go* to bed and try to sleep it off.

As she hung up, Marcus parked in front of the Wilkinses' house, and turned off the engine.

"Have you ever been drunk before?" he asked.

Not like *this*. So, she shook her head.

"A lot of guys away from home for the first time party their way right out of baseball," he said. "Or college, for that matter. Or, at least, squander their skills by not taking care of themselves."

Who died and appointed *him* God? "I had one bad night," she said. "You're already writing off my career?"

"I don't want *you* to write it off," he said.

She had a few damn beers. So what?

"The curveball and change weren't working, and you didn't have much command," he said. "It happens. You learn from it."

She really didn't feel like listening to someone *else* tell her what a bad pitcher she was.

"And you might be mad at me right now for breaking it up with Hector," he said. "But, tomorrow, you're both going to be *glad* that our stud lefty pitcher didn't have a public make-out session with our center fielder."

"We weren't making out," she said. Although she damn well wished that they *had* been.

"Hey, if you think that's a good career move, go for it," he said. "Next time, I'll just shake my head and go home."

Good. Might give her a chance to live her own god-damn life. But, instead of responding, she opened the door and staggered her way out of the car. "Thanks for the ride."

"Make sure your phone is charged," he said. "I'll call you early, so that you don't miss team stretch."

She acknowledged that with an abrupt nod, and then concentrated on making it across the uneven grass, stumbling more than once. She also managed to drop her house keys twice, while trying to open the back door—only to figure out that it was already unlocked.

Mr. and Mrs. Wilkins must already be asleep, since most of the lights were off, but the harder she tried to stay quiet, the more noise she made. Of course, it didn't help that she kept tripping over things.

She managed to get down to the basement without falling, at least. Then, she was on her way to the bathroom when she heard someone, and focused blearily up the stairs, where Mrs. Wilkins was standing, in her bathrobe and slippers.

"Are you all right, Jill?" she asked.

"Yup," Jill said. Except that was probably *way* too loud. "Just turning in."

"Are you sure?" Mrs. Wilkins asked.

"Yup," Jill said. "Sorry. Was trying to be all quiet and stuff." She wrenched at the bathroom door—and was surprised when it actually opened quite easily. "Oops. Um, good night. I better get some sleep." Then, she closed the door, without waiting for an answer.

It didn't seem like she was going to throw up—whew—and she drank a bunch of water from the sink faucet, scooping it up with her hands and not worrying that she spilled a lot on her clothes. She was about to change out of them anyway, right?

She left her polo shirt and khakis on the bathroom floor, and pulled on a T-shirt, not really caring that it was inside out—and had been in the laundry basket. She set several alarms on her phone, since she couldn't remember what time she was supposed to wake up. Then, she flopped down on the bed—

and fell asleep in what felt like about forty seconds.

When the first phone alarm went off, she slowly woke up, still lying facedown. She listened to the annoying sound for a minute, feeling exhausted, disoriented, a little sick to her stomach, and quite unsteady.

And, briefly, panicked, since she might have overslept. So, she lunged for the phone, relieved to see that it was only nine-thirty, and she had plenty of time. Maybe? She actually wasn't sure when today's game was. Or even what *day* it was.

She sat on the edge of the bed, rubbing her face and trying to shake off whatever drunkenness remained. Hard to believe people did this on a regular basis, if they woke up feeling this lousy.

A few minutes later, her phone rang. Marcus, of course.

"I'm up," she said.

"Good," he said.

She was going to look like an idiot, but— "What time is the game today?" she asked.

"Six o'clock start," he said. "But, you'll have an early session with Sofia before team stretch, so get there by noon, at the latest."

Right, okay. "See you at the ballpark," she said.

"Yeah," he said, and hung up.

After a very long shower, and chugging a cold Gatorade from the mini-refrigerator, she felt functional enough to attempt going upstairs. Mrs. Wilkins was in the kitchen, and Mr. Wilkins was—she hoped—off golfing.

"Good morning," Mrs. Wilkins said, as she poured herself a cup of coffee.

"Um, good morning," Jill said. "I'm sorry I got home so late last night. I hope I didn't disturb anyone."

Mrs. Wilkins shook her head, but definitely looked tight-lipped.

She should probably apologize—or was it better to pretend that nothing had really happened? And what if Mrs. Wilkins didn't realize that she had been drunk?

And what if a large group of leprechauns came in and started dancing around the room and making breakfast for them?

"Are you hungry?" Mrs. Wilkins asked.

God, no. Although it would be too much of a cliché to shudder. "It's pretty early," Jill said. "I thought I might just have some juice, and maybe a piece of toast."

"Do you need aspirin?" Mrs. Wilkins asked.

Probably, yeah. But, she was damned if she would admit it. "Um, it was very inappropriate for me to come rolling in drunk last night, and wake you up like that," she said. "I'm sorry. It's not something I plan on doing again."

Mrs. Wilkins looked startled. "Oh. That's direct."

Better than letting it fester. "I had such a bad game, that the guys wanted to cheer me up," Jill said, "but I got *too* cheerful, I guess."

Mrs. Wilkins studied her for a moment, and then fixed a

second cup of coffee, which she handed her. "If it makes you feel better, it's not exactly unprecedented. We've almost never had a player stay here who hasn't had some ups and downs."

The thought of milk in her coffee seemed gross this morning, but Jill added a good amount of sugar. "And yet, you keep inviting us back," she said.

"You seemed pretty clean-cut," Mrs. Wilkins said, and smiled at her. "Until I started getting to know you."

So, apparently, her coming home roaring drunk was the secret for making them relax a little with each other? Well, whatever worked, right? She didn't want to remember all of the stupid things she had done last night—but, it occurred to her that there was a phone call she really ought to make.

"I think I upset a friend of mine last night," she said. "Do you mind if I take a minute and call her?"

"You're actually *living* here this summer," Mrs. Wilkins said. "You need to try and start feeling at home."

Jill nodded, and went out to the dining room, speed dialing Lauren on the way. "Hey," she said.

"Are you all right this morning?" Lauren asked.

Somewhat. "I'm sorry that I was so stupid," Jill said. "I— well, I guess I drank quite a lot."

"No," Lauren said, "*really?*"

Understatement, yeah. "I was completely inconsiderate, and I apologize," Jill said.

Lauren laughed. "Don't worry, I just went ahead and

knocked a whole bunch of points off your score."

Hell, she probably *had*—which meant that the running total must be pretty low, at the moment. "I'm kind of off my game today"—on a thousand different levels—"but, you're kidding," Jill said, "right?"

Lauren just laughed.

She was kidding. Probably.

"For what it's worth, I was keeping score last fall, too," Lauren said, more quietly, "and you *aced* that one."

They almost never talked about those weeks in the hospital—the endless hours during which Lauren rarely spoke, and Jill didn't, either, trying to sit so unobtrusively that even Lauren's parents often seemed to forget that she was there, and witnessing all of the pain, fear, indignities, not enough medication—or, sometimes, *too much* medication, with awful side effects. It was all mostly a blur, but she remembered one night, when Lauren's mother had lurched off to get coffee or something, or maybe just breathe fresh air, and they had held hands, and Lauren cried silently, so Jill did, too—without either of them looking at each other. "Well, it's good to have data," she said aloud.

Lauren laughed again. "Oh, yeah, the more, the better." Then, she paused. "*Was* Marcus being okay last night? You were pretty upset."

A lot of which was embarrassingly foggy. "I think he's really mad at me, but he was just trying to help. I mean, I don't even want to go over to the park today," Jill said. "All of the guys are probably—" Part of the evening suddenly flashed very clearly in her mind. "Oh, God, Hector and I were *all over* each other. Jesus, I'm not going to be able to show my face in the clubhouse."

"Is he the beautiful one?" Lauren asked.

Was he ever. "Yep," Jill said. "Flat-out gorgeous."

"How far did it get?" Lauren asked.

Good question. A few too many details were—murky. "I think Marcus broke it up before we actually started making out," she said. Hoped so, anyway.

"Luckily you have a guardian angel," Lauren said.

Yeah, the good one pacing nearby, while the bad angel kept whispering, "Oh, come on, just *do* it, you know you want to." "Why didn't I spend more time screwing up in high school?" she asked. "Get it out of my system? Or, at least, learn *how* to do it."

"Because you're usually a totally boring straight arrow," Lauren said.

Yeah. Not only had she always been worried about whatever workout or game she had the next day, but she had also generally spent time at parties or dances feeling out of place, and awkward, and impossibly *tall*.

"I'm not going to make fun of you," Lauren said, "although it's *very* tempting."

No doubt. "Am I going to live it down?" Jill said.

"Well, don't walk in there today and throw your arms around him," Lauren said, and paused. "At least, not immediately."

Yes, there was humor in this. There was even probably some humor to be found in giving up nine damn runs in a single inning.

Maybe.

CHAPTER 26

After an "I'm fine, just didn't pitch well" conversation with her mother, she decided to call Theo, too, even though she wasn't sure whether he was supposed to take calls at his internship. But, she knew he would pick up—which he did immediately, and she told him everything that had happened the night before, and then *retold* him other things—and wished like hell that they were in the same room together, and could just talk for hours.

"Have you been telling Mom this stuff?" he asked. "Other than vague little details sometimes?"

There was no point in fibbing, since he knew the truth. "Not really," she said. "I mean—well, I don't want to upset her."

"God, you two drive me crazy sometimes," he said. "Neither one of you is at all as fragile as the other one *thinks* she is."

It probably did go both ways, although Jill rarely looked at it like that.

"Plus," he said, "you know, the part where she isn't stupid, and knows perfectly well that there's always a lot going on that you never say. So, do *better*."

An entirely deserved chiding, she suspected. And—she would try.

"Anyway, we saw the press conference, when they showed it later," Theo said. "You were amazing." He laughed. "You and your *trope*. Hell, you probably *earned* the right to go get smashed."

One young man's perspective. "I thought that guy was going to ask if I thought *Dad* would have been ashamed of me," she said.

Theo was silent for a minute, and she started worrying that their father *might* have felt— "Do you remember Bunky?" he asked, unexpectedly.

Ancient blast from the past. "You mean, Bunky the Balloon Dog?" Jill said.

"Yeah," he said. "Or the Balloon Fox or the Balloon Lion, or whatever he was supposed to be."

Bunky had been lopsided, and misshapen, and malformed— and she had brought him home proudly, after making him at a birthday party when she was about eight, and insisted upon displaying him on the table in the front hall for one and all to admire. "Mammal of undetermined species," she said. "And you popped him." The tragic coda, a week or so later.

"It was a mercy popping, believe me," Theo said.

Maybe. Although she remembered crying, and throwing a book at him as hard as she could. "That was like, ten years ago," she said. "What made you think of that?"

"Dad was *impressed* by Bunky," Theo said. "And I don't think he was just being nice to you. He actually thought you were showing imaginative creative flair, or whatever it was that Mom said to make you feel good. He *gushed*."

"So, that's why you popped him?" Jill said. Sibling rivalry, being what it was sometimes.

"No," Theo said without hesitating. "He was an atrocity, and needed to be destroyed. The point is, Dad was *always* proud of you, even when you didn't really deserve it. And in this situation, when you totally *do* deserve it, he'd be over the moon."

For a second, she felt tears in her eyes, and wondered if Theo had also instinctively reached for his dog tag. "He was always proud of you, too," she said. "Remember how he said you did it just right, so it popped with a real *bang*, instead of sadly deflating, or whatever?"

Theo laughed. "Yeah, actually. And when you beaned me with that stupid little cat book, he said something like, 'Look at her *velocity*.'"

She didn't quite remember that—but, it sounded like exactly the way he would have reacted.

"Jill," Mrs. Wilkins said from the dining room door.

She looked up, and Mrs. Wilkins tapped her wrist. So, she

checked the wall clock—which had twelve bright little flowers, instead of numbers—and saw that she was in grave danger of running late. "I need to hurry, if I'm going to get over there in time for, you know, my *fluffing*," she said to Theo.

"And I'm not making a lot of friends here in the lab today," he said.

Which made her appreciate his answering the phone just that much more.

When she got to the stadium, she wasn't the only one slinking across the parking lot in dark sunglasses. Raffy gave her a weak wave on his way inside, and her wave back was similarly feeble.

Scott was slowly getting out of his host family's car, and she waited for him to catch up with her.

"I feel awful," he said, looking red-eyed even behind his shades, his hair sticking up in several directions.

"I bet I feel worse," she said.

"No way," he said, and opened the players' entrance door with an effort. "Remind me not to get that wasted ever again."

"Only if you remind me, too," she said, and he nodded.

After getting changed, she stood outside the clubhouse door for a minute, trying to get up the nerve to go inside.

"Is that a hungover little ladybug?" someone asked from behind her.

She turned, still wearing her sunglasses, and saw Dimitri, who looked alert and energetic. "*You* look cheerful," she said— maybe rather ungraciously.

"It was fun," he said. "I mean, *I* had fun. It does everyone some good to rock out, every now and then."

She might beg to differ—but, she nodded, as though she agreed, and followed him into the clubhouse. When Owen saw her, he laughed, and pretended to stagger around like a drunk, and there was a lot of joking around, some of it at her expense—but, no one seemed to be connecting her with Hector, so maybe Marcus *had* stopped things just in the nick of time. She was too embarrassed to meet eyes with either of them, though, and went straight to the training room.

"Good morning," Sofia said. "Let's start with—" Then, she stopped, sniffed the air, and looked exasperated. "Oh, are you *kidding* me?"

On the way indoors, she had noticed that Scott still reeked of beer—so, apparently, she must, too. Jill shrugged, not looking at her.

"Get on the bike," Sofia said. "See if you can sweat some of it out."

"I'm just tired," Jill said.

Sofia looked at her grumpily. "Shut up and pedal. Go at least thirty minutes. Forty-five would be better. We'll have to work on your arm and shoulder later."

The exercise felt as though it was taking *hours*, but she gutted her way through it, pedaling extra hard to try and perspire as much as possible. Perspiration that did, indeed, have kind of a sour alcohol smell, she noticed.

The lights were way too bright, and she kept her sunglasses and cap on, with the brim pulled down low over her eyes.

"Here," Sofia said, and slapped a large bottle of Gatorade into her hand. "Drink *all* of it, and then keep hydrating, you irresponsible infant."

On the planet of People Who Did Not Suffer Fools Gladly, Sofia was probably a *queen*. So, Jill drank, and pedaled—and had just enough time to wipe the bike down with a towel, before making her way outside to team stretch on wobbly legs.

Bannigan zeroed in on her right away, with rather slitty eyes, and she wondered why it was so utterly obvious that she had— overindulged—last night. But, he didn't say anything, and she found a spot to stretch behind Scott and Danny—who looked almost as bad as Scott did. Actually, half the team appeared to be in lousy shape—or, at least, *really* tired—and most of their stretching was sluggish, at best.

"What I'm seeing here isn't what I expect out of professional ballplayers," Bannigan said, sounding disgusted.

Caleb laughed. "You don't get around much, then, because as far as I know, this is *exactly* what ballplayers do."

Bannigan was not amused. "You're supposed to show up in shape to play," he said.

"Hey, man, *I'm* in shape to play," Caleb said. "Don't blame the rest of us, for the ones who are wusses."

Bannigan was still not amused. "Less talking, more stretching," he said.

After stretch, Jill went inside to have Sofia work on her shoulder and arm, and also did some light resistance band and weight work. Then, she took her second shower of the day, before heading out to BP. Caleb spent most of the time regaling everyone in the outfield—half of whom didn't speak English, of course—about how incredibly *hot* the girl he'd met last night had been, and how she'd invited him over to the apartment she shared with two other "chicks"—and a number of graphic details about his evening that she would really rather not have known.

She had been going out of her way to avoid Hector, but he was in the last BP group, and motioned her off to the side, as she was leaving the field. So, she went over, hesitantly, and they both leaned against the backstop, standing about five feet apart.

"So," he said. "It got pretty crazy last night."

Very much so. She nodded.

They stood there.

This was mortifying. "I know you were just really drunk," she said, "and I was acting dumb, and—well, let's never bring it up again, okay?"

"I wasn't, actually," he said.

That woke her up. "What?" she asked.

"I mean, yeah, okay, I was pretty buzzed, but I made a move on you on purpose," he said. "I *wanted* that to happen." He looked sheepish. "Or, anyway, *almost* happen."

It was a relief—and a surprise—to discover that they both

felt the same way about it. "Me, too," she said.

They stood there some more.

"You're a really good guy, and I wish it wasn't so completely—implausible," she said. Impossible, even.

He glanced over. "If we kept it quiet, maybe no one—" He stopped. "Not really going to play, is it?"

With the team inevitably finding out right away, and gossiping enthusiastically, until it went very public, and destroyed what little baseball credibility she still had right now? She shook her head.

"Damn," he said.

Which pretty much said it all. Unfortunately.

After taking a *third* shower, right before the game, she started to feel pretty close to normal, although she kept as low a profile as possible. Since Caleb was charting tonight, he was much less—voluble, which was a relief. But, she still stood as far away from him as she could, as she leaned against the railing to watch the game.

The team didn't play well, and poor Danny was still so sick to his stomach, that he actually had to leave the bullpen and go lie down in the clubhouse for the last few innings. They lost, six to nothing, and were collectively lousy enough for Adler to snarl at them all for a few minutes, when it was over. But, he didn't knock anything down, or swear too much, and she figured that they had gotten off pretty easily.

Naturally, there were some guys who went out drinking

almost every night—especially, she had noticed, when they were on the road—but the sheer number of hungover players today must have been too blatant for him to ignore.

The next day, Caleb pitched, with Ramón catching—which meant that Marcus was going to be much harder to avoid. So far, they hadn't interacted much, beyond a couple of hellos, and a few nods here and there. She was still embarrassed, and she assumed that *he* was furious at her.

Even though she had heard that Caleb had been out catting around again the night before, he pitched incredibly well. His fastball sat reliably and effortlessly in the high nineties, and the batters were pretty well baffled by his cutter and slider. He would probably move up to Low A within a week or two.

After three innings, he had six strikeouts, and no one had really even gotten the ball out of the infield yet. The other team *did* have a hit—but, it was a soft grounder that had just been too slow for Owen to get the guy at first.

In the bottom of the third, Marcus joined her up at the railing, and they nodded at each other, and then watched in silence as Scott was retired on a fly ball, and Dimitri and Schwartzman both struck out.

"You've been pretty scarce, the last couple of days," he said. "Are you not speaking to me?"

Wasn't it the other way around? "I thought you were mad at *me*," she said.

He shook his head.

Well, that was good news. "I wasn't very nice to you," she said.

He smiled faintly. "No, but I may have been a little patronizing towards *you*."

She nodded.

"The thing is, we only needed *one* fool with a cell phone to see the two of you, and the next thing you know, it would have been uploaded somewhere, and—" He sighed. "I'm sorry, I just didn't want to see you caught up in that."

God, she hadn't even considered the full implications of how it all could have played out—and that *would* have been a disaster. "Thank you," she said. "I was maybe not thinking very clearly."

He grinned, and then looked curious. "Do you like him?"

For some reason, she hadn't expected him to come right out and ask. "Well, I—" Did she? "Of course, I do," she said. "I mean, he's really nice, and God knows I'm attracted to him, but—" Did she? "I don't know."

Marcus nodded, and she couldn't quite read his expression, but it looked—*complicated*, somehow.

She glanced around, to make sure that no one else was paying attention to them. "Can I tell you the truth?" she asked.

"Of course," he said, although he looked more uneasy than he sounded.

"They all want me to be this perfect role model," she said. "You know, the ideal of what a female baseball player is supposed to be. That I have to be *exemplary*, in every possible way. But, I'm pretty sure that the person who they want me to be is entirely sexless, and I think I'm in the habit of suppressing that whole part of myself, you know?"

Marcus nodded, somewhat cautiously.

"And Hector was looking at me as a normal *dateable* woman, and I *liked* it," she said. "And that's who I felt like being, and—well, it was disappointing to have it cut off."

He nodded again.

"The idea of having to spend months, and maybe *years*, that way is—I don't know. Depressing." She looked over at him. "And I kind of have the feeling that you know exactly what I mean, about how tiring it is, sometimes, to try and be so damn *exemplary*."

He nodded. "Did you know that my father's a preacher?"

Actually, she hadn't, so she shook her head.

"So, I'm not precisely in your position—and I'm glad that I'm not, because I don't envy all of that extra pressure," he said. "But, I do know what you mean about the burden of trying to be exemplary."

Which she had been sure that he would, for a lot of different reasons, and being a preacher's son would just add to all of that. "I guess we can look forward to some very interesting bus conversations," she said.

His face relaxed into a smile. "I daresay we can," he said.

CHAPTER 27

They both watched, as Caleb pumped his fist on his way into the dugout, after getting yet another strikeout.

"He's very good," she said.

Marcus nodded. "Yes, he is."

"Better than I am," she said.

He glanced over. "You don't generally fish for compliments."

And she wasn't now. "Just looking for confirmation," she said.

"Okay. He's a physical specimen in a way that you won't ever be," Marcus said. "And he probably has more talent than anyone on the staff—although I think Andrew's upside is a little under the radar."

All of which pretty well matched her own observations.

"You're *never* going to be the most gifted player on the field again," he said. "You wouldn't have been in Division I, either, for the most part. And the reality is that most of the players are going to be much physically stronger than you are, and many of the pitchers will throw harder, and quite a few of them are going to be more talented, too."

Well, she could always count on him to be a straight shooter.

"*But,*" he said, "you have intellect, and courage, and command. Play your own game, and don't worry about what anyone else is doing. *That* is what's going to give you a shot at making it. Comparing yourself to anyone else will just drive you crazy."

Easier said than done, but it did have the ring of truth, so she nodded.

"You can't let a guy like that get inside your head," he said. "I mean, you've pretty much gone off the rails since he showed up, and you can't allow that to happen. You're going to run into a lot of players just like him, the higher up you go."

Of course, it begged the question of whether she wanted to be in a profession where she was going to have to deal with people like that on a regular basis.

They both watched, as Caleb strutted around, damn near *demanding* congratulatory high fives from people, although some of the ones he received in return were more enthusiastic than others.

Marcus shook his head. "When I first saw him the other

day, I said, 'Hello, Caleb, it's good to have you here.' Do you know what he said to me?'

Probably nothing that friendly.

Marcus put on a cocky, disdainful expression—which was really quite a good imitation of Caleb's typical look. "Hey, Grimes, aren't you glad you don't have to try and bat against me anymore?'"

Ouch. "He's a delight," she said.

Marcus nodded. "I could definitely have done without that."

"But, he'll be able to get away with being—brash—as long as he backs it up on the field," she said.

"True of most pro athletes, I think," he said.

No doubt.

"All things considered, you're an astonishingly polished pitcher, but you need to do a lot of work on *this*," he said, tapping his own forehead.

So, now she was a head case? "It's not that easy," she said, defensively.

Marcus shrugged. "Did you expect it to be?"

Well— "No," she said. "But, it's so much more—I don't know—*relentless*, than I thought it would be. Sometimes, it's— daunting."

"Jill, I have complete faith in you," he said.

God, she hoped so. "Do you really?" she asked. "I mean, genuinely?"

He looked her right in the eye. "One thousand percent," he said.

Which was one of the nicest things he could have possibly said to her. "Just for the record," she said. "I'm very glad we know each other."

"That one is mutual," he said.

They both nodded, and then looked out at the field to watch the rest of the game.

Her next start was going to be in Hudson Valley, against the Tampa Bay affiliate, and, okay, she was maybe dreading getting back out there. Once she was in the outfield, doing some preliminary jogging and stretching, she tried to concentrate on clearing her mind. Focusing. Locking in. Trying to learn how to improve the weakest damn aspect of her game.

There was another standing-room-only crowd tonight, and it looked as though at least a couple of hundred media credentials had been issued—but, she wasn't going to pay attention to that. Her last start didn't have to govern *this* one. She'd had a bad game, that's all. It wasn't necessarily going to happen again.

She hoped.

Her pitches in the bullpen were okay. Not terrific, but not awful, either. With luck, she would be better, once the game started, but she could work with what she had. Everything was going to be fine.

She hoped.

After warming up, she was relieved to locate a sweet-looking little girl with no trouble, and paused to hand her the ball. The girl was so stunned that her eyes filled with tears, and Jill gave the kid a hug—because, really, how could she *not*?

"Enjoy the game," she said, when she let go.

The little girl nodded, with a huge smile, even though her eyes were still very shiny.

As they continued to the dugout, none of them spoke, but Sawyer was shaking his head, and Marcus was looking amused.

In the top of the first, the guys scored a run, so, once again, she was starting off with the comfort of a lead, however small it was.

She felt her dog tag through her jersey, put on her cap, and picked up her glove. Then, after one last deep breath, she stepped out onto the field, and strode towards the mound.

Game on.

She was scraping some dirt off her cleats, when Scott came over to talk to her.

"Are you lost, son?" she asked, then pointed towards left. "The outfield is that way."

"Try something new tonight," he said.

Was there anyone *anywhere* who didn't have an opinion about what she should be doing, and when, and how, and why she should be doing it? It was a struggle not to scowl at him.

"It's a game," Scott said. "So, forget the work part tonight. Just *play*. Each pitch isn't going to change the world, you know."

Well—it was a point of view. "Okay," she said. "Thanks."

"The game's way better, when you enjoy yourself," he said. "So, have *fun*." Then, he clapped her lightly on the right shoulder, and trotted out towards his position.

Fun. Well, if she could manage that, it would be a nice change.

Marcus came out, and handed her a new baseball. "Focus on the glove," he said.

She nodded, vaguely noticing that the public address system had started playing some music, although she didn't ever pay much attention to the wacky stuff that happened between innings in minor league parks.

"I think tonight's going to be a good one," Marcus said. "So—" He stopped, also listening to the music. "Wait a minute, is that—?"

She listened, too. Yes, it *was* an old recording of "Thank Heaven for Little Girls," and most of the crowd was laughing. Along with both dugouts, the media, and everyone on the field, including the umpires.

"Well, gosh," Marcus said.

They stared at each other, and there really wasn't anything to do *but* laugh. Then, Jill tipped her cap at the announcer's box—where they must have been planning to do this for *weeks*—and Marcus went back behind the plate.

She wished her father was here for a thousand reasons— but, at the moment, the primary one was because he would have thought that having this song play was *hilarious*. She touched the dog tag fondly, and then threw her first warm-up pitch.

The song kept playing, and the fans were suddenly laughing harder, and when she looked at Marcus, he was, too—to the degree that he was having trouble staying in his catcher's stance. They all seemed to be looking at the outfield, and she turned to see that Scott, Hector, and Schwartzman were all waltzing with imaginary partners—and that even Schwartzman looked somewhat graceful.

She watched them for a few seconds, with great amusement, and then continued her warm-up tosses, finishing just as the song ended.

Marcus fired down to second, and then walked out to the mound, intercepting Owen's underhand throw before it got to her.

"How's your focus?" he asked.

Not the sharpest it had ever been—but, she was certainly *relaxed*. "I think I need to strike out the side," she said.

"That sounds like an excellent plan. And," he grinned at her, "if you get the first two guys, you can freeze the third one with Uncle Charlie, and I'll take the heat from Sawyer."

Well, okay, then. What other enticement could she ever possibly want?

The first guy went down swinging, on a four-seam fastball that was up and out of the zone. The next one was overeager, too, and she kept the ball low, getting him on a two-seamer that had the kind of late movement that made a pitcher's heart sing.

The third hitter wasn't quite as quick to chase, but the two-seamer was her magical friend tonight, and grabbing just enough black, so that she got two easy strikes. Going a little bit more outside would probably be the correct call, since he had to protect the plate now—but, they went with the curve. A great, vicious, *ruthless* curve. The guy started to swing—and then stared at the ball with his mouth hanging open, as it pretty much dropped out of sight for the third strike.

Three up, three down—and she was on her merry way back to the dugout.

Oh, yeah, she was bad.

So bad.

"Keep it up," Sawyer said, as she passed him.

She nodded, waving Sofia off, and just putting her jacket on, instead, because—well—she really *preferred* it that way.

She set them down in order in the second, and again, in the third.

And then, the fourth. Nine strikeouts so far, and nothing even *close* to a runner reaching base.

No one said much to her, which was fine, because she *liked* to be able to hear herself think. She had no idea what the crowd was doing—and didn't care, one way or the other. The same went for the damn media. Let them amuse themselves, or boo, or—whatever. It was their dimes.

The first batter in the fifth grounded out to Raffy, who

hurried his throw, but Dimitri reeled it in with no trouble. The second guy struck out on a changeup so deceptive that it actually surprised *her* a little.

She'd overwhelmed the next hitter back in the second inning, by coming in on his hands *every single time*—so, she was half-expecting him to try and lay down a bunt, which he did. But, she was ready, and dashed in to snatch it up.

Marcus pounced on it before she could. "Get out of the way!" he yelled, as he scooped the ball barehanded, and whipped it to first, beating the guy by two steps.

And, that was the fifth. Fifteen up, fifteen down.

Gosh. She didn't get *bellowed* at very often. "Woof," she said. Since they were, after all, Retrievers.

Marcus frowned at her, as he gathered up his mask. "How about 'Thank you for the well-executed and timely play'?"

God, he could be insufferable. "Woof," she said.

"Yeah, that's about right," Owen said, passing them on his way to the dugout. "Mother barks a lot."

How rare to agree with Owen.

She got two quick outs in the sixth, and was getting ready to take down the third guy—except that Adler was heading out to the mound, which was the last thing she would have expected, especially when she was in a groove. But, she stepped off the rubber to wait, as Marcus came out to join them.

"So," Adler said.

Jill nodded, wondering what she could possibly have been

doing wrong—and then realized that Eduardo was standing by the bullpen gate, clearly warmed up and ready to come in. What in the hell was *this* about?

"Here's the thing, Cafferty," Adler said, after a minute. "Pittsburgh called in the fourth, and then in the fifth, and they just called again."

Suddenly, she realized why he was out here. "Pitch count," she said.

He nodded. "We could let you go the rest of the way, milk some more headlines and magazine covers—or maybe we could decide *not* to risk your arm."

But, she was *pitching a perfect game*. She only needed ten more damn outs. She could *get* ten more outs. Were they really going to yank the Holy Grail away from her, when she *almost* had it in her hands?

"Is it worth arguing to stay in?" she asked.

He shook his head. "No. But, I'm going to give you two choices. I pull you right now, and you lift your cap, and get some applause—or you can finish the inning, and not come back out for the seventh."

That one was easy enough. "Then, go back to the dugout, sir," she said. *Immediately*.

Adler smiled. "Yeah. That's what I figured."

She let herself stand there and take a few seconds to feel *really* disappointed, then shook it off, and focused on the signals Marcus was flashing her. Fastball, curve, *whatever*. She was fine with any of them.

The first two strikes were easy—and Marcus looked out at her, and she looked in at him. Then, he signaled for the four-seamer.

She had expected him to ask for the curve—and she *wanted* to throw the curve—but, he was right. The *hitter* was going to think he was calling for a curve, too.

So, she threw the fastball, and threw it *well*, and the guy swung and missed—and that was the inning.

Eighteen up—and eighteen down. Twelve strikeouts. Six perfect innings. Emphasis on the word *perfect*.

Marcus came out to the mound to meet her, and they headed for the dugout.

"You finally *pitched* tonight," he said.

She nodded.

"I thought you might shake me off there," he said.

It had certainly crossed her mind. "Mother knows best," she said.

"Right," he said, and glanced over at her. "Is that a swagger?"

Probably, yeah. "Think it suits me?" she asked.

"Well—it's different," he said.

Yeah. It was. She raised her cap at the little girl in the stands—who was still clutching her pre-game warm-up baseball—and then looked back at Marcus.

"Was I going to do it tonight?" she asked. Because, after

all, baseball games were random, and a ball could have dropped into no-man's-land, or she could have missed the plate, or—all kinds of things. But, still. Eighteen up, and eighteen down.

He nodded. "Yes," he said. "I think you were."

So did she.